Amish Romance;
Torn Series

The Complete Collection
Boxed Set – Books 1 to 4

SARAAH SOWELL & NICOLE WRIGHT

Other Books By Saraah Sowell

TORN SERIES
1. Amish Devotion
2. Amish Bride
3. Amish Loss
4. Amish Mystery

FOLLOWING ORDNUNG SERIES
1. Amish Secrets
2. Amish Rebellion
3. Amish Past
4. Amish Nobility

AMISH FREEDOM SERIES
1. Amish Freedom to Love
2. Amish Freedom to Choose
3. Amish Freedom to Live
4. Amish Survival

MYSTERY IN AMISH COUNTRY SERIES
1. Amish Autumn
2. Amish Courtship
3. Amish Falsehood
4. Amish Christmas Wishl

www.facebook.com/saraahsowellbooks

Published in USA by:

SARAAH SOWELL & NICOLE WRIGHT

© Copyright 2016

ISBN-13: 978-1523934430
ISBN-10: 1523934433

About the Authors

Saraah Sowell loves the Amish community. She likes the way they run their lives from healing, to farming, to seeing how they are so independent from the outside world. She has a desire to spread the love she gets from this unique community through her stories.

Many of her stories are based on her encounters with them, although, of course, all the names, events, and places that may resemble or are similar to living people are only coincidental and are fiction. She is married with three kids.

Nicole Wright graduated in 2011 from Hollins University with a degree in English, with a Concentration in Creative Writing. Once she learned to read and write, she frequently stayed up past bedtime with a flashlight and notepad to write as a child.

As an adult, she still stays up late and writes, but this time she reads her stories out loud to her almost two-year-old daughter. She spends the majority of her time running after said daughter and reading through cookbooks for dinner ideas. Now a full-time mother and writer, Nicole lives in Colorado with her tight knit Coloradan family and enjoys living in the Rocky Mountain State.

INTRODUCTION

This is a boxed set by bestselling author Saraah Sowell & Nicole Wright. It contains one complete series of 4 books and one bonus book specially for you.

No.1 - Amish Devotion (Amish Romance)

A new Amish love relationship approaches. But obstacles emerging...

Aubrey Forrest's Rumspringa is quickly approaching. She knows all too well what the ramifications can be for choosing to leave the community. Although she's not to discuss it, the pain is still very real for her. After witnessing the excommunication of someone she loved dearly, Aubrey is not too keen on going through this rite of passage herself.

Jamie Miller's Rumspringa is approaching too. His feelings about it may be very different, but that still doesn't make his decision any easier.

A sweet friendship develops between Aubrey and Jamie, but there are rules to be followed. As Aubrey's heart grows fonder for Jamie, some rules prove to be difficult to obey. Neither wants to keep secrets in this very disciplined world, but some secrets are necessary in order for their love to bloom.

This is the first book in the Torn trilogy. Can Aubrey and Jamie reconcile their personal struggles and find a happy medium that will allow them to love freely?

A clean Amish romance story of friendship, romance, love, rebellious, hope, loyalty, and faith to God.

No.2 - Amish Bride (Amish Romance)

An union is emerging... Will true love prevails? Can they stay together?

Jaime and Aubrey are ready to start their lives together, but they are plagued by events that neither they, nor their small Amish community can forget about.

Jaime's father is disapproving and Aubrey's shunned sister is prepared to wreak havoc on their pending union. Winning over Jaime's father's approval will not be easy, but learning to rely on each other will bring this couple together.

They have a long battle ahead of them, but if they can manage to hold on and let go of their self-doubts to strive for what they want most.

This is the second book in the Torn tetralogy. Can Jaime and Aubrey move past the obstacles that stand in their way and stay together?

A clean Amish romance story of union, love, betrayal, hope, loyalty, and faith to God.

No.3 - Amish Loss (Amish Romance)

Are they going to live a normal life?

Their new life together should be simple, but when chaos finds them again, what they'd worked so hard to achieve, stands in the balance.

Aubrey and Jamie have endured the hardest battles of their young lives. Tough choices have been made already and remnants from the past should be long gone, but when Aubrey's sister, Emma, returns to their tight-knit Amish community and a past love interest soon follows, the next phase in Aubrey's life is threatened.

The young couple will have to hold on tightly to what they'd fought so hard to obtain or risk losing everything, including their growing family.

Are Aubrey and Jamie strong enough to weather the storm that has crept back into their lives and hold steadfast to each other forever?

A clean Amish romance story of marriage, romance, love, suspicion, hope, and faith to God.

No.4 - Amish Mystery (Amish Romance)

Will a past mistake ruin their future?

Life has been filled with constant turmoil for Aubrey and Jamie Miller since the events of last Spring and their future together hangs in the balance.

After an emotional goodbye to Aubrey's sister Emma, the young couple is haunted by rumors that threaten their life and their love. Now, expecting their first child, they should be relishing in all that joy that parenthood brings, but instead their lives are marred by the vicious cycle of fact vs. fiction.

The young couple will have to muster up the strength, look past the rumors and hold on to the love they share or be forever haunted by a secret that neither yet ready to explore.

Will Aubrey and Jamie be able to withstand the storm that has plagued their lives or will a peaceful existence be too far out of their reach?

A clean Amish romance story of mystery, marriage, love, suspicion, hope, and faith to God.

These books are sweet, clean and Christian themed Amish Romance stories.

1.AMISH DEVOTION

EPIGRAPHS

"According to Greek Mythology, humans were originally created with four arms, four legs, and a head with two faces. Fearing their power, Zeus split them into two separate begins, condemning them to spend their lives in search of their other halves." -*Plato, The Symposium*

"She buried her ears into the calm of his heartbeat, and in a matter of of seconds, fell terribly in love with the way her loneliness fell softly and suddenly asleep in his chest." -*Christopher Poindexter*

AMISH JARGON

Before reading this book, get to know the various dialects or jargon of the Amish culture.

- Englischer – Englisher (Non-Amish; the term is used among the Amish for talking about "Englishers"; they are often not comfortable using the term to non-Amish directly as it is a bit of a derogatory term)
- Gott – God
- Mann – Man
- Shtamm – Family
- Bruder – Brother
- Haus – House
- Kaffe – Coffee (Amish men are particularly fond of coffee, but soda is an especially appreciated treat by Amish families)
- Jah – Yes (some books say Ja)
- Ach - Oh
- Fraa – Wife
- Danka – Thank you
- Nee – No

- Kapp – Cap (such as female's prayer cap: prayer kapp)
  - Gut – Good
  - Daett or Daed – Dad
  - Shveshtah – Sister
  - Grohs-mammi – Grandmother
  - Kins-kind – Grandchildren
  - Bobli – Baby
  - Kinner – Children
  - Kinder - Kids
  - Mansleit – Men folk
  - Ordnung – Order (Church)
  - Wunderbaar – Wonderful
  - Maemm – Mom
  - Ant – Aunt (Very seldom are words like "aunt" and "uncle" used as a title by the Amish. The relationship does not mean much in the community, probably because of the practice of intermarrying among the Amish, leaving nearly everyone an aunt or uncle. Children and adults refer to each other by their first name, unless they are a direct authority such as mother, father, or a grandparent)
  - Dochtah – Daughter
  - Brau – Brown
  - Schaffe – Work
  - Weiss – White
  - Wuhnt – Lives
  - Aaduh – To dress, to put on
  - Aadreffe – To meet
  - Fashtella – Changing one's appearance
  - Rumschpringe or Rumspsringa – Translation

means "the running around years." It's a period of adolescence in which boys and girls are given greater personal freedom and allowed to form romantic relationships, usually ending with the choice of baptism into the church or leaving the community (in some Amish communities). Communities autonomously choose what they permit for their children during this period. Many communities opt out of it completely.

ᴄᴙ CHAPTER 1 ᴔᴑ

Aubrey Forrest buried her fingers in the rising dough and began to knead the fleshy mixture expertly. The smell of freshly baked bread wafted through the morning air.

"Don't you love the smell of freshly baked bread?" Aubrey asked. She smiled over at Hannah Byler, working alongside her.

Flour dusted the front of Hannah's apron and her hands were also buried in bread dough. "Jah. It always smells good in here." Hannah pulled the dough free from the floured counter, setting it neatly in a bread pan. "I hear Englischers say that all the time to your maemm."

Fingers sticky with dough, Aubrey dipped her hands in a bowl of flour. "I know. Mama is very happy with how well business is going."

"I hope it continues like this until winter. Daed says most likely the bakery will have to shut down because no one will be coming in." Hannah said.

Aubrey grimaced at the thought. She enjoyed working in the bakery with Hannah (when she had the time) and

Katie along with her sister Sadie and brother Isaac, who diligently washed the dishes before they both walked to school. They used to walk every morning, something that Aubrey did not mind, but Daniel had hired an Englischer to taxi them when Katie started having trouble breathing. The short trips to the bakery had given her a little bit of time to relax and not worry about responsibilities.

Her stomach grumbled hungrily and reminded her that she had skipped breakfast to help Sadie tuck the soft strands of her blonde hair under her white kapp and then pin it securely.

"I think I will ask Mama if I can take a quick break and eat," she said, turning to face her best friend, who was busy rolling out a pie crust.

Hannah gave a brief nod. "Okay. Hurry back before the breads are done baking."

"I will." She grabbed her bag from beneath the neatly organized counter and headed to the front of the bakery. "Is it alright Mama if I take a quick break? The breads are baking and we're about to start on the pies."

Katie stood behind the cash register with Sadie. Today the both of them wore matching gray dresses with white kapps and had the same freckles dotting their cheekbones. Hours out in Colorado's bright sun during all the seasons spotted and toughened their skin. "Jah. If there is time. You need to eat before coming to work, Aubrey. I can't have you fainting with how busy it has been." Katie said.

"I know. I'm sorry."

She hurried out of the store, which was brimming with Englischers. Most were passing through and stopped to buy something to eat along the way through Monte Vista. There were a few who came to observe and ask odd questions about their way of life. Aubrey shook her head. She never understood what was so fascinating about their lives that strangers had to come and watch them.

She leaned back against the warm walls of the bakery and inhaled deeply. If she had to chose a favorite season, it would be late summer. The air was always dry and crisp with the faint scent of dry grass lingering. Today it would be very hot, judging from how warm it was already for early morning. She thought of her Papa, carving furniture in the blazing heat with sweat beading on his forehead. Daniel owned and ran a furniture business called Forrest Furniture that kept steadily busy throughout all the seasons. Levi, her oldest bruder, worked there as well, but mainly did the books instead of crafting the furniture.

She had just taken a bite from her apple when the door creaked open behind her. She looked over her shoulder and saw Sadie exit the store. The guilty look on her sister's face told Aubrey that she had confessed to Katie about sleeping in and had been sent out to apologize.

"You don't have to apologize." Aubrey said.

Sadie leaned dejectedly against the wall beside her. "Mama sent me out here to, though," she said, shrugging. "I didn't sleep very well last night."

"Why is that?" Aubrey asked. She had noticed the bloodshot eyes and puffy dark bags under her sister's eyes, but had been too busy rushing to get everyone ready for the day to ask.

Sadie hesitated for a moment. She glanced over at

Aubrey, studying her intently and then letting out a heavy sigh. "I was thinking about Emma."

Her whispered words pierced their hearts with a sharp knife and then jerked the blade violently. Aubrey blinked against the tears in her eyes. They were not supposed to talk about or even say Emma's name, not since her excommunication from the church.

"I know I'm not supposed to," Sadie continued, tears also glimmering in her hazel eyes, "but I can't help it sometimes. I can't forget how hard Mama cried that night or the look on Emma's face when the bishop told her that she was shunned."

Aubrey sought to control her emotions. She remembered that afternoon vividly. Emma had suddenly announced while sitting down for dinner that she was leaving because of her soon-to-be marriage to Thomas Fields, a highly-respected church member whose wife had died from pneumonia several months prior. He was favored to replace the minister Isaac possibly, whose healthy was slowly declining.

Emma had originally been excited about their courtship, but it slowly ebbed away to fear and doubt over time. She had confessed to Aubrey one night that she had sinned with Michael, her previous love interest, during *rumspringa* and her courtship with Thomas. She refused to confess to the church out of humiliation. When Michael confessed to sinning of the flesh, the Amish church had pressured Emma to confess as well and face the punishment. Emma had refused and left the next day with only the clothes on her back.

The church had excommunicated her after that. She was as good as dead, even though she was alive and out in the world somewhere.

"I know, Sadie." Aubrey said, coming back from her reminiscing. She offered a small tired smile to her sister. "It'll be alright in the end. We can not doubt Gott's will at this time. Go on and get inside before Mama comes looking for you."

Sadie nodded, wiping her cheeks dry with the sleeves of her dress. She disappeared back into the bakery.

The sun crept an inch higher in the clear blue sky. For a while she gazed at the mountain range surrounding their small community, her thoughts stuck on the lone key hidden under a floorboard in her room.

CR80

Hannah Byler wore the blue dress that she had worn to her wedding in November, the color bringing out the hazel flecks in her eyes. Aubrey admired the color and fabric from the corner of her eye. Jacob Byler sat on the other side of Hannah across the aisle, and every once in a while the two shared a loving smile. Aubrey watched their exchange with a stab of envy.

This Sunday morning, they were seated side by side on wooden benches in the Helmuth's barn, where church was being held. Aubrey's eyes itched from the hay bales stacked around the walls and she rubbed at them in aggravation as the hymns came to an end.

"Tonight I'd like to announce that we have a family

joining our community," Abraham, the bishop of their church, said. He stood tall and strong for a man who was nearing his seventies. His long beard was grey and his skin was tough from many years of being out in the sun. "They have come from Lancaster, Pennsylvania and will be attending church next Sunday for the first time here. I hope you all will give them a warm welcome."

Abraham's blue eyes twinkled as he gazed around the barn in pride. They ended in prayer and the youth promptly began to gather for night singing.

"I'll see you later, jah?" Hannah said, hugging Aubrey briefly before going to Jacob's side. The two disappeared in the hot afternoon to visit family nearby.

"That will be you one day, dochtah." Katie said, coming up behind Aubrey. She rested her hands upon the curve of Aubrey's shoulders. "Why don't you stay behind? Your father and I can get the kinner to bed."

Aubrey gave a small shake of her head. A headache was beginning to make its presence known in her temples and having some quiet time sounded more appealing. "Nee. I will come home. I am not feeling well."

She waved a quick greeting toward Levi, standing with his wife Rosella on the other side of the barn. Levi returned the wave, grinning widely, before Aubrey slipped out of the barn with her remaining family in tow.

The walk home from the Helmuth's barn was over a mile, but none of them complained. Aubrey walked alongside Daniel down the dirt road, and for a while the sound of crickets chirping and rocks crunching under their shoes were all they heard.

Daniel's strong arm brushed hers occasionally as they walked. She took the time to take in his profile, with the sunlight highlighting a strong jaw underneath his beard and high cheekbones. Years of hard work in the fields and carving furniture had made Daniel a fit man who sometimes seemed more frightening than welcoming. She admired his ability to lead others and keep a level head in desperate times while humbling others with his own humbleness.

"Is there a particular reason why my face has captured your interest?" Daniel asked, a smile tugging at his lips.

Aubrey laughed softly and twined an arm through his. She felt Daniel's calloused hand reach up to give her fingers a fond squeeze.

"I'm sorry, Papa. I was only admiring you," she said, resting her head on his muscled shoulder as they walked.

Behind them, Katie walked with Sadie and Isaac. She glanced over her shoulder to watch Sadie talk animatedly about learning how to knit and sew properly.

"Next week the Miller family will be here." Daniel said casually. "They will not arrive until late at night on Wednesday. Levi and I have built some furniture for them since they are bringing very little."

"I can spare a few blankets of mine and make more later," Aubrey offered. She could knit a heavier blanket during her free time, before the harsh winter season came barreling down upon them.

Daniel smiled proudly at her. "That would be wholly appreciated. Make sure to have six plates of food to spare for Wednesday night as well," he said, and they turned down a long pathway that led to their home.

They fell into their normal routines of finishing up whatever chores needed to be done before night descended upon the house.

Aubrey perched herself on the window seat and stared up at the stars, drawing the fabric of her cotton nightgown along her bare legs. In the center of her palm the key felt cold against her clammy skin. She'd had the key for several months, along with Emma's letters. Somehow she had managed to sneak the key into Aubrey's room, along with a short letter explaining where the P.O. box was. Aubrey feigned sickness shortly after that to sneak over to the post office outside of their community and found a letter waiting there already. Her sister had found a place to live with the meager savings she'd had and had applied to a college in New York City to study art. She began to send various articles and books on art to Aubrey, who shared the same passion for knowledge and art.

The guilt and secrecy nearly drove Aubrey to hand it over to Daniel. She knew that keeping contact with Emma would cause her to risk being punished, but she missed her sister. Aubrey had cried just as hard as Katie had when she'd left.

Rumspringa was coming shortly and both of her parents had given her permission to participate if she desired. Hannah had gone two years prior to her baptism and marriage to Jacob. She said it had been the most exhilarating and terrifying time of her life, but Jacob was more appealing than a life without the Amish church and her family. She knew who she was within their community.

A wave of fatigue crashed over Aubrey. She yawned deeply before sliding off the window seat and slipping under the freshly washed linens. Maybe she would talk to Daniel about *rumspringa* in the morning.

CRYS

The chance to talk to Daniel didn't come until Friday morning. Aubrey rose before the sun could spill its warmth and light over the rugged terrain. She quickly finished the chores that needed to be done before heading to the bakery with Katie and found Daniel sitting at the dining table, where she knew he would be relaxing with a steaming mug cradled in both hands, the smell of kaffe strong in their kitchen.

"Morning, Papa." Aubrey said, leaning down to kiss him on the cheek. The coarse hair of his beard tickled her skin and the taste of soap lightly clung to her lips. She noted his half full mug. "Would you like some more kaffe?"

"Danka," he said when Aubrey carefully poured the dark liquid into his mug. "You've finished your chores earlier than normal."

Doubts clouded her mind about telling Daniel that she had been thinking of *rumspringa*. She rubbed the back of her dry knuckles anxiously, like she always did whenever something bothered her.

Daniel noticed it as well, his brow furrowed in apprehension. He gestured for her to sit down on the chair next to him. "What is it, dochtah?" he asked once she had seated herself on the edge of the wooden chair, the skirts of her gray dress tucked around her legs neatly.

"I-I," Aubrey closed her eyes, gathering what little courage she still had within her. "I've been thinking about our conversation… about *rumspringa*."

A pregnant pause followed.

Aubrey opened her eyes to find Daniel sitting rigidly in his chair. The hardening glint in his eyes told her exactly what he was thinking. She flushed hotly in shame at even mentioning it to him and opened her mouth to retract her words, but Daniel began to talk.

"If that is what you wish, Aubrey. I will allow it. You have the choice to go out into the outside world and decide," he stated curtly. His fingers tightened noticeably around the mug and brought it up to his lips, sipping long and hard.

Aubrey began to scramble. There had only been a few times in her life that Daniel ever was angry at her and it was always for a good reason. "I'm sorry, Papa. I won't go. I have no desire to see what the outside is like. Hannah told me all about it and that's enough for me," she rambled, forcing an apologetic smile.

A thick tension settled in the room as the pale blue morning light filtered through the curtains. It felt like a long time before Daniel finally stirred to life and slowly lowered the mug back to the table. His fingers absently traced the rim and looked back up at Aubrey. Several emotions shimmered in Daniel's eyes and they disappeared before she could decipher any of them.

"Listen to me, Aubrey," Daniel said, reaching out to grab her hand and hold it tightly in his own, "I do not wish to impose my opinions or feelings onto you. Joining the church is a personal decision that only you and Gott make together. Sow your wild oats if you have to. I pray that you will come back, but I cannot bear losing you because I could not let you go out of fear."

The soft vulnerable tone of Daniel's voice plucked hard at her heart strings. While they had swept up the dust Emma left behind and tried to hide it beneath the rugs, she still existed within them. Daniel never mentioned Emma's name or talked about her like he once had, and now Aubrey could see that it had broken his heart just as much as hers.

They were incredibly lucky to have a loving man as a father. Aubrey had heard rumors of other men hitting their wife and children and taking child brides. Daniel had never been like that. He showered them with love and looked down upon that type of behavior.

Aubrey squeezed Daniel's fingers assuringly. The desire to leave, to see Emma, to go to college and learn art faded away like the pale blue light in their kitchen as it transformed into a sunny glow. For now, she would let it go. "You won't lose me, Papa. I promise to pray harder about it." Aubrey said.

Footsteps clambered noisily down the stairs. Isaac entered the kitchen, rubbing at his eyes sleepily and hair damp from where had Katie smoothed the stray hairs down. His white shirt was crisp and black trousers free of lint. "Morning, Pa," Isaac mumbled, giving him a brief hug before doing the same to Aubrey.

Aubrey went about the kitchen to ready breakfast for them and was setting a loaf of bread she had baked the day before on the table when Sadie rushed to her side.

"I have to tell you something," Sadie said excitedly. "It's really, really, really exciting and I promise you will think so too."

Aubrey couldn't help but laugh at her younger sister's enthusiasm. The tension between her and Daniel had already floated away, but Sadie's excitement erased the lingering traces of it.

"Slow down, Sadie," Daniel chuckled, handing a piece of buttered toast to Isaac. "What is so exciting?"

Sadie sucked in audible breath. "Jamie Miller came to the bakery yesterday to personally thank Aubrey for all the delicious breads and cookies." She rolled her eyes dramatically. "I, of course, didn't tell him that I helped bake those too, but he's been looking for you."

Aubrey blinked once, and then twice. *Jamie Miller was looking for her?* She tried to process the information. The Millers had arrived earlier that week and beforehand Aubrey had set the loaves of bread and plates of cookies on the table for them, along with plates of food for dinner like Daniel had requested.

She bit her bottom lip and sat down on the edge of her chair again.

"He sounds like a nice young man." Daniel said, smiling across the table at Aubrey.

"He's also not married, right Pa?" Sadie asked.

A mischievous smile spread across her sister's

freckled face. When Aubrey had turned sixteen, she had received permission from Papa to begin courting. It had been exciting initially to know that she could begin searching for her husband, the one Gott had designed for her, but it had faded to disappointment. Several of the boys in and around her age didn't feel *right*. Maybe it was the romantic side of her, the one that daydreamed about feeling that sudden spark and a fluttering sensation in her belly, that made her too picky.

Aubrey changed the topic by asking where Katie was.

"She's upstairs," Sadie replied, clearing the dishes from the table.

The open door to Emma's old room spilled morning light out into the hallway. Aubrey's heart hammered. The floorboards creaked beneath her sneakered shoes and she peered cautiously around the doorframe.

Katie sat with her back toward the door, on the edge of Emma's neatly-made bed, staring distantly out through the window across the room. Her white kapp sat beside her on the quilted blanket and the blonde strands of her long hair fell freely down her back.

"Mama?" Aubrey called softly so as not to startle her. Daniel had closed the door after Emma left and ordered it to stay shut until they could convert it into a different room. None of them ventured into it and she had a feeling that Katie did so when no one was looking or around.

"Hmm?" Katie hummed, turning to look at Aubrey in the doorframe. Wet trails streaked her freckled cheeks and the whites around her eyes were tinged red. "Oh, Aubrey. I shouldn't be in here and neither should you."

She stood, the blue skirts of her dress swishing gracefully at the movement. Katie wiped away the tears lingering and offered a quivering smile while she quietly shut the door behind her. The conversation with Daniel replayed in Aubrey's mind and she felt her skin twitch painfully in response. Guilt mixed with bravery opened her mouth to confess about the key, about everything, the tip of it on her tongue when Daniel yelled at them from downstairs that their ride had arrived.

The drive to the bakery was filled with chatter. Daniel conversed about fishing with the Englischer, who drove them to work and back every day, with Isaac occasionally jumping in with advice. Sadie talked to Katie about what she'd read in school and her arm brushed against Aubrey's whenever she reached up to tuck a stray hair behind her ear. With the windows opened and warm air blowing in, Aubrey noted with exasperation that Sadie's errant strands of hair were because she had messily pinned her hair underneath her kapp.

Aubrey diverted her attention to the scenery passing them by in a blur of dry green and brown colors. In a few months, the summer season would give way to a much cooler one. The green trees would transform into tones of fiery reds and bright yellows and she would collect the leaves once they fell. A chill would settle along the stretches of green fields and then creep down into the ground, plants and animals slowly going dormant.

She looked up at the sky, a light blue that stretched on behind the mountains, and a shiver of anticipation went through her. Like the world below it, the sky would turn into a pure shade of blue that reminded Aubrey of the clear and deep mountain springs.

Most of all, she wondered whether Jamie Miller liked the changing seasons.

☙ CHAPTER 2 ❧

Jamie Miller stood in front of the newly-erected fence that surrounded his family's house and farm. He leaned against the wood to catch his breath, head dizzy from the thin air and high altitude. They'd arrived in Colorado only a few days before and he was still not used to the altitude. Even his daed and oldest bruder had to take frequent breaks to drink water and catch their breath.

"I have to give it to Pa. It is beautiful out here," Henry said, wiping a layer of sweat from his forehead with a leather glove. "Just hope that we can get used to all this thin air and not being able to farm like we used to."

Jamie kept his expression blank. Farming had been their main job within their community back in Lancaster, and when their had Pa announced that they would be moving to Colorado, his heart had plummeted. The idea of doing something beside what he had been doing his whole life was daunting, but he had followed obediently, knowing that Henry and Aaron also felt the same level of anxiety. "It is beautiful here," Jamie agreed. He raised his eyes to the mountain range that loomed on the horizon, the tips of them white. "Nothing like Lancaster. Has Pa talked about the furniture store with you yet?"

Henry nodded, draping his long arms on the fence and leaning backward to rest against the wood as well. He tilted his head upward toward the sun, bearing down on them relentlessly, and closed his eyes briefly. "He said that we will start later this week. Daniel Forrest owns the store and he will be showing us how to make furniture. He insisted on us taking the time to get used to things here. He supplied all off the furniture we didn't bring," Henry said.

The house had been generously built by the community in preparation for their arrival and also supplied with items they'd had to leave behind, mainly furniture and blankets, but also a few clothes. Their pantry was well stocked with canned goods and bags of potatoes and onions. Daniel Forrest had even offered Henry and Jamie jobs until they found their own ways of living.

"That's very generous of him. We will have to thank him," Jamie replied, swatting away a fly that buzzed near his face annoyingly.

"Let's get going. I bet Ma and Lily have lunch ready by now."

The two brothers gathered their tools and walked down the dusty road back toward the house. Sunlight bounced off the top of their heads and Jamie constantly smoothed a hand over the gold strands of hair to make sure that his scalp was not burning like the rest of him.

As they drew closer to the house, Lily's distressed

voice reached them through the open windows. "It's ruined, Ma! I can't believe I ruined it. I have never ruined bread before."

The smell of burnt bread wafted strongly throughout the house. Lily stood near the stove with Sarah, her solid gray dress splattered with flour and face red with humiliation. She turned to look at Jamie as he entered through the back door. Tears welled in Lily's eyes as she turned back around to stare at something on the stove.

"What's going on?" Jamie inquired softly.

He rested a hand on Lily's trembling shoulder. Their move from Lancaster had been a hard adjustment for everyone, but Lily had taken it the hardest. She didn't want to leave her friends or Brian, her current love interest, and had cried the whole trip to Colorado. Aaron luckily was in a forgiving mood for Lily's emotional outbursts, but Jamie was starting to worry that his sister was crossing a thin line and testing his patience.

"She burnt the bread," Sarah replied. She turned to look away from the stove and the corner of her lips twitched, a indication that she was trying to keep a smile at bay. "This high altitude is going to prove hard on baking too. You boys look hungry. Let me make you something to eat."

Jamie came to a stand beside Lily and took in the blackened mass that had twisted and shrunk in the pan. He tried to keep his amusement under control for the sake of his sister, but a snort disguised as a laugh escaped.

Lily rounded on him with furious eyes. "You think that it's funny?! Well, it's not. You try baking and see how it turns out." Lily snapped at him.

"Lily," Sarah's voice cut through Jamie's laughter, a warning lacing her soft tone. "Don't speak so harshly. It was an accident and your brother shouldn't poke fun."

Jamie clicked his jaw shut and sat down next to Henry at the table. Their shoulders trembled in silent laughter as Lily stomped around the kitchen and threw the loaf out the back door. Sarah's lips pursed into a tight line of disapproval.

After their stomachs were full, the two brothers scoped out the piece of land Aaron had marked with sticks earlier that morning for plowing. They were too late for planting season, but Aaron wanted to plow the earth and have it ready for spring. Jamie pulled a stick free from the dirt and stuck his finger into the small hole, feeling the hot dirt crumble into dust. He sighed heavily, crouching easily on the balls of his feet.

"How did Pa say they water here?" Jamie asked, frowning up at his brother, who stood alongside him.

Henry pointed to the mountains. "They somehow irrigate the snow that melts into water. Pa says they can't rely on the snowfall and rainfall here like we did in Lancaster. The seasons are too unpredictable. One winter they'll get several feet of snow and the next winter it'll be mild, with hardly any snow."

"We will have to ask how they irrigate." Jamie said.

He watched a hawk circle in the sky before swooping down into the dry field and then bouncing back up effortlessly, with something clutched tightly in its talons.

CRENO

The Forrest family was a respected one. Jamie found that out by talking to various community members who brought baked goods, fresh vegetables, and whatever else they could spare. Daniel Forrest owned Forrest Furniture and his wife Katie owned Forrest Bakery. They had two daughters and two sons.

"You're such a kind young man. How old are you again?" Almina Wagler asked.

The older Amish woman smiled pleasantly as Jamie offered an arm to help her step off the stairs of their home. She'd stopped by to bring a pot pie for them.

"Seventeen, ma'am," he answered respectfully.

"You are the same age as Aubrey Forrest. Such a sweet girl. She spent two days baking breads and cookies for your family."

After finishing his chores, he had taken the moderately-long walk to Forrest Bakery to meet Aubrey and thank her for the tasty bread and delicious cookies that had been eaten with gusto. Along the way, he planned to stop by Forrest Furniture and ask what time Daniel wanted him to start work.

Forrest Bakery was a modest white building with a little porch in front and an elaborately-painted sign with pine trees nailed to the side of the building to attract passing cars from the road. Only a few cars were parked in the gravel parking lot and a group of Englischers stood alongside the building, each happily eating a large sugar cookie. A Englischer girl with bare legs and shoulders watched him approach curiously.

Jamie dropped his eyes to the ground as he walked by the group and up onto the front porch. The smell of sugar and flour wafted through the screen door when he pushed it open and stepped inside the hot bakery. Clean display cases of cookies, pies, and pastries lined the back wall while small aisles filled with various breads were tidy and clean.

Behind the register, a young girl wearing a gray dress and with blonde hair framing her freckled face underneath her white kapp watched him curiously.

"Hi," she chirped as he approached the counter, a puzzled frown on her face. "Are you one of the Millers? I've never seen you before."

Jamie smiled politely and tipped his head forward. "My name is Jamie Miller. I was hoping to find Aubrey and thank her for the delicious breads she made for my family. They were greatly appreciated and tasty," he stated.

The younger girl blinked a couple of times and stared at him again curiously. Jamie arched an eyebrow questioningly.

"Oh, right," she replied hastily, a pink hue coloring the center of her cheeks. "I'm Sadie Forrest. Aubrey isn't here. She had to take our little brother Isaac home after school and watch him."

Disappointment weaved through him. Sadie was a beautiful young girl with her blonde hair and delicate features. He was curious to see whether Aubrey was just as beautiful as her sister and as pretty as everyone in the community had described.

He didn't even know Aubrey and a part of him was

already curious about her. He blinked in surprise at that. Back in Lancaster Jamie had never really been interested in any of the girls around his age.

"Well, please tell her that my family and I appreciated it," Jamie added, clearing his throat. "I hope to meet her sometime soon or at church this upcoming Sunday."

"I'll tell her." Sadie smiled at him and gave a short little excited wave that made Jamie smile in amusement. The screen door screeched to a close behind him and the bright afternoon greeted him once more.

The small town teemed with life; horse hooves clipped along the pavement and the occasional roar of car motors echoed in the afternoon. The pace was much slower and relaxed than Lancaster's had been whenever Jamie had ventured into town to help Aaron with selling their vegetables and fruit and whatever canned goods Sarah could sell.

He casually tucked his hands into the pockets of his black trousers and strolled toward Forrest Furniture. Today would be his last real day of free time since arriving at Monte Vista before he settled back into the routine of working from sun up to sun down again. There were plenty of chores around the house and farm that needed to be done before and after work. Aaron had warned them that they would be working much harder here.

By the time he reached the large building, he was out of breath and dizzy again. Instead of venturing inside, Jamie rounded the corner and went to the back. There he spotted Daniel Forrest in large work area that looked similar to a barn with a vaulted ceiling and several pieces of crafted furniture stored neatly while the in-progress ones were in the middle of the room.

A large pile of wood shavings sat next to Daniel's booted feet. He looked up, sensing a presence, and immediately straightened at the sight of Jamie. His clothes were covered in wood chips and dust and a couple of chips dangled from his brown beard.

"Good afternoon, sir," Jamie said. "I am Jamie Miller."

Daniel smiled warmly and slipped his leather gloves off, tossing them onto the table he was sanding. He extended a tanned and calloused hand to shake. Aaron had taught him how a handshake could tell you how strong someone was and the firm squeeze around Jamie's fingers told him that Daniel was strong. Very strong.

He squeezed back just as firmly and watched the smile on Daniel's weather-beaten face widen.

"Nice to meet you, Jamie. Well met," Daniel said, his voice deeper than Aaron's and slightly rougher. "I was not expecting you until later this week. Are you all setting in well?"

Jamie nodded his head. "Jah, sir. We are settling in well. I wanted to come here and thank you for the furniture," he remarked, leaving out the part about thanking Aubrey for the bread and cookies. He knew that in Lancaster some fathers refused to let their daughters court because they relied on them to maintain the household.

"Of course. Please come in if you have the time and have some water," Daniel offered.

He moved to retreat further into the storage area, but Jamie caught sight of the clock hanging above the door leading to the front of the store. A stab of disappointment went through him.

"I'm sorry, sir, but I must get home before my Pa gets off work," he said, smiling apologetically at the middle-aged Amish man. "He is working construction and will be off soon so we can plow the ground. I just wanted to thank you and your family for all your hospitality. When did you expect Henry and I here?"

Daniel returned to the roughly-sanded table and slipped his gloves back on. He picked up the piece of cured sand paper and adjusted it back on the black sanding block.

"The taxi picks us up at 7:00am and then we work until 5:00pm. Will Friday be enough time for you all to settle here?" Daniel asked.

"More than enough, sir. Thank you," Jamie said.

The sound of sand paper scratching away at the wood was the last thing Jamie heard as ventured out into the hazy and hot afternoon.

Cʒଛ୬

They finished plowing the ground the next day and took the horses swimming down in a lake that Jamie had found the day prior.

"Are you ready for work this week?" Henry asked, clinging easily to the back of his horse.

Both were submerged to their chests as they allowed their horses to swim deeper into the lake. Jamie wrapped his arms around the strong muscles of his horse's neck and allowed his legs to float out behind him.

"Jah. I met Daniel Forrest yesterday," Jamie answered.

Henry turned to look at him in bafflement. Droplets of water clung to the golden strands of his hair.

"You met him yesterday? Wait a minute," Henry frowned, contemplating something before he spoke again. "Lily mentioned that you had gone to town to thank Aubrey Forrest for the bread and cookies. Is that where you actually went?"

Jamie looked away to avoid his brother's penetrating stare. The last thing he needed to hear was Henry's teasing about having a crush and not doing anything about it.

"I thought it would only be polite-" he started with a indelicate sniff, but Henry swooped in and began to laugh.

"You don't even know her and yet you act like you are courting her. What was she like?" Henry asked.

They steered their panting horses back toward the edge of the lake. The sun began to dip down below the trees and Aaron would be home soon from his construction job. Though their chores were completed, Aaron would still give them a tongue lashing for getting their clothes wet with lake water and treating their horses like family pets.

Jamie shrugged indifferently before submerging his burnt face into the cool water. "She wasn't there," he answered, wiping his mouth clean of the murky taste of the water. "Her sister Sadie was the one behind the register."

Rocks crunched and clinked together under the

hooves of the horses. They took a moment to wring out some of the water from their drenched clothes and smoothed out the water from the horses' hair.

Their youngest sister Matilda walked hand-in-hand with Lily from the barn, their gray dresses matching. Matilda spotted them first and waved eagerly in the same fashion Sadie had done the other day. They both waved back as they trotted closer.

Lily's nose wrinkled at the smell of lake water clinging to their clothes and horses. She looked up at them, a scowl beginning to spread across her face. "Please tell me that you didn't go swimming in the lake in your freshly-laundered clothes," she sighed, exasperation lacing her tone.

Henry shrugged indifferently. He flung a few drops of water at them and Matilda giggled while Lily danced away from them.

"Okay. Is Pa home yet?" Henry asked.

"No, not yet. I suggest you get dressed in fresh clothes though, before he does. You know he doesn't approve of you treating those horses like family pets," Lily asserted, continuing down the road and back toward the house.

"Well," Henry began, after feeding the horses and letting them dry outside in the field. "It was nice having some free time to relax. Back to work tomorrow."

Jamie grinned at him. They walked side-by-side down the road, boots making an uncomfortable squishing noise from the water trapped inside. Crickets chirped loudly as the evening sun began to slip below the horizon and pink light spilled across the sky.

"I like to work," Jamie said. For the past few days he had felt rather lost without work, and though he was anxious about learning a new craft, he was also excited to return to some sort of normalcy. "Pa can't support all of us on one job. We have to help out too. It's tough to live here, despite how much more room there is."

"I know that," Henry agreed, sighing deeply. "I just enjoyed having the time to look out here and see Gott. It was so congested in Lancaster and hard to take in things like you can here. The pace and feel is so much slower."

After changing into fresh clothes, Jamie set his clothes outside on the porch railing to let them dry and make it easier for Lily and Sarah to wash them. The back door opened behind him and he turned to see Lily exiting from the house. The smell of roasting chicken followed through the door after her.

"Dinner is almost done," Lily informed him. She looked at their clothes hanging off the porch railing and smiled appreciatively.

Jamie nodded and made to go inside, but Lily stopped him by gingerly resting a hand on his arm. He arched an eyebrow in confusion at her.

"Can I talk to you?" Lily asked quietly. She peered up at him, the top of her kapp barely reaching his shoulder. The orange glow from the evening sun darkened her sunburned cheeks.

"Sure."

Lily lowered herself to the porch step and folded the fabric of her dress around her legs. They sat quietly for a while, relaxing with the peaceful sounds of the horses grazing in the distance and chatter from the neighboring houses and farms.

"I don't think I'll be able survive here," Lily almost whispered, breaking the companionable silence between them.

Her words drove a knife through Jamie's gut. She didn't offer any further explanation, but Jamie knew exactly what Lily meant. *Rumspringa* was approaching for both of them. Sarah and Daniel had already approved if they wished to participate before deciding to join the church or leave.

He rushed to calm his sister's doubts. "You *will* survive here. All of us will. It'll just take some time to adjust." Jamie said.

Lily turned to look at him. Tears welled in her eyes and then slowly began to trail down the contours of her cheeks. She shook her head solemnly, a wavering smile turning her lips up slightly. "I can't even bake bread here, Jamie. What kind of wife will I be if I can't even bake something simple? I know Mom and Dad are upset with me because I can't stop talking back or crying over the littlest things. I can't help it though. I just miss Lancaster and Brian so much. He wanted to marry me, but then Pa decided that we had to move. What if I don't ever find someone like Brian again? What if he was *the one*?" Lily sobbed, curling up into his side.

Jamie sighed as he rubbed Lily's trembling shoulders in a soothing manner. "You will figure it out in time, Lily. You will make someone a very happy husband, who won't care if you burn the bread occasionally," he announced, grinning at the choked laugh that escaped from Lily. He waited while Lily wiped her cheeks dry and regained control over herself before nudging her playfully. "How about this? I'll ask Ma and Pa if you can come with me to work sometime this week and we can walk to the bakery—what?"

Lily stared at him with a knowing smile on her face. "See!" she exclaimed, poking him in the arm with a finger. "I told Henry that it's fate that Aubrey Forrest keeps getting brought up. Everyone keeps mentioning it to Ma, saying you two would be perfect for each other."

To Jamie's horror, he felt the center of his cheeks flare. For some unexplainable reason his heart thrummed a little bit harder at the mention of Aubrey's name.

"It's not a big deal," Jamie shrugged, but his sister grinned widely at him. "Stop smiling like that. You and Henry are making things up in your head again."

They were interrupted by Aaron's whistling from down the road. He lifted his hand in a wave and began to trek the gravel road to their home. Lily rose with a sigh, straightening out the wrinkles in her dress and patting Jamie fondly on top of the head.

"Danka bruder. You are always good at cheering me up," she noted with a smile and slipped through the door to help Sarah set the table for dinner.

Aaron eventually strolled up to him, white shirt covered in dirt and trousers smudged with what looked like cement. Out of all of them, Aaron was the only who wasn't sunburned. His forehead was only tanned and toughened from being out in the sun.

"Beautiful evening." Aaron said to Jamie, pausing beside him on the porch steps. "Why are your clothes drying on the porch?"

"We took the horses swimming because they were hot after plowing." Jamie said, not bothering to lie to Aaron. Since as long as Jamie could remember Aaron was good at detecting lies, and he found that their punishments were less severe if they told the truth. "Sorry. It won't happen again."

Aaron shook his head and sighed heavily, hands on his hips. He leveled a stern glance down at Jamie. "Don't let it. Those horses are for work and transportation," said he advised simply before disappearing into the house.

Jamie gazed at the darkening sky for a moment longer before following Pa inside. He wondered what Aubrey Forrest was doing at that exact moment.

ભ CHAPTER 3 ૯

The bakery was blazing hot and stuffy as the sun sat high in the sky. Aubrey used the sleeve of her cotton dress to wipe away the line of sweat beading at her hairline and fanned herself with a piece of paper. She was in charge of the register at the moment, giving Katie a break to eat lunch in the back of the bakery, and watching a group of teenage Englischers browse the aisles of bread.

She waited patiently for them to make a decision, mentally making a list of things to do. She still needed to pull a couple of old loaves from the shelves and clean the inside of the glass display classes, but couldn't move from her spot until they paid and left. The bakery had been unusually quiet all morning, with the occasional customer venturing in, but neither Aubrey or Katie were complaining. It gave them the much-needed time to clean, stock, and organize their inventory.

"Do you ever get hot in that?" One of the girls from the group asked, setting two loaves of friendship bread down on the counter. A sweet smell clung to her tanned skin and it was overwhelming.

"No. I don't," she replied politely, keeping her eyes averted from the bare skin that popped out everywhere.

The Ordnung, their code of conduct, taught them to never be confrontational or openly express their differing opinions unless asked, and even then it had to be in subtle hints. Aubrey bit the inside of her cheek and kept quiet. As the girl handed over a credit card, Aubrey tried not to picture Emma exposing the same amount of skin and slid the thin plastic through the card reader like Katie had taught her.

"Well, it looks like it would," the girl stated, taking the card back after it went through and sliding it in the front pocket of her shorts. "And it's kind of a shame. You're a really pretty girl, even without any makeup."

She smiled widely and then grabbed the loaves. The sweet smell still lingered in the air even after they exited the bakery.

Aubrey let out a pent up breath and stepped out from behind the counter. Her sneakers squeaked on the linoleum floors and she gathered an armful of bread loaves that were a few days old. After work, she would help Katie and Sadie deliver them to their neighbors.

She had rounded the metal shelves that Daniel had put up years ago when the screen door screeched open and then thudded closed. Aubrey turned to greet whoever stepped in, but the words froze on the tip of her tongue and the rest of her followed suit.

Even though Aubrey had yet to meet or see Jamie Miller since his arrival in Monte Vista, she recognized him right away from how Sadie and Daniel had described him. His hair, a rich honey color, shimmered in the light and a few strands brushed against his burnt forehead from under his wide-rimmed hat. His tall and strong frame was like most Amish men, hard from years of work toiling on a farm. The sleeves of his white shirt were rolled up on his forearms and the straps of his black suspenders dangled by his side. Blue eyes, a shade that reminded Aubrey of the fall sky, focused intently on her and a dizzying smile spread across his sharp face.

Aubrey's heart thundered wildly and so loudly that she feared that Jamie could hear it. A fluttering sensation in the pit of her stomach made her jolt slightly and the loaves of bread fell free from her arms to the ground. She grimaced inwardly at her clumsiness and the sides of her neck flared in embarrassment.

"Are you Aubrey Forrest?" Jamie asked softly, the silky deep tones of his voice penetrating the stillness of the bakery.

She managed a small nod. Jamie's boots thumped loudly on the floor and he crouched gracefully in front of her, picking up the loaves. When he straightened, their eyes met and she smelled freshly-cut wood on his clothes. The top of her head barely reached the center of his chest and she controlled the urge to bury her head there.

"I wanted to thank you for the bread and cookies," Jamie said simply. He smiled almost shyly down at her, long eyelashes curled and framing his eyes. "They were delicious. My sister wants to know your secret."

Aubrey cleared her throat against the sudden

onslaught of dryness and smiled. "Thank you for those kind words. Tell your sister the trick is increasing the baking soda and adding a little bit of water with the flour," Aubrey explained. Baking at high altitudes was difficult and she had a inkling that Jamie's sister had recently found that out.

Jamie nodded and carefully set the loaves on the counter, next to the register. At that moment, Aubrey was glad that there were no customers around and that Katie was in the back eating her lunch. For the past couple of days, Jamie had played in her thoughts constantly. To finally see him there, standing in front of her with a smile on his face and blue eyes sparkling, eased a curious ache that she didn't even know she had deep within her.

"How are you and your family adjusting?" Aubrey asked.

"Gut. It is very beautiful out here," Jamie said.

Aubrey smiled genuinely. He loved the outdoors just as much as she did. "Wait until the seasons change. Each one is more beautiful than the next," she informed him.

Jamie's eyes focused on her once again and rooted her to the spot, studying her like she was the most fascinating person in the world. A shiver crept up Aubrey's spine in response. Her skin tingled under the weight of a stare that almost penetrated right into her soul. She wondered faintly if it was possible to feel so exposed under someone's eyes while fully clothed.

"I will look forward to the seasons changing then. I am working with your daed at the furniture store," Jamie went on, eventually breaking the silence. He rubbed at the back of his neck absently with a hand. "I wanted to introduce myself since everyone else has suggested that we meet."

Aubrey laughed breathlessly. White teeth flashed briefly when Jamie grinned widely. His eyes flicked upward to the clock above the door that led back into the kitchen and then settled on her again.

"Your daed gave me a half hour to eat lunch and I have to return shortly," Jamie said, smiling apologetically at her.

"Of course," Aubrey answered, returning the smile. "I understand. Papa's peeve is tardiness."

Their arms brushed when Jamie took a step past her and a sizzling sensation rushed through Aubrey's veins. With one hand pushing open the door, Jamie turned partially to look over at her one last time.

"I will see you at church at Sunday, jah?"

"Jah."

"Gut. I look forward to seeing you there."

A loud whoosh of air escaped through Aubrey's clenched teeth after Jamie stepped out. She felt light-headed and dizzy from the adrenaline pumping rapidly throughout her. No other boy had ever uttered those words to her before and made her heart flutter in excitement.

Aubrey jumped when Katie's curious voice spoke up from right behind her.

"Who were you talking to?"

"Ach! Mama, you nearly scared me to death."

She placed a hand over her already-wildly beating

heart and turned to face Katie with a relieved smile.

Katie stood in the doorframe of the kitchen and read the excitement etched plainly over Aubrey's flushed features. Her eyebrows arched high in a silent question and almost disappeared underneath her white kapp. "Well?" Katie prompted when she didn't answer right away. "Who were you talking to that has all you excited? I heard a boy's voice."

"Jamie Miller. He came in to introduce himself and thank me for the bread and cookies," Aubrey answered, barely containing the excited tremor in her voice.

The front door squeaked open and customers trickled through. Aubrey used the distraction as an excuse to move about the bakery, dusting the shelves and wiping down the display cases.

It was unexplainable, the jittery feeling still rushing throughout her. The rational side of her chided such feelings when she barely even knew Jamie. The other side tantalized her with their conversation, no matter how brief it had been, and what could possibly transpire over next Sunday. Church would be at Hannah's parent's barn, and even though night singing wasn't for another couple of weeks it would actually give them time to have a conversation. It would also give Aubrey the chance to prove that she was not always so clumsy or air-headed.

She rolled her eyes at herself for making a great first impression. She spent the rest of the afternoon busy in the kitchen, with Jamie not too far from her thoughts.

CRICO

Jamie's heart pounded in the caverns of his chest. He had gone to the bakery during his lunch break expecting Aubrey to be gone or running errands, but had been pleasantly surprised to find her there pulling loaves of bread off the shelves.

She was more beautiful than he could have imagined. Her pale blue eyes shimmered innocently at him and her skin, a lightly golden hue, had freckles peppering her cheekbones. Strands of light blonde hair peeked out from beneath her white kapp and hidden beneath the fabric of her gray dress and white apron he could see her short and very slender frame. *Delicate*, he thought as he walked down the sidewalk and back toward the furniture store. She was very delicate and yet so full of life and strength.

"Aubrey," he whispered to himself, shivering at how her name rolled off his tongue.

The afternoon felt even hotter than the last couple of days. Maybe it was the heat or the selfish need to think about Aubrey that made Jamie feel lazy and scuff the bottoms of his boots on the sidewalk.

It was alarming, the effect she had on him with that brief encounter. He hadn't expected the instantaneous attraction. Aubrey felt the same way, he was sure of that. She had dropped the bundle of loaves in her arms in surprise when he walked in and looked at him in the same fashion as he'd looked at her.

Daniel had just sat on the wooden bench outside the store and opened his lunch pail when Jamie walked up.

"The store is slow at the moment. Henry went to the

general store to buy a sandwich," Daniel told him, patting the empty spot next to him on the bench. "Business will pick up tomorrow since it's Saturday. How are you liking it so far?"

Jamie sat on the bench and stared out at the empty field alongside the building. All morning Daniel had taught him how to hand-select certain pieces of wood for certain types of furniture and pay close attention to the grains in the wood when glueing. He'd also taught him about the two types of styles that Forrest Furniture supplied: the Mission and Shaker Styles. Englischers from the surrounding area loved their work and nothing lasted very long on the sales floor.

"It's very interesting work, sir. I like it more than farming," Jamie stated politely but truthfully. He'd enjoyed learning the craft all morning and it was nice to be in the shade the majority of the day versus being in the sun from dawn until dusk. Next week Daniel had promised to let him work on a dining room table with a set of chairs as a training and test session.

The afternoon sweltered away with Levi Forrest, the oldest son, appearing from the front of the store and introducing himself as the oldest of the Forrest children. While Henry and Jamie worked, he occasionally spouted advice or showed them a easier way of using a certain tool. By the time the store closed and they began the long trek home, Jamie had decided that he liked the Forrest family. He could easily relate to them and that had to be another sign. Jamie had gotten along with every family in the community back at Lancaster, but he never had felt such a click.

The small town disappeared behind them the further the two brothers walked toward their settlement and they soaked in the quiet afternoon.

"Where did you go for lunch?" Henry asked, turning to look at him curiously. "You left before I could ask if you wanted to get a sandwich from the general store."

Jamie's stomach rumbled hungrily. He felt lightheaded from the heat and having not eaten since breakfast. He should have bought a pastry or cookie, but seeing Aubrey for the first time had erased any trace of appetite and kept him full for the rest of the afternoon.

"I went to the bakery," Jamie muttered, and he looked away from the teasing glint that immediately sparked in Henry's eyes. A part of him wanted to keep their conversation, their *first* conversation, to himself and not let any others look into it. However, he knew Henry well enough to know that he wouldn't let up until Jamie told him the details. "Aubrey was there and we didn't get to talk long, but I'm going to try and talk to her after church Sunday."

Henry smiled widely. "I'm glad you got to meet her, bruder. When is the next night singing here?" he questioned as they turned down a more isolated road.

"I don't know," Jamie replied. He would find that out on Sunday after church.

A sudden thought popped into Jamie's head and made his stomach churn uneasily. It was the same thought that he'd had the first time meeting Daniel Forrest.

Henry watched the grimace on Jamie's face and

frowned in concern. He laid a sweaty hand on Jamie's tense shoulder and opened his mouth, but Jamie beat him to it.

"What if her daed doesn't allow her to court?" Jamie asked anxiously. He looked over at Henry in distress. "There were several daed's back at Lancaster who didn't allow their daughters to court because they preferred them to stay home and help with the house and kinner."

"I'm not sure, bruder. Have you asked him about it? You won't know unless you ask," Henry mentioned.

Their farm came into view down the road and they could both see Aaron's tall figure in the distance, moving around the side of the barn, a pail in one hand. Matilda's shorter figure darted from inside the barn with a pail clutched tightly to her chest and followed Aaron toward the horses grazing in the field.

Henry was right. He wouldn't know unless he asked, and if the answer was no, then perhaps Jamie could persuade Daniel.

"No, not yet. But I will," Jamie promised and then smiled gratefully at Henry.

Tomorrow he'd ask Daniel about Aubrey. Or Sunday if they were too busy.

CRESO

Church was at the King's barn a mile down the road. Aubrey walked along the gravel road with a basket of bread and cheese cradled in her arms. The rest of her family followed behind and their cheerful conversation was distant to Aubrey. With each step closer to the King's farm, she grew more nervous and jittery.

She constantly replayed her conversation with Jamie over and over in her mind, analyzing the words and the small gestures that were so ordinary but exciting. The past couple of days had ticked by slowly, with the normalcy of chores and spending time with her family.

The barn had been swept clean, but a couple of pieces of hay and dirt lingered on the floor. Wooden benches were pushed into rows and at the front one of the ministers of their church, Isaac, stood with Samuel King. Families filtered in slowly, greeting one another with handshakes and placing food on the long table outside of the barn.

Hannah appeared at Aubrey's side the second she'd set down the basket of food on the table and twined an arm through hers, tugging the two of them away from prying ears.

"So?" Hannah asked excitedly. "How did meeting Jamie go?"

Aubrey frowned at her. "How did you know that I met Jamie yesterday? I haven't seen you for a couple of days."

"Jacob saw Jamie walking out of the bakery," Hannah explained. She squeezed Aubrey's arm and practically bounced from foot to foot. "Tell me! What are the details?"

A smile worked its way across Aubrey's face at Hannah's enthusiasm. She knew she shouldn't divulge in gossip and should reprimand Hannah for it, but the jittery feeling inside of her was threatening to burst.

"We didn't get to talk much, but he's so handsome,

Hannah. I don't know what it is that is so different, but I just can't stop thinking about him..." Aubrey trailed off with a dreamy sigh and then blushed at the teasing look Hannah sent her. "It's stupid, I know. We've only talked for like five minutes and we don't even know each other."

Hannah laughed. "If Gott is telling you that he's the one made for you, then you should trust it. I felt that way about Jacob and we only courted for a month before we were married. We felt were a match," she said and then smiled tenderly at Aubrey, grabbing her hand. "You deserve this happiness, Aubrey. Just as much as anyone else here. Don't let what happened make you question otherwise."

At that moment, Jacob called Hannah's name from inside the barn. She squeezed Aubrey's hand comfortingly before dropping it and disappearing into the barn to find Jacob. Aubrey stood by the table for a moment, blinking away the tears that had surfaced there suddenly at her friend's kind words.

For the first time since Emma had left, a glimmer of hope flickered within Aubrey. Even though her family wasn't shunned for Emma's decision, there were subtle consequences and whispers. Daniel had also been favored from most of the community to replace Minister Isaac after he stepped down, but that had changed naturally. How could a minister tend to the community's spiritual wellfare if he could not manage his own family? The church kept a close eye on them, and Aubrey in particular had become a constant target of the whispers.

Aubrey sighed heavily and a headache began to pound

in her temples. *Maybe it could be possible*, she thought, *to be loved by someone here possibly*. Maybe she didn't have to venture out of the community to find love or happiness like Emma had done.

"Good morning, Aubrey."

The gravelly tone told her right away that it was their minister Isaac standing behind her. She was partially tempted not to turn around and face Isaac's keen eyes, but knew what sort of tongue-lashing that would ensue for being disrespectful to a member of the church. Aubrey inhaled a calming breath and then forced a pleasant smile on her face.

"Good morning, sir," Aubrey responded, hastily wiping her eyes dry before turning around to face him. "How do you fare today?"

Up close Isaac looked every bit of his old age from the wrinkled and brown spotted skin to the slight trembling in his stiff fingers. The only feature of him that had not aged was the luminous blue eyes that could peer right into one's soul and know their deepest and darkest secrets. It was when he stood in the middle of a barn or a house and preached memorized scriptures that no one would believe him to be in his seventies.

"Wunderbaar," Isaac said, his smile showing the few teeth he had left. "I noticed you standing over here by yourself while everyone has taken a seat. Something troubling you?"

Aubrey glanced around and realized with a jolt that everyone had indeed gone inside the barn. She mentally scolded herself for not paying attention to her surroundings and kept the same smile trained unwaveringly on her face. "No, sir. Forgive me. I was only thinking of something small," Aubrey said, bowing her head.

She moved to step by him, but Isaac reached out a gnarled hand and halted her with a firm grip to her upper arm. A tremor of fear shot through Aubrey instantly. She knew that the Amish didn't believe in violence of forcing themselves upon one another, but she had heard rumors of such things happening in other communities.

"Your father tells me that you are thinking about *rumspringa*," Isaac commented.

The tension in Aubrey lessened a little, but not completely. She shifted uncomfortably against the rough fingers that circled and dug slightly into her arm.

"Yes, but I do not think I will be participating," Aubrey said, hoping that answer would satisfy whatever Isaac was seeking. "Mama and Papa need me here to help out with the bakery."

Isaac's pale blue eyes threatened to carve holes into her own and a strange expression glazed them over. Neither one of them moved as he assessed her answer for a minute before his fingers released her arm.

Aubrey immediately took a step back, resisting the urge to reach up and rub at the sore muscles there.

"Do not fear the church, Aubrey. We are only here to help guide you through troubling times. If you wish to speak to me privately about this matter, I will be more than happy to converse," Isaac said.

He smiled warmly down upon her and wrapped an

arm lightly around her shoulders. The smell of kaffe clung strongly to Isaac and threatened Aubrey's queasy stomach. She walked tensely alongside him as they entered the barn and discreetly shifted out from under Isaac's arm to the spot Katie saved for her. Both Katie and Daniel watched her enter the barn with Isaac's arm draped around her shoulders and a concerned frown graced their faces.

If they suspected anything, they didn't get the chance to ask. Aubrey sat down on the edge of the bench and clenched her fingers tightly in the fabric of her dress. As the barn began to fill with hymns, Aubrey felt a pair of eyes on her. She looked up from the ground and to the right, to find Jamie staring directly at her from across the aisle.

Several emotions rushed through Aubrey at the sight of those warm blue eyes that she had been thinking about since the day at the bakery. She was so utterly relieved to see him sitting there, singing along with everyone else, and yet his attention was on her. More than anything she wanted to sit down alongside him and soak up the warmth that radiated off of him.

"Are you okay?" he mouthed to her.

The genuine concern on Jamie's face made tears surface again in Aubrey's eyes. She blinked against them and nodded, offering him a small smile before turning to face the front again.

When Isaac concluded with one last hymn, they ventured out into the hot air to eat and socialize for the rest of the afternoon.

"What happened outside with Isaac?" Hannah asked her, biting into a piece of cheese. "You looked like you were about to throw up afterwards."

Aubrey let out a pent up breath and looked down at her plate of food, all of it untouched. Her stomach churned at the idea of eating. The two of them sat on a patch of grass a couple feet away from the table. Kinner ran around them occasionally, laughing joyfully.

"He asked me about *rumspringa* because daed mentioned to him that I was considering it," Aubrey said quietly, picking at a stray thread at the hem of her dress. "I know that the church is concerned about my spiritual well being, but I don't want to go anywhere at the moment."

Her eyes floated over to where Jamie stood by his daed's side, half listening to Miriam Bender. Jamie sensed her stare and looked away from Miriam, a smile gracing his face. She couldn't help but smile back.

"Because of Jamie?" Hannah prodded gently, watching the exchange.

Aubrey nodded. "Some part of me is telling me to stay here and I don't want to question that like my sister does," she answered.

The instant the words left Aubrey's mouth, she realized they were the wrong thing to say. Hannah's eyes shot to Aubrey's and she stared at her in puzzlement, a frown slowly shaping its way across her face.

She was saved from explaining when Jamie approached them. Aubrey sat back, cupping a hand over her eyes to look up at him, and a fluttery sensation, the same one from the bakery, filled her again. They stared at each other silently, until Hannah broke it off with a impatient sigh.

"How about you two sit and talk instead of just staring at each other?" Hannah said, rolling her eyes at them dramatically, all traces of her frown gone. She stood, brushing grass from her blue dress, and left them wordlessly. There had been several times in Aubrey's life that she was thankful to have Hannah as a friend and now was one of them.

Jamie folded his long and lean frame down next to her, keeping a respectable distance between them. The faint spicy smell of whatever soap he used permeated Aubrey's senses. This morning his face was clean shaven from the prickly beard that had dotted his jaw at the bakery and his skin was a little less burnt.

"Is everything okay?" Jamie asked. He draped his arms casually around his bent knees and looked at her in concern. "I noticed that you were standing outside with the minister and then you came back in looking pale. You still look pale."

Color filled the center of Aubrey's cheeks at his rather keen and accurate observation. She cleared her throat and feigned indifference. The last thing she wanted to do was spend their second conversation talking about her spiritual crisis and Emma.

"I was a little sick from the heat this morning is all," she said and then rushed on when Jamie arched an eyebrow at her, clearly not buying it. "I've been here forever and I still have trouble with the heat and altitude at times. How are you adjusting?"

For a split second, she feared that Jamie wouldn't let it go from the way he looked at her, but he slowly shrugged his shoulders. Aubrey exhaled in relief.

"Now that all my original skin is burnt off, I'd say that I'm adjusting," Jamie answered, grinning widely.

Aubrey burst out laughing, all traces of unease floating away. For the next hour she listened to him talk. Nothing serious or spiritual, just talking about random things from his life. She learned that Jamie was an energetic person and had to keep busy from the he way talked. He constantly shifted, picked at the grass, looked at her with a beaming smile, or picked at his long fingers while she sat motionlessly alongside him.

When families began to trickle back down the road to return home for the evening, a heavy weight settled in Aubrey's stomach. She wanted to stay at Jamie's side and listen to the syrupy rhythms of his voice and feel his eyes on her.

"I better get going. My daed is waving me over," Jamie commented.

Aubrey spotted her family also waiting near the table, picking up their baskets and whatever else they had brought. "Me too," she said, and couldn't keep the glum tones out of her voice.

Jamie smiled. He rose gracefully to his feet and then leaned down, offering a calloused hand to help her up. Aubrey hesitated, knowing that inappropriate touching was frowned upon, but told herself that Jamie was merely being a gentleman and helping her up.

Her breath hitched inside her throat when she placed her much smaller hand into the palm of his. The feeling of Jamie's calloused, but incredibly warm, skin enveloping hers in a strong grip was one of the most heart-pounding experiences Aubrey ever felt in her life. Tingles of energy shot up her arm as he hoisted her up effortlessly.

Aubrey expected him to drop her hand, but his long and strong fingers squeezed hers. She raised her eyes, breathless from his close proximity and the spicy smell that was uniquely his.

"I'll see you soon," Jamie promised.

His own voice was breathless and her heart thumped even harder. The second Jamie's fingers slipped from her own, a emptiness clung to them. As she watched Jamie walk away, she couldn't help but think of people as anchors.

They sometimes anchored you down in such a way that you struggled to breathe, while others anchored you in such a way that you didn't mind drowning.

ଔ CHAPTER 4 ଶ

Aubrey rose and crept quietly about her room, mindful of the floorboards that groaned loudly, and lit a candle on her desk. Soft light flickered to life and erased the darkness that had occupied her room and dreams.

She had dreamt of Emma again.

Sometimes her dreams were of her brushing the tangles out of Aubrey's hair and the feel of Emma's soft fingers on the nape of her neck. Other times it would be talking together in the living room as they dressed in front of the wood stove and warmed their chilly nightgowns before running up the stairs to their separate beds.

This time she'd dreamt of Emma's tombstone in a graveyard outside of Monte Vista. The skies were overcast with black clouds and a bitter wind ripped at her dress. Her heart was shattered and the pieces were pumping at different rates, some slow and others fast. The piece that belonged to Emma was clutched tightly in her sister's grasp below the ground. She could feel her sister's fingers tightening fiercely on the piece.

"This is what happens, Aubrey," Isaac's gravelly voice spoke up. He stood in front of the tombstone clothed in black. The surrounding darkness made his luminous eyes appear brighter. "This is what a life of wickedness does to you. Let it go. She is gone, dead. Let it go or you'll be in here with her."

She woke after that with a choked sob caught in her throat. Sweat covered every inch of her skin and the sheets were damp and tangled around her limbs. It had only been a dream, but she had to check. She had to make sure that Emma was alive.

The loose floorboard was beneath her bed. Stomach pressed against the cool wood, she slid her way beneath her bed. Using her fingernail to pry the board up, she set the board quietly to the side and pulled out the various objects stored there.

She tiptoed her way over to the desk and set everything down there, listening to the stillness of the house before easing into the chair. She rifled through the envelopes of letters and found the most recent, the envelope still sealed. It had come over a week ago, and with Jamie serving as a distraction, she had completely forgotten about it until now.

Aubrey took the sewing scissors from the drawer of her desk and cut the top of it open so that the sound of paper ripping wouldn't wake Katie or Daniel, whose room was located right next to hers. She eased the letter out and the faint smell of perfume, the one Emma wore now, spilled out as Aubrey's eyes greedily took in the neat cursive words:

Aubrey,

I am writing this from a plane. Imagine that! This is my first time being on one and it is the most thrilling experience to be flying high above the clouds and close to heaven. I wish you were in the seat next to mine, enjoying it with me.

I am going to New York City to attend college at Columbia University. They have one of the best Fine Arts programs in the United States and accepted me on a full ride scholarship. Turns out that people are willing to help people like us out more. I told my case worker about you and she said that if you wish to leave that you could easily have the same future I have. I got a list of my textbooks and I think you would enjoy them. I will send you copies to read at night or early morning.

I know that the church would have a heart attack thinking of New York City, but it's not so bad out here. Every place is different. Every person is different. There is good and there is bad. There's also tons of gray areas.

This letter is shorter than I intended it to be. My heart is too full and anxious to even write you. Once I am settled in the city and find a job, I will send you a letter with my updated address.

Please give Mama and Papa a huge hug for me. I miss all of you so much. I sometimes spend the evenings imagining conversations with all of you. I wish things didn't have to be the way they are now.

Love you always,
Emma

Tears rolled down Aubrey's cheeks. Her sister was

alive and well, traveling across the country to a city. She gently folded the letter and put it back in the envelope. She placed it on the top of the small stack of the other letters from Emma and then pulled out her large leather journal. Aubrey raked her fingers over the supple, tough leather and inhaled its comforting smell. Tucked in the very back were lined pieces of paper that Emma had sent for her to write on instead of wasting the paper of her journals. She pulled a piece free and made to write, but her hand remained motionless.

What would Jamie think?

The sudden thought was enough to make her drop the pen. Emma had sacrificed everything she ever cared about to pursue the outside world. She knew her sister well enough that if she truly was happy on the outside, she would not be writing letters and asking about their family. There would be nothing if she was happy.

To follow meant losing Jamie, and she wasn't sure if she was exactly willing to do that just yet.

CREO

"You're up early."

Aubrey looked up at the sound of Daniel's voice, hands submerged in the basin of soapy lukewarm water, and shrugged tiredly. His tall figure filled the doorframe of their tiny laundry room and he looked mildly surprised to see her awake.

"I couldn't sleep, so I came down to get a head start on the laundry," Aubrey replied. She had managed to start one load of laundry without waking the household from the gas motor roaring to life and now she could hang the clothes to dry outside before heading to the bakery.

"The rugs needed to be washed at 5:00am?" Daniel asked, disbelief coloring his words. "Come, doctah, there is something you aren't telling me."

She stared down at the little soap bubbles floating on the water's surface and a wave of fatigue crashed over her, harder than before. Even her bones ached from exhaustion. Daniel's hand brushed the side of her head before pushing a few errant strands of hair away and then resting his palm on the surface of her warm forehead.

"You have a low grade fever," Daniel noted quietly, hand retreating.

He gently pulled Aubrey's hands from the water and she leaned gratefully against the wall, breathing in deeply. After Daniel rang the excess water out of the rug, he clipped it to a line and guided Aubrey to the living room. Once they settled on the couch, pale light started to leak in through the windows.

"What is going on?" he asked.

Aubrey rubbed her forehead and then pinched the bridge of her nose in despair.

"I don't know, Papa. I had a dream that Emma was dead and that Minister Isaac told me I would be dead too if I didn't let Emma go. I couldn't get rid of this horrible feeling, like something bad is about to happen. Am I a bad person for missing Emma? Am I going against the church by missing her or wondering if she's okay out in the outside world?"

The words tumbled out of her in a soft whisper. It was only the partial truth of what was bothering her, but she had asked the one question plaguing her constantly. Was it entirely wrong to miss someone who'd left?

She half-expected Daniel to reprimand her for thinking or saying such things, but he surprised her by smiling gently.

"No, of course not. You are not a bad person or going against the church for missing Emma. It's all part of a process of grief, Aubrey. Emma may be alive, but she is gone and we all feel the loss. I do too sometimes," Daniel replied.

"You do?" Knowing that Daniel thought of Emma even when they were supposed to ignore her made the weight on her shoulders more tolerable. If someone as strong in their faith as Daniel also had doubts sometimes, it made her own doubts seem normal.

Daniel nodded. "Of course. I am only human, Aubrey." He smiled wanly. "It is normal to feel this way at your age. Questioning Gott and the church is part of accepting Jesus in the end. He gave us the choice to choose and imperfect emotions. We just have to stay true to ourselves and in the end it will work out."

The quiet shuffling of feet down the stairs alerted them that Katie was venturing downstairs to start breakfast and morning prayers. She looked surprised to see them sitting closely on the couch, with Aubrey's hand in Daniel's and tears on her cheeks.

"Katie," Daniel called, holding out a hand for her to take. "Let's all three of us pray together this morning for strength. I fear that I am not the only who had despairing dreams."

Aubrey bowed her head as Daniel began to pray. Though she felt better knowing Daniel wasn't angry at her for missing Emma, she knew he would be furious about the letters tucked in her floorboards and the one letter she had eventually written before doing laundry.

☙❧

Jamie practically sprinted to the bakery. The store had been busy with Englischers and he began to select the wood for the dining room table Daniel asked him to build, but all of that was distant from his mind now.

He wanted to see Aubrey.

The town was also busy, and he figured it had to do with the lunch hour. Henry had gone the opposite direction to buy a sandwich at the general store. Sarah had been so busy the past couple of mornings with Matilda and organizing the house that she'd left Lily in charge of Henry and Jamie's lunch. In their lunch pails, the sandwiches, which consisted of cheese and a slice of ham, always spoiled in the heat, and both brothers agreed to talk to Lily privately about the matter later.

In a way, Jamie didn't mind. It gave him the excuse and time to head to the bakery.

He bounded up the porch steps and pushed the door open, a wide smile plastered on his face. Except Aubrey wasn't standing behind the register this time. Katie Forrest stood behind it, dressed in a gray dress that was covered in flour and her white kapp sitting delicately on her blonde hair.

"Can I help you?" Katie asked.

Jamie felt his heart clench in painful disappointment. He distracted himself by pointing to a strawberry pastry in the display class. "Yes, ma'am. I was wondering if I could buy that pastry. I hear it's the best in town," he said.

Katie's eyes continued to assess him. She reached in the display case and pulled the pastry from the tray. She set it carefully on a napkin and then slid it across the counter.

"It's free," she told him, a brief spark of genuine warmth flickering in her eyes. "Daniel tells me how helpful you are at the store and that it's nice to have someone young and strong to lift things for him. He hurt his back a few years ago after falling from the barn roof and Levi is only good at the numbers part."

The pastry was soft and sticky under his fingers when Jamie picked it up from the counter. He nodded at Katie.

"I'm grateful for the work he has given my family. I will make sure to not let him lift anything heavy while I work with him."

Katie smiled, a small smile, but Jamie took it the nonetheless. He stepped out of the bakery, his appetite now gone, and was about to turn back down the road toward the furniture store when he caught sight of Aubrey's petite frame walking down the sidewalk. He thought she'd never looked lovelier than she did with her fair head bowed and hands twined together at her stomach. Her small steps were light, barely audible on the sidewalk, and when she glanced up concern rose in him.

Even from afar it was easy to see the dark bags under Aubrey's eyes and her normally radiant skin was pale, like he had seen at church the previous Sunday. Her shoulders were slumped with an invisible weight. Their eyes met, the innocent blues of hers plagued with an indescribable emotion that was immediately wiped clean with a joy to see him.

Jamie waited patiently for her to reach him. It was hard not to reach out and touch her. The contact of their hands last Sunday at church had thrilled him to no end and it was even harder not to reach out and grab her hand.

"Hello," Aubrey said, smiling shyly up at him. She came to a standstill in front of him, with a foot of air between them, mindful of propriety.

"Hello." Jamie returned the smile and impulsively took a step forward, closing the space between them ever so slightly. Even though her appearance was haggard, he could not help but admire the details of her face. "How are you this afternoon?"

"Fine," she replied, the word tense on her tongue. Her eyes flicked down to the pastry in his hand and smiled. "I see that you have bought a pastry this time. I bet Mama was happy to see you actually buying something."

"She said it was free for helping your daed," Jamie said, shrugging nonchalantly. His eyes trailed up the sidewalk in the direction that Aubrey had come from. "Where were you coming from?"

The last time Jamie had been in town he had taken the time to note all the streets and memorize them for faster travel. The direction Aubrey had come from led out of

Monte Vista and onto the highway.

"I went for a walk. I-" Aubrey paused, biting her bottom lip in uncertainty. The small gesture caught Jamie's full attention. "I am not feeling well and thought a walk in the fresh air would help."

Jamie frowned.

The steady clip of horses' hooves on the street drew their attention behind Jamie. A middle-aged Amish man with a black beard and hair stared at them as he trotted past, sitting high up in his buggy.

"I better go inside," Aubrey said, anxiously watching the man go up the streets. "Mama is waiting for me."

She made to step by him, but Jamie anticipated the movement and blocked her path. Aubrey arched her eyebrows at him in confusion.

"Why aren't you feeling well?" he asked. Something nagged him about the direction Aubrey came from. The longer he looked at her, the more clear it became that Aubrey had a secret and was hiding it from everyone and especially from him.

It intrigued him to no end.

The question threw Aubrey off. She looked down at their feet and a bright pink color trailed up the sides of her neck before coloring in her cheeks.

"I-I-I-" Aubrey stammered. Her dainty hands twisted around themselves nervously. "I just didn't sleep well is all. I had bad dreams."

"Bad dreams?" he echoed, frowning. "What sort of bad dreams?"

Aubrey's eyes rose to his suddenly, a blaze of irritation

and defiance in them. "Why do you care? You don't even know me," she snapped, shoulders squared for a fight.

Jamie reeled back in shock at the sudden change of temperament. The last thing he had ever expected to come from Aubrey was a slip in anger. They were always mindful of their emotions, filtering through them, and dealing with them privately.

Shame filled Aubrey instantly at the outburst. "I'm sorry! Please, forgive me," she rambled, face trembling with her wavering emotions. "I did not mean to take out my foul mood on you. I am just so tired."

At that moment, Jamie didn't care if there were curious eyes watching them from somewhere nearby. All he knew was that his heart ached to see tears welling in Aubrey's eyes. He reached up and curled his fingers along the soft skin of Aubrey's jaw, holding her there tenderly. His stomach flipped when Aubrey's head turned into his touch, eyes slipping closed and a deep sigh escaping her lips.

"I am trying to know you," Jamie sighed, his voice a pitch lower than normal. "Can't you see that? I want to know who you are. Who Aubrey is beneath that white kapp."

A trembling smile graced Aubrey's face and a choked giggle escaped. She reached up, hesitantly at first, and then wrapped her small soft fingers around his wrist.

"There is not much to me," she whispered, eyes still closed and unaware of the world around them.

"There is. I can see it from a mile away."

ᑞᏏᎧ

Something was bothering Katie. Dinner was unusually tense, with Katie barely speaking to anyone and only glancing over the table at Aubrey, eyes narrowed slightly. When finished with their meals and prayers, Sadie and Isaac went outside with Daniel to feed the animals, but Aubrey had a sneaking suspicion that it was to give them privacy. After they'd cleaned up the kitchen in a thick silence, Katie finally turned to Aubrey.

"Can we talk, doctah?" she requested. Her stern tone indicated there was no other option.

Aubrey's stomach tightened in dread. She tried to read the tight lines around Katie's eyes, but could not pinpoint her mother's need to talk. If someone had seen her going to the post office to send her letter to Emma there would be no waiting to talk about it after dinner.

Something else was bothering her.

They went into the living room and sat on the couch, their legs brushing one another's in the process.

"Thomas Byler mentioned to me that he had seen you and Jamie Miller outside the bakery engaging in an intimate gesture," Katie stated.

Aubrey looked away from the disapproval shining brightly in Katie's eyes. She should've known better than to let Jamie touch her when Thomas Byler had ridden by, watching their every move. She hadn't meant to let it happen or to allow herself to engage in something inappropriate, but when it came to Jamie it was hard to remember all of the rules.

"It wasn't intimate, Mama. I was-he-I-" Aubrey stammered.

Katie stared at her unblinkingly and then laid a soft hand on Aubrey's bouncing knee.

"Your daed told me that you had a bad dream about Emma last night," Katie started, her tone gentle and understanding, "and also about what you have been feeling lately. Aubrey, you are our daughter and we love you. If there is something going on, please don't keep it to yourself."

That was the thing though, Aubrey thought, nodding her consent. She had to keep it to herself or risk being shunned from everyone, including her family and Jamie.

"I promise, Mama. I will be fine in time."

"Gutt. Now, tell me what happened this afternoon."

"It honestly wasn't a big thing, Mama. I was tired from not sleeping well and Jamie comforted me."

"Okay," Katie nodded, satisfied with the answer. "Just remember the rules of courtship."

"We aren't courting."

Yet. The word seemed to linger between them, but neither acknowledged it.

Katie smiled. "Jamie seems like a good young man. He comes from a very good family back in Lancaster. I remember what it was like before I married your father. We courted for over a year before we were allowed to marry. I know how tempting-"

"Ma!" Aubrey exclaimed.

"It is when you meet someone who you're attracted to and how how exciting it is-" Katie continued like

Aubrey hadn't spoken.

"Ma, please. I know and we wouldn't even dream of doing so."

A bright blush filled the entirety of her cheeks. There had been one conversation about what happened between a man and a woman in a marriage and that was enough to make Aubrey want to avoid it as long as possible. Of course, time had changed that since she was now a woman ready to marry when the time was right, but that was not a conversation she wanted to have with Katie at the moment.

Her mind drifted to what Jamie had said to her earlier. I want to know who you are. She shivered at the sound of the dark sugary folds of Jamie's voice echoing in her mind and she curled her knees up to her chest. Who was she? The question seemed so simple, but it was inexplicably hard to answer. She honestly didn't even know who she was anymore.

♋

"Can I talk to you for a moment, Jamie?"

The question stopped Jamie mid-step down the porch steps. He turned around to look at Aaron standing in the doorframe, dressed in black suspenders with a blue button-up shirt with the sleeves rolled up.

"I'll wait for you," Henry offered when Jamie turned around to look at him. The two exchanged confused glances before Henry began to walk up the road to give them privacy.

"I won't keep you long since you have to walk into town," Aaron acknowledged, still cradling his cup of kaffee. "I wanted to ask you what your intentions are with Aubrey Forrest."

Jamie stiffened. It was not normal for Aaron to ask questions like that. Courting was usually private and not talked about.

"What do you mean?"

"You know exactly what I mean," Aaron said, leveling a glance at him. "I heard from three different sources about what happened yesterday in front of the bakery."

"Oh... that."

"Yes, that."

Jamie looked at Aaron carefully. Something else was bothering him. It wasn't uncommon for the occasional hand holding or innocent touches with the younger kids.

"I'd like to court her," Jamie stated. He tipped his chin up and met his father's hardening stare. "If that is what you are asking..."

Aaron's face tightened with disapproval. "How much do you really know about Aubrey? Or the Forrest family, period?"

The first stirrings of anger sparked inside of Jamie at the implications behind Aaron's tones, but he managed to contain them. Years of being taught to control your emotions and not to let anger dictate decisions kicked on inside of Jamie.

"They're a good family," Jamie said defensively. "Have been around for a long time and the community respects them. I'd like to get to know Aubrey more so-"

"I don't think so," Aaron cut in, his voice as sharp as steel. "You know nothing of what has happened to that family."

"Like what?" Jamie asked. "What more do you know than me?"

He was skating on thin ice and knew it, but didn't care. Aaron's heavy boots thumped on the porch as he approached Jamie. For a wild moment Jamie thought he would strike him, but Aaron never raised a hand against them. His tongue was much more effective.

"Thomas Fields alerted me of the Forrest's daughters after seeing you with Aubrey during Fellowship," Aaron stated.

Jamie's heart began to thump faster in dread. Various scenarios rushed through his mind and none of them he wanted to believe.

"Aubrey's older sister, Emma, was arranged to marry Thomas Fields and it would have been a powerful match with Thomas's position of replacing Minister Isaac. Three days before the marriage, Emma left the church and her family. There have been concerns that Aubrey will be following suit."

No. The denial shot hotly through Jamie. Not Aubrey. Not the young Amish woman who unknowingly attracted him like a moth to the flame. He wracked his brain over the conversation he'd had with her Sunday after church. She had seemed so genuinely happy to be around him, laughing at his jokes and listening to his every word.

Earlier flashed through Jamie's mind. She was hiding something, an apparent spiritual crisis, and hearing Aaron's words clicked it all into place. It was never easy when someone was excommunicated from the church and banned from speaking or seeing any family members or friends. He couldn't even imagine not being able to talk to his family or see them outside the limited contact.

His thoughts were broken when Aaron spoke again, either unaware of the tumult of emotions within him or ignoring it completely.

"It might be a good idea to stay away from Aubrey, son. You don't want to put that shame on yourself or on your family."

Jamie didn't reply.

∝ CHAPTER 5 ∾

Two weeks passed without any sight or word of Jamie. With each afternoon that ticked by with no sight of his blue eyes sparkling down at her or that smile that made her knees wobbly, Aubrey felt that little flicker of hope begin to fade. She had no doubt in her mind that someone had said something to Jamie and he was keeping his distance for a reason.

A part of her wanted to seek him out, mainly out of a selfish need to cling to his comforting presence, but business at the bakery had increased since Katie had decided to close down during the winter. By the time chores were finished around the house, she collapsed in exhaustion every night and didn't have the strength to seek Jamie out and discover his reasons to stay clear of her.

For that reason, she was wary and mildly surprised when Jamie sought her out at church that Sunday and asked if they could talk.

They walked toward the garden behind the Byler's barn, carrying their plates of food. They were still in sight, but far enough to talk in privacy. She walked carefully next to Jamie, their arms occasionally brushing and her arm tingling at the contact.

Aubrey sat on the little stone bench facing the garden. Jamie sat alongside her, staring out at the neat rows of peas that were ready to be picked and canned before September was upon them. The afternoon light shimmered off Jamie's blonde hair as he took off his wide brimmed hat and set it between them. From the corner of her eyes, she admired the way the suspenders were pulled tightly along Jamie's back and then quickly admonished herself for entertaining those wicked thoughts.

She tapped a fingernail anxiously against the rim of her plate as another minute of silence went by. She finally gave up waiting for Jamie to speak and turned to him, in need of a distraction from her thoughts.

"How are you?" she asked and offered a smile when Jamie only turned his head to look at her.

He leaned forward and rested his elbows on his knees, looking back out at the garden. A deep breath escaped him. Aubrey turned around to see if anyone was watching them before reaching over and placing a hand on Jamie's shoulder. Bone and muscles shifted beneath her palm and she could feel the warmth of his skin through the stiff fabric of his shirt.

"What's wrong, Jamie?"

He inhaled deeply again before turning to lock eyes with Aubrey. Several emotions flickered in the sapphire depths she was beginning to love, but there were too many to read. She waited patiently for him to talk.

"I heard something about you the other week," he blurted, watching the grimace on Aubrey's face. "And I-I-I had to think about what this person said to me."

Aubrey's teeth clicked loudly when she clenched her jaw shut in silent indignation. She should have expected that someone would eventually tell Jamie about her family's history. She hadn't even thought of staying in the community long enough to be interested in someone. Jamie had that effect on her.

He made her stop and hesitate.

"What did this person say to you?" Aubrey asked, striving to keep control of her voice. She wanted to remain calm and collected, unlike the last time he had seen her.

"Thomas Fields told my daed about your sister, Emma, and said that there are concerns that you are going to leave too," Jamie explained. His eyes flicked over her face again, gauging her reaction. "I just...I don't know, Aubrey. It made sense to me when Pa told me what he had heard."

Aubrey reared back at that. Her hand dropped from his shoulder blade and fell to the hot stone between them. She stared at him, unshed tears beginning to sting the back of her eyes. "I see." Aubrey whispered. "If that is how you feel too, then I will leave-"

She grabbed her plate and made to stand, but a strong hand circled her elbow and tugged her firmly back down onto the bench.

Jamie shook his head in exasperation at her and scooted close, so that there was only a couple of inches of free space between them. "That is not how I feel. You didn't let me finish what I wanted to say."

"I already know what you are going to say," Aubrey said bitterly. "I've heard it a million times already. I just don't want to hear it again from you-"

"Stop, Aubrey," Jamie commanded sternly. His long fingers squeezed her elbow pointedly and she raised her eyes to meet his. "I'll admit that I think you are hiding something, but not because you want to keep secrets. You just don't know how to confess those secrets without getting into trouble and you don't know who to trust. Maybe someday you will trust me enough to share whatever it is that is causing your doubts. In the meantime, I don't care what others think or what my family may think. I already told you once before. I want to know who you are."

Aubrey remained motionless as she absorbed Jamie's words. Her heart hammered wildly against her rib cage at the intense and determined glaze in his eyes. She was utterly speechless and it took several seconds for her even to formulate a response.

"I'm nothing special, Jamie. There's plenty of other Amish girls who could love you better than I ever could."

Jamie shook his head. He reached up a hand, the one that had been holding her elbow, and tucked an errant strand of her blonde hair back behind her ear. "Maybe," he admitted lowly, "but I've courted those types of Amish girls before. None of them drew me to them as I am drawn to you."

Warning bells went off in Aubrey's head. Not because she wasn't enjoying the attention, but because she was enjoying the attention too much and they were in clear sight of the whole community. *Pull back*, she told herself, *pull back before you do something brash.* Except Jamie wasn't letting her move away easily. He reached out and grabbed her hand with his free one, as if sensing her thoughts, and placed her palm over his thumping heart.

"You can't tell me that you don't feel what I feel. I know that you do," Jamie continued, his deep voice intoxicating her. "I don't quite understand it either, but give me the time to prove what we both feel is right. To show the church that you aren't leaving and want to stay here, because I think you do. You just never had anything to keep you here."

"I-" Aubrey started, trying to control the surge of blood coursing through her. Her body and mind were reacting in a way that sent Aubrey's senses reeling in different directions. She closed her eyes and swallowed. "I do have things to keep me here. My family. They keep me here."

"There is a stronger love that exists."

"You don't love me. You don't even *know* me."

"True. I don't love you, but I will in time if you let me."

CRSO

Jamie watched Aubrey as she talked to her youngest sister Sadie. The two girls stood side by side, arms casually twined, with their white kapps close together, and wondered what they were talking about. Aubrey tilted her head, sensing his stare, and the corner of her lips curled up into a smile.

"Jamie."

He turned around. Aaron stood directly behind him, face tight with disapproval and watching their exchange closely.

"Do you remember what we talked about?" Aaron asked quietly.

Families were leaving the Byler's barn and beginning to venture down the road to socialize with other families. The youth gathered excitedly around the barn and readied for night singing.

"Yes, sir. I talked to Aubrey and she assured me that she was not planning to leave," Jamie said. He left out his plan to take Aubrey home tonight and start courting if her daed let her. Aaron glanced over at Aubrey and the two stared at each other for a moment before she dipped her head down, blushing brightly.

"Just be careful, son," he said simply.

Jamie watched Aaron walk over to Sarah and take the armful of dishes she had propped on her hip as she reached for a basket. The two shared a smile, the type of smile Jamie had seen Aubrey give him, before Lily graced his side.

"Are you staying behind for night singing?" she asked, envy thick in her tone.

She longingly watched a group of Amish boys wrestle their way playfully into the barn. Lily had yet to receive permission from Aaron to start courting, because he didn't believe she was ready to have those types of interactions.

"Yes, tonight I am," Jamie said. He smiled at the jealous noise that escaped his sister's throat and tugged on the string of her kapp fondly. "Don't worry, sister. Pa will let you court once he thinks you're ready."

Lily mumbled something incoherent under her breath before going to Sarah while Aaron gathered Matilda from a group of children playing around the barn. Jamie was pretty sure it was along the lines of "yeah right" and couldn't help chuckling at his sister's expense.

The Forrest family stood talking to Minister Isaac when Jamie walked up to them. Isaac took notice of him approaching first and smiled widely.

"Good afternoon, Jamie Miller!" Isaac boomed in his gravelly voice. He extended a trembling hand and there was surprising strength behind the minister's grip when he shook Jamie's hand vigorously. "Wonderful day, jah?"

Jamie smiled politely. "Yes, sir. Wonderful service too," he said, looking over to Daniel Forrest. "I was wondering if I could talk to you privately, sir, before you leave."

Daniel nodded. "Yes, of course. Excuse us, Minister."

Aubrey caught Jamie's eyes before he turned to follow Daniel, her brow furrowed questioningly, and he smiled assuredly at her.

"What can I help you with, young man?" Daniel asked once they were a few feet away from the group.

The nervous flutter in Jamie's heart began again, but he forced himself to remain calm and steady. He was confident that Daniel would allow him to court Aubrey, but the possibility that Daniel could say no still lingered in the back of his mind.

"I was wondering, sir, if tonight I could take Aubrey home after night singing and court her." He breathed in relief that the words came out evenly spaced and not rushed like the pounding of his ears.

Daniel looked at him in genuine surprise and then began to laugh, a full-bellied laugh that surprised Jamie. "You had me worried that something was sincerely wrong. Of course, sir. Nothing would make me happier than to know that a good man like you is courting my daughter."

Daniel clapped Jamie firmly on the shoulder, grinning broadly at him. Jamie felt dizzy with the rush of adrenaline and relief. He returned to Aubrey's side and gently touched her elbow. She turned to look at him expectantly.

"Stay for night singing. I will take you home afterward," he said.

Aubrey's eyes widened dramatically as the meaning behind his words processed fully. Behind them, Sadie let out a "oooh" and then flew into a fit of giggles when Aubrey whipped around to glare at her. "Is it okay, daed?" she asked Daniel.

"Of course, of course. Have fun. Don't stay up too late since you both have work tomorrow morning."

They walked back into the barn side by side, both too lost in their nerves to even speak. He could feel the waves of anticipation rolling off Aubrey and onto him, making his own blood rush through his veins. He wished at that moment that night singing was over with and that they could walk back to Aubrey's home, but they took their respective seats across from each other and sang with the other youth for the next few hours.

By the time ten o'clock rolled around, the barn was hot. Sweat gathered under the brim of Jamie's hat and he wiped it away with his shirt sleeve. He stood by the barn doors, waiting for Aubrey to finish talking with Martha Hilty, when a hand tapped his shoulder.

"Hi." Miriam said, smiling up at him. "What are you doing over here all by yourself?"

Jamie returned the smile a bit forcefully. "Just waiting for someone," he replied.

Miriam's brown eyes sparkled in interest. "Oh, who would that be?" she asked, eyes still fixated on him.

Jamie shifted uncomfortably, sighing inwardly at the hopeful glimmer on Miriam's face. He didn't think badly of Miriam; she was a pretty girl with brown hair and delicate features and would undoubtedly make a good wife, but the few conversations he'd had with her didn't spark anything within him.

Not like the spark Aubrey evoked. "Aubrey."

Miriam blinked in surprise. She turned to look at Aubrey hugging Martha goodbye and then back at Jamie with a bewildered frown. "Aubrey Forrest?"

"Yes," Jamie replied, tensing at her skeptical tone. "That Aubrey. Why?"

"You do know about her sister, Emma, right? Don't get me wrong," she added hastily at the anger sparking in Jamie's eyes, "She's a really nice girl and they are a good family, but I just figured you would want someone who isn't...struggling with their faith."

Jamie gritted his teeth to keep his temper under control. He knew Miriam meant well, like Aaron had, but he was confident in Aubrey's faith after their conversation earlier.

"Have you ever struggled with your faith?" Jamie asked bluntly.

Miriam took a step backward, startled by the question, and blushed in embarrassment. "Well, I-yes. Of course. Who hasn't it?'

"So how would it be different for Aubrey?"

No reply came from the trembling girl in front of him. Tears flooded her eyes. Guilt for letting his frustration made Jamie reach out and pat Miriam on the shoulder rather awkwardly. "I'm sorry, Miriam. I didn't mean to snap at you like that."

"It's okay. I deserved it," Miriam replied meekly, bowing her head. "I was only speaking out of concern for you, but I wish you two luck and happiness." She brushed by him and out into the night, down the gravel road to walk home alone.

Jamie leaned back against the doorframe and thumped his head back against the wood. What was wrong with him? Never had he felt so defensive or protective over a decision in his whole life.

"Is everything okay?" Aubrey asked, coming to his side. She followed Miriam's slumped form down the road until she rounded a corner and disappeared from their sight. "What's wrong with Miriam? She said she was staying behind for night singing."

He opened his mouth to explain what had happened,

but thought better of it. He would apologize to Miriam later. In the meantime, he didn't want the night to be ruined. "I don't know. We should probably get going," Jamie said.

He started down the road, not giving Aubrey the chance to question it any further. At the edge of the driveway Jamie waited patiently for Aubrey to catch up to his long strides before heading in the direction of Aubrey's home. Without the lamplight from the barns and house, it was hard to see the road stretching before them. A moist earthy smell from the irrigated fields clung to the night air.

"How do you like Colorado so far?" Aubrey asked, her soft voice echoing in the night. She walked alongside him, hands clasped in front of her and head bowed as dirt crunched beneath her shoes.

Jamie shrugged noncommittally. "It seems like Lancaster so far, except the air is thinner and I feel closer to the sun," he answered, and smiled when Aubrey laughed in response.

"Well, you are if you think about it. I don't think Lancaster's elevation matches here."

"It doesn't. So, I guess it's different. There's much more space here too, and it's a lot quieter if you can believe that."

"How so?"

Her hand brushed against his before pulling away, and he swallowed against the sudden dryness in his throat.

"For starters, there isn't nearly the amount of Amish here like in Lancaster. Pa decided to move because it was getting too congested there. The community was large and there were tons of families."

"That's hard to imagine. It's always been so quiet and small here. I think it's better that way, because it keeps us humble and less distracted by other people's lives. So we can concentrate on our own lives."

Their hands brushed again. Jamie's hand twitched compulsively at his side and he couldn't resist anymore. He reached out and found Aubrey's hand, weaving his fingers through her smaller and softer ones. His heart gave an excited thump when Aubrey squeezed his hand.

"How do you see your life going?" Jamie asked curiously.

The starlight sparkled in Aubrey's eyes when she looked upward at the night sky and a lazy smile spread across her face. Their pace slowed as they walked hand in hand down the road. In the distance he could hear muffled laughter and voices.

"The same way any Amish girl dreams of it going. Getting married, having children..." She trailed off with a heavy sigh, the smile slipping from her face.

"You don't seem entirely thrilled about any of that," Jamie commented quietly.

"No, I really am. Those things keep my heart full. I wouldn't know what to do without Mama or Papa," Aubrey answered.

They reached a driveway that led to a two-story farmhouse with a screened-in front porch. Aubrey tugged his hand and led him down the gravel road, past a field where a couple of horses grazed happily.

"But you miss your sister," Jamie said, and felt

Aubrey's fingers tense between his. He turned to apologize, but was silenced by Aubrey shushing him with fingertips on his lips.

"Do me a favor, Jamie. Let's stop talking about my sister and everything revolving around that. I am barely holding on by a thread here, and that thread is you."

☙❧

Jamie's lips felt petal soft under her fingertips. Their eyes met, neither one blinking as her words settled between them. Her lips tingled from Jamie's warm breath, the taste of him on the tip of her tongue, and she wanted to reach up and close the distance between them. Jamie's head tilted downward to listen to her and his nose bumped hers slightly. Aubrey parted her lips.

A high pitched giggle startled them both.

Aubrey hastily stepped back from Jamie, reluctantly letting of his hand and turned around to peer out at the dark fields behind him.

"Was that someone giggling?" Jamie asked, frowning in confusion. He too looked out at the surrounding darkness.

The rustle of fabric near a large oak tree caught Aubrey's attention. She turned in time to see a flash of white disappearing around the trunk and her fists curled in irritation. Aubrey opened her mouth, ready to call Sadie out from her hiding spot, but thought of a better idea.

She held up a finger to her lips at Jamie, who merely nodded, perplexed by what she was doing. She slipped off her shoes, using the cover of darkness to tread silently in her socks toward the tree. Placing a hand on the rough bark, Aubrey leaned around the trunk slowly to spot Sadie crouched on the other side. She held her breath and silently counted to three before leaping forward.

"BOO!"

Sadie screamed and fell backward ungracefully. The horses in the field started in surprise at the sound and trotted away in fright. Jamie stepped around the oak tree to find Aubrey doubled over in laughter, holding her stomach and tears streaming from her eyes.

"Aubrey! I probably have grass stains on my dress now and this was my favorite!" Sadie complained. She brushed off blades of grass and dirt from the folds of her dress.

"Maybe next time you'll think about spying on me then," Aubrey chuckled, crossing her arms.

In the dark the two sisters glared at one another before Sadie brushed by them to stomp down the road and toward the house. Katie stood on the front porch step, looking out at them in concern. Aubrey sighed in annoyance and turned to look at Jamie apologetically.

"I'm sorry. My sister is annoying sometimes," she explained, rolling her eyes. "She's jealous that I'm allowed to court and she isn't yet."

Jamie chuckled. "No worries. My sister Lily can be the same way too. She's almost sixteen and keeps asking Pa if she can court yet."

"Yeah, but I bet she doesn't try to spy on you when you're about to get your first kiss." She mumbled without thinking and then flushed hotly when she realized what she'd just said. She was very grateful at that moment that it was dark outside so Jamie couldn't see her expression nor could she see his.

"You've never been kissed before?" Jamie asked slowly.

"No. I mean, once, but it wasn't really a kiss. It was more like-" Aubrey paused to think of the right word. David Lapp had kissed her when she was fourteen behind the school house, but it was because they had thought they were in love at the time. She still remembered his cracked lips pressing against hers quickly and the scrambled eggs on his breath. "Okay. I don't know how to explain it beside it being terrible."

"I find it hard to believe that a beautiful woman like you hasn't been whisked away for marriage yet."

Aubrey laughed breathlessly at that. "It's not that hard to believe obviously, because I'm standing right here with you."

Jamie's fingers slid along the inside of her wrist and then twined through her fingers. *A perfect match*, she thought, relishing the feeling of his fingers between hers.

"And I have a feeling that I will have to fight off other suitors now that everyone knows I took you home tonight," Jamie noted.

Heat flickered in the pool of her belly at the protective tone in his voice and the way his fingers tightened around hers. She shivered, and it had little do with the cooling air. "I wouldn't want any other suitors anyway."

"So, the odds are in my favor then."

"Seems like it."

White straight teeth flashed at her in the dark. Jamie reached up with his free hand and traced her cheekbones. "I guess it does seem like it."

His head tilted downward again, the taste of him strong on Aubrey's tongue, and she was tempted to let him kiss her with Katie standing on the front porch waiting for Sadie, but instead gently pulled away. At Jamie's confused look, she smiled and whispered, "If you kiss me in front of my whole family I won't ever hear the end of it."

Jamie's fingers twitched slightly from where they rested on the curve of her cheek. He smiled down at her in the moonlight. "Next time I'll just have to make sure we're alone then."

‹ CHAPTER 6 ›

The sky changed overnight and with it the hot air. A sapphire color peeked out from behind the gathering clouds on the horizon and the distant boom of thunder promised rain. In their stalls, the cows mooed uneasily and shifted at the noise. One of them nearly knocked Aubrey off the wooden stool she sat on.

"Oh, relax," she cooed, reaching up to soothingly stroke the cow's belly. "It's only a bit of thunder. You aren't going to be out in the storm."

She readjusted the tin pail so that it balanced evenly on the hay-riddledground and began the process of milking again. The sound of thunder and milk hitting the pail in a strong stream echoed in the barn. Earlier that morning, Sadie had complained of a sore throat and the chore of milking their cows passed to Aubrey automatically. Her least favorite chore to do.

Word had spread fast about Jamie courting her. The whole week anyone who came into the bakery asked about Jamie and wished them the best of luck. It was utterly embarrassing to be the center of attention, but Jamie didn't seem to mind it. Every day he walked up to the bakery to buy a cookie or some sort of pastry so they could talk outside.

"Because I don't want to go a day without seeing you," Jamie had said, kissing the back of her hands.

Aubrey smiled widely, not caring at that moment when she was nudged off her stool again as thunder boomed closer this time. She looped her arm through the pail's handle and hoisted it up, a wave of milk splashing against her apron. When she exited the barn, she found Isaac carrying a basket of eggs from the chicken coops and the two walked side by side back to the house.

"Papa says that Jamie is coming over this evening," Isaac said, looking up at her. "He says that we are going to go fishing."

Isaac's eyes shimmered in excitement when Aubrey nodded in confirmation. She watched him bound up the porch steps and disappear inside. She knew the rules of courting kept the sins of flesh at bay, but the idea of fishing with Isaac and Sadie around didn't sound as exciting as Isaac imagined. She wanted to be alone with Jamie and away from everyone else.

"How are the cows?" Katie asked when Aubrey stepped into the kitchen, carefully setting the pail on the counter so as not to spill anymore. She smiled at the irritated look Aubrey slid her direction.

"I was knocked off my stool four times," Aubrey said. "I don't know why they are so afraid of thunder. There's no lightning out yet."

Katie glanced worriedly out the window above the sink. "Are you sure about fishing today? I worry about you kinner down at the river with this storm brewing."

"Yes, Mama," Aubrey replied, rolling her eyes. "We've worked out in the storms before and it'll probably be done by the time we get to the river."

Katie sighed in resignation, turning back to continue chopping vegetables to go with dinner later that evening.

"Mama!" Sadie called from the living room, "Mama, have you seen-"

Sadie stopped in the doorframe when she caught sight of Aubrey's narrowed eyes. She crossed her arms over her chest and raised an eyebrow.

"Sounds like your throat doesn't hurt too much if you are yelling," she accused.

"Mama fixed me some tea," Sadie replied defensively. "It still does hurt a little bit."

Aubrey's chin jutted out skeptically. "You just didn't want to do chores," she countered, shaking her head.

"That's not true!" Sade shot back. "I really wasn't feeling good."

"Then maybe you shouldn't go fishing, since it might start raining," Aubrey said.

"No!" Sadie said quickly, shooting a beseeching look in Katie's direction. "I feel much better after the tea. I want to go fishing too."

Katie frowned, taking in Aubrey's words, and then looked at Sadie with an apologetic smile. "I'm sorry, Sadie, but Aubrey's right. You can go fishing another day. You don't want that sore throat to get any worse. Not right before canning season."

Aubrey grinned triumphantly at the downcast expression on Sadie's face. If she had to spend the evening with Isaac tagging along with them, she wouldn't complain. Isaac often went off on his own and didn't care about what others were doing. It was the closest thing to having privacy.

When Jamie arrived, Aubrey and Isaac were waiting for him on the front porch, fishing poles balanced on their shoulders.

"Where's Sadie?" He smiled at Aubrey and her heart swelled at the sight. She wanted to throw herself down the porch steps and embrace him, feel his hands in her hands again, but told herself that was not a how an Amish woman acted.

"She's not feeling well," Aubrey replied. She rested a hand on Isaac's shoulder and nudged him forward. "So it's just going to be us."

Jamie shrugged his shoulders. They set off down the road at a leisurely place, listening to the thunder boom in the distance with the smell of rain thick in the air.

"I hope it doesn't rain," Aubrey mentioned, glancing at Jamie walking alongside her. "That way we can stay down at the river as long as possible."

Jamie studied the clouds for a few seconds. "It could rain," he said, "but it looks like the the storm will pass by us."

"You don't know Colorado weather. One minute it can be sunny and the skies clear, then it can turn cold and rainy," Aubrey said.

Their hands brushed before Jamie twined their fingers and swung their hands lightly between them. Isaac led them down a dirt pathway, eagerly talking to Jamie about the different fish in the river and easily maneuvering over logs that were strewn across their path. Jamie helped Aubrey over them, his hand never letting go of hers the whole time.

They walked through the pine trees, listening to the roar of the river grow louder the closer they approached. Dry pine needles crunched beneath their shoes before the trees cleared and revealed a large river with smooth boulders surrounding the bank. The smell of algae and fish was strong in the air when Aubrey set her pole on the ground.

"This is beautiful," Jamie commented, smiling at their surroundings. "I will be honest though and admit that I haven't fished in awhile."

Aubrey laughed and crouched lithely, fingers scooping through the wet dirt. She pushed the dirt aside into a small mound and dug until the slimy skin of earthworms were visible to them.

"Do you remember how to bait a hook?" she asked. At the negative shake of his fair head, she pulled a worm free of the dirt. "Slide the hook in here and then wrap them around it so it makes a knot. That way the fish will bite the hook instead of nibble around it."

Jamie stared down at the squirming worm on the hook and grimaced, but cast it easily into the fast-flowing river. A few feet away, Isaac sat on a smooth boulder and focused on his line bobbing in the water.

"You are definitely not what I'd ever expected," Jamie commented, reeling in slightly.

Aubrey stood by his side, hands folded in front of her, and kept a watchful eye on Isaac's still form.

"Why is that?" she asked curiously, tilting her head to look up at him.

A breeze picked up and stirred the folds of her dress and threatened to knock Jamie's hat off his head. A loud groan filled the air when the trees swayed in response to the oncoming storm.

"Well, for one, by looking at you I wouldn't assume that you know how to bait a hook," Jamie laughed. He drew the pole back and then cast again, Aubrey stepping out of the way so as not to get snagged by the hook. "You just seem very in tune with the nature and weather around here, which not many people take the time to notice."

"I've been here my whole life," Aubrey replied softly. "I used to explore the woods all the time with Levi and spend all my time outside when I wasn't doing chores. If I had a choice, I would be outside all the time instead of being inside the bakery or in the kitchen."

"I bet it was wonderful growing up here," Jamie said.

The pole jerked hard in his hands and Jamie looked at Aubrey in surprise. "I have a fish already?" He reeled in hard, Aubrey tugging the pole forward, and a fish plopped unwillingly onto the bank near their feet.

"You got a fish?" Isaac called, scowling at them. "We can't leave until I catch two fish."

The fish flopped around on the rock surface before going still. Aubrey crouched down and freed the hook from the fish's bottom lip, weaving a piece of rope through it, and tied the end off so she could throw it back into the water, to keep it fresh until they were done.

"I bet I can catch more fish than you!" Jamie yelled.

He grinned at the determined glare Isaac shot him. "You're on!"

By the time the wind picked up and threatened to blow them over, they had ten fish strung on the rope. When they emerged from the forest and started down the road, dark clouds spread across the sky and lightning danced from cloud to cloud.

"Hurry!" Isaac yelled at them, sprinting down the road. "It's going to start raining any second now."

Aubrey pumped her legs, dress flying behind her as she ran beside Jamie. The wind pushed against them and the first cold drop of rain splattered on her cheek. In an instant, rain began to pour down and surrounded them in a gray sheet of wetness.

The wind ripped at her kapp and it slipped free from the pins holding it to her hair. She laughed as her hair fell free to the middle of her back and soaked up the rain.

She turned back, moving to chase after her kapp, but a hand on her elbow stopped her. Aubrey turned around to find Jamie standing right behind her and his arms wound tight around her waist. She shivered at the feeling of muscles shifting under the fabric of Jamie's now-drenched shirt.

They stared at each other as the rain came down hard around them. Aubrey wasn't sure who moved first, but in the next instant Jamie's mouth was on hers, rubbing softly and firmly all at the same time. The taste of him intermingled with rain water strong on her tongue.

Thunder boomed above them and a white light flashed around them. Aubrey drew back, dizzy from the kiss. She started to laugh.

Jamie looked at her in confusion, a half smile on his lips. His hands moved restlessly on the small of her back.

"What?" he shouted over the roar of the rain. "What is so funny?"

"You have any idea how cliché it is that we just kissed in a rain storm?" Aubrey yelled back, still laughing.

"I told you that I would get you alone next time." He reached out and drew a strand of Aubrey's soaked hair over her shoulder, tugging on the end of it fondly.

"We better get back before we both get sick," he said, taking her hand in his again.

Halfway back down the road the rain let up just as suddenly as it had began. Jamie turned to her with arched eyebrows.

"I told you that you don't know Colorado weather."

CRSO

"Thanks for dinner, Mrs. Forrest."

Katie smiled at Jamie from where she stood behind the sink, dress sleeves folded up to her elbows and arms submerged in soapy water.

"Of course, Jamie. Please come by again. We enjoyed your company."

Jamie nodded. He shook Daniel's hand before

following Aubrey out of the warm house that smelled of pan fried fish and into the balmy evening. The rainstorm had disappeared just as it had began and left the earth beneath his feet moist.

They walked down the driveway and back to the main road, stopping at the bend. There Jamie gathered Aubrey in his arms again and kissed her, the unique taste of something sweet intermingled with vegetables on his tongue. He felt Aubrey shift in his arms and then pulled back, her cheeks flushed with the kiss and embarrassment.

"My breath must taste like fish," she said shyly, keeping her head tilted down so as not to breathe on him.

"No. It tastes like vegetables."

She smacked him hard on the chest and then buried her head there, listening to his heart beat. He rested his chin on top of her head and closed his eyes, listening to the buzz of crickets around them and horses whinnying in the distance. He tried to recall the last time he had ever felt so content, holding Aubrey close to him, and enjoying an evening as much as he was.

"Do you really have to go?" her voice mumbled into his chest, filling him up.

Her hands clutched at the back of his shirt and held tightly. He smiled and reached up behind him, detaching her hands from his shirt easily and squeezing them.

"Yes. I told Pa I would be home before dark to help finish chores."

At the disappointed pout on Aubrey's lips, he leaned down to kiss her one last time before taking a reluctant step back. She lifted her hand in a wave before going back down the road and he watched her go, making sure she made it back into the house before heading down the road.

Lily sat on the front porch in a rocking chair when he arrived home, fabric draped over her legs and a needle held delicately between her fingers.

"Where's the fish at?" she asked, frowning at his empty hands. "I was looking forward to Ma frying fish up for dinner."

"We had to fry it all up so it wouldn't spoil in the heat."

"Oh."

"What are you doing?"

"Starting on blankets and watching the sun set. Pa says we need to start stocking up on things for the winter."

Jamie nodded. "Jah. Might be a good idea since the weather is so unpredictable."

She looked back down at the blanket she was currently sewing and he left her there with her thoughts. Sarah glanced up from wiping crumbs from the table when Jamie entered and smiled at him.

"Did you have fun?" Sarah asked, straightening. "I thought you would be back later."

"*Daed* asked me to come home before nightfall to help him."

Sarah frowned, but didn't reply. She knew Aaron didn't want him to spend too much time around Aubrey because of what he had heard and would attempt to limit their contact as much as he could. If Sarah disagreed with her husband's view, she didn't voice it. She would stand alongside her husband and support him. That was the way things worked.

He found Aaron standing in front of the plot he'd marked with Henry, the two of them talking about what to plant.

"Potatoes and onions grow well here," Henry was saying when Jamie walked up to them. "Ma could easily make something with those. Beans too. They grow well here too."

"I can ask Aubrey if they scan spare some extra beans once they can them," Jamie pointed out, shoving his hands into the pockets of his pants. "I also saw tomatoes at the Byler's garden, and carrots too."

Aaron turned to look at Jamie. "Let the Forrest family keep their own vegetables for the winter. The Bender family supplied us with extra jars of vegetables and preserves. The Bender girl, Miriam I think her name was, brought them over with her brother. Nice young lady."

It was a harsh slap in the face and Jamie fought to keep it from showing. His fingers curled into fists. Never before had he felt the urge to hit something, but at that moment he did and immediately felt ashamed for it. He looked away from Aaron to stare at the fields and the darkening skies, and silently prayed for strength and forgiveness for his thoughts.

"Yes, Pa, she is," was all he managed to say.

At Aaron's pointed glance, Henry started toward the house. He grasped Jamie's shoulder in passing and gave a small squeeze before clambering up the porch steps to give them privacy.

"How was your fishing trip?" Aaron asked.

Jamie shrugged indifferently. "Gutt."

"You're wearing different clothes," Aaron commented then, frowning deeply at the baggy fabric. "Where are your clothes?"

"It rained when we were fishing," Jamie explained, not meeting Aaron's gaze. "Daniel let me borrow some dry clothes to wear while we ate dinner."

Aaron's lips thinned, but he didn't say anything. Instead he motioned for Jamie to another marked spot in the ground.

"Next Saturday we are going to build a chicken coop. The Hilty's agreed to give us five chickens to get through the winter with and cows for milk," he told Jamie and then turned to sweep a hand toward the fields. "The community also agreed to a barn raising to help us before the winter season. We'll start on that two weeks from next Saturday."

"Why can't we do it during the week too?" Jamie asked, a part of him already knowing the answer.

"Saturdays are the days we will work on this. Tell Daniel you and Henry aren't working on Saturdays anymore."

The final tone in Aaron's voice told Jamie there was no arguing about it anymore. When his father put his foot down, that was it and he wasn't easily dissuaded. He sighed heavily and lowered his head, still praying for strength.

"Did you hear me, Jamie?"

"Jah, sir."

Aaron studied him, sensing the turmoil, and then laid a hand on Jamie's tense shoulders. "I am only trying to do what's best for you, son," Aaron explained quietly.

"By keeping me from Aubrey?"

"By keeping you away from someone who is struggling with their faith. Aubrey is a nice girl, Jamie, I know that she is. I don't doubt her feelings toward you, but I worry about her repeating her sister's behavior. Do you know what will happen if she leaves and you knew about her contact with her sister?"

Jamie nodded. "Bann," He said softly. "I know that, Pa. Aubrey wouldn't put me in a position to be shunned."

Aaron sighed in exasperation. "You say that like you've known her for years, when you've only known for a few weeks and just started courting her. I know this decision is up to you, as it is part of *rumspringa* to figure things out on your own, but I am asking you to be careful of where your heart and loyalties lie."

Jamie stared at his father, taking in the proud stance and hard glint in his eyes. This was a man who followed the Ordnung and would side with the church, even if it meant losing his family. The Amish faith was deeply rooted within Aaron and for a glimmering second Jamie felt himself doubting his own faith. He closed his eyes at the despair quickly building in him and began to think of ways to convince himself and his father.

The air, still tinged with moisture, felt chillier than it had the previous week. He shifted to fight off the cold. "What would convince you?" he asked, opening his eyes to look at Aaron.

"You know what would convince me and yourself."

CR80

"So, he kissed you?"

Aubrey bit her lips, grinning. She stood in the back of the bakery with Hannah as they slid bread loaves into bags and twisted them shut. Hannah had arrived to help out after Jacob left for work at his construction job, but also to socialize. They had moved into their own house a few months ago and when Hannah finished with chores, and with Jacob's consent, she helped Aubrey at the bakery.

"Yes. In the rainstorm last Saturday," she said, the memory still replaying in her mind.

Hannah smiled teasingly at her. "So, can I expect a wedding announcement here soon?"

"Oh, shut it."

The two girls fell into a fit of giggles that was interrupted by the door screeching open at the front of the bakery. Aubrey immediately wiped her hands free of flour dough on her white apron and peeked around the door, smiling at the sight of Jamie.

"Afternoon, Mrs. Forrest. Is Aubrey free for a few minutes?"

"Yes, she's- oh, right here," Katie jumped when Aubrey appeared suddenly at her side, smiling widely.

Jamie returned the smile, but not with the normal sparkle in his eyes. She faltered at that and took in the bags under Jamie's eyes. Dread built in her stomach again.

"Actually," Katie continued, pulling out a white envelope from alongside the register. "If you both have the time, I need this to be dropped off at the post office. If you don't mind walking on your lunch break."

"Not at all," Jamie said.

Katie handed the envelope to Aubrey and the two of them walked out of the bakery. Storm clouds, typical of August weather, were beginning to gather on the south horizon over the mountains. A static energy filled the air and the hair on Aubrey's arms stood on edge as they headed in the direction of the post office.

Aubrey walked along, her heart sinking further and further when Jamie didn't reach out to grab her hand like he usually did now that they were courting. She turned to look at him, reading the exhaustion and tension in his body. "What's wrong?" she questioned softly.

She reached out to touch Jamie on the shoulder, but he shifted away and her hand fell uselessly between them. Aubrey blinked against the sting of tears in her eyes and focused on the ground.

"My Pa wants me to end our courtship," Jamie blurted suddenly.

The words slapped Aubrey hard on the face. She tried to keep her face neutral, but it contorted into a painful grimace on its own. They stopped walking and stood next to each other on the sidewalk, but kept their eyes away from each other's.

"I see. If that's what your Pa thinks is best..." Aubrey trailed, voice trembling. It hurt deeply to think of ending her courtship with Jamie, but she knew it would be better to end things now rather than later. It wouldn't do either one of them any good if they continued and hoped to marry, but didn't have the approval from the church or their parents.

Jamie turned to her suddenly and grabbed her firmly by the elbows. His eyes bore down in hers. "I don't want that, Aubrey. I think we have a shot at this, at a future. My Pa will allow us to keep seeing each other if we join the Church."

She blinked, sucking in a harsh breath. "You mean if we get baptized?" At Jamie's nod, she shook her head. "Jamie, this is sudden for me. We are supposed to take our time before joining."

"I already know what I want. I've never questioned it. I just want to know if you feel the same way."

"Of course I do. I just-"Aubrey closed her eyes, fighting to keep control over the swell of emotions steadily rising within her. "I just want to make sure I am making the right decision instead of regretting it later."

Jamie wrenched his hands from her elbows and stared at her in disbelief. His shoulders trembled as anger slowly made its way to his eyes. "You're saying that if you joined and we got married that you would regret it later?"

"No!" Aubrey cried, reaching out to console him. "No. I'm not saying that. I just don't know why it has to be *now*."

"Why not now? What are you waiting for, Aubrey? What is the excuse?"

Her temper roared to life at the onslaught of questions. She took a step back from him, fingers clutching the fabric of her dress and meeting his angry stare. "You can't make me do something I don't want to do. That's the whole point of *rumspringa* ... to let us figure things out on our own instead of being pressured into it."

Jamie laughed, a dark laugh, shaking his head. "It's all so clear now. All very clear now," he said to himself, rubbing his face with both hands.

"What's clear?"

"You can't make up your mind whether you want to be here or out there with your sister. You want the outside world. Do yourself a favor and admit it."

"Fine," Aubrey snapped, throwing her hands up in the air. "I do want the outside world. I want to go to school because I like to learn something new everyday. I want to learn the art. I want to go to art museums and fill a gallery with my own paintings. I can't do that here and it breaks me into pieces because I can't even think about it without wanting to go crazy. I want to know who Vincent Van Gogh is."

"Who?"

"Exactly! Who is he? I want to know."

She was spouting off things from Emma's letters and knew that Jamie had no idea what she was talking about. They stared at each other, Jamie's arms crossed and chin jutted out stubbornly. It hit her then that Jamie was anchoring her down only one way, and that was the Amish way. He wasn't going to accept her any other way.

Aubrey turned on her heel and continued up the sidewalk toward the post office. She felt Jamie's eyes on her the whole time and when she turned to look back at him, he was going the opposite direction.

Her fingers numbly pushed the envelope in the drop off box before she slipped into the cool post office and walked to the PO box. She pulled the key from her sock, feeling how hot the metal was, like it had absorbed all her anger, and quickly shoved it into the keyhole. The box was full of envelopes that were thick and thin.

Aubrey held them to her heart and tears slipped from the corner of her eyes.

"God, give me strength," she whispered.

C3 CHAPTER 7 80

I know nothing *with any certainty, but the sight of the stars makes me dream.* Aubrey stared up at the night sky, repeating the words silently to herself as she threw a fistful of chicken feathers into the garbage pail next to her. When she closed her eyes, the copy of the painting *Starry Night* that Emma had sent appeared in her mind in a brilliant scheme of blues and yellows.

Katie came into the kitchen, a bowl of fresh beans propped on her hip, and stared down at the chicken feathers fluttering around the ground from the night breeze. She sighed in exasperation at Aubrey, who turned around to look at her, blinking back from whatever thoughts she had been submerged in and then taking in the feathers on the ground.

"Aubrey," she started, "where has your head been this past week?"

"I'm sorry," Aubrey muttered, crouching down to grab them. She tossed them into the garbage pail and continued to pull feathers free from the rubbery skin of the chicken, until it was bare.

"I've noticed that Jamie hasn't been around the bakery all week," Katie commented, taking in Aubrey's stiff back and shoulders. "Are you two no longer courting?"

Aubrey shrugged. "I don't know. Probably not..."

She ripped a few more feathers free and slid the chicken into the baking dish for tomorrow night's dinner. Tears stung her eyes and she kept them focused on the counter, determined not to cry.

"What happened?" Katie asked.

Aubrey shook her head tiredly. "No offense, Mama. I just don't want to talk about it with anyone right now."

"Of course, but whatever is, please pray about it."

"Yes, I will," she replied distantly. "The chicken is plucked for tomorrow. May I go outside for a walk to clear my thoughts?"

Katie nodded. "Be back in time to pray before bed."

Wet dirt and grass permeated her senses as she walked down the road. Halfway there, a tall figure rounded the bend and began to walk toward her. She paused, trying to discern who it was, until she recognized Jamie's face from the dim starlight and she took a step backward, surprised to see him.

"Don't run away," he said, voice cutting through the darkness.

"What are you doing here?" she asked, folding her arms across her chest. "I'm not really in the mood to fight, if that's why you came here."

He came to a stop less than a foot away from her. Shadows danced across his face and starlight sparkled in his eyes, pinning her there to the road.

"I'm not here to fight. I walked down here to talk to you."

Aubrey tensed at those words. She swallowed thickly, bracing herself for the end of their courtship. After a few seconds of silence, she broke it with a moody sigh and raised her chin to look Jamie directly in the eye. "Look, if you're here to end our courtship, just do it."

Jamie's eyebrows shot upward in disbelief. He looked at her aghast and reached toward her.

"That's not what I'm here to do." When her hands remained tucked in her chest firmly, Jamie grabbed her shoulders instead. "I'm here to say I'm sorry about yesterday. It wasn't right of me to try and pressure you into joining just so we can keep courting. I just thought-I thought it was the right thing to do at the time."

"And it's not?"

Crickets chirped loudly from the field next to them. Aubrey stared up at him, waiting for his answer, when he took her by surprise and bent down to kiss her. They broke apart minutes later, breathless and hearts racing. He brushed his forehead against hers.

"I know that *we* are right." When Aubrey opened her mouth, he laid a finger on her moist lips and hushed her. "I also know that you think it's crazy that I feel the way I do for you when we barely know each other. All I'm asking for is a chance to prove to you that it can work."

"Your daed won't allow it, Jamie. You already said-"

"My daed is stubborn, but I will change his mind in time."

"I-we-" Aubrey closed her eyes in defeat, out of excuses. "I'm just so confused about what I want, Jamie. I don't want to hurt you if I decide to leave."

The pad of Jamie's calloused thumb rubbed her temple soothingly, fingers slipping underneath her kapp and stroking the soft strands of her hair.

"If you really wanted to leave, you would have already done it by now," he commented softly.

Aubrey's eyes fluttered closed, tears leaking out of the corners of them and leaving warm trails on her cheeks. "You're making this harder on me, Jamie."

"Just think about what you are doing not only to yourself, but to your family, by leaving. What is out there that you want so badly?"

She let out a trembling laugh. "I don't know," she paused, thinking of Emma's letters and the copy of Starry Night in her room. "I honestly don't even know what I think is out there. I just-maybe I'm being tempted by sin for a reason, to be stronger."

"All of us are tempted by sin at some point, but I don't think that is why you want to go outside. What's the real reason?"

Aubrey bit the inside of her lips, shaking her head. "If I told you, you'd think I'm horrible."

Jamie smiled gently. "I doubt that, but give me a try."

She reached up to grab his wrists, curling her fingers around them and holding on tightly there.

Jamie's fingers tightened their hold on her in response.

"You have to promise me something then," she

whispered.

He kissed her again and it took a few minutes to recollect herself. "What's the promise?"

"That you won't tell anyone. Not even the church."

She opened her eyes to read his expression. Jamie watched her curiously, slowly nodding his consent.

"Okay. I've been talking to my-"

"Aubrey?"

Daniel's voice called out into the night, the sound of heavy footsteps approaching them. Aubrey whirled around, startled by the sound of Daniel's voice, and then took a hasty step back from Jamie. "I have to go."

Before she could slip away toward Daniel, Jamie's voice stopped her.

"Don't think I'll forget about this, Aubrey. The one time you let your guard down."

ᘓᘓᘔᘓ

"Can we name the chickens, Pa?"

Matilda curled her fingers around the chicken wire and peered in at the chickens clucking happily around in their straw pen. She looked up at Aaron with hopeful eyes.

"Nee, Matilda," Aaron said, fondly running a hand along his daughter's head. "We cannot name the chickens. They are for food and eggs."

She pouted at him, but didn't argue it any further.

Jamie watched his youngest sister reach a finger in through the wire and touch one of the chickens' backs, a startled squawk coming from it.

"You did a good job building the chicken coop."

Jamie turned to look at Miriam, standing behind him with her small hands clasped shyly behind her back. The afternoon breeze stirred a few pieces of hair from beneath her kapp and tangled in her eyelashes.

"Danka."

He turned to meet Aaron's warning stare. They had yet to talk to Aaron about not ending his courtship with Aubrey and things had gotten tense between them. He loved his father, but Jamie was determined to prove him wrong and convince him otherwise. In the meantime, to save himself a argument, he turned in resignation to talk to Miriam. The Bender family, including Miriam, had arrived with chickens, and like the gracious hosts Sarah and Aaron were, they'd invited them to stay for dinner in gratitude for all their help.

"Would you like to go for a walk around the fields?" Jamie asked suddenly. He shrugged his shoulders to ease some of the tension out of them and fidgeted on his feet. He was in desperate need of distraction and time to think.

Miriam looked startled, but nodded her head. She followed him quietly out into the fields where the horses were grazing happily. The grass swished around their feet in glimmering waves of green and they stood side by side for awhile, looking toward the mountains.

"Your father seems really nice," Miriam spoke up, breaking the silence. "He has been most gracious, and your mother too. I don't understand why you seem so angry toward him."

"I'm not angry."

The lie slipped out surprisingly easy. Jamie kept his eyes focused on the mountains, feeling Miriam's stare on him.

"You are. You've barely spoken a word to anyone," she observed, laying a tentative hand on his forearm. "If there is anything you'd like to talk about, I can listen."

Jamie discreetly shifted from underneath Miriam's hand. "Miriam," he started, sighing heavily. She flinched as though he had slapped her and immediately took a step back from him. "I don't know what my father has told you-"

Miriam shook her head. "He didn't say anything. I overheard him talking to my daed about how he wishes for us to court and I-" she broke off, her voice trembling, "I just thought maybe if I tried harder, you would consider it. Not that I don't like Aubrey, but she's always had boys asking for her and she never acknowledges any of them. No one's ever asked to take me home or..."

He watched as tears slid from the corner of Miriam's eyes and down the round curves of her cheeks. Anger toward his father threatened to rip him into pieces. Unknowingly, he had given Miriam hope when there was none.

"Someone will find you someday," Jamie said, reaching out to wipe a tear from her cheek. "And that man will be very lucky to have you as a wife. Don't give up hope on that. God will let you know when the time is right."

"Does God tell you that about Aubrey?"

He stiffened visibly and withdrew his hand from her cheek.

Miriam peered up at him curiously. "I only wish to know if you hear God telling you that Aubrey is right. How do you know?"

The wetness of Miriam's tears clung to his fingertips and he rubbed them together, drying his skin. "I don't know, Miriam. It's just an instinct, to love, and to fight for it, because we may never get it again."

"But how do you *know*?"

Jamie rubbed at his face tiredly, starting to regret his decision to ask Miriam to come with him to the fields. He wanted silence and to get away from the tension between him and his father. "It's a *feeling*," he finally answered lamely.

Miriam frowned deeply. She reached down to pluck a blade of grass and rolled it between her fingertips. "What's the feeling like?"

"Well, for one, I feel different when I'm around Aubrey. I feel connected to her in a way that isn't describable."

"Despite what she's going through?

"I feel closer to her because of it."

They fell silent again. He eventually felt Miriam leave his side, her dress swishing around her legs, leaving him alone with his thoughts in the middle of the field. If he focused hard enough, he could see the pine trees swaying in the breeze on the mountain top, and then looked down the road in the direction of Aubrey's home. His heart stretched the road toward her and for a moment he considered leaving.

"God help me," Jamie muttered under his breath.

The next morning Jamie walked by himself to the Hilty's farm. He rose before anyone else in the house and left a note for his parents that he would meet them for church. He wished to speak to the minister before church. Martha Hilty greeted him first, a broom in one hand and dustpan in the other. He smiled at her, coming to a stop in the entrance of the barn and peering in for any sight of Isaac.

"Morning, Jamie."

"Morning. Is Minister Isaac here?"

"Inside with Ma and Pa having coffee. Knock on the back door."

Jamie rounded the house and climbed up the concrete steps, rapping his knuckles gently against the wooden door. He took a step back as a middle-aged Amish woman opened the door, smiling at him.

"Morning, sir. What can I do for you?" she asked kindly, black apron stirring in the morning breeze.

"I was wondering if I could talk to Minister Isaac for a few minutes before church," Jamie requested.

"Of course, of course."

She ushered him into the rather small kitchen and dining area where Isaac sat, a cup of *kaffe* cradled in his hands.

Isaac blinked in surprise to see him and waved him closer to the cluttered table. A middle-aged Amish man sat on the other side of the table also with a cup of kaffe in hand. The smell of scrambled eggs still lingered inside the house, and upstairs he could hear footsteps on the floorboards.

"Can I talk to you privately, sir, for a few minutes?" he asked.

"Certainly."

They walked out into the dewy morning and toward a metal swing set. Jamie curled his fingers moodily around the chain and sat down, scuffing his boots on the wet grass. Families began to come from the road, arms full of food.

Isaac lifted a hand in greeting to those who waved at him. "What would you like to talk about, Mr. Miller?"

Jamie twisted his hands nervously. "You probably already know about Aubrey and I courting." At Isaac's nod, he continued, "My father will only allow us to court if we both join the church, and Aubrey is still questioning it, as you probably know too."

"*Rumspringa* is about sowing your wild oats. It is very natural for Aubrey or anyone her age for that matter to feel the way she does. We can only pray that they accept Jesus in the end," Isaac said, sagely.

"Right, but she mentioned something to me the other day that got me thinking."

Isaac leaned forward in genuine interest. "I see. And what was that?"

"She told me she loves to paint and I was thinking that maybe, with your approval and the church's, that she could paint and possibly sell her work to the Englischers. I think this is the one way it could keep her here."

Silence followed.

Jamie looked up Isaac, trying to read the minister's thoughts. He stared contemplatively up at the sky and a small smile curled up his lips.

"Have you prayed about this?" Isaac asked.

"I prayed about it last night."

He had thought of it last night while replaying his last conversation with Aubrey. Back at Lancaster, some Amish women sold their paintings and sketches at various festivals. He had yet to see it in Monte Vista, but it was something that he could give Aubrey to convince her to stay with him.

"Aubrey will decide on her own whether or not she wants to stay with the community. As for the painting, I see no issues with it in the meantime," Isaac acquiesced.

Jamie grinned, relieved. He stood and shook Isaac's hand before leaving the minister to return to the Hilty's kitchen to finish his kaffe. If he could give Aubrey one reason to stay, he would be happy. Even if she decided to leave in the end.

CRSO

"I have something for you." Jamie whispered.

He kissed her on the apple of her cheek. Despite their previous conversation still lingering in her mind, Aubrey's curiosity piqued at the eager expression on Jamie's face. They were generally not allowed to give gifts unless for a special occasion, but Jamie had shown up at her home with something in his arms.

They were currently seated outside on the front porch of Aubrey's house, watching lightning streak across the afternoon sky. On Jamie's lap a square and bulky object was covered with a blue quilted blanket. Whenever he shifted his legs to rock, something clinked beneath the blanket.

"What's that?"

Jamie grinned. "Close your eyes."

At her skeptical look, he reached out and gently closed her eyes with his fingertips. The fabric of the quilt swished away and something solid rested on her thighs. She buried her fingers in her dress to keep them from reaching out and touching whatever was in her lap. Something soft tickled her nose and then brushed along her lips. Reaching up to swipe at it, she giggled at the sensation.

Jamie's fingers, then tangled with her own. "Okay. Open your eyes."

Her eyes widened drastically at the items set neatly on her thighs. Several pieces of canvas were folded neatly on top of a large sketch pad and a small wooden box, partially opened, was full of sketching pencils and paintbrushes. Various colors in plastic containers sat neatly in a row on the porch railing in front of her. Speechless, she trailed her fingers over the items.

"What do you think?" Jamie asked, still grinning.

He held a thin paintbrush between his fingers and trailed the soft bristles across the back of her hand.

"How-how did you get all of this?" She looked up at him, breathless. "Is it okay to-to.."

"Yes." Jamie nodded. "I asked Minister Isaac if it would be okay and he didn't have any issues with it."

A slow grin spread across Aubrey's face. She looked over at Jamie, touched by the simple gesture, and her heart surged with appreciation. He had taken it upon himself to give her something that she wished for badly. All she could do was lean across her rocking chair and kiss him, hard, harder than ever before, to try and show him how much it meant to her.

She poured herself into the kiss, hands clutching at the side of Jamie's neck, and broke away with a smile. "Thank you, Jamie. Thank you so much."

She eagerly slid a pencil free from the book and set the rest of the items on the porch next to them, splaying her hands on the white page of her new sketchbook.

"Look over there," she said, pointing to the right.

Jamie arched an eyebrow at her, mock scowling at her. "Maybe I don't want to be drawn."

"Too bad. I'm sketching you."

He relented then, turning to look across the field at the horses grazing. Her heart swelled as Jamie casually propped his legs up on the front porch railing and propped his hat on top of the rocking chair. She studied every line and hard curve of Jamie's body resting on the rocking chair, memorizing him.

For a while they were quiet, with Jamie's eyes focused on the storm twisting above them and Aubrey's eyes flicking between the page and him. She felt herself relaxing at the strokes of the pencil against the sketch paper. The world felt far away as she continued to sketch that moment, keeping it alive forever.

"You shouldn't be drawing me," Jamie spoke up.

Aubrey's lips curled. "I know, but I think it can be our little secret. Just don't think too much of yourself afterward."

A low chuckle resonated in Jamie's chest. He turned his head, blue eyes sparkling over at her and a wide smile on his face.

"That depends on your artistic skills. For all I know you could be really bad and I wasted all my money on you."

"Look back over there," Aubrey commanded, pencil still on the paper. "I guess you'll just have to wait and see. Where did you get all this stuff by the way?"

"I paid an Englischer to pick the supplies up. He drives my daed to work."

She snorted softly, shading in the outlines of Jamie's legs. "I beat your daed loves that you spent money on art supplies for me."

Jamie shrugged, shifting in the rocking chair. "He doesn't know about it and it'll stay that way." He paused for a moment and then started to laugh. "If I don't show up to the bakery one afternoon, you'll know what happened."

"I'll keep that in mind."

She glanced up to find Jamie staring at her again, hands laced on top of his head and clearly bored with sitting still.

"Keep looking that way. I'm not done yet."

Jamie shook his head stubbornly. "I want to see."

"Too bad. You can't see it until I'm done."

In less than a few seconds, Jamie snatched the sketch pad from underneath Aubrey's hands and she blinked in surprise at his fast relaxes. Aubrey jumped to her feet and tried to grab it back from him, but he danced out of reach. Jamie laughed, easily stretching it out of her reach.

"Jamie! Give it back." She tried to jump up and grab it, but failed again. A piece of hair slipped from beneath her kapp and Aubrey blew it out of her eyes, glaring up at him. "You're impossible! Are you going to be this impatient all the time?"

An arm snaked around her waist and pulled her close. Jamie leaned back against the porch railing and carefully balanced the sketch pad on the railing alongside them. He rested his hands on the curve of her waist and tugged on the ties of her apron.

"Are you happy?" he asked quietly.

Their foreheads brushed as Aubrey wrapped her arms loosely around Jamie's shoulders. She bit her bottom lip and relished in the feeling of Jamie's hands absently rubbing circles along her lower back.

"I am." She kissed him again. "Are you happy?"

Jamie's lips curved up against hers. "I have no complaints." He laughed when she smacked him on the shoulder in response. His arms tightened around her waist until she was standing between his legs and they remained there in each other's arms, watching the dark clouds twist and threaten to spill rain any second.

For the first time, Aubrey thought to herself, *I am happy.*

The admission startled her. The longing to be on the outside, to see Emma, had gone away the second Jamie had given her the sketchpad and art supplies. It was a new reason to stay behind with him. The one thing she had desperately wanted, he gave to her.

She stared at him, tilting his head back to look up at the rain drops starting to splatter on the roof above them.

How was it possible to know someone so giving? It was the Amish way to avoid selfishness, but Jamie was a physical manifestation of being compassionate. She was lucky. Beyond lucky.

For the first time in several months, she didn't want to leave. She wanted to stay forever in Jamie's arms, on the porch with the rain beginning to pour down around them and lightning flashing about them.

Her eyes landed on the sketch pad next to them, papers flapping in the breeze. A couple rain drops managed to find their way to the paper and gray streaks trailed down it. Despite the water splattering the page, the image remained the same, but Aubrey realized then that she didn't need it to remember that moment because it was in her heart.

When Jamie looked at her again, she knew. She had to tell Emma goodbye.

She only prayed that she had the strength and courage to do it.

⊂ℜ CHAPTER 8 ℠

The air conditioning in the post office hummed loudly. Aubrey tilted her head back to enjoy the cool air blowing across her hot skin as she waited in line behind a elderly Englischer to purchase a large envelope and stamps.

She hugged the carefully-folded sketches to her chest, casting a nervous glance over her shoulder outside. Today would be the last day she would be here in the post office. Today would be the day she said goodbye to Emma. She would do this for Jamie, for herself. She repeated that to herself several times as she paid for the envelope and stamps before retreating to the corner and out of sight from any passing eyes.

Aubrey slid the sketches into the envelope and read the letter she had written the night before.

Emma,

This is the last time I will be writing you. I just wanted you to know that I am alright and that no one is forcing me to stay behind.

I want to stay behind. I met someone and he's the one who bought the supplies for my sketches to make me happy.

I miss you every hour of the day, sister. This is right for me, to say goodbye and live my life without wondering about yours. I drew Mama, Papa, Sadie, and Isaac, for you because I knew it would make you happy to see them again. They don't know that I drew them, but that's what I found out about art. It's better when it's unexpected and it's beautiful.

I am praying for you.

Farewell.

Love always,
Aubrey

She sucked in a trembling breath and pressed her lips to the page before placing it in the envelope as well. She scribbled the address down and opened the PO box to check one last time.

"Aubrey?"

Her hand smacked up against the metal of the PO box and she whirled around to see Jamie, taking in the envelope clutched in her hand and the opened box with a bewildered frown. They stared at each other in surprise. Jamie blinked a couple of times and slowly approached her.

Aubrey's breath caught in her throat and tried to think of an explanation of what she was doing.

"What are you doing?" Jamie asked.

"I-I-"she stuttered. Panic filled her. How could she even explain this to Jamie without getting them both into trouble?

Jamie took a step closer and looked at the key jutting out of the PO box. She glanced away guiltily when he looked back at her.

"Well?" he prompted, crossing his arms over his chest. "What's going on, Aubrey?"

She shook her head frantically. "Nothing. It's not what you think."

Jamie's eyes narrowed, anger starting to spark in them. "Oh, really. Then please explain it to me, because the last time I checked we didn't receive mail from a private PO box."

His voice raised a pitch higher and sliced through the air at her. Aubrey shrunk back at the sound, bowing her head to look at the ground and twisted her hands anxiously.

"It's hard to explain."

"Try me."

She gaped at him. Her skin prickled hotly under Jamie's narrowed gaze and she briefly considered bolting from the post office, but thought better of it. Jamie would easily catch up to her or seek her out later.

"I don't know what to tell you," she faltered, voice trembling with fear. "If I tell you-"

Jamie growled in frustration, rubbing his hands over the front of his face. He stared at her in aggravation. "I think I've done a lot for you to prove that you can trust me, Aubrey. If you are going to run around with your secrets constantly and expect me to be okay with it, you are horribly mistaken." He turned on his heels then, stomping out of the post office.

Aubrey hastily shut the door to the PO box and threw the letter to Emma inside the envelope, sealing it with shaky fingers. She dropped it in the little slot that said DROP OFF and hurried out the door after Jamie, who was already a couple blocks down the road. "Jamie, wait!"

Her sneakered feet pounded into the concrete sidewalk and she dodged anyone who was walking by, earning bewildered glances from Englischers. She reached Jamie's side and grabbed his arm, stopping him.

"Please, let me explain," she pleaded, stepping in front of him when he shook her off his arm. "I'll tell you if you just stop for a minute."

Jamie took a step back and then crossed his arms, waiting for her to talk. She closed her eyes briefly and prayed for forgiveness, for Jamie's understanding, for strength to confess finally.

"I've been writing to my sister, Emma. She got the PO box for me so we could write each other letters and so that she can send me things. Mainly art things that she's learning in school because she knows that I've always liked to draw. I've been writing to her awhile and today I was writing her a goodbye letter, to tell her that I'm not going to leave."

The words tumbled out of her. A small bit of weight lifted from her shoulders. She stared up at Jamie, panting from the heat as he took her words in and processed them with wide eyes.

"You've been talking to your sister without the church knowing about it?"

Aubrey gave a brief nod.

Jamie whistled out a breath through clenched teeth. He leaned back on his heels, rubbing the back of his neck, and started to shake his head. He gazed at her with a troubled expression.

"Oh, Aubrey... that is... I can't even think how much trouble you are going to be in. To talk to someone who is kicked out is-"

"I know!" she cried. "It was stupid of me. I should've told Papa about it, but I couldn't. I wanted to hear about art and life on the outside. Now that you're here, I realize that I have to give her up to be with you and I am. I was writing her to say that I was staying behind."

Tears stung her eyes. She reached up to palm them dry and they were quiet for a few moments as people walked by them on the sidewalk.

"You know that you have to confess," Jamie stated plainly.

Aubrey looked up, startled by the cool edge of his voice. He stood rigidly, blue eyes hard glints and his expression neutral.

"What do you mean?"

He took a deep breath. "I'm joining the church, Aubrey. This is the life I want and it's the life I want for my family in the future. If you want to be with me, you have to join the church. To do that, you have to confess what you have been doing. I can't be with you knowing all this and knowing you never confessed to doing something wrong."

A pulse of anger went through her. Aubrey's chin jutted out as she stared back at Jamie. "Is that an ultimatum?" she challenged.

"Take it whatever way you want. Think about what you really want, because once you choose there's no going back."

He brushed by her and continued down the sidewalk back to work. Aubrey watched him go, her heart splitting in two. What weight she had thought lifted from telling Jamie slammed back down upon her, harder than before, and it left her trembling in weakness.

Aubrey thought about the envelope she had tossed in the box. The paper had been moist and tearing from her sweaty hands. She felt like the envelope, torn and crumpled, and unsure whether she could or even wanted to confess to the church.

One thing was clear though. If she wanted to be with Jamie, she had to do it. The only question lingering in her mind as she walked back to the bakery was whether Jamie worth letting everything go for.

C33&0

Never before in all his life had Jamie felt so furious and scared all at the same time. With a grunt, he swung the axe down hard. The sound of wood splitting and then toppling to the ground lessened the knot in his chest. He bent down to retrieve the split wood and tossed them into the growing pile a foot away.

"...*I have to give her up to be with you and I am.*"

Jamie shook his head to rid himself of Aubrey's soft voice. She had said those words to comfort him, but he was far from it. Doubts clouded his mind, turbulent and dark, like the summer storms that graced the skies now. He didn't know what to think of finding Aubrey in the post office when he had gone to drop off some mail for Sarah or what she had told him afterward.

All he knew was that it made sense.

Except now Aubrey's secret turned into his secret and it felt unbearably heavy on his shoulders. He knew that he should tell, but his loyalty toward Aubrey held him back. After all, she had said that she was staying.

His frustration levels rose dangerously close to boiling over just thinking of it and the knot in his chest tightened again.

The axe swung down hard on a log he propped up, shards of wood spraying the ground and his legs. He tossed the pieces into the pile again and had bent to retrieve another log when Henry emerged from the kitchen.

"Whatcha doing?" Henry asked, coming down the steps.

He frowned at the pile of chopped wood on the ground. He looked at Jamie's tense face and wordlessly stepped behind Jamie to gather the chunks of wood. He set them in a neat row along the backside of the house and began to stack as Jamie continued to chop, until he could no longer swing the axe.

"Thank you," Jamie panted as he sat down on the large log he used to split the wood, sweat glistening on his forehead. "I know Pa wanted to stack it over there. I just needed to chop."

"Sure," Henry replied, coming to sit on the other side of him. "What's going on?"

Jamie didn't answer. He wrung his leather gloves in agitation and searched the windows of the house for any sight of Aaron.

"Where's Pa?"

"With the horses in the field. One of the horses is pregnant, he thinks."

"I have to tell you something that you can't tell anyone about. Especially Pa."

Henry's eyes widened in alarm. For as long as he could remember, Jamie had always been honest and never secretive. The storm swirling in his eyes made Henry's heart clench in genuine concern. "Okay..." he said slowly, nodding his head. "I'm listening and I promise I won't say anything."

The next few minutes Jamie told him about finding Aubrey in the post office, her comments and behavior, and about keeping contact with Emma even though she was excommunicated.

"You have to tell Pa, Jamie," Henry stated, shaking his head. "If you are going to take the kneeling vow soon you have to confess, and it's better that Pa finds out from you than from the church."

"I know. I just-" Jamie paused, sucking in a breath. "I understand what Aubrey is going through and I want to help her. I do think she wants to stay. She just doesn't know how to let go without facing the consequences."

"Jah, but you are risking yourself getting into trouble too. You know how it works, Jamie. Do you really want to risk punishment?"

"Pa would have no problem punishing me." Jamie replied bitterly.

Henry sighed. "He's worried about you. Frankly, I am too now, with what you've told me."

Jamie didn't reply. He kept working the supple leather of his gloves between his fingers, watching it stretch and crinkle. Deep down he knew that his brother was right. He didn't want to be shunned for Aubrey's indecisiveness, but he couldn't turn away from her either.

It just wasn't simple like he wanted it to be.

Cₓₓₒ

The house was eerily quiet, without the usual echoes of chatter and footsteps on the floorboard. Aubrey sat in the living room, still dressed in her nightgown even though it was well past mid afternoon, and stared blearily out the window. Her body ached from the lack of sleep and nausea that had plagued her all night long.

"Rest," Katie had told her, tucking the blankets around Aubrey tightly. "I can't have you being sick with the canning season in a couple of weeks."

Sleep was elusive. Her mind wouldn't allow it, constantly replaying the look on Jamie's face and the moment that her heart had plummeted to the center of the earth. She knew that look well. It had been the same look on Emma's face right before she left.

Detachment. Taking the hooks out and freeing themselves. That's what that look said.

She drew the fabric of her nightgown over her bare toes. It seemed that no matter how hard she tried to make things right, they only got worse. Even when she had confessed to Jamie about writing Emma and wanting to be on the outside, the weight of her sin didn't feel any smaller. It had only grown in size and now Jamie carried a part of it with him.

The guilt of it made her sick.

A warm breeze filtered through the open window and blew the envelope resting on the living room table to the floor. Aubrey slid down from the window seal and picked up the envelope, listening to the quiet again out of habit.

"One last time," she whispered before tearing the envelope open.

Aubrey,

I have exciting news! I met someone and his name is Derek. He serves in the military (I know) and is an art student like me. He's really sweet and ambitious; he wants to open up his own mental health clinic someday for war veterans to deal with PTSD (post traumatic stress disorder). Anyway, I know you don't know what that means, but here's the real reason why I am writing you.

I know that the kneeling vow is coming up for you. I told Derek about our lives and how close you are to me. He asked me to move in with him and he has an extra room to spare if you want to leave.

It's a huge decision, I know. Think about it. By the time this gets to you I will be arriving in Colorado. Don't worry about sneaking out because I'll find you. Have a bag packed if you want to come.

Love,

Emma

"Ach, Emma."

Her heart pounded furiously as she reread the letter. She checked the date on the envelope and blanched. According to Emma's letter she would be here by tonight or tomorrow. She immediately stood and went to the front porch, not caring if someone walking by would see her in her nightgown.

Aubrey ran her eyes along the tree line, but when no movement caught her attention she retreated back inside the house. She hurried up the stairs to Emma's room and opened the door, holding her breath the whole time.

Nothing.

The window was closed and the bed undisturbed. Aubrey swallowed against the thickness in her throat and closed the door before retreating to her room. She tucked in the sheets and blankets of her rumpled and unmade bed, ears straining toward every noise. She quickly washed and dressed before checking the rooms once more and settling down in the living room to sketch and relax her nerves.

A few hours later the front door of the house screeched open and a stampede of feet echoed in the hallway. Aubrey looked up from her sketchpad as Sadie entered the living room.

"What's that?" Sadie asked, tilting her head to look at the sketch pad. "Are you drawing?"

Aubrey pulled the sketchpad out of Sadie's sight, hugging it close to her chest.

"Yes," she said, raising her chin a silent challenge.

"Jamie got it for me so I can draw."

Sadie frowned. "Does Papa know about it?"

"No."

"I thought we weren't supposed to-"

"Jamie asked Minister Isaac about it and he said it was fine," Aubrey snapped, uncurling from where she had been sitting on the couch facing the window. "Let's get started on chores. Isaac, go feed the chickens and Sadie, the laundry outside needs to be folded."

"I thought you were sick."

Aubrey turned around to glare at her younger sister, who stood with her arms crossed, eyebrow raised at her. "Even when we're sick things still need to get done. You should remember that in the future next time you feel sick."

Sadie scowled at her before stomping out the front door to the laundry lines. By the time Katie and Daniel both arrived home, all the laundry was folded neatly and a ham was roasting in the oven.

"That smells wonderful," Katie commented, opening the oven door to peer inside. "You did a good job, doctah. I imagine you are feeling better then?"

Aubrey nodded. "Yes, Mama. I am feeling much better now."

Aubrey forced herself to eat, even though her stomach was turning in on itself. She chewed through a forkful of beans, watching the expressions on her parents and sibling's faces as they talked about their days. When Katie turned to her, eyes sparkling with warmth and laughter still clinging to her lips, the impulse to tell them about Emma coursed through her. She knew what sort of heartache it could cause them if she left.

No matter what the church said about limited contact with a excommunicated member, it was never easy to just forget someone. They stayed alive inside of you.

Sadie's voice interrupted her thoughts. She looked up from her plate of food to find that everyone was looking directly at her. "I'm sorry, what?"

Daniel's jaw tensed as he slowly lowered his fork back to his plate and leaned back in his chair. "Your sister just informed the table that you have been drawing," he said. "Is that true, Aubrey? That you have been drawing."

She hesitated before answering. Disapproval radiated off Daniel in powerful waves. Aubrey curled her fingers tightly around her fork and lowered her gaze, avoiding his eyes.

"Yes, Papa," Aubrey whispered.

A vein on Daniel's forehead throbbed at the admission. "I see. And where did you get the supplies from?"

"Jamie." At Daniel's furrowed brow, she added, "He bought them for me. He said that Minister Isaac said it would be okay... He even said that I could sell them to the Englischers."

Daniel still looked suspicious, but relaxed a little at those words. He picked his fork back up from his plate and resumed eating.

"I wish you would've told me, Aubrey," he said. "As long as you follow the Ordnung and don't paint anyone without their permission. I will be asking Minister Isaac about this tomorrow."

Too late, Aubrey thought, biting her lower lip. She caught sight of Sadie's glowering face across the dinner table and sighed deeply. She briefly wondered if she had been the same way toward Emma when she was Sadie's age before helping clean up the kitchen table.

They were in the middle of prayers when the startled sounds of the horses followed by barn dogs barking loudly interrupted Daniel.

"What's going on?" Katie asked.

Daniel rose to his feet, peering out the window and then drew back, muttering an oath underneath his breath.

"Bears," he answered grimly. "Helmouths lost some of their cattle last night. They're coming down from the mountains to eat before going into hibernation."

"Can I go, Papa?" Isaac asked, following Daniel out of the living room and into the hallway. "I promise I'll stay right beside you."

Aubrey leaned out the open window to peer into the darkness. In the distance, horse hooves pounded into the ground and a hot breeze stirred the strands of Aubrey's hair.

What if Emma was out there? The thought made Aubrey's fingernails dig into the wooden window frame and pieces of paint dug into her skin beneath her nails. She turned to look at Daniel as he emerged from the utility room, shotgun in hand.

"Stay inside, all of you. Don't come out until I say it's safe," he ordered before opening the front door and disappearing into the night.

"Will Papa be alright?" Sadie asked, coming to Aubrey's side. "It's only him and a bear out there."

Katie smiled nervously and smoothed a hand down the back of Isaac's head. "He will be fine," she said, and then turned to Aubrey and Katie. "Come, all of you. Lets get ready for bed. We have a busy day tomorrow."

They trudged up the stairs, listening to dogs bark in the distance. As Katie ushered Isaac in the direction of the bathroom, Aubrey and Sadie lingered in the hallway. Aubrey shifted on her feet anxiously as they waited for Isaac to finish in the bathroom.

"I'm sorry."

Aubrey's head shot upward at Sadie's voice. She arched an eyebrow at her confusion.

"You know," she continued, a pink color filling in the center of her cheeks, "for trying to get you into trouble with Papa."

"It's fine." They stared at each other awkwardly before Aubrey spoke again. "Why *did* you try to get me into trouble by the way? I've never done that to you."

Sadie lowered her head. The lamp light glinted off of the top of her kapp and filled the hallway with a dim light. "I know. I just thought if I got you into trouble that, you know, you wouldn't leave," she whispered softly.

"I'm not going anywhere, Sadie."

Aubrey gathered her younger sister into her arms and rubbed soothing circles along the curve of her back. The door to the bathroom opened and Isaac, hair wet from a quick wash, emerged with Katie following him.

"Go on. Let's get ready for bed," Aubrey said.

Their eyes met and Sadie nodded. She spent the rest of the night brushing the tangles from Sadie's long hair and listening to her talk about Eli Hilty annoying her at school. By the time Aubrey retreated to her own room and slipped into bed, she was exhausted from the past couple of days.

Her eyes had just slipped closed when an odd noise startled her. Aubrey rolled over onto her back, blinking away the sleep that had just barely clung to her eyes. The house was still and quiet, with no traces of light leaking through the crack of her door, telling her that Daniel had arrived home and gone to bed.

Aubrey rubbed at her eyes tiredly and rolled back over, about to drift back into sleep, when a voice hissed through the stillness

"Aubrey!" Another noise, a pebble hitting her window, echoed in her room. "Aubrey!"

She jolted upward, heart hammering in her chest. She clambered out of bed, throwing the blankets away from her legs. Aubrey unlatched the window and slid it open, leaning out to stare down at the slender figure hooded in darkness. Familiar blue eyes looked up at her, a smile showing off straight white teeth.

She sagged against the window, knees weak from adrenaline. "Emma."

⌘ CHAPTER 9 ⌘

"Emma."

Aubrey stared down at the slender figure shifting anxiously from foot to foot surreally. Moonlight danced across the contours of a sharp face with pronounced cheekbones and covered in the makeup Aubrey saw often on *Englischers*. Strange markings, black and bold, were spread across the bare skin of arms and clavicles and silver glinted from the round curves of small ears.

This could not be her sister, her beautiful older sister who always looked fresh and radiant in her chore dresses and blonde hair always pinned perfectly under her white *kapp*. Her Emma would never have dreamed of wearing tight black pants that sat low on her hips and an equally-tight white shirt that didn't cover her flat stomach fully. Her fingers sought the tender skin of her inner forearm and pinched hard. She opened her eyes and looked down again, but nothing had faded away or changed.

"Is everyone asleep?" Emma whispered, wary eyes scanning the other windows. When Aubrey didn't answer, she looked at her in exasperation. "Aubrey! Snap out of it. It's really *me*. Is everybody asleep?"

"*Jah*," Aubrey whispered back. Her throat was dry and thick from the turbulent emotions coursing throughout her. "Stay there. I'll come down through the back porch."

"Pack a bag if you want to leave. I have a car waiting down the road."

Emma stepped back into the darkness and hurried around the corner of the house before she could reply.

Mindful of the squeaking floorboard, Aubrey pulled on the boots she wore whenever it was muddy in the barn and wrapped a blanket around her cotton night gown. She hesitated in front of her door, peering around her room, and then tiptoed to her desk to grab her sketchpad and journal.

The house was motionless and quiet beside the occasional snore from Daniel drifting through the walls. She feared that her pounding heart would wake everyone up. She side stepped boards that squeaked in the dark hallway and walked down the stairs on her toes, keeping the majority of her weight of the stairs.

She hurried through the kitchen, grabbing a lamp they used when walking back from the barn at night, and slowly unlocked the door. Cool night air rushed to greet her and goosebumps pimpled Aubrey's legs in response. Shivering, she secured the blanket around her more tightly and closed the door quietly behind her.

Emma immediately appeared from behind the tree and rushed forward. Her arms were around Aubrey in an instant, hugging her tightly with surprising strength. A vanilla smell mixed with cigarette smoke clung to her sister's smooth skin, and soft silky strands of blonde hair streaked black brushed against Aubrey's cheek as she tentatively hugged her back. She couldn't help but think she was hugging a skeleton of her sister from how bony and thin she felt in her arms.

"I've missed you, *shveshtah*," Emma whispered, gently reaching up to cup Aubrey's jaw with clammy fingers. "You look so grown up and beautiful."

Aubrey smiled faintly. "*Danka.*"

Movement near the tree Emma had appeared from caught her eyes and a tall figure slowly emerged from the shadows. A well-muscled man walked cautiously toward them, clean shaven and with barely any hair on his head. His eyes, a green color, were kind when Aubrey looked at him nervously.

Emma turned, hearing his approach, and then took Aubrey's hand comfortingly.

"This is Derek. Remember? I wrote about him."

"Nice to meet you," Derek said, holding out a hand. "Emma's talked nonstop about you."

Aubrey gingerly shook his hand, feeling thick calluses and abnormal strength behind them. His hands were strong for an entirely different reason than farming or holding leather reins.

"We should go to the barn to talk," Emma said. "That way no one will hear us talking or leaving. I think if *daed* saw me he would have a heart attack."

Emma smiled grimly before leading them across the grass toward the barn like she had never left. Before following them into the barn, Aubrey turned to glance one last time at the dark windows of Katie and Daniel's room before slipping into the barn. She slid the barn door shut while Emma took the lamp from her.

A soft yellow glow partially filled the barn. They stood for a moment in an awkward silence before Aubrey broke it, unable to contain herself anymore.

"Emma..." she started, shaking her head at her sister in perplexity. "What's happened to you? You've got strange marks all over you and you look like you haven't eaten since you left."

"Stress does that to you," Emma replied, shrugging her shoulders. "And they're called tattoos and piercings. You've seen them on the *Englischers* before."

"But you're not an *Englischer.*"

Tension filled the barn. Emma's eyes hardened as she crossed her arms over her chest.

"I am, Aubrey. By definition, I am. Look," she saind and pulled the hemline of her shirt further down. "These are sparrows. They are symbolic of freedom and undying love. I have five of them."

Tears filled Aubrey's eyes. She looked away from them and down at her sister's right forearm, freezing at the familiar words tattooed there in black words.

"Be not conformed to this world," Aubrey read out loud, looking up at her sister in bafflement. "You tattooed Romans 12:2 on yourself."

"I thought it was weird too," Derek cut in, shaking his head at Emma. A small fond smile curled his lips. "Yet she insisted on getting it done, along with the bird tattoo.

Stubborn little minx."

Emma turned her head to smile at Derek and leaned toward him, brushing a light kiss on his cheek.

An indescribable emotion filled Aubrey as she stared down at her sister's forearm. For how hard Emma had tried to escape her Amish faith, she still had it etched on her forever. She still followed their faith. They were Amish through and through, no matter what they did.

"How's *maemm* and *daed?*" Emma asked.

Derek interrupted again before Aubrey could answer. "Sorry, but talk in a language I can understand. I don't understand d-what is it called again Emma?"

"Pennsylvania Dutch," Emma answered, without looking at him. "Derek hasn't had much time to learn about the Amish yet. He just returned from duty only a week before we flew out here to talk to you."

"Duty?"

"Yes, he's active military. He gets only a certain period of time off before going back to Iraq."

Aubrey blinked at the strange word. "Iraq?" she repeated, stumbling over the pronunciation.

Derek looked at her strangely. "You don't know what Iraq is?" he asked in disbelief.

She shook her head, cheeks flaring in embarrassment, and hitched up the blanket around her so the bottom of it didn't touch the hay-ridden floor.

"I told you, Derek." Emma said, sighing impatiently. "Schooling ends at the eighth grade and the Amish don't believe in violence. I didn't know what Iraq was either until I left."

Discomfort gave way to annoyance. She opened her mouth, ready to point out that Emma was Amish, but quickly calmed herself.

Derek raised his eyebrows in incredulity. He smoothed a hand over the top of his head and the simple gesture made Aubrey's thoughts instantly stray to Jamie. At that moment, she wished more than anything that he was with her.

"I *get* the whole simple lifestyle to keep you humble, but not learning about the rest of the world seems a bit bizarre to me," Derek mentioned.

"Family is more important than the rest of the world," Aubrey retorted, voice sharp.

He didn't reply. Instead Derek's eyes focused intently on the barn door, a frown spreading across his face.

"Are you sure no one heard you coming down here?" he asked.

Panic filled Aubrey. She rushed over to the barn window, peering out the window at the dark house. Some part of her expected Katie or Daniel coming toward the barn, wondering what she was doing out here in the middle of the night.

"Stop being paranoid," Emma said. She also peered out into the night. "No one heard her. If Mama or Papa heard her leave, they'd be out here by now. Have you thought about what we've talked about? About leaving with us?"

Aubrey glanced away from Emma's probing eyes.

This was it. The moment that she needed courage to decide what her heart wanted. She took a deep breath, staring down at her hands folded tightly in her lap. Without even thinking about it, she began to pray quietly under her breath.

"Why are you praying for strength?" Emma asked, a sharp edge to her voice.

"Because I don't know what is right or wrong anymore."

"For heaven's sake, Aubrey. You've had plenty of time to figure what's wrong or right."

"Do you?" Aubrey lifted her gaze and looked her sister directly in the eye. "Do you know what's right or wrong?"

Emma's jaw tensed and her eyes fluttered shut, a tell-tale sign that she was trying to control her temper.

"I thought this is what you wanted. To be on the outside, to go to school, to draw and paint. That's all you wrote about for the past couple of months."

"I do... I mean, I did. But then Jamie bou-"

"Whose Jamie?"

"He moved into our community a couple months ago."

"I see. And how old is he?"

"It's not an arranged marriage, Emma," she stated, knowing that her sister's thoughts immediately went to that. "And he not older either. He's my age and about to take the kneeling vow. He wants to marry me someday."

"Have you announced it yet?"

Aubrey frowned. "Announced what?"

"Marriage. I may have been gone for awhile, but I haven't forgotten things." She smiled thinly. "Look, I'm offering you a chance to see the world. It's not like what the church claims it to be."

"I can't do it, Emma. I can't do what you did to Mama and Papa. I can't leave Jamie behind." Aubrey shook her head. She didn't even want to think about how Jamie would feel if she left after all the effort he'd put in to persuade her to stay. "I love him. He's really the sweetest boy. He bought me art supplies so I can draw because he knows that I wanted to study art."

Emma scoffed loudly at that. "What do you know about love, Aubrey? You're only seventeen years old."

"What do you know of it?" she shot back, fingers curling up into fists and staring hard at Emma. "You think you know more about love because you left and traveled all over the place? You aren't wise, Emma. You aren't in love, because to love someone you can't be selfish, and that is exactly what you are. Selfish. You didn't run out on the community. You ran out on *us*, the people who always loved you and always will."

"Could you have done it then?" Emma whispered, tears filling her eyes. "Could you, Aubrey? Think about it real hard. Imagine knowing you couldn't marry Jamie because you were tied to someone else. It's easy for you to sit there and reprimand me because of what I've done when you aren't facing what I was. It's easy to judge when you haven't even been in anyone else's shoes."

Aubrey looked away.

"That's what I thought."

Fingers grabbed her own. She stared down at them, at the rings and the cross tattoo above her pointer finger, trying to imagine her hands looking like Emma's.

"Think about what you are deciding. If you come with us, you'll have tons of freedom. You can get married to someone who you truly love instead of settling on one because they are the only person around."

"How can you say that?" Aubrey snapped. "You didn't have anything to complain about until Thomas Fields wanted to marry you because his *kinner* needed a mother. Everything was fine until then. How many men have you courted before Derek?"

"That doesn't matter-" Emma started, shaking her head.

"It *does* matter, because I don't see any difference in what you are trying to tell me. If the outside is so wonderful for you, then why are you here? Why did you sneak that key into my room and write me all these months? Why do you ask about Mama and Papa?"

Her skin felt hot and tight with anger. The short leash she kept on her temper was unraveling fast. Emma stared at her in speechlessness.

"I don't want to be like you. I don't want to carry that guilt on my shoulders like you do. You've tried so hard to run away from it, and yet you have it tattooed all over you. I'm not going to be torn between two places like you are."

Aubrey's voice echoed in the barn. She winced, not realizing her voice had risen with her emotions. The lamplight cast a dim glow on Emma's tense form.

"Then you'd better decide." Emma said. "I came here because you wanted me to. Do you really not trust me anymore?"

The vulnerable tones in Emma's voice struck her. This was her older sister who had come from the other side of the country and snuck back into the community to help her. Before she could reply, the barn door slid open behind them with a loud bang that even startled the horses in the distance.

All three of them jumped at the unexpected noise. Aubrey whirled around, her heart dropping to the pit of her stomach as she took in Daniel's pale face and furious eyes that threatened to burn them all alive if he could. Katie lingered behind her husband, her face pale and streaked with tears as she took in Emma with wide eyes.

The silence that stretched on was painstaking. Aubrey desperately tried to scramble for an excuse, for an explanation, but her voice buckled under Daniel's wrath that filled the entire barn.

"What are you doing here?" Daniel asked, pointing directly at Emma, who took a stumbling step backward. "You know that you are not allowed back here. You are not welcome here."

Emma's eyes filled with hurt. She looked over at Katie, whose own eyes were filled with tears, but didn't try to ask for her mother's intervention. She knew just as well as Aubrey that Katie wouldn't go against their father.

"I-I-I-"

"She's here because we've been writing each other," Aubrey blurted out. She looked down in shame at the barn floor when Daniel's eyes rounded on her. "I knew she was coming and I didn't tell you."

"Aubrey," Katie breathed out.

Hot tears spilled down Aubrey's cheeks. She could feel Daniel's eyes boring holes into the top of her head.

"Don't punish, Aubrey, *daed*," Emma spoke in a trembling voice. "I was the one who convinced her it would be okay to write me."

"And you were trying to convince her to come with you?" Daniel asked, his voice an eery quiet for the anger on his face. "Look at yourself! Covered in tattoos and piercings and no weight on your bones. Bringing a strange *Englischer* into my barn. What sort of *Englischer* have you turned yourself into?"

The implication behind Daniel's words drove a knife right into Emma's heart and twisted it around violently. The wince on her face spoke volumes of what she felt at his words and it rendered everyone silent.

"Listen, man," Derek cut in defensively, going to Emma's side. He wrapped a steady arm around Emma's trembling shoulders and looked Daniel squarely in the eye. "I know your faith goes against what Emma left for, but there's no need for you to hurt your own daughter. She still loves you. She's a good woman, no matter what you think, and we're going to get married soon."

Aubrey's jaw fell open in shock. She stared at her sister, completely floored that she had left out that one detail until now. Emma wouldn't meet anyone's eyes.

"She's not my daughter. Get out of my barn, *now*."

Daniel grabbed Aubrey by the elbow, his fingers digging in painfully, and pulled her stumbling into the dark night. The blanket she had wrapped around her tightly fell to the ground when he whirled her around to face him.

"If you want to go with your sister, go. I will not stop you. If you leave, you're also no longer my daughter."

He left her there, trembling as sobs began to wrack through her, and walked up the back porch steps. Katie trailed behind him, a hand covering her mouth to stifle her own cries as she brushed by Aubrey without looking at her

Her knees gave out and she fell to the ground. She began to pray for forgiveness. She had done the worst thing possible, betraying her parents and hurting them. The guilt threatened to swallow her whole.

Footsteps approached her from behind. She raised her head to look up at Emma's eyes, which had glossed over in numbness.

"*Daed's* right. He won't stop you if you want to go."

Aubrey continued to stare up at the physical vessel that had once been her sister. Come tomorrow, no doubt, she would be confessing her sin in front of the Church and facing disciplinary action. Facing the hurt she inflicted on her family seemed more daunting by comparison and at that moment she wasn't sure if she could ever forgive herself or receive forgiveness.

She had crossed a line and running away in the darkness with Emma seemed much easier than facing what would happen next.

CXEO

Daniel Forrest didn't show up to work until well into the afternoon. Jamie tried not to let the concern or dread show on his face as he worked, sanding down a table that would need to be stained next. Something was wrong, horribly wrong, from the look that had been on Levi's face when he showed up half an hour late with the keys to open the store.

So when Daniel finally did arrive, eyes bloodshot and appearance haggard, and asked for Jamie to come outside, the dread and concern increased to the point that he felt sick with worry.

"What's going on, sir?" he asked, following Daniel into the hot afternoon. "Is Aubrey alright?"

"She's fine," Daniel answered, a faint smile on his lips. "She's fine, considering what's about to happen."

Jamie tried to read his face anxiously, but whatever emotions Daniel was feeling were well guarded.

"What happened?"

"I have to ask you a question first and I expect an honest answer."

Daniel leveled a stern glance in his direction, all traces of a smile gone. Jamie swallowed and nodded his consent.

"Were you aware of Aubrey talking to her sister Emma or that Aubrey had considered leaving?"

The pit of Jamie's stomach threatened to fall out of him and it made him breathless. Did Aubrey leave without saying anything to him? He shook his head. *No.* No matter how much she yearned to be on the outside, she still loved the inside too much to just get up and leave without warning.

Something else had happened.

"She never directly said if she was or wasn't," Jamie answered carefully. "She did express to me though that she wanted to paint and draw, so I had bought her the supplies for it with Minister Isaac's permission."

"I noticed," Daniel said curtly. "What about writing to her sister? Were you aware of that?"

Jamie hesitated. He was spared answering when Daniel read the reluctance on his face and then sighed heavily, shaking his head.

"I'll never understand this phase of secrets. I never kept secrets from my *shtamm*."

Daniel walked over to the wooden bench outside the warehouse and slumped over wearily, elbows resting on his knees. Jamie slowly followed him and sat on the edge tensely, his mind racing. He forced himself to wait patiently.

"I suppose Aubrey or someone else has told you about what happened with Emma." At Jamie's nod, he continued. "Last night Emma snuck into the community to talk to Aubrey about leaving and-"

"She didn't, right?" Jamie cut in. His body felt tight with tension and blood pounded in his ears as he waited for Daniel to answer. "Tell me she didn't leave. She wouldn't leave without saying goodbye."

"No, she didn't leave."

A whoosh of air blew through Jamie's nose when he breathed out in relief. He slumped back against the wall behind them.

"She stayed behind and told us everything."

"I'm glad. I'm glad she finally told you."

The urge to see Aubrey vibrated within him strongly. *She had stayed.* The thought exhilarated him to no end. The future, the one he hoped to build, flashed through his mind unchecked.

"I know you are excited to hear this. Aubrey told me that you have been trying to convince her for weeks now to stay behind and take the vow."

Jamie nodded. "I've been trying, sir. She has her own mind about things."

Daniel chuckled slightly at that. "Yes," he agreed. "She does have a streak of stubbornness in her."

Jamie laughed. They sat in silence for a few minutes, watching cars and buggies go by.

"Has she confessed to the church?" Jamie asked quietly.

"*Jah.* This morning I took to her to the church members to confess."

His heartbeat sped up anxiously. "What's going to happen to her?"

"They are setting up a disciplinary action for her to follow for the next six weeks."

"*Bann?*"

"*Bann.* Only for a while." Daniel turned his head to look at Jamie, face grim. "I wanted to tell you in person. Aubrey's contact with everybody is going to be limited. I know it'll be hard for the both of you, but please follow the church's actions. Aubrey needs a strong spiritual leader, and she'll look to you to be that. More so, the church will be watching you as well, to see if you two are suitable for marriage."

Jamie nodded his understanding. As men, they were supposed to be steadfast and able to take care of their families spiritually.

"Of course, sir. I understand," he said.

It would be hard. It would take every bit of his self control not to go against the church's order and have contact with Aubrey. It would give her time to think more thoroughly and pray. He told himself that this was for the better, that this was what he had asked Aubrey for originally. He had known what the consequences were going to be.

"I will be praying for her," Jamie promised.

Daniel smiled. "I will tell her that you are praying for her, as the whole community will be."

Certain things were private within the community, but a spiritual crisis rarely was because prayers were often asked for and needed. That meant his family would hear of it either at church or via word of mouth. It would give Aaron another reason to disapprove.

"I have to be honest, sir," Jamie said, looking at Daniel with a heavy heart. "Once my family hears of this, I'm afraid my father will disapprove and try to persuade me to end the courtship."

"If he does, do not go against him," Daniel replied. "Courtship is the last thing Aubrey needs right now. It will best for that to come later. I have told Aubrey of my wishes for your courtship to end for the time being. She did not agree, but that is up to you two."

Jamie scuffed the bottom of his boot in the dirt. He looked up at the cloudless sky and began to pray silently.

"I understand, sir. If you don't mind, I would like to tell Aubrey in person."

Daniel nodded, patting him on the back. "Of course. I am sure the church would understand."

Jamie only hoped Aubrey would understand.

⊂ℜ CHAPTER 10 ⅏

Fall was coming. Aubrey could feel it in the air when she stepped out, a wicker basket of wet sheets and blankets propped on her hip. She walked along the green grass to the laundry lines and began to clip them up. The sunlight felt warm on top of her kapp, but there was a marked coolness in the air and her skin pimpled in response.

The afternoon was quiet beside the occasional moo from a cow in the field or horse hooves crunching on gravel as a buggy traveled down the road. She didn't mind the quiet. It was something she needed after the past few days' events and since her confession to the church.

Bann. Six weeks of limited contact with her family, with her community, with Jamie. The church and her parents believed the *bann* would help her realize what the consequences of her actions could have entailed.

The first two days of eating separate meals from her family and not being able to work at the bakery with Katie sent a clear message. Sitting away from everybody in church, some ignoring her pointedly, felt like a punch to her nose and made her eyes water. She didn't how much longer she could take staying at home and not being able to interact with anyone fully. Six weeks seemed like six years to her.

She knew how Emma felt now, and didn't like it.

Aubrey brushed off a few blades of grass from the sheets and took the basket inside. After chores, which naturally had increased since she was home, Aubrey sat in the living room and began to pray. A few hours out of the day she'd dedicated to prayer and reflection. Other times, she sat numbly on her knees, staring out the window or down at highlighted scriptures that were about strength and being tempted with sin.

She took a deep breath and decided to chop vegetables to roast with the chicken. In a few minutes her siblings and parents would arrive home from their days. Their happy voices would fill the house and remind Aubrey that she was not allowed to be a part of it.

How could she have tempted herself in such a wicked way? She kept asking herself that over and over. She had been too lost in imagining a life outside of the community, taking in Emma's words, to realize that it had been wrong. She had gone about it all in the wrong way. Daniel had given her permission to participate in *rumspringa*, to run around and sow her wild oats (as they said), but she had done the extreme version of that.

The front door opened and then closed. Aubrey looked over her shoulder as Sadie entered the kitchen. She frowned when no one else followed her.

"Where is everyone else?" Aubrey asked.

"Down the road still," Sadie said, taking a step toward her. "I told them that I had to use the bathroom."

She peered at her, chewing on her lower lip. Aubrey turned back around, scooping up the freshly-chopped onions and dumping them into the baking dish.

"Were you really going to leave with Emma?"

Aubrey's eyes drifted closed. She cleared her throat, not willing to meet Sadie's burning stare. "We aren't supposed to talk about it, Sadie. You aren't really supposed to be talking to me," she said.

"Mama says that Emma was trying to convince you to leave."

"I wasn't going to leave." Aubrey's fingers curled tightly around the hilt of the knife. She sliced through a carrot with more force than necessary. "I was trying to tell her that I wasn't going to go with her. I couldn't leave even if I wanted to. All we need to do now is pray for her."

And for me, Aubrey thought, but kept that part to herself.

"How did she look?" Sadie asked curiously. "I overheard Mama say that Emma looked like some sort of harlot."

Aubrey smiled thinly at that. She knew Emma would never engage in such behavior, but her sister certainly had taken on the appearance of one and either was comfortable with it or unaware of how she looked like to others. "Sort of. She had tattoos and piercings."

"Tattoos?" Sadie drew closer to Aubrey's side. "What are tattoos? I know that Englischers pierce their ears sometimes."

This was how it had started for Aubrey; asking Emma questions about the outside and growing curious for more information. She took in her sister's pale and innocent face underneath her white kapp, hanging on her every word. She couldn't imagine Sadie surviving on the outside without their family.

"I don't know," Aubrey said, shrugging her shoulders. "She didn't really explain the process to me."

She reached for the pitcher of water, but Sadie grabbed it for her and poured the water into the baking dish. She stepped away right as Daniel and Katie entered the kitchen with Isaac in tow.

They danced around her wordlessly, aware of her presence, but not acknowledging her directly. Katie spoke simple commands or made little comments as they prepared dinner together. Daniel just ignored her outright.

When Katie pulled out the roasted chicken, Aubrey stood back and waited for everyone to be served before dishing a plate for herself. She went into the living room and sat down on the couch. She was excluded from meals, one of the times for no one but family, and it was by far the most painful. She listened to Daniel say a blessing over the food before happy chatter broke out and she began to eat, listening to Katie talk about closing the bakery down in a couple of weeks. She needed the help, but couldn't ask Aubrey to help her until her punishment expired.

Guilt squashed Aubrey's appetite. Earlier that morning when dressing, she had noticed that her dress was looser on her frame and pinned the fabric differently. It wasn't that surprising since she had barely eaten for the past few weeks.

She waited until the scuff of chairs against the wooden floors diminished and went to the kitchen to help Katie wash dishes.

"You are losing weight," Katie commented quietly.

They stood side by side, with Katie's hands buried in soapy water and Aubrey drying the dishes with a small towel. She stiffened at her mother's observation. "I'm fine."

"You need to eat."

"I said I'm fine."

"Don't think I haven't noticed that you are pinning your dress differently."

"Maem," Aubrey turned to look Katie the eye. "You aren't supposed to be talking to me. Remember?"

Katie's lips thinned. "I know, but that doesn't make me worry about you any less. Did you see your sister? Nothing but bones. I will not see you look the same way."

"I just haven't had much of an appetite is all." Aubrey fiddled with the damp towel, absently tugging at a stray thread. "It's been hard not eating with all of you."

Katie opened her mouth, but was interrupted when a knock came from the front door. They heard Daniel get up from his spot near the wood stove and open the front door, his voice soft and distant.

"Who would be here on a weekday at this hour?" Katie asked, frowning.

Aubrey took the roasting pan from her mother's soapy hands and dried it quickly before placing it back in its cupboard spot.

"Aubrey."

She looked up, startled to hear Daniel's voice for the first time in a couple of days, and stared at him with a glimmer of hope. He refused to look at her, staring down at the kitchen floor with a hard glint to his eyes.

"There is someone here to see you at the front porch."

Aubrey dried off her hands with a towel and left the kitchen. She opened the front door to find Jamie standing behind it.

Her heart lifted at the sight of him. It took everything in her not to throw herself into his arms and breathe in his clean scent.

"Jamie." She cast a nervous glance over her shoulder. "You shouldn't be here. If my daed sees you-"

"He invited me to come talk to you," Jamie interrupted, a strained smile on his face. He shifted on his feet and played with the rim of his hat anxiously. "Can you come outside for a few minutes?"

Aubrey nodded. She stepped out on the front porch, folding her hands in front of her stomach, and waited for Jamie to talk. After church on Sunday, she knew that the whole community knew by now, and that included Jamie. He wouldn't meet her eyes the entire time at church and he had yet to talk to her.

She didn't blame him. She expected it.

"Your daed thinks it's a good idea for us to slow our courtship down," Jamie said, not looking at her.

He kept his eyes focused on the boards of the front porch. His words washed over her in a numb haze. A couple of days of preparing for it still didn't make it any easier.

"I know," Aubrey whispered, tears stinging in her eyes. "He told me that he wishes for our courtship to end for now."

"It'll only be for a awhile," Jamie mumbled.

Aubrey looked at him closely then. His expression was glum and strained as he stared out along the fields. She reached out and laid a hand on his shoulder, smiling in relief when he leaned into her touch.

"I'm sorry, Jamie. Things weren't supposed to happen like this."

He reached up and grabbed her hand, bringing it up to his lips. Jamie's eyes sparkled dimly when he looked back at her. "They never do."

CRSO

After hymns concluded, the bishop of their community stood.

"I would like to announce," Abraham said, gazing about the room with a smile. "An upcoming marriage between two of our recently-baptized members. Please join me in congratulating the pending union of John Lapp and Miriam Bender."

Jamie clapped with the rest of the room. He caught Miriam's eyes from across the aisle and smiled widely at her. The center of her cheeks flushed with a pinkish hue before he lost sight of her as a swell of bodies surrounded her.

The excitement in the barn was hard to ignore. Voices echoed in the barn rafters and there was a sea of wide smiles. Despite the past few days and the ache currently residing inside of him, he felt excited for Miriam. He wanted to see her happy.

Jamie offered his congratulations to John Lapp, who shook his hand and then stepped outside to enjoy the warm air. A hint of coolness still clung to the air and he tilted his head back to let the sunlight warm him.

"You okay, bruder?"

Henry came to a stand alongside him and grasped his shoulder, squeezing briefly.

Jamie smiled faintly at him. "Jah. I am fine."

He caught sight of Aubrey slipping out of the barn, head bowed as she walked down the road. Jamie watched her go, his heart following her every step of the way, even though he remained standing with Henry. He knew the news would hit Aubrey hard even though she wouldn't have shown it and hugged Miriam in congratulations. She was embarrassed enough over having the whole community know about what happened with her sister arriving in the middle of the night.

There were several questions about it, but he only had one for Aubrey, and it was the one he planned to ask her in a few weeks. *Was that brief glimpse of the outside worth all of this?*

"It must be hard," Henry commented quietly.

"What is?"

"Not being able to talk to her for another couple of weeks."

"It's what the church thinks is best for now," Jamie responded.

"But if you plan to marry her, it won't be until next Fall. That's over a year from now."

"Courtships can last as long as need be."

"You know that daed isn't going to let you court her again until you both take the kneeling vow."

Jamie's eyes drifted over to where Aaron stood in line for food with a few other Amish men. Their conversation the day before while working together in the barn still lingered in his mind. Aaron had expressed his wishes for them not to court until enough time had passed, and even then he didn't trust Aubrey. It wasn't customary for him to worry about his father's opinions when it came to courtship, but it was customary not to go against the community and his family.

"*If* he does let me court her again," he replied. "Only time will tell if Pa will change his mind. It may take years."

They both smiled at their father's stubbornness. Henry's head titled to the right suddenly and focused on Elizabeth Yates, a recent widow, who was staring at them. The two shared a smile, and when Henry turned to look back at Jamie, he blushed at the knowing expression on Jamie's face.

"How long has this been going on?" Jamie teased.

"Only a month. I didn't want to tell you with everything that has been going on with Aubrey."

He had been so lost in Aubrey and trying to win her over that the rest of his life had slipped away. Now, his brother was in a courtship and had kept it secret because he knew of the turmoil inside of Jamie.

"You could've told me. I am happy for you."

Henry smiled hesitantly. "Danka. I just imagined how you must feel and decided to keep quiet."

Jamie didn't honestly know what to feel. He was torn between loyalty toward his own family and heart, while the other part wanted Aubrey and nothing else. In a short amount of time she had won him over without even trying. That's all the time it had taken for him to fall in love with her, flaws and perfections.

Except now it was gone.

Or, as he reminded himself, *put on hold for the time being.*

He spent the rest of the afternoon in the warmth of fellowship. His mind constantly wandered down the road to the Forrest home, to where Aubrey had undoubtedly gone. He was about to leave when the bishop and minister called him.

Jamie walked with them away from the barn and into a field, away from prying ears. His heart began to beat a bit faster. Though he wasn't in trouble for knowing what Aubrey had been doing, he still was uneasy about the church looking at him closely.

"How are you holding up?" Isaac asked.

"I am fine, sir," Jamie replied. As an afterthought, he forced himself to smile.

Bishop Abraham placed an aged hand on Jamie's shoulder. He gazed at him in kindness with his hazel colored eyes.

"I wanted to take some time to talk to you about Aubrey," he said and after reading the tension in Jamie's eyes, went on assuredly. "I promise you are not in any trouble with the church. Aubrey confessed that you had known about her correspondence with her sister, but tried to convince her to stay here."

"Yes, sir. I tried to give her a reason to stay here."

Dread curled in his stomach. It wasn't an every day occurrence to have the bishop and minister consulting someone. He tried to read their expressions, but their faces remained guarded.

"We hope you understand," Isaac began, "that the church believes courtship and marriage for Aubrey right now is not possible nor in her best interest. Daniel has told us that he has asked of you to end your courtship for now."

Jamie looked at the ground. He had known that this was coming. He had prepared for it after talking to Aubrey, who had no other choice but to obey the disciplinary action if she wanted to stay in the community. It still didn't lessen the tightness in his chest.

"Yes, sir. He has told me that he wishes for us to end our courtship."

Abraham patted him sympathetically on the shoulder. "It is hard, we know, to end a courtship. It is hard to be young and in love," he stated wisely.

"To be honest," Jamie started, looking Abraham directly in the eye. "I want to marry her someday. I realize that now is not the right time, but in the future."

"In time, perhaps, we will see. For now," Abraham leveled a pointed stare at him, "there will be no courtship. It is best for the both of you."

The two older Amish men nodded their goodbyes to

him before walking back down to the barn. Jamie watched them go and a bitter disappointment filled him. A young Amish boy crossed paths with them, waving at them in greeting, before sprinting down the pathway. His delighted laughter reached Jamie's ears and if he tilted his head the right way, the boy almost looked like a mixture of Aubrey and himself.

His feet started on their own accord down after the bishop and minister. *Give me strength*, Jamie prayed, *to convince them of our courtship.*

CℜℬↃ

Aubrey took solace in the open dirt road and walked aimlessly around the community for the next few hours. She couldn't remain behind for fellowship, when everyone within the church pointedly looked the other direction, when Miriam Bender was getting married to John Lapp.

Tears surfaced in her eyes and she swiped at them in mild annoyance. *Stop crying*, she told herself, *you've done enough of it the past year.*

Houses and farms were empty as she passed by them. She stopped at one of the fields to scratch a horse on the nose gently and then continued on her way toward home, relishing in the peaceful afternoon. Fellowship would end soon and Daniel had mentioned to her that they would be home shortly afterward. He expected dinner to be cooking by the time they were home and her chores to be done, since she'd decided not to stay behind. It was one of the few ways Daniel sought to keep her busy during her punishment.

She had reached the driveway leading home when Jamie's voice rang out in the afternoon.

"Aubrey!"

Startled, Aubrey turned back around and cupped a hand over her eyes. Down the road, Jamie jogged lithely toward her. He came to a stop in front of her, sweat beading on his forehead.

"Where have you been?" Jamie panted. "I've been looking for you for the past hour. Your daed said that you would be home."

"You're not supposed to be talking to me."

She went to turn back around, but Jamie grabbed her firmly by the wrist and tugged her toward him.

He stared down at her sternly. "Where've you been?" he asked.

Irritation flickered inside her. "Nowhere," she replied, breaking free from his hand. "I just went for a walk around the community to clear my head and pray. I find it a little hard to do that at church now that everyone ignores me. You are supposed to be ignoring me."

"I need to talk to you," Jamie said.

Aubrey sighed impatiently. "You aren't supposed to-"

"Be talking to you, I know," Jamie interrupted, waving his hand in a shooing manner. "Good thing no one is around then to see us talking then."

Her stomach did a little flutter, like it always did whenever Jamie said things like that to her. She quickly reined in her self control, even if it was tattered at the moment, and fought the feeling by focusing on the irritation inside of her.

"I have to start dinner before everyone comes home." She stopped when Jamie made to follow her down the road. Aubrey scowled at him when he grinned at her, not in the mood to fight off the feelings Jamie would involuntarily stir up.

"What are you doing here?" she asked, irritation now lacing her tone. "I thought you would be with your family for fellowship."

"They don't know I'm down here. I told them that I was going to Jacob Byler's farm to look at one of their cows they are giving us for the winter."

"So, you lied to them?"

"Partially. I really was there for a few minutes. I wanted to come talk to you."

Her curiosity piqued despite the nervousness twisting around her in stomach. Since her punishment, Jamie had only spoken to her once, about ending their courtship for the time, and otherwise kept his distance.

"About what?"

"About *us*."

Aubrey's eyes closed at those words. She sucked in a deep breath, willing her heart not to beat so fast.

"Jamie," she shook her head in dismay, "there isn't any us. You know that there never will be if we don't win my daed's or the church's approval again."

He took her hands in his larger and stronger ones, squeezing her clammy fingers. "So we will convince them then."

"How? We're already breaking the rules of my punishment."

"I talked to the bishop this morning after church," Jamie said.

His blue eyes began to sparkle again with their normal warmth. Impulsively, she slid a hand free from his and curled her fingers around the smooth skin of his jaw. A flicker of hope began in her stomach. "About what?"

"About not ending our courtship."

Aubrey's heart hammered. "And?" she prompted, clutching Jamie's hand tightly. "Did they say anything?"

"It took some convincing, but they agreed to us marrying next Fall if we both wish it."

"Really?" A grin began to spread across Aubrey's face. "They really agreed to that?"

Jamie shook his head affirmatively. "Yes, but," he said in a warning voice, "we have to convince your father first and then take the vow. From what I hear, he isn't very open to the idea of us courting anymore until he believes that you are straightened out."

She was dizzy with adrenaline. After making the decision to stay, she hadn't been sure if it was the right one. It had been far more tempting to leave after the prospect of losing Jamie, one of the reasons she had stayed, her anchor, became a frightening reality.

"I know. He hasn't said one word to me since the night Emma was here."

"How was seeing your sister?" Jamie asked. "After all those questions about the outside, was it worth it to see her?"

Aubrey's hand fell from Jamie's jaw and onto his shoulder. She then rested her palm over his heart and soaked in the feeling of his heart beating strongly underneath her hand. "It was…" she paused, thinking of the right word, "not like I had thought it would be like. She looked so lost and frail. I've been praying really hard for her."

"I will pray for her too," Jamie promised.

She smiled appreciatively, and without thinking brushed a light kiss on Jamie's lips. His arms wound around her waist and pulled her close. She had to stand on her tiptoes to kiss him properly and wrap her arms around his shoulders.

"You'd better go before my daed comes home," Aubrey said, pulling away reluctantly. "He will be furious at the both of us if he sees you here when we are not supposed to be talking."

Jamie kissed her one last time before stepping back. His hands slipped from hers. "Guess we better keep this a secret then."

Aubrey laughed breathlessly.

"No more secrets. They got me into trouble last time."

"Some secrets are worth keeping."

She watched him go, cutting across the field and then in the direction of his own home. *Yes*, Aubrey thought with a smile, *some secrets were worth keeping.*

End of Book 1

2.AMISH BRIDE

CR CHAPTER 1 &)

"We have an announcement to make this morning." Bishop Abraham said.

He stood in front of a sea of white kapps and black wide-rimmed hats. He smiled at all of them, eyes scanning the rows of patient and eager faces peering up at him. A curious and excited static clung to the air. It was the month of October, and it was also the Sunday when upcoming wedding announcements were made public.

Aubrey Forrest twined a clammy hand through Hannah Byler's. The two squeezed hands and rested them on the bench. Her heart pounded furiously with the nerves and blood surging through her veins.

She closed her eyes and waited.

"There will be a marriage next month between Jamie Miller and Aubrey Forrest."

At first there was a deafening silence. Or there was at least to Aubrey, as she waited for someone to object, or worse than that, to wake up from this surreal dream she seemed to be in. When a chorus of cheers and applause broke out, she started in surprise. Faces beamed at her and arms swept her into tight embraces. Excited chatter broke out as Aubrey tried to answer questions and not get overwhelmed by the response she really did not expect from the community.

Not after what had happened the previous summer.

It was Jamie's strong and familiar hands resting on the curves of her waist that helped Aubrey begin to relax finally and accept that her surroundings were a reality. They were really getting married and it wasn't the same cruel dream she oftentimes had.

"I've never seen so many excited Amish over a wedding," Jamie said.

His warm breath that smelled of a crisp autumn morning stirred the hairs around her ear. A shiver went up Aubrey's spine in response and she leaned her head back, resting it against the muscles of Jamie's chest.

"Jah," she agreed softly. "It was a bit surprising."

Tradition would've had them at home, cooking together, when they were published. Except the bishop had offered for them to see their community's reaction and Jamie had convinced her to come to church.

She glanced upward and absently traced the curve of Jamie's jaw with a pointer finger. A few blonde bristles that Jamie had missed while shaving earlier poked her in the fingertip. Her heart filled with an affectionate warmth.

"Over a year later and here we are," Jamie said, shaking his head wistfully. "I bet you never imagined last summer that things would end up this way."

Six weeks after bann she was finally allowed to eat

meals with her family once again and she had spent the next couple of months mending her relationships, including the one with Jamie. Somehow along the way they had convinced Daniel to let them resume their courtship on the assurance that they were both planning to join the Amish church, their rumspringa days well beyond them. Afterward, Jamie and Aubrey started the eighteen-week class that took place during church to prepare themselves for their baptism.

Aubrey still remembered that day vividly, kneeling before Bishop Abraham as he asked her about her commitment to living a Christian life, renouncing the devil and committing to Christ while accepting the Ordnung. Her voice, by some miracle, never shook once while answering "yes" before the deacon poured water over her head and hair. She was then a part of the church and fully committed to Christ. Nothing made her feel stronger than that. Breathless, she had caught Jamie's proud eyes and whatever doubts that had clouded her mind had faded.

All of last summer had been erased and didn't seem so important anymore.

"Let's get something to eat," Jamie offered.

His fingers dug deeply and playfully into her waist, knowing well that it would send her into a giggling fit. Aubrey danced away from his hands and both retreated from the barn into the unusually warm October afternoon .

Sadie flocked to Aubrey's side the second that Jamie slipped away to grab a plate of food.

"Can I help you sew your wedding dress?" Sadie asked

eagerly. "I promise that I'm really good at it now."

"Maybe, Sadie," she replied. "You know that it is the bride's responsibility to sew her own wedding dress."

"I know."

The glum expression on Sadie's face brought a smile to Aubrey's face that she hid with her hand. After Sadie's fourteenth birthday a few weeks before, she had become increasingly interested in courting and their daed was a bit exasperated over her sudden interest. Aubrey suspected (with dry amusement) that Daniel couldn't wait until all his daughters were married off so he could focus on Isaac as he grew to his teenage years. Sons were just less complicated than daughters, according to Daniel.

"Tell you what," Aubrey said, twining her arm through Sadie's. "You can help with the quilt. I'm sure Mama will have a quilting bee here in the next week or so."

Sadie's mood brightened at that. She slipped away from Aubrey's side a few moments later to talk to one of her friends. Aubrey watched her go, a fond smile ghosting her lips. She had made sure that one of the relationships she mended was the one with Sadie, and had spent the winter months doing that exactly.

As the afternoon melted away into a noticeably crisper evening, Aubrey gathered the baskets they had brought for Fellowship. She turned to find Jamie already approaching her.

"I'll see you tomorrow afternoon at the bakery?" he asked, even though it really wasn't a question. They spent their lunch breaks together sitting on the front porch of Katie's bakery.

"Jah. See you for lunch tomorrow."

Jamie kissed her on the cheek before returning to his family. Lily Miller waved cheerfully from where she stood between her parents. She returned the wave with a smile. Her eyes caught Aaron's and he gave her a brief nod of acknowledgment. Aaron's attitude toward her had changed tremendously since her union with the church. He had at least been accepting of their courtship and their soon-to-be marriage then.

I bet you never imagined last summer that things would be this way.

No, Aubrey thought to herself, she'd never imagined things to be the way they were now. She only hoped and prayed that it would remain the same when it felt so fragile.

ᔆᔆ

"What do you think, bruder?"

Henry took in the piece of land that would soon have a house and barn with fields for horses and cows. The area would soon be Jamie's own stretch of land, and he nodded in approval.

"Very gutt. The earth is nice here for plowing."

"Jah," Jamie nodded, taking in the land with a swell of pride. "I promised Aubrey that we would plant a couple of apple trees along with a peach tree."

Henry smiled broadly. "More like you promised yourself a couple of apple trees and a peach tree. I suspect you love her apple and peach pies more than her."

"The pies happen to come along with her, but it's a

tie sometimes between the two."

They laughed and turned to walk back up the grassy hill. A chill had yet to set in, but the grass was slowly wilting and turning a shade of dry yellow. The crisp afternoon air promised one soon.

Jamie stepped up into their family buggy as Henry grabbed the reins and flicked them. Their family buggy jerked beneath them as the horses started forward in the direction of their home.

He slid into the wool coat that he'd left behind in the buggy and sighed in relief when it warmed his skin. Winters in Lancaster had been brutal in their own way, but Jamie wholeheartedly agreed with Aubrey when she insisted that the winters in Colorado were worse. The constant chill that went bone deep combined with the thin air had made last a winter a miserable one. Sickness frequently plagued Matilda and she'd stayed inside the majority of the winter, coughing delicately from her room. They chopped wood before and after work for months on end, throats sore from inhaling the glacial air as they worked.

Aubrey and Lily, during a sewing frolic, had knitted several scarves and mittens for them to wear while working outside. Jamie wore the blue scarf that Aubrey had personally knitted for him every day now that the mornings and afternoons were markedly cooler, with summer giving way to fall.

He reached up and adjusted the scratchy but warm scarf around his neck more properly to keep himself warm.

"When will we start building?" Henry asked. He too tucked his scarf more carefully around his neck.

Jamie smiled at him gratefully. His brother never failed to offer help or advice.

"This weekend. I asked Daniel for the time off. He offered to help us after work as well."

"Extra hands will help if you wish to have it done by next spring."

It still felt like a surreal dream to him knowing that next month he would be married to Aubrey in the eyes of the church and Gott. The prospect thrilled him to no end. He looked forward, albeit selfishly, to having Aubrey to himself day in and day out. Only seeing her for a few hours of the day simply wasn't enough anymore. He was also secretly thankful that they had decided to wed in a month. The attraction between him and Aubrey was beginning to blossom to a rather intense one that he oftentimes feared would drive them both to do something before their wedding vows. Just thinking about it made Jamie shift uncomfortably in his seat.

Patches of bright yellows and reds painted the mountainsides. The few trees they passed were also slowly turning to a shade of yellow and a couple of leaves trickled down. In a matter of weeks or possibly days, depending on the first freeze, the trees would lose all their vibrant color and become bare.

Saturday night he planned to take Aubrey up into the mountains so they could enjoy the colors and give Aubrey the chance to paint a quick canvas. After her bann, she'd admitted that she had desired to paint the vibrant fall foliage, but couldn't. She would be happily surprised when she found out where he was taking her.

Jamie smiled at the thought. He raised his eyes to the dark blue sky hovering above them, the sun already dipping down to the horizon even though there were two hours left in the afternoon. He prayed and gave thanks quietly then, listening to the horses' hooves crunch down the road until the sight of their home and barn appeared in view.

Smoke curled around the chimney, and the closer they drew, the stronger the scent of beef stew became. Together they unhitched the horses from the buggy before leading them into their stalls to be brushed and fed.

"How is Elizabeth?" Jamie asked.

"She is gutt. Feeling much better after a week of rest," Henry replied.

The relief was evident in Henry's tone. A few weeks prior, Elizabeth's health had declined rapidly from the exhaustion of taking care of her farm and preparing for the winter months. Henry had helped her as much as he could, and Jamie also volunteered a chunk of his time to help with canning. In all honesty, Aubrey had helped Elizabeth can and he'd chopped wood to keep her and her kinner warm during the winter months.

He had been partly surprised to hear that he and Aubrey were the only ones marrying next month. He was more than sure that Henry and Elizabeth would marry, but with her husband's death only a year prior to courting Henry, their courtship was a slow and sensitive one.

"She has not mentioned marrying again?" Jamie asked carefully.

Henry's eyes clouded with frustration. "No, not yet.

Maybe next year, she said. I worry about her keeping up with that farm and house all by herself with no husband to help."

"Give it time. She loves you and will eventually marry you."

"I can only hope," Henry sighed, rubbing his face tiredly. He glanced over at Jamie and smiled thinly. "I remember giving you advice over a year ago and now it's switched. How did that happen?"

Jamie shrugged. "Things have a habit of working out in time. You'll see."

Or so he hoped.

Last summer still lingered in the back of his mind like a sour aftertaste. It had faded over the winter with Aubrey joining him in their classes for baptism, but every once in a while old doubts resurfaced. Particularly when he caught glimpses of apprehension floating in Aubrey's eyes, but he'd never mentioned any of it out loud.

He didn't want test the seemingly calm waters.

CREESO

Aubrey carefully packed her canvases, oils, and brushes in a bag that Katie let her borrow. She slipped the strap of the bag over her shoulder and also grabbed the small easel Jamie had crafted for her to paint on.

Katie looked up from her sewing when Aubrey came into the living room and arched an eyebrow at the items she carried. "You're bringing your canvases along?"

"Jamie said to bring them."

She had no idea what Jamie was up to exactly. He'd only mentioned to her to have all her chores done by noon and have all her art supplies packed. Their destination was a secret, but he'd promised that she would love it once they were there.

"And you have no idea where you are going?" Katie asked.

Aubrey shook her head. "No, Mama. I'd tell you if I knew."

"It's a good thing that we like Jamie, or else I'd be demanding to know where he is taking you."

A swift knock on the door ended Katie's mumbling. Aubrey opened the door, a breeze of lukewarm air greeting her along with Jamie's smile.

"Ready?"

"Ready. Let me grab my coat."

"Make sure to dress warmly. It's cold where we are going."

"Where are you two going exactly?" Katie asked, entering the hallway. "It better not be somewhere dangerous or outside of Monte Vista."

Jamie grinned as Aubrey slid her arms into her wool coat and buttoned it securely. She then slipped her gloves on and wrapped a scarf tightly around her neck.

"When have I ever made you doubt me?" Jamie asked.

Aubrey bit the inside of her lips to contain her laughter at the exasperated look on Katie's face. She kissed Katie briefly on the cheek before stepping out on the front porch and stopped when she caught sight of another buggy up the road, with Lily sitting alongside a boy Aubrey recognized as Martha Hilty's younger brother, Mark Hilty.

"Am I seeing things correctly?"

Lily lifted a gloved hand from where it rested on the heavy blankets around her and waved excitedly. She waved back and turned to look at Jamie, who was scowling down at the porch boards.

"You're seeing right," he said.

The protective tones in Jamie's voice brought a smile to Aubrey's face. A few months ago, Lily had turned sixteen and Aaron had given her permission to start courting. Jamie hadn't been too thrilled with knowing his sister was courting.

Jamie took the easel and bag from her arms as they walked toward his buggy. She absently stroked one of the horses' brown necks before stepping up into the buggy and waiting for Jamie to sit down so she could wrap both of them in the heavy blankets. It gave her the excuse to cuddle into his side and soak up the warmth that radiated through his winter clothes.

"So, where are we going exactly?" Aubrey asked.

The trot of the horse hooves along the road echoed in the quiet afternoon. They slowly drew closer to the mountains that were splattered with aspen trees changing colors.

"You'll see."

Jamie's eyes, the color of the clear blue sky above them, sparkled with mirth. He leaned down and to the side, cold lips brushing hers in a soft kiss that immediately heated her up. She pulled back before either one of them could act on the heat building between them both. It was becoming harder lately to kiss Jamie and not feel the physical yearning inside of her.

"Why did I have to bring my supplies?"

"You'll see."

She mock-glared at the vague answer and earned a deep chuckle in response. Jamie easily held the leather reins in one hand and wrapped his arm around her shoulders.

"My answer doesn't please you?" he asked teasingly.

Aubrey smoothed the wrinkles from the blanket around her legs. "It surely does not."

"You don't like surprises, do you?"

"I hate surprises. So do me a favor and tell me where we are going."

"Not a chance. I can't be a romantic soon-to-be mann if you can't accept surprises. Where's the fun in knowing everything?"

"It is fun, knowing everything," she insisted.

A pink color tinged her cheeks and she wasn't sure if it had to do with gradually cooling air or her body's response to the word mann.

In a month Jamie would be her husband and it still didn't feel real to her. The past winter didn't feel real after what had happened and how close she had been to losing all of it. Apprehension started to mix with the excitement. Or at least it did for Aubrey. She was more than sure that Jamie wasn't anxious about their wedding or wedding night.

Aubrey glanced away as the thoughts crossed her mind. She didn't want to ruin their afternoon by confessing to Jamie about her nerves.

Lily's laughter rang out in the afternoon over the clop of horse hooves. Jamie's arm lifted away from her shoulders and he leaned out of the buggy to glance behind them, where Mark Hilty followed in his buggy. Aubrey laughed when she caught sight of the protective glare Jamie sent behind them. She rested a hand on his tense arm.

"Stop it, Jamie. They aren't doing anything wrong."

"I don't know why Pa insisted they come with us," Jamie mumbled, facing forward again. "The last thing I want to do is watch my sister court somebody."

"Maybe that's why he wanted you to watch her. He knows you are the protective brother."

They continued further up the road and to the mountainside. Aubrey tilted her head back to look up at the leafy canopy above, shivering from the crisp air that greeted them as Jamie steered their buggy further up the mountain. The afternoon sunlight filtered through the vibrant leaves and cast a red hue along the rocky road as they crossed over a small bubbling creek.

"Here we are," Jamie announced.

He slid out from beneath the blanket and helped Aubrey down, grabbing her art supplies and easel.

Aubrey glanced around them in bewilderment. The road continued up the mountainside, too steep for horse or buggy to continue, and they were surrounded by a cluster of aspen trees. Yellow leaves shuddered in a breeze and the sound filled the forest.

"Where are we exactly?" she questioned.

Jamie only grinned at her. Looping the leather reins around an aspen trunk, Jamie turned as Mark and Lily came up the road. When a scowl spread across his face, Aubrey pointedly smacked him on the arm and then forced a neutral expression.

"Isn't it beautiful up here?" Lily exclaimed.

She shifted out from beneath the blanket covering them and jumped out of the buggy, the fabric of her dress flying behind her before she landed easily on her feet.

"Beautiful," Aubrey agreed, smiling. "Do you know why we are up here?"

Lily opened her mouth to answer, but Jamie cut in over her. "Don't give it away. Come, let's go this way."

He took Aubrey's hand and started to walk through the cluster of trees, but stopped when Lily and Mark didn't follow behind them.

"We're going for walk," Lily stated, meeting Jamie's irritated stare bravely. "You and Aubrey want some privacy like we do."

"No, absolutely not. I promised Pa that I would keep an eye on you. Plus, Aubrey and I are about to be married."

"We won't go far."

"Lily-"

Aubrey stepped in before the argument could continue any further. She twined her arm through the crook of Jamie's arm and tugged him away pointedly.

Lily smiled appreciatively at her before wrapping an arm through Mark's. The two disappeared into the yellow foliage.

"They won't go far from us, Jamie. Don't spoil the surprise by starting a fight."

She somehow managed to tug Jamie in the direction

he had been originally walking and patted him soothingly on his tense shoulder.

"Relax. What are they going to do in the middle of the forest?"

A mischievous smile spread across Jamie's face then. She shrieked between laughter when he wrapped his arms around her waist and hoisted her up, booted feet dangling in the air. The fabric of her dress tangled in the tree trunk behind her as their bodies pressed together and mouths found each others' in a heated kiss.

When Jamie's hand brushed against her forehead and knocked her kapp loose, she forced herself to pull back. Only one more month and there would be no more boundaries or reasons to stop. Her body thrummed in anticipation.

"If that's what can happen in the forest, maybe you should keep an eye on your sister."

Jamie chuckled. He took a step back to put much-needed distance between them and watched as Aubrey expertly pinned her kapp back in place.

"Exactly my point, but that's not why I brought you out here."

She followed him through another cluster of aspen trees until they were standing on a large rock cliff that jutted out into the open air. The San Luis Valley sat before them, and a patchwork of fields and neighborhoods stretched on for miles. A few fields had managed to keep their green color, but a majority of the colors now shading the valley were brilliant yellows and deep reds. In a matter of weeks it would covered in snow.

"You mentioned that you wanted to paint the fall colors last year, but couldn't," Jamie explained when she turned to look at him, eyebrows arched in confusion. "So I brought you up here to paint the colors, since you have the time to do it."

Aubrey's heart swelled as it always did knowing that in a month she would forever have Jamie as her husband. She kissed him again before he set up her easel in front of a rock large enough for her to perch herself on and paint.

"How are you so good to me?" she asked, dipping a paint brush into the blue oil.

From the corner of her eye, she watched Jamie stretch out on his back on the rock beside her. He kept one long leg extended outward while the other one he kept bent and rested his head on his interlaced hands.

"It takes effort."

He smirked when Aubrey kicked him playfully in the legs. They were quiet for awhile, listening to the brush smear paint across the canvas and the breeze stirring the aspen trees behind them.

"Are you almost done?" Jamie asked.

Aubrey smiled as she rubbed a bit of paint across the canvas. "Almost. Impatient for me to finish?"

"No, I'm impatient for other things."

"Oh, really. Like what?"

Jamie's eyes fluttered open when Aubrey turned on the rock to look at him. He smiled almost demurely at her and a longing filled his eyes. Since their announcement of marriage, Aubrey oftentimes found Jamie looking at her with an odd longing in his eyes.

"Do I really have to say?"

She cleared her throat, a blush filling the center of her cheeks. "You sure know how to make a girl blush, Jamie Miller."

"Whatever keeps you wanting to stay here, darling."

Jamie winked before closing his eyes. He didn't need an answer or assurance. He already knew that she was going to stay. She wasn't going to risk it again.

Her paintbrush stilled as she took in Monte Vista. Since her baptism, Jamie's confidence in her faith had been unwavering and she wished that she could return the same confidence in herself. She didn't dare tell him what thoughts and doubts were beginning to circle inside of her heart.

❧ CHAPTER 2 ❧

The first frost came sometime during the night and breathed its white breath across the valley. Blades of grass crunched noisily under Aubrey's winter boots as she ventured out into the chilly morning to greet the Englischer Brandon, who drove them to and from work every morning and afternoon.

"Morning, Aubrey."

His breath puffed out in front of him like a distant cloud in the sky. Today he wore a thick flannel shirt and a blue knitted hat, the one Katie had made for him over a year ago to show her thanks, with a cup of kaffe in his hands. He smiled at her warmly from where he sat behind the wheel, with his window rolled down to talk to her as she approached.

"Morning, Brandon."

Aubrey smiled at him, reaching the idling car. She slid into the back passenger seat and closed the door, thankful that he'd turned the heat on full blast.

"It'll just be me today," she informed him. "Daed

took the buggy to work this morning and maem is staying home with Sadie. She woke up with a cough."

Brandon turned in the driver's seat to look at her in concern. "Is Sadie alright? There are some nasty bugs going around at this time of the year. My oldest kid caught one two days ago and has been sick ever since."

"I'm sorry to hear that. She will be fine. Maem is keeping an eye on her."

"And Isaac?"

"Daed took Isaac with him this morning."

"Okay then."

He put the car into drive and drove in silence. Aubrey watched the houses and fields blur together as they drove to the bakery. When they drove by a buggy, too fast for Aubrey to see who it was, the previous night's dream stirred in her thoughts.

She was dressed in her wedding dress, the fabric a beautiful blue and perfectly sewn, not a thread out of place, and in a buggy with a heavy blanket draped along her legs. The buggy drew closer to her home, horse hooves clopping surely on the gravel road, and her heart began to pound with each second that ticked by.

Jamie was there. The whole community was there, waiting for her to arrive. She was late to her own wedding and she rushed forward.

Her fingers clutched the leather reins in a death grip and the horse jumped slightly, sensing her jitteriness. Clouds from her own breath distorted her view of the several buggies in front of her parent's house. Panic swelled within her, violent and sudden as an onslaught of a hailstorm during the spring season.

She couldn't marry Jamie. She couldn't marry him.

"I'm sorry, Jamie," she whispered, before jerking the reins to the right.

Cold air ripped her kapp free as they galloped away, further and further from what she had thought she wanted.

Sadie's coughing had roused Aubrey from the dream in a layer of cold sweat and heart pumping furiously.

She rested her head back against the fabric of the back seat and closed her eyes, breathing in deeply. The dreams stirred an uneasiness inside of her. Maybe it was normal to have wedding nerves, the rational part of her reasoned. It was the other half of her that knew the dreams were stemming from what had happened last summer and wondering where Emma went after Aubrey had stayed behind.

Her sister would be marrying sometime soon. She briefly wondered whether Emma had the same dreams and thoughts sometimes.

Hannah stood at the front door of the bakery, waiting patiently for the car to drive up. Her pale face, paler than normal, stretched into an exhausted smile when Aubrey bid goodbye to Brandon and walked toward her. Up close, Aubrey took in the bags under Hannah's eyes and the slightly green tinge on her cheeks with concern.

"Where's your maem?" Hannah asked.

"Home with Sadie. She woke with a bad cough this morning. Are you feeling well?"

"I'll tell you in a minute. Open the door so we can warm ourselves in front of the ovens."

Aubrey unlocked the front door and they slipped inside the cool bakery. Hannah flipped on the lights as they ventured to the kitchen to fire up the ovens and warm their hands.

"So?" Aubrey prompted, turning to look at her best friend. "What is wrong? If you're sick, I'm closing the bakery and taking you back home."

Hannah's eyes watered as her lips spread into a tremulous smile. "Please do not say anything just yet to anyone else, but Jacob and I are expecting a child."

Aubrey's mouth fell open in shock before she let out a shriek of excitement and hugged Hannah tightly, their laughter echoing in the kitchen. "When did you find out?" she asked, grinning.

"A few days ago. I had to tell you. It might be hard explaining why I'm puking every thirty minutes between rolling out pie crusts and baking cookies."

"You shouldn't be working then. I'll call Brandon and have him-"

"No!" Hannah cut in, shaking her head. "I want to work. The midwife told me to try and keep to a normal routine. It will help with the fatigue and nausea if I'm not concentrating on it."

Aubrey went to the fridge where they stored their milk and eggs. She searched for the ginger root Katie had bought the previous day and sliced a couple of chunks off into a mug of water to warm over the stove.

"This will help with nausea," she said, stirring the liquid with a spoon. "And no heavy lifting of any kind, and if you feel sick we will close and go home. Mama would understand."

Hannah smiled widely. "You are going to be a good fraa and mother someday, Aubrey Forrest. You're always thinking of others before yourself."

The dream from last night surfaced again inside her mind. Aubrey looked away from Hannah and focused on the mug, trying not to let those thoughts ruin the moment.

Unfortunately, Hannah's keen eyes glimpsed the expression on Aubrey's face. "What? What is it?"

"Nothing. It's nothing," Aubrey replied quickly.

Hannah's eyes narrowed. "Don't lie to me. I'm pregnant and hormonal."

Aubrey laughed. Stirring the mug's contents one last time, she handed it to Hannah for her to sip on as they worked. "It's really nothing. Just bad dreams is all."

"About the wedding?"

"Did you have dreams about your wedding?"

"All the time." Hannah sipped at the mug, gloved fingers holding it tightly to her chest. "I used to have dreams about Jacob calling the wedding off or I couldn't remember the vows."

Sighing, Aubrey shrugged out of her wool coat and set it on the counter. She peeled off her gloves and set them on the counter alongside her coat. "I wish that were true for me. I have dreams all the time about me leaving Jamie," she confessed softly.

"It's normal, Aubrey, to feel nervous before a wedding. I was really nervous before mine too."

She wished more than anything that she was like Hannah, strong in her faith. Hannah was right, it was normal to be nervous, as it was a huge a decision that meant spending the rest of her days with Jamie, but that still didn't quell the anxieties building within her.

Aubrey closed her eyes in prayer, asking for strength to stop the next few thoughts that crossed her mind.

CR&SO

The bakery was busy when Jamie stepped into the warm building. The usual smells of pies and bread baking greeted him, along with Aubrey's tired smile. She slid a plate across the counter toward him, a slice of apple pie in the middle, his favorite dessert. Aubrey baked a pie for him every morning and always had a slice waiting when he came into the bakery to spend his lunch break with her.

"Danka."

"You're welcome."

He waited patiently as Aubrey talked with customers, shoveling bites of pie into his mouth with speed. He only had half an hour from the store to eat and talk with Aubrey, so he ate at a quick pace.

Once the bakery emptied, Aubrey leaned across the counter to kiss him lightly on the cheek. "I can't have a long lunch break today," she told him. "Mama is home with Sadie and Hannah is not feeling well either."

Jamie arched his eyebrow. "Are you sick too? Because if you are, don't kiss me. I don't want to get sick."

Eyes glinting mischievously, Aubrey began to cough loudly and in exaggeration in his direction.

He scowled at her and took a step back. "That's not

funny."

"I'm not sick."

"You look sick."

Aubrey barked out a sarcastic laugh. "Thanks, Jamie. That was really nice of you to say."

"You look beautiful too. You just look like you barely slept last night. Bad dreams?"

He gauged her reaction carefully. Since their wedding announcement, he'd kept a close watch on Aubrey. Her physical health was often a result of her emotional health, and whenever she looked worn out it told him that it was either from dreams or thoughts that would keep her awake at night.

He told himself that he was being reasonable about keeping a close watch on her. After all, they were to be married, and it was part of his responsibility as a mann to watch for her spiritual well being.

Shadows flickered in her blue irises, but Aubrey guarded her emotions from his inspecting gaze. Faint annoyance flashed in her eyes. "Stop it."

"Stop what?"

"Trying to read me like a book. I just didn't sleep well is all."

The first flicker of irritation started in Jamie. He sucked in a deep breath to control it, not in the mood to argue. Not when the past few months had been wonderfully blissful and simple. "I wasn't trying to read you. I was just asking a general question about how you were feeling."

"Well, I'm fine. Believe me when I say that I am. I

have to get back to work."

Aubrey leaned over the counter once more and lightly brushed her lips on the center of his cheek. Before he could reach out to bring her back for a proper kiss goodbye, she rushed away and then disappeared back into the kitchen with such fluidity that it startled him.

He stared at the area where she had been standing, her unique smell of soap and sugar lingering behind.

"That's the thing though," Jamie muttered under his breath as he exited the bakery. "I don't believe you when you say that."

The chilly afternoon made him grateful that he had worn his wool coat to the bakery. Jamie moodily shoved his hands into the pockets and picked out wood shavings before curling his fingers into tight fists. For the first time in months, since their baptism, he felt the same as he had last summer--irritated and anxious.

He was confident that Aubrey wasn't harboring any secrets like corresponding with her sister. She took her vows seriously. It was something else, and it had to do with him and their upcoming wedding.

Jamie raised his eyes to the sapphire sky and sighed heavily, breath streaming out from his mouth in a white cloud. Whatever it was, Jamie planned to spend the next month trying to figure out the reason behind Aubrey's distant behavior and lack of sleep.

He would be damned if he let the summer's previous events repeat themselves.

CR80

The rest of week passed by in a blur of Sadie's violent coughing during the night and Hannah's bouts of morning sickness. By the time Saturday arrived, Aubrey had never been so thankful to have a day that just consisted of chores around the farm instead of running the bakery and coming home to double chores. Not that she mind entirely, the chores and business keeping her mind occupied, but it was still exhausting.

"So, Hannah has been sick every morning for the past week?"

Katie sat in the rocking chair across from Aubrey and picked up her sewing from the basket next to the chair. The glow of their oil-fueled lamps filled the living room with a soft light along with the comforting sounds of a fire crackling within the wood stove. Outside, the chilled air threatened to seep in through the cracks, and no matter how they tried to stuff towels or blankets between the doors and windows, a draft of cold air always found them.

"Jah," Aubrey nodded, looking up from her own stitch-work. " Brandon said there has been some nasty bugs going around. Or at least that's what he told me."

"I see. And how far along is she?"

A knowing smile tugged at Katie's chapped lips as she threaded a needle and began to patch a hole in Isaac's trousers.

"I didn't say she was pregnant."

"I've had four of you kinner. You think that I don't recognize a pregnancy symptom when I see it?"

Shaking her head, Aubrey laughed at the pointed

glance Katie shot her. Though they weren't supposed to openly discuss pregnancy, as such things were private and personal, the signs of one didn't go entirely unnoticed. She sat back against the couch pillows and stared down at her own patchwork, a dress that Sadie had torn while climbing over a barbed wire fence.

"Not very far, a month or so. She is nervous, as it is early still."

Katie nodded. "Understandable. Hannah shouldn't fear anything. She is quite young, healthy, and can carry well."

Memories of Hannah puking sporadically throughout the morning flashed through Aubrey's mind and she grimaced. "She's not healthy at the moment. I think she lost five pounds this week from throwing up all morning and barely ingesting anything beside ginger tea," she noted.

"That's normal, Aubrey. I was sick with all of you every morning for the first couple of months, but in time it passes. Pregnancy is a beautiful blessing from Gott."

She was temped then to repeat Katie's words to Hannah next week. Having seen her mood swings firsthand, however, quickly changed Aubrey's mind. She finished her sewing by clipping the thread and draping Sadie's dress over the back of the couch.

"I hope I won't get sick every morning."

Katie glanced up, her concentration broken. She stared at Aubrey with a teasing sparkle in her eye. "Thinking about a bobli already?"

The comment made Aubrey's cheeks flare in embarrassment. True, it was every Amish girl's dream to be married and have a large family, but the last thing Aubrey wanted to do was discuss those sort of topics with her mother.

She wouldn't admit out loud that Hannah's newfound pregnancy entertained thoughts inside of her own head about being pregnant with Jamie's child. More so, she wouldn't admit how scared those thoughts made her from the excitement that came along with those images of the future with Jamie. She supposed it was natural to think that way. After all, it was bound to happen shortly after their wedding, or whenever Gott saw fit for them.

"That reminds me," Katie continued, not taking heed to Aubrey's hesitance to answer. "I will pick up some fabric from Alma and you can start on your wedding dress."

Grateful for the change of topic, Aubrey listened to her mother's soft voice, like a summer breeze on a hot day, talk about her own wedding dress, which had been ruined during a buggy accident that had torn her dress to shreds and bed-ridden her for over a month to recover from her injuries.

This was what Emma had to miss the most, spending the evenings with their mother and listening to her stories. This was what Aubrey would have missed the most.

Unbeknownst to Katie, Aubrey silently gave thanks for having her mother well and sitting across from her in the rocking chair. She couldn't imagine her life without her mother's gentle hands and words of guidance.

She only prayed that one day she would be like Katie; a dutiful wife and mother, strong within their faith and always loving without a hitch.

CRUSO

After church concluded, Jamie went straight to Aubrey's side.

"Can we talked in private?" he asked.

Confused by the urgency in his tone, Aubrey nodded her consent. They left the crowded living room of the Lapp's house and ventured out into the crisp morning. The two walked to the edge of the farm, away from curious ears and eyes.

"What is it?" she asked, concern threading her tone. "Is everything alright?"

"Everything's fine. I just need to talk to you about something."

"About?"

Jamie rubbed the back of his neck anxiously. "I had a dream last night that got me thinking of a few things..."

Aubrey tensed visibly. She hugged her wool coat closer to her delicate frame and shivered from the cool air lingering in the morning air. He forced himself to wait before reaching out to warm her.

"*Ach?*"

At her prompt, Jamie told her.

He was standing in Aubrey's bedroom, their bedroom now. He didn't know what prompted him to crouch down on the floor alongside the neatly-made bed with their wedding quilt spread over it neatly, but the loose floorboard beneath the bed caught his eye.

Sliding underneath the bed, he pried the floorboard loose with his fingernail and tentatively reached a hand into the dark hole. His fingers brushed against paper and he hooked his finger on a string, pulling something moderately heavy up to his eyesight.

They were letters, and lots of them.

Jamie slid out from underneath the bed, letters clutched tightly in his hand. He opened the first letter on the stack and the most recent one.

Aubrey,

Meet me tonight at the barn at 10:30 if you want to leave.

Emma

The dream, the letter, the sinking feeling in his chest, all had felt real. He had awoken shortly after the panic had set in and he had been unable to rest for the rest of the night.

Aubrey's face remained impassive during his explanation of his dream. She let out a soft sigh and reached out to rub a thumb across his cheekbone. Her pale blue eyes more startling this morning with the cold air and frostbitten fields rolling endlessly behind her.

"If it makes you feel better, daed nailed the floorboard shut."

Jamie smiled faintly at that. "A little bit," he admitted, reaching out to wrap his arms around Aubrey. "I just don't want to lose you after finally getting you."

"You aren't going to lose me, Jamie. I promise. I took the vow to prove that to you, to everybody."

"You shouldn't have joined if you were only trying to prove something."

Her eyes flashed with anger. Jamie caught her retreating hand and clutched it tightly in his own when she began to tug it away discreetly without causing a scene. The last thing either of them wanted were rumors to start the month before their wedding.

"I'm sorry. I shouldn't have said that. I just don't want you to regret marrying me when you feel like you had something to prove."

"What do you want me to say then?"

"I don't know." He sighed heavily, dropping his head. "I just feel that there is something going on inside of you that you aren't telling me."

It was Aubrey's turn to sigh heavily. She turned to gaze out along the frosty fields, breath steaming in front of her. When she looked back at him, her eyes were soft with tears. "It's just normal wedding anxieties. Everybody has them beforehand."

"You're having them too?"

"Aren't you?"

Aubrey peered up at him shyly, eyelashes framing her pale skin. The apple of her cheeks colored as she waited for his answer.

"Of course I am. Hence the dreams," he said.

Grinning when Aubrey rolled her eyes, he swept her into an embrace and hugged her to him. Aubrey rested her head on the center of his chest, her own arms wrapping around his waist. Jamie's chin rested on top of her kapp and he inhaled deeply, the smell of Aubrey's shampoo and mountain air swirling in his lungs.

This was what made him believe her. The feeling of her delicate frame pressed against his and feeling her nuzzle into his chest, feeling her clutch him like he was her anchor. They were each other's roots to the ground, unwilling to let go, and they would either flourish or wilt from it. He simply refused to believe that she could be planning to leave again, despite the dreams and anxieties plaguing him.

Wedding anxieties, as Aubrey put it.

They walked hand in hand back to the Lapp house to enjoy Fellowship with their community. Before they could make it up the front porch steps, however, Elizabeth Yates came flying out the front door with tears streaming down her cheeks, with Henry close at her heels.

Alarmed, Jamie managed to step hastily out of the way to avoid being trampled. He watched as Elizabeth jogged down the gravel road, blue scarf flying out behind her.

"Elizabeth! Elizabeth!" Henry yelled after her, still standing on the porch.

"What's going on?" Aubrey asked.

Henry buried his head in his hands. When he looked up at them, his face was contorted into a distressed frown. "I mentioned to Minister Isaac that I wished to marry Elizabeth," he told them, voice strained.

Aubrey looked at him aghast, and moaned in dismay. "Ach, Henry. Why did you do that?"

Jamie, however, was confused. He watched Elizabeth disappear around the bend in the road in a blur of grey and wool before turning to look at Henry in confusion.

"What's wrong with saying that? You love her."

"Because, Jamie," Aubrey started, sighing at him in impatience. "She's been having a hard time accepting her husband's death. I'm sure the idea of marrying Henry makes her feel like she is cheating on her husband."

"But he died though," Jamie stated, still lost. The only time marriages ended within their Amish community was when a spouse died unexpectedly, and most of the time the widow remarried.

"That doesn't make the idea of marrying another person any easier," Aubrey remarked.

She shook her head at him in exasperation before walking up the front porch steps and squeezing Henry's shoulder as she passed by him.

"Give her time to think. I will attend to her kinner."

Aubrey disappeared through the front door. Henry sank down on the front porch step with a heavy thump and rested his head on his knees. White clouds floated from the sides of his face. Jamie sat down alongside him, resting a hand on his bruder's tense back.

"I know how you feel now," Henry muttered.

Jamie smiled thinly at that. "How do I feel exactly?"

"Frustrated over things you can't control, including the person you love." Henry raised his head and their eyes met. "Afraid that you'll slip in faith if the person you love slips in faith."

The conversation with Aubrey earlier and his recent dreams swelled within him. He had spent the latter half of the winter trying to pinpoint what it was that bothered him so deeply about Aubrey's possible departure from the community.

That was exactly it. He was terrified of slipping in his faith, and he was more than confident that if Aubrey slipped again, he would too.

His faith was twined to Aubrey's, and the thought alone was a terrifying one.

"Elizabeth is talking about leaving," Henry spoke up, staring distantly in front of them. "She wants to take her kinner and live with her maem's shveshtah somewhere back east."

From the displeased tone in Henry's voice, Jamie assumed that Elizabeth wanted to live with an Englischer.

"How did you convince Aubrey to stay here?" Henry asked suddenly.

Jamie looked away uncomfortably from the hopeful glint in his bruder's eyes. "I didn't convince her to stay," he said, picking at a stray splinter in the porch step. "Aubrey decided for herself to stay here. She didn't want to lose her family or community."

"That's why I think Elizabeth doesn't want to leave. She'd miss her family too much. Maybe Aubrey could talk to Elizabeth about it?"

The innocent question tied Jamie's stomach muscles into a painful knot. He was spared an answer when the front door opened and families begin to file out, ready to head home or visit with other family.

They were to be married in four weeks. The last thing he wanted was to have Aubrey talking to Elizabeth about leaving the church. Even more so, the last thing he wanted was to have old feelings stirred up again when there was something already simmering underneath the surface.

ᑲ CHAPTER 3 ᔆᑯ

Four weeks. In four weeks their wedding would take place in the eyes of Christ and the Amish church, with their community to bear witness of their union. Four weeks since they were published by the church.

Aubrey stared down at the rows of celery stalks, ready to be harvested for the wedding, and a rush of excitement went through her. In a couple of weeks, Hannah would be over to help decorate with the celery and use whatever was leftover for the main meals.

Her breath steamed in front of her. The sun had long since set and darkness was beginning to blanket the clear sky. Daniel had taken the buggy to run an errand in town and was due back any minute. Aubrey tried not to let her impatience grow, absently pacing in front of the celery rows.

She ran over a checklist in her mind of the things that needed to be done for the wedding. She was determined to concentrate only on the wedding, in hopes that it would calm her anxieties.

The steady clop of horse hooves down the road brought Aubrey's attention to her family's buggy slowly making its way toward her. Daniel smiled down at her as he easily maneuvered the buggy. His forehead was beet red from the cold air. The only parts of his skin that weren't red were protected by the auburn-colored beard, which reached the center of his chest. Little streaks of grey were starting to become more noticeable.

"Going somewhere, dochtah?" he asked, a teasing glint in his sparkling eyes.

Aubrey reached out to scratch their horse's nose gently in greeting. "Jah. I am going to Elizabeth Yate's house to check on her."

And to ask her a question, but Aubrey didn't voice that part. After church on Sunday, she had decided to strike up a friendship with Elizabeth. Partly to help Henry win her over, since the two deserved happiness, but also because Elizabeth was a kind young woman who Aubrey suspected needed a friend that understood. Rumors had surfaced within the past two days that Elizabeth had turned down the idea of marriage to Henry because she was planning to take her kinner and leave the church.

"That's very kind of you," was all Daniel said.

He slid easily out of the buggy and offered a gloved hand to help Aubrey up. She gathered the leather reins in her fingers and smiled down at him.

"Tell Mama I will be back shortly."

Daniel lifted a hand in farewell before walking up the back porch and disappearing into the house and undoubtedly to his chair right next to the wood stove.

There was no heat in the storage room of the furniture store and she always felt a chill in Jamie's fingers whenever he came into the bakery.

Half a mile down the road, Elizabeth's farm and house was a white dot in the distance. Smoke curled from the chimney and from the road she spotted Elizabeth's petite frame gathering chopped firewood in her apron.

Elizabeth looked up at the sound of the approaching buggy, her hazel eyes wary at first and then warm at the sight of Aubrey. She straightened and lifted a hand in greeting.

"Hello," Elizabeth smiled, her pale cheeks tinged red from the cold air as well. "To what do I owe this unexpected visit?"

Aubrey slid out of her buggy, landing easily on her feet. "I just thought you'd like a friend to visit with. Perhaps help you make dinner? I know your hands are full with your kinner being so young."

"Jah. That would be lovely and much appreciated."

She followed Elizabeth through the back door and into the tiny, but neatly organized kitchen. Upstairs, delighted laughter echoed, followed by the sound of the patter of tiny feet on the floorboards.

"There is chicken there in the pan to roast." Elizabeth motioned to the pan where a bare chicken, cut up in neat pieces, sat next to the oven. "I will add some wood to the fire and gather the kinner. They are upstairs playing with each other."

Elizabeth's eyes, worn out as they were, filled with a burning love at the mention of her kinner. She left Aubrey to season the chicken and set the dinner table as a stampede of little feet came down the stairs and hallway a few moments later.

Naomi and Simon Yates looked exactly like their parents, from their sharp facial features to matching hazel eyes. Their dark-colored hair, almost black, was neatly combed and free of tangles.

Elizabeth rested her hands fondly on top of their heads. "Aubrey is helping us make dinner tonight. What do we say?"

"Danka," they echoed in unison before rushing to Aubrey's side. Tiny arms hugged the folds of her dress before Simon darted back to Elizabeth's side, peering at Aubrey shyly. Naomi lingered by her side, asking to help toss chopped vegetables into a baking dish and to place a plate of bread on the table.

By the time they'd finished dinner, cleaned the kitchen, and participated in prayers before bed, Aubrey had stayed well over what she'd expected. She didn't mind however, sensing that Elizabeth needed the little break, and finished whatever chores still needed to be done.

When Elizabeth came into the kitchen to find it spotless, with the dishes cleaned, dried, and put back in their places, tears surfaced in her hazel depths. "Danka, Aubrey." She hugged her tightly, offering a watery smile. "I didn't realize how tired I was until you arrived and did all the chores."

"Of course. Sit down. I will make us some tea."

Once both of them were cradling mugs of steeped mint leaves, Aubrey reached over and grabbed Elizabeth's hand. Calluses covered the edges of her fingertips, but her skin was still soft to the touch.

"How are you holding up?"

Elizabeth stirred the mint leaves around with her pinky. "I don't have to tell you. Everyone in the community has talked about me leaving."

"Are you?" Aubrey asked softly.

"I don't know. If I leave, then the church will excommunicate me. I don't know if I could handle being on the outside with the Englischers and not having contact with my family. Ma and Da will always side with the church before siding with any of their kinner..." Elizabeth trailed off with a heavy sigh. She rubbed at her eyes tiredly and freed her prayer kapp, revealing dark tresses of hair. "After Eli died, I just couldn't help but wonder why Gott would allow this to happen? We've devoted ourselves to Him and done nothing wicked. I started thinking that maybe the church isn't right about everything."

Aubrey was quiet for awhile. She too had thought of those same things after Emma left the community. She sometimes still did, despite her baptism and renewed sense of faith.

"I think about those same things too sometimes. Your mann died and you have every right to question it."

"Even when it goes against our faith?"

Their belief systems were so ingrained inside of them, believing that when something happened, including a death, that it was Gott's will, and if things needed to be changed, He would change them. A part of Aubrey believed it wholeheartedly, but the other part of her still questioned when she shouldn't. Her thoughts were turning wicked again, and the last thing she wanted to do was turn Elizabeth away from the Amish church when she needed the community.

"I'm obviously not the best to give advice right now," she replied, smiling thinly. "All I can say is that if you leave, it's not going to go away either. What about Henry? You two have been courting each other for awhile now. He would be heartbroken if you left. He loves you and the kinner."

Color filled the center of Elizabeth's cheeks at the mention of Henry's name. She looked away from Aubrey, staring at the tabletop as she nibbled at her bottom lip.

"I know. I just-" Elizabeth paused, her eyes briefly closing. "I just don't know if I'm ready to be married again. With Eli, I was so anxious for the wedding and couldn't wait for married life. We built this farm and house together. We started a family together. Throughout all of that, I fell in love with him. When he died, a part of me went with him, and I'll never get it back. I'm scared of it happening again if I marry Henry. I don't have very many pieces of my heart left to spare."

Tears wet Elizabeth's eyelashes. She looked every inch a confused and grief-stricken widow from her scarily thin frame to her haunted hazel eyes.

Sitting across the table from Elizabeth, it occurred to Aubrey that that had been part of her anxieties about getting married to Jamie. Losing him, after building a life together and looking toward the future, would break her in several ways that could never be repaired. Her heart would always still belong to him, even if she were to marry again.

Soft but calloused hands grabbed her own suddenly. Aubrey raised her eyes tentatively to meet Elizabeth's.

"I don't want to scare you away from marrying Jamie. I know how nerve-wracking the month before your wedding is. Don't listen to me. You deserve every bit of happiness."

"Danka. You do, too."

"I've been meaning to ask you," Elizabeth started, focusing on Aubrey intently. "How was your shveshtah?"

Aubrey tensed at the abrupt change of topic. She hadn't spoken about seeing her sister with anyone beside her family and Jamie. It was still a sore subject and she was unsure of whether talking about it would stir up all those feelings again. She knew Elizabeth was merely curious. At one point the two had been good friends, prior to Emma's leaving.

"That was the wrong thing to ask, I'm sorry."

"Nee. I'm sorry. I don't think it is best for me talk about it. I have done my best to forget about it and move on."

Elizabeth nodded empathetically. "Of course. You should, when you have so much to look forward to in the next month. I am assuming that Hannah is your matron?"

"Yes." She hesitated for a moment, reading Elizabeth's face carefully. "I came over here to ask if you would also stand at my wedding as well. Henry is obviously standing for Jamie."

She expected Elizabeth to decline, understandably in

Aubrey's opinion, but to her surprise Elizabeth beamed in happiness. "Jah! I would love to. What other things do you need help with?"

They spent the next hour talking about wedding preparations, before Aubrey left to fetch her horse from the field to hitch up to the buggy. The stars above sparkled brightly and illuminated the road back home. Aubrey hugged the heavy blanket closer to her body to fight off the chilly air. The conversation with Elizabeth swirled inside her. While she had done her best to comfort Elizabeth's doubts and fears about marrying, she had managed to stoke the fire of her anxieties.

It was already hard to think of Jamie as her mann. The idea of losing him as her mann threatened to steal the breath out of her though.

When she reached the barn, her thoughts were on Elizabeth gathering firewood in her apron while trying to start dinner for her kinner and not fall apart in front of them. She, like Aubrey, had been so eager and excited to marry, without realizing what marriage really meant. A deep kind of love that could shatter someone completely and cause them to lose faith in everything and everyone around them.

There was only one question surfacing inside of her mind.

Could she handle such possible heartbreak?

ᑕᔕᗝ

"That dresser is looking very gut."

Jamie looked up at the sound of Daniel's voice. He smiled, looking down at the freshly-stained wood and perfect drawers with brass knobs. A pang of pride went through him. Every piece of furniture he crafted himself sold, usually within a few days of sitting on the sales floor.

"Danka, sir."

Daniel bent down until he was eye level with the dresser top, checking the levelness, and brushed the pad of his thumb along a smoothed corner. He straightened, and nodding his head, took a step back to admire it from afar.

"Business has increased since you've started working here, Jamie. More Englischers have been coming in to buy whatever you have crafted. I think you have a real talent at this. You could run your own furniture store someday."

Jamie swelled with pride again. Though he loved farming and being outside, he loved hand-crafting furniture and watching others enjoy his work. It was the first time that Jamie understood why Aubrey loved to draw and paint. Watching other people react to your work and enjoy it was an extremely satisfying feeling.

"Have you thought about running your own business before?" Daniel asked.

"Once before back in Lancaster. I thought about opening up a farming equipment store, but I've never been good at the numbers side of it."

Daniel chuckled. He stuck his thumbs through his black suspenders. "I never have either. Levi gets his math skills from his maem."

"What about Aubrey? What has she gotten from all of you?"

"Hmm," Daniel tipped his head back and gazed upward, contemplative for a few seconds."I would say Aubrey has a very good mix of Katie and I. Gentle nature, but very stubborn."

"That fits her alright," Jamie said, laughing.

He wiped his hands clean of the wood stain and glanced across the storage area to the clock above the door. Aubrey's lunch break would start in thirty minutes and his mouth watered at the thought of the slice of apple pie she would have waiting for him.

"Have you started building your haus?" Daniel asked.

"Jah. Henry and I have the floor and walls, but the weather has been hard to predict."

"Has Aubrey seen it yet?"

Jamie shook his head no. He wanted it to be a surprise once it was completed. It was tradition for the mann to live with his fraa's parents until the following spring, when they could finish their own home, but he was sure Aubrey expected a new haus at some point.

The thought of having their own space and privacy from others sent his body thrumming in excitement. The past couple of nights, since the church had published their intent to marry, his thoughts had wandered to what it would be like falling asleep with Aubrey curled up in his arms. He wondered if Aubrey thought of the same things as well.

"I want her to see it once it's completed or when you can at least see the rooms," Jamie explained.

"Well, you will need new furniture. Feel free to use the wood supply when there is the free time."

"Danka."

Daniel nodded before leaving to grab his own lunch pail. The afternoon sun bore down on him as he walked up the sidewalk to the bakery, but there was little warmth to it. He looked up at the sun and smiled a little.

Maybe, just maybe, things were looking up finally.

CRO

Saturday night was a frigid one. The thick grey clouds that had lingered all day, trapping in moderately cold air, now threatened to trickle out the season's first snowfall.

Aubrey prayed that it wouldn't snow. She kept her attention focused on the window above the couch, waiting for any signs of snowflakes to appear. The weather had taken a particularly cold turn, colder than normal for the fall season. The crops had yet to be harvested, with only a couple more weeks left until November.

Since tomorrow was their free day from chores and no church, Jamie had ventured over to help Daniel drape heavy fabric over their crops in an attempt to fight off the biting nip to the air. She tried to wait inside and bid what Jamie had asked her to do, to stay away from the cold, but she couldn't help it any longer.

Her thoughts focused on the celery stalks still growing for their wedding.

Aubrey went to the hallway and grabbed her wool coat, sliding her fingers through her gloves and tying a fur-lined bonnet securely to her head. She exited the house with a spare lantern in hand, gasping when a wave of icy coldness threatened to swallow her whole.

"Dear Gott! It is so cold."

In the distance, lanterns danced in the dark. She spotted Jamie's lean frame moving about in the dark with graceful movements. Aubrey started in their direction, rocks crunching underneath her boots. When she reached the edge of the field and slipped through the fence, the lantern light illuminated Jamie's face enough to show that he was scowling at her.

"I told you to stay inside the house," Jamie said.

"I can't stay in the house. Not when I'm thinking about the celery freezing."

Heavy footsteps and the sound of fabric trailing on the ground signaled Daniel's approach. He frowned at Aubrey in disapproval. "What are you doing out here? You should be inside. I don't want you getting-"

"I won't get sick," she insisted, rolling her eyes at them. "I want to help. We're wasting time just standing here."

Jamie sighed at her in exasperation, but didn't comment any further. He wordlessly handed over a piece of fabric that was coarse and thick.

"Drape them over the crops gently. Your daed and I will work on the other vegetation."

She went straight to the celery crop and laid the fabric down the neatly planted rows. Shivering from the cold, Aubrey crouched low to the ground and inspected the green leaves for any signs of wilting. Thankfully, the little leaves showed no browning or yellowing from the cold.

"Please, Gott, protect our crops," she whispered, her

breath creating puffs of white smoke in front of her.

If their crops froze, the harvest would be minimal and that meant their food supply would also be very small. There were a few things that Katie bought from the Englischer's store that the Amish were not able to supply themselves, but they prided themselves on their vegetation.

Above them, the stars twinkled more brightly and vividly from the cold night. She gazed up at them, wondering why the stars were always so beautiful in the late fall and winter seasons.

"Did you honestly think that I would let the celery crops freeze?"

She rose from her crouched position, cold air rushing up through the fabric of her dress, and turned to face Jamie as he approached her.

"No, but I couldn't help it. You and daed had the other crops to worry about."

Jamie shook his head. "The celery crops matter too. We wouldn't let them freeze without attempting to save them."

Her heart clenched painfully in fear. Blankets of impenetrable darkness lay across their vegetation and she prayed again that their actions would be enough.

"Do you think the freeze will kill the crops and vegetation tonight?"

"I don't know. Your daed says this freeze is earlier than normal. I better get home to help my Pa and Henry cover our gardens. They've been complaining about me spending too much time over here."

By they, he meant Aaron. It was custom that once married, the mann and fraa live with the fraa's parents for the first few months, while they built their own home and established their own crops. Next spring they would have a house of their own.

On the weekends that they didn't have church on Sunday, Jamie walked or took the buggy over to help out with the farm and spend time with Aubrey. Even though Aaron was accepting of their soon-to-be marriage, he still needed the help on their own farm.

"Of course. Let me brew you a cup of tea to take with you."

They walked back to the house. The heat from the wood stove, logs crackling happily from the living room, hit both them in a dizzying blast of hot air. Sweat immediately gathered at Aubrey's hair line and she shrugged out of her winter wear while Jamie mimicked her.

In their small pantry, Aubrey found a jar of mint leaves. She boiled some water on the stove and dropped a couple of leaves into the bubbling water. The scrape of a chair against the wood floor told her that Jamie had sat down at the kitchen table to wait patiently for tea.

"Henry told me that you asked Elizabeth to stand with you at our wedding," Jamie commented, his tone not giving away his thoughts.

"Jah..." She turned around, arching an eyebrow at him. "I thought it would be a good time for both Elizabeth and Henry to spend with each other."

Jamie folded his arms across his broad chest. It wasn't hard to see the disapproval swimming in his eyes.

"You do know that she is planning to leave the church, right?"

Aubrey sucked in a long breath to keep her patience in check. She didn't want to argue anymore than what they already had done over the past few weeks.

"I don't think it's wise to talk about this, Jamie. Especially about someone who has lost her mann in a horrible way."

"I don't want you talking to her, Aubrey. Not after what happened last summer."

"I'm only trying to help her through a hard time."

"It's not a good idea to-"

Her thinly-veiled patience ripped apart. "Why not?" she demanded, looking Jamie directly in the eye. "Why isn't it a good idea to be compassionate and understanding?"

Jamie stared stonily back at her, nonplussed by her outburst. If anything, he was starting to learn that as gentle mannered and soft spoken Aubrey was, she had a fiercely stubborn streak.

"All I'm saying is," he continued, his tone irritatingly pacifying. "That it may not be a good idea for you to be friends with Elizabeth right now."

Aubrey gaped at him in silent outrage. A thousand comments, none that were nice, flashed through her mind, but she kept herself quiet. That was not how an Amish woman treated her mann, but in all fairness she didn't think Jamie was treating her correctly either.

She curled her fingers into tightly clenched fists and looked down at the table top, anger dusting her cheek bones with a light pink shade.

"I will think about it." Aubrey forced out in a clipped tone. As an afterthought, she added, "If that's what you want."

The chair scuffed against the floor again. Jamie came to stand in front of her, looking down with those blue depths that were the color of the fall sky. Blonde bristles dotted his tense jaw and he reached out to grab her limp hand in his own. "Just try to see things from my side, okay? I love you."

He pressed a kiss to the corner of her lips and then disappeared out the back door before she could reply. Frustration built up in her again over their argument (again) and she busily poured herself a cup of tea, needing a distraction from what had just transpired.

The back door opened a moment later. Daniel emerged from the dark night, cold air following in after him.

"Where is Jamie off to so quick?" he asked, frowning.

The apprehension on his reddened face caught Aubrey's attention. She set down her cup of tea, suddenly feeling uneasy. "He has to return home and help his daed. Why?"

Daniel froze. The color drained visibly from his face. "He left?"

"Jah. Papa, what's going on?"

"There are wolves out there in the tree lines. I had to bring in the horses and cattle before they could attack."

A sickening dread filled her whole body and tasted like spoiled milk. She grabbed the thick and itchy wool sleeve of Daniel's coat. "They can't get him in his buggy can they?"

"He didn't take the buggy, Aubrey. He's walking home."

❧ CHAPTER 4 ☙

There were only two occasions in Aubrey's life wherein she'd felt so terrified that it stole her breath away and stopped her heart. The first had been when Isaac was two years old and choked on a grape; his little face had turned a violent shade of purple as his sticky fingers grabbed at her in sheer panic. The second was staring down at the blood-soaked bandages wrapped tightly around Jamie's left calf and the blood-soaked blankets around him.

Those had been the times that she'd prayed the most. That is what she was now doing, praying for Gott to keep Jamie alive, for the chance to say she was sorry for their argument earlier and that she loved him.

A painful groan escaped his lips when Katie quickly began to tie another bandage around his left forearm, pushing her palm firmly on the bite wound. Jamie's fingers clutched at hers so tightly and fiercely that she worried he would break her bones just by squeezing. Instead, she hid her grimace of pain and squeezed back reassuringly.

"Everything will be fine, Jamie. I promise," she told him. "My daed went to get your parents."

Jamie lifted his head to look at her with narrowed eyes. His face had paled drastically from the loss of blood and nerves. A fine layer of sweated beaded along his forehead as he breathed heavily. "Great. Since the wolves didn't get a chance to kill me, Gott decided to let my daed get a chance at it."

He hissed when Katie pressed a cloth against the side of his neck. The smell of alcohol filled the living room, which already had a strong metallic aroma.

Aubrey breathed in through her mouth to control the nausea churning in her.

"Don't talk like that, young man," Katie ordered briskly. She pressed the cloth harder into Jamie's neck and to Aubrey's relief, blood didn't soak it right away. "You are going to be just fine. You should not have gone out there without your buggy. What were you thinking at this time of the year? You know that there are wolves out here."

Jamie's body began to tremble. He opened his mouth to respond, but no reply came.

"Jamie?"

He turned his head to look at her through unfocused eyes. She reached up with her free hand and rested her palm on his shoulder. Through the fabric of Jamie's shirt came waves of feverish heat. Jamie mumbled incoherently before slumping backward into the couch to stare distantly at the ceiling.

Panic surged through her with such force that it winded her. Aubrey looked up at Katie, whose hands and sleeves were stained with Jamie's blood. Tears flooded her eyes. "He's dying, Mama! Do something!" she cried hysterically.

Aubrey grabbed Jamie's hand tightly in her own and began to shake his arm violently.

"Aubrey!" Katie's sharp tone caught her attention quickly. She looked up at her mother, holding a cloth to the side of Jamie's neck. "He's not dying, I promise. Stay calm and try to keep him awake until his family arrives."

"Please, Gott. Don't let him go," she pleaded under her breath, gently taking Jamie's much larger and calloused hand in hers. "Jamie, listen to me. You have to stay awake for a little bit longer."

Jamie only blinked in response, but kept his hazy gaze fixated on her. Barking from their barn dogs alerted them that Daniel had arrived with Jamie's parents. The back door banged open and Sarah Miller rushed forward with a cry. Katie moved out of the way to allow Sarah a place next to Jamie's side and wordlessly allowed her to take the rag from Jamie's neck.

Larry Brenneman, the local doctor for their community, strode into the room with a leather bag in hand. His grey eyes swept over the blood-soaked blankets and to where Aubrey sat next to Jamie, clutching his hand tightly.

"Move," he ordered. When Aubrey hesitated, Larry glared at her in annoyance. "Did you not hear me? Move."

Blinking away tears, Aubrey let Jamie's hand slip away. She retreated to the other side of the living room and looked away as Larry bent over Jamie's leg, peeling back the bandages. Her eyes were met with Aaron's cold ones. A tense silence filled the room. Jamie's hisses of pain occasionally intermingled with the fire crackling in the wood stove. Finally, after what seemed like hours, Larry stood up and addressed them.

"He'll be fine. Katie did a good job of dressing the wounds and cleaning. He's dizzy from blood loss, so it's best to get him home and let him rest for a few days."

A loud rush of air whooshed through Aubrey's teeth. Her knees trembled with relief and tears slipped from the corner of her eyes. She took a step toward Jamie, who was now slumped over unconscious, but Aaron's clipped voice directed right at her stopped her in mid step.

"What happened? Why wasn't he in his buggy?"

Aubrey opened her mouth several times to explain, but couldn't find her voice. She was absolutely terrified of Aaron as he swelled with silent rage.

"There's no need to try and blame, Aubrey," Daniel replied before she could say anything. "It was an accident-"

"An accident that could've been prevented. What happened?" Aaron demanded. His eyes focused on her unblinkingly.

"It was-I-we," she swallowed thickly. "We had an argument, but I didn't realize at first that he'd left without his buggy..."

Her voice trailed off when Aaron's eyes closed briefly, hiding whatever thoughts he had, and then started toward Jamie.

"Come, Sarah. Help me get Jamie into the buggy."

Between the two of them, and with Larry's help, they managed to get Jamie into their family buggy. Aubrey trailed after them, slipping her arms through her wool coat hastily.

"I'll wash your blankets," Sarah said to Katie, hugging the woman briefly. "Thank you for saving my son."

Katie smiled thinly. "Of course. We will pray for a fast recovery."

Aubrey had just stepped onto the wooden step of her family's buggy when a steely hand clamped down on her elbow and pulled her down. She looked up into Aaron's eyes, so similar to Jamie's, but lacking warmth or love.

"Where do you think you are going?" he demanded.

Aubrey tilted her chin upward and met his gaze bravely for the first time that night. "I'm going with you to see that he gets home alright."

"Nee," Aaron tersely responded. Before she could reply that he was not her father and had no right to tell her what to do, he continued with narrowed eyes, "I wouldn't want you getting attacked by wolves either."

He left her there then, standing in a cloud of dust, shivering from much more than the cold.

CR80

"You are not getting out of this bed for the rest of the week, Jamie Aaron Miller."

Jamie rolled his eyes half heartedly at Sarah as she fretted about his bedside, tucking in the sheets around his legs tightly. He inhaled sharply when her fingers accidentally brushed against his left calf and hot pain flashed through his leg.

"I'll be fine by tomorrow, Ma. It's just a dog bite."

Sarah's eyes narrowed until the blue color was barely visible. "It is more than just a dog bite, Jamie. You were bit on the leg, forearm, and neck-"

"I was scratched on the neck," he cut in, but Sarah continued like he hadn't spoken.

"-And you are going to be lucky if none of those bites get infected. You don't know what type of diseases wolves carry."

"Mrs. Forrest cleaned them with alcohol. I doubt that they will get infected."

Sarah threw her hands up in exasperation. "You are lucky that your daed and I love you, because it is tempting to kill you ourselves."

A ghost of a smile touched her lips. Jamie grinned at her, effectively masking the pain radiating around the bite marks.

"You would miss me too much to kill me," he replied.

The anger in Sarah's face softened. She leaned down to brush a fond kiss on the top of Jamie's head, running a hand over the golden strands. Jamie leaned into the touch, eyes slipping closed on their own accord at the contact.

"I would miss you. I'm glad you are safe."

The door to Jamie's bedroom opened. Aaron stepped in, holding a lantern aloft. Unlike Sarah, his face had yet to soften or show any relieved emotion. Instead, his face remained impassive and his eyes hard glints. "Tea, Sarah. If you have the time."

"Of course." Sarah bowed her head and stepped back from his bedside. "I'll be back to blow the candle out."

Jamie wanted to call out and ask her to stay, but knew it was futile. His father wanted to talk privately with him and there was no room to argue otherwise.

The whole trip back home, and throughout Larry Brenneman's examination of his wounds, Aaron had remained in a stoic silence. Not once had he uttered a word of relief or directly addressed him.

Getting attacked by wolves seemed much more pleasant to Jamie than the storm that was about to be unleashed by his Pa.

Jamie leaned back against the headboard, raising his head to look Aaron directly in the eye. For a minute they stared silently at each other, before Jamie broke it.

"Go on. Punish me. Yell," he challenged defiantly.

The lantern clanged down on Jamie's desk with a loud noise. Aaron towered over the end of his bed, hands placed on his hips. Shadows danced across the sharpness of his face and the lantern light gave off enough glow to show the vein throbbing at his father's right temple. Without hesitation, Aaron began to speak in a very loud and sharp voice.

"What were you thinking, Jamie? Leaving your buggy behind on a cold night with wolves in the forest? Do you realize what could have happened to you if Daniel hadn't come down the road with his shotgun?"

Jamie flushed hotly under the rage radiating off of Aaron. He shifted uncomfortably, clenching his jaw tightly when the movement caused his leg to throb again. "I'm sorry. I-"

"You're sorry? Think about what you would have done to this family if you'd died. Your mother and siblings would've been heartbroken."

Would you be? Jamie bit his tongue hard to restrain himself from asking that question. As loving as their father could be, he was just as emotionless at times. It was one of those times now that he wished Aaron was the loving type.

"I wasn't trying to get killed. I didn't think about it when I left. I just wanted to go for a walk," he explained.

"Because of your argument with Aubrey?"

Jamie's eyes instantly shot to Aaron's in surprise. "How did you know about that?"

"How do you think?" Aaron shook his head at him. "Aubrey told me that the two of you had a fight and that you had left without our buggy."

That part was true at least. He had been so angry that a walk home in the brisk night seemed like the only way to calm his temper down and he'd failed to notice the luminous eyes blinking at him from the tree line. Not until an angry growl had alerted him that his irrational decision to walk home had been the wrong and nearly fatal choice.

Guilt intermingled with the pain coursing throughout him. Jamie looked away from Aaron and focused his attention on the quilted blanket. He pulled at an errant strand of thread. "I'm sorry, Pa," he said softly.

Floorboards creaked as Aaron shifted on his feet. He snuck a glance at Aaron, but found no reprieve in the still-hard glints of his father's eyes. A part of him didn't expect it.

"I think it's a good idea for you to call the wedding off," Aaron demanded, his voice neutral. "You've been spending too much time over there and-"

"Isn't that what a mann does? Spend time with his fraa?"

"Aubrey is not your fraa yet. How do you think your marriage will be if you two are arguing now? For Gott's sake, Jamie! Try to see things from my perspective."

The anger building within him was more painful and dizzying than a wolf's teeth ripping through his skin and muscle. Jamie fisted his hands in the quilt and strove to keep himself under control. "If you're trying to blame Aubrey for what happened tonight-"

"I do blame Aubrey for what happened tonight," Aaron interrupted, tugging at the end of his beard in irritation. "None of this would have happened if you would've stayed here tonight like I asked you, to help with the crops."

"She is my soon-to-be fraa," Jamie started, his voice trembling from anger. "And there is nothing that you can do to stop that."

A heavy pause filled the room.

"The wedding's off." Aaron's words cut through the room. He turned on his heel, boots stomping down on the floorboards and blew the candle out. The wall shook as the door slammed shut and a smothering darkness filled the room.

Jamie slumped back against the headboard. He quietly began to pray.

$\text{C}\mathcal{R}\text{S}\text{O}$

The sunlight held little warmth when it rose Monday morning. Aubrey stood in the cold utility room that they used as a storage and laundry room, pinning damp clothes to the line.

She took a step back to look more carefully at the sleeves of her mother's dress, which had been stained with Jamie's blood. Cold water and soap had somehow lifted the crimson stains out of the cotton fabric, but Aubrey could still see it perfectly in her mind.

Shaking her head clear of those images, she left the room to start breakfast for everyone. She had barely cracked an egg when Katie stepped into the room, holding something behind her back.

"Morning," she said, smiling. "I have something for you."

"Ach?"

The gentle swish of fabric echoed in the kitchen as Katie held up a large piece of blue fabric. Aubrey gasped, the wooden spatula falling from her fingers to the stove top with a soft clang. She took a step forward to look more closely at the fabric Katie held aloft.

"It's beautiful," Aubrey murmured, running her fingers over the soft fabric. "Is it for me?"

Katie smiled widely. "Jah. I traded a few pies with Alma for the fabric, since you need to start sewing your wedding dress soon."

Her excitement and happiness quickly dissipated as the past weekend flashed through Aubrey's mind. She drew her hand back, tears stinging her eyes.

"I don't know, Mama. Jamie's daed is very angry. He blames me for what happened to Jamie. He wants to end the wedding."

"Nonsense, Aubrey," Katie said sternly. She frowned at her daughter. "Where did you hear such things? You have not seen or talked to Jamie since Saturday."

Aubrey buried her hands in her face. She tried to regain her composure, but found herself quivering as the past few days' emotions finally caught up to her. She was tired…so tired of things going wrong or someone disapproving.

"Lily stopped by Sunday afternoon when you and Papa were over at the Byler's visiting. She told me that Aaron is trying to convince Jamie to call off the wedding."

"Ach, dochtah," Katie's arms wrapped soothingly around her. Just like that she was five years old again, crying into her mother's slender shoulder and inhaling the clove and nutmeg spices that always clung to her.

"Listen to me." Katie pulled back so their eyes could meet. "Jamie's daed had quite a fright this weekend. He nearly lost his son. You are not a parent yet, but do you remember your daed that night Emma arrived? It's not so different. Fear makes us say things we normally would not say."

"I know, but what if this is a sign from Gott? Maybe He is telling me that now is not the right time."

"Do you love Jamie?"

"Of course, I do. I can't picture my life without him."

"Then it isn't wrong. What is really bothering you?"

She looked away from Katie's keen stare and focused on the blue fabric draped over the back of a chair. Starting tonight after chores and prayers, she would begin sewing her wedding dress. Her throat thickened at the thought of Jamie seeing her in her dress and without it.

There were certain topics she could talk to her maem about, but that was not one of them. Such matters were better left unsaid. She heard Sadie's voice echoing from down the hallway and quickly palmed her eyes dry.

"Normal wedding nerves, I suppose. Thanks, Mama. I will start on the dress tonight."

Aubrey hugged her mom briefly before Sadie walked by and immediately gasped at the sight of the fabric. Her younger sister rushed over, picking up the fabric.

"Is this the material for your dress? It's beautiful. You will be beautiful in this color." Sadie rubbed the fabric together between her fingertips and stared down longingly at it.

She smiled despite the anxious knot inside her chest. "Danka, Sadie. Perhaps you can help me tonight?" she asked, already knowing the answer.

"Jah! I would love to."

Sadie beamed happily at her before carefully folding the fabric and handing it over to Aubrey for her to put away. She left the kitchen as Sadie wordlessly scraped a forgotten egg from the frying pan into the kitchen sink and cracked a new one.

She set the fabric on top of her small dresser. Through the curtains, morning light spilled in and onto the floor. Closing her bedroom door quietly, Aubrey laid down in the middle of the patch of light on the floor and stared up at the ceiling as she quietly prayed for the one thing that might never happen again.

Aaron's acceptance.

CRSO

By Thursday there was still no word from Jamie or any of his family. Henry had taken the week off to help around the farm and the news crushed Aubrey's hopes of finding a way to see Jamie.

Anger had filled her as the week passed. She understood Aaron's anger for what had transpired and fear over nearly losing his son, but Jamie was her soon-to-be mann. She had every right to know of his well being.

Or that's what Aubrey told herself repeatedly as her horse trotted surely down the road toward the Miller's farm and barn. It was barely past four o'clock and the sun had already begun its descent the sky. An orange glow filled the surrounding area, and despite the cold air, it filled her with a contented warmth that only came from afternoons like these.

Her hands shook with nerves as she unhitched her horse and led her to the field to graze for the time being. Flower beds were perfectly pruned, but were slowly starting to wilt and lose color with the dipping temperatures at night. The fire-colored leaves barely clung to any of the trees anymore.

Aubrey softly rapped her knuckles against the front door and took a step back. As footsteps approached the door, she prayed that it wasn't Aaron answering the door.

To her immense relief, it was Henry who opened the door. "Aubrey?" His brow furrowed in confusion, but he smiled warmly at her. "What are you doing here?"

He took a step back and opened the door wider, motioning for her to step inside. The smell of a freshly baked apple pie wafted strongly through the house and the fire roared happily from the fireplace.

"Oh, wait. I know why you're here," Henry said, laughing. He took her wool coat graciously and hung it on a peg in the hallway. "I know you didn't come all the way out here to see me."

Aubrey laughed. "It's still good to see you, too. My daed says he misses you both at work."

"Jah, well, I miss working there too. We'll be back next week."

Her heart swelled in happiness at the word "we'll." Before she could inquire about Jamie, Sarah came down the hallway with a kitchen towel in hand.

"Hello, Aubrey. I'm glad you came," Sarah said, smiling. "I have your mother's blankets freshly washed for you to take back to her. Will you be staying for dinner?"

She had a feeling that she wouldn't receive such a friendly welcome from Aaron and politely declined with an apologetic smile. "Nee, but danka though. I have to get home before dark. I wanted to see how Jamie is doing."

Henry instantly frowned at that. "You have not been getting his letters?" he asked, exchanging a glance with Sarah.

"No." Aubrey shook her head, heart pounding

furiously. "He's been writing me?"

"I don't get it, Ma. I've been giving Jamie's letters to Pa to del..." Henry trailed off.

Neither of them addressed the rest of his sentence. Sarah glanced up at the clock over the wood stove and ushered Aubrey up the stairs.

"Jamie's bedroom is the third door on the right. You have about an hour before it gets dark out."

An hour before Aaron comes home, Aubrey said to herself, but went up the stairs nonetheless. She stood in front of the third door on the right, listening to papers shuffling around and Jamie's soft breathing. She rested her hand briefly on the wood before knocking gently.

"Come in," Jamie called out.

Aubrey opened the door, her heart beating furiously. Jamie sat on his bed, dressed in his day clothes and looking incredibly bored from the book he was flipping through absently. Her soul lifted at the sight of the healthy glow back in Jamie's cheeks and the obvious healing to the gaping wound on his neck, now a series of small red dots.

Sapphire eyes glanced up from the pages and he froze when they landed on her. "Aubrey?"

Jamie blinked a couple of times, peering at her like she was a ghost. A slow grin spread across his face.

"Hi." Was all she could say. She was so relieved to see him smiling and alive that it left her speechless.

"Come here," he said, opening his arms. When Aubrey didn't move, he rolled his eyes, "I can't walk over there to hug you, so you have to come here."

It was improper for her to be up here in Jamie's

bedroom, but at that moment the rules didn't apply anymore. She rushed forward without another hesitation and buried herself in his arms.

Jamie held her tightly as she cried into his shoulder, her fingers clutching his shirt tightly.

"I'm fine, I promise," Jamie muttered into her hair, nuzzling the side of her face with his. He inhaled deeply. "I've missed you. Where have you been? I wrote you a couple of letters."

They pulled back, but their hands remained twined together like the root system of the aspen tree, tangled together forever. She hesitated in answering, not wishing to cause a bigger fight between Jamie and his father.

"Henry said he had been giving your letters to your daed to deliver."

Jamie's eyes narrowed as he processed her words. He sighed heavily, shaking his head. "I'm sorry. I should've known better than to trust my father with those. It doesn't surprise me that you never got them."

"He still wants you to call off the wedding?"

"Jah, but don't worry," he rushed to say when tears flooded Aubrey's eyes. "He will change his mind. I will change it for him."

Aubrey shook her head solemnly. She reached out to gently caress the side of Jamie's neck, feeling the bumps from the scabs dotting his skin. "He won't change his mind, Jamie. He's stubborn."

Jamie leaned forward and kissed her. They broke apart, her stomach flipping in on itself as it always did whenever Jamie's lips were on hers.

"Just wait and give it time. You'll see." He smiled confidently, but it didn't quite reach his eyes.

"We'll see," she replied.

She only hoped that if and when the answer came back she could still marry Jamie after the weekend's events.

ᏣᏛ CHAPTER 5 ᎒᎒

Somehow, by miracle, Jamie managed to convince Sarah that he was well enough to take the family buggy and invite neighbors and friends to the wedding. He was determined to fulfill his role as a soon-to-be mann and inviting neighbors was part of his responsibility. Aubrey had enough to do as it was with helping her maem with the bakery and planning a wedding within a short period of time.

He stopped at John and Miriam's newly built farm and home. Since their wedding last fall, the two had spent the winter with Miriam's family, and when spring finally graced them, they began to build their new home.

The front door opened right as Jamie pulled the buggy to a halt and began to climb out. Miriam appeared on the front porch, wiping her hands dry on her apron.

"Jamie, hello," she greeted, smiling warmly at him. "To what do I owe this surprise visit? John isn't in at the moment, if you are looking for him."

"That's alright. I wanted to invite you both to mine

and Aubrey's wedding on November fourth," Jamie said.

Miriam grinned widely. "Of course! You know that we will be there. How exciting. Would you like something warm to drink before John comes back?"

"Nee, but danka though. I have to get to the bakery for Aubrey's lunch break," Jamie said.

"Okay." Miriam's eyes then focused on Jamie's bandaged arm. Concern threaded her tone when she spoke. "What happened to your arm? There is blood seeping through the bandages."

Glancing down, he grimaced at the red-stained bandages. His leg and neck had been bit superficially, but his forearm had taken the deepest bite when he had waved his arm around to defend himself. It never seemed to stop bleeding even when he rested the wounded limb.

"Wolves," he replied, rolling down his shirt sleeve to cover the bandage. "Tell John to be careful at night, because they are hunting for the winter."

"Jah, I will. Thank you for warning us. Are you sure you're okay?"

Jamie smiled assuredly. "Jah. Do not worry about me. It's just a scratch. Tell John I stopped by and that I'll need his help in the next few months to build."

They exchanged goodbyes before Jamie hopped back into his buggy and went back to the road toward town. With the past few weeks' events and the weather, the haus he had been building with Henry's help had crept to a stop. He hoped to have it done by early spring so he could have vegetables and fruits planted in time for the following harvest.

He wanted privacy from the community, from his family, even from Aubrey's family. They had spent so much of their time the past year and a half dealing with the church and their families' opinions. He wanted alone time and planned to have tons of it once the wedding passed.

The bakery's parking lot was full of cars. Since Katie had announced that during the winter season the bakery would be closed, business always picked up before winter. Jamie kept going down the road toward the furniture store to save time before Aubrey's lunch break.

Daniel looked surprised to see him when he stepped into the storage area. "I wasn't expecting you back until next week with Henry," he stated. His eyes swept up and down in an assessing gaze. "How are you feeling? We've been praying for your fast recovery."

"Gott answered our prayers then. I am feeling fine. Much better."

He kept his left arm behind his back in case blood had soaked through his bandages and into the fabric of his shirt. Part of that was true at least, he told himself. He did feel better, compared to two days ago when his muscles had felt like they were on fire.

The storage room was full of half finished furniture and the smell of wood glue was poignant in the cold air. Jamie stared guiltily at a freshly-sanded table that needed stain.

"Looks like you've been busy," he commented.

Daniel smoothed his hands across the table. "Jah. We've been pretty busy this past week. What are you doing?"

Shrugging out of his coat, Jamie had picked up a paintbrush and dipped the coarse bristles into the stain. "Helping. You're behind because of me."

"I'm not behind on anything. We've had more orders, jah, but we are not behind."

Jamie shook his head in disbelief at the scattered furniture around the storage room. "You look behind to me."

"Listen, Jamie." Daniel grabbed him firmly by both shoulders and leaned down slightly so that they were eye level. "If you expect to marry my daughter, you have to take care of yourself first and foremost. You can't take care of her if you aren't around. We can handle things here until you are ready to come back."

He wanted to reply that he had been working on the farm since two days after he had been attacked, but a wave of exhaustion silenced him.

Daniel continued, "Now you go home and get some rest. We will get by in the mean time. Don't worry about things here. I've gotten through without you before."

When he pulled up to the bakery, Aubrey came out the front door. He thought she'd never looked more beautiful than she did right then with her pale cheeks peppered with freckles and dark eyelashes framing blue eyes that were lighting up at the sight of him.

"What are you doing here?" Aubrey asked breathlessly. "I thought you were supposed to be on bed rest for the next week."

He wrapped his arm around her shoulder and pulled her into him, keeping his bloody one out of the way. His nose bumped the top of her prayer kapp.

"I was going crazy sitting at home. I haven't even been on bed rest."

Aubrey pulled back to look at him with narrowed eyes. "What do you mean?" she asked, propping her hands on her hips huffily. "You're supposed to be resting, Jamie. If you aren't well enough before our wedding-"

"I will be," Jamie interrupted assuredly, squeezing her slender shoulders tenderly. "I promise I will be. I just wanted to come here and see you. Is that such a bad thing?"

She opened her mouth to reply, but shook her head resolutely and sank into him like he knew she would. They stood there for a little while soaking in each other's warmth against the chilly morning air. When Aubrey spoke again, her voice was muffled from her mouth pressing against his chest.

"Have you talked to your daed yet?"

Jamie cringed at the question. He quickly averted his eyes when Aubrey tilted her head back to hear his answer. "Nee. Not yet, but-" he rushed on at the crestfallen expression gracing Aubrey's face rapidly. "I promise to talk to him tonight about it."

She slipped out of his arms and danced lithely out of reach when he tried to pull her back. "How am I supposed to plan for our wedding when you haven't even talked to your father yet?"

"I know. I'm sorry."

For the second time that morning, Jamie swallowed down the guilt building in his stomach. He hadn't even attempted to talk to Aaron, simply because he was too exhausted and in too much pain to argue his point. Convincing his daed would take hours of exchanging words, and even then he would be lucky to get a word in edgewise. Aaron was well known as an unquestionable authority figure and challenging that wasn't going to go over well.

"Why haven't you talked to him yet?"

"I haven't had the time to. It's better to let him cool down before breeching the subject again."

Aubrey sighed tiredly. She pinched the bridge of her nose and tears began to surface in her eyes and wet her eyelashes. "Maybe this isn't right, Jamie. Maybe this is Gott trying to tell us that it isn't the right the time."

"How can you say that?"

Jamie took a step forward, and ignoring her attempts to back away, wrapped his arms around her tense shoulders. He pressed a kiss against her right temple and inhaled deeply, the scent of raw sugar clinging to the blonde strands of her hair.

"I know you are overwhelmed trying to plan for this wedding and I'm not helping, but I promise it will be alright. I will take care of it. Okay?"

Her chest brushed against his briefly before she exhaled loudly in wordless defeat. He had Aubrey convinced for now.

He only had his daed left to convince.

CRLSO

Katie announced Thursday morning that they were going to close the bakery down early for a quilting bee.

"And you can start on your wedding dress, Aubrey," Katie said, grinning excitedly.

Sadie grinned too. "And I can start on my bridesmaid dress too!"

Aubrey quickly asserted control over the excitement surging through her. She didn't want to get anyone's hopes up, including her own, when Jamie still hadn't talked to Aaron yet about letting the wedding plans continue.

"I don't know-" she started, but Katie shot her an exasperated glance.

"Aaron is not going to deny his son a wedding. He knows that Jamie loves you." A car horn blared in the silence, signaling the end of their conversation. Aubrey piled into the car with her family and spent the rest of the morning rolling out pie crusts while trying not to think about the uneasiness in her stomach.

After serving the last customer for the morning, Aubrey glanced out the window as Katie and Sadie slid into their wool coats. Her heart dropped when she didn't find any sign of Jamie walking toward the bakery. A part of her didn't expect it, since he was still recovering from his wounds, but yesterday loomed heavily on her mind. She had hoped that he would show up, grinning in that particular way that made her knees week and carrying news of Aaron's acceptance.

The only thing that the early afternoon carried was dark grey clouds and a miserable cold rain that pattered on the roof of their house as they brewed tea for their guests, who sat in their living room in a small circle.

"That is a really beautiful fabric," Hannah complimented, rubbing the soft fabric with a smile. "You will look beautiful in this color. I am jealous."

"Yours is beautiful too," Aubrey said.

She draped the fabric over her thighs and picked up a pair of scissors, fingering the cool metal.

"It is beautiful," Elizabeth said. She sat on the other side of Hannah, a half-knitted blanket on her knee. "The fabric is much softer than normal fabric. Make sure to wash it in cold water so it doesn't stiffen over time."

Aubrey forced herself to nod and smile in Elizabeth's direction. Alongside her, Sadie's fingers nimbly threaded a needle and began to work eagerly on her bridesmaid dress.

Katie emerged from the kitchen carrying a tray of tea mugs and a kettle of boiling water. The smell of freshly crushed mint was soothing to Aubrey's already-strained nerves.

"So, how are the wedding plans coming along, Aubrey?" Martha King asked from beside Hannah.

"Gut," Aubrey replied.

An awkward silence filled the living room. She caught Katie's warning stare and continued in a high cheery voice. "We've done all the invitations and the celery is close to being harvested."

"It is always so exciting to see you young couples getting married," Bertha Bender said. "There's nothing more beautiful than the start of a new family. Ach, I cannot wait for my dochtah to have a bobli."

She beamed over at Hannah and Aubrey as her fingers

expertly worked a needle through the fabric. Hannah shifted in her seat, a tell tale sign that she was uncomfortable with the conversation. They kept pregnancies quiet until it was noticeable, and such talk was uncomfortable sometimes when one was expecting.

"Why aren't you sewing your dress, Aubrey?"

Aubrey tensed at Almina Graber's voice. She looked up to find the older Amish woman's eyes focused on her and groaned inwardly. Almina was famous for speaking her mind, despite her Amish upbringing, and making brash comments.

"I am," she countered, gesturing to the scissors in her hand.

Almina's eyes continued to study her unblinkingly. She shifted back in her rocking chair, the wood creaking at the weight and movement. "You haven't even started. Most new brides have their dresses sewn by now."

It was a hidden insult that didn't go unnoticed by anyone in the room. Aubrey glowered at the older woman, wishing her maem had not invited her. Almina was one of the best sewers, but the hardest to deal with.

"I've been busy helping maem with the bakery," Aubrey said defensively.

She caught Katie's warning glance again and curled her fingers into the wood of her chair to keep her wavering anger in check. Heat began to build in the center of her cheeks.

"Ach?" Almina said, arching an eyebrow indifferently. "I just thought it was because Jamie has called the wedding off."

The words slapped Aubrey hard on the face. The scissors fell from her fingers and landed on the floor with a loud clang.

Katie quickly took control by speaking in a strained and bright voice, "Why would Jamie do that, Almina? They both have been published by the church and baptized."

Almina didn't break eye contact with Aubrey's glaring ones. She sniffed indelicately and continued to make perfect stitches in the blanket draped along her lap. "I wasn't saying that none of that didn't matter. I was only saying that I wouldn't blame the poor boy for wanting to call off the wedding with everything that has happened."

Silence filled the room again. Aubrey stared down at the floor, heart hammering loudly in her chest cavity. The room felt unbearably hot and stuffy with everyone looking away from Almina, who either didn't care or notice their reactions.

Hannah's soft hand rested tentatively on Aubrey's arm. "Aubrey?"

She jerked at the sound of Hannah's voice. A faint dusting of pink colored Hannah's pale cheeks and everyone else was studiously avoiding her gaze.

She had to get out.

Aubrey stood up abruptly. The blue fabric fell from her legs in a blue wave and to the floor. She ignored Almina's eyes that were radiating disapproval and crossed the room toward the front door.

"I'm going for a walk. Excuse me."

"Aubrey, wait-"

Aubrey grabbed her wool coot from its peg, snagging

the material in her haste to get out the door, and ignored her mother's calls to come back. She slammed the front door and hurried out into the cold rain.

She jogged down the road and in the direction of the one thing that only made sense to her anymore.

◯ঽ৪৹

The following Sunday after singing Jamie wrapped an arm around Aubrey's slender shoulder's and ushered her out into the chilly night.

"It's so cold," Aubrey complained, breath puffing out in front of her. "I wish we lived somewhere warmer."

She coughed into a handkerchief that she'd brought with her to church. Occasionally during the sermons Jamie heard her muffled watery coughs as she tried to keep as quiet as possible. He insisted on her going home with the rest of her family after Fellowship, but she remained behind for singing and for him to take her home.

Jamie climbed up into the buggy next to her and pulled out the heavy blanket to drape across their legs. He gathered the leather reins and clucked softly. The wooden wheels groaned as they started forward down the dark road toward Aubrey's home.

He kept one eye trained on her, studying the expressions on her face. Something was wrong, from the visible tension in Aubrey's neck to the way she refused to look him directly in the eye. She also had yet to reach out and touch him now that they were alone.

"So," he started casually, gathering the reins in one

hand. "How was the rest of your week?"

"Fine," Aubrey replied softly. Before he could prod further, she turned to look at him with a forced smile. "Yours? I forgot to tell you that you look better. Like you actually stayed in bed and rested."

He shrugged indifferently. "Wounds eventually heal in time, but jah, I've had time to rest these past couple of days."

"Gutt."

They continued down the road in silence. Not able to stand the tension anymore, Jamie pulled the buggy over to a stop alongside the road and turned to look at Aubrey.

She glanced around in confusion and shifted slightly in her seat. "What are we doing?"

"We need to talk about whatever is bothering you."

Just as he'd expected, a flash of defiance crossed Aubrey's already watery eyes. He smiled to himself sardonically. Over a year together and he knew what certain reactions would be to certain topics.

"Nothing is bothering me."

"Really?" Jamie scoffed. "Then why haven't you even tried to kiss or hug me?"

"Because I'm sick and I don't want to get you sick while you're recovering still."

"I don't care about that."

Aubrey scooted away from him hastily when he went to kiss her. At his pointed glance, she bowed her head and began to tug at a thread in the blanket absently.

"My maem organized a quilting bee for me on Thursday."

He arched an eyebrow in confusion at her solemn tone. "Isn't that supposed to be a good thing?" He didn't know much about quilting bees, but they were generally done a month before a wedding and the quilts were often wedding gifts.

"Jah, but Almina Graber was there."

Jamie hung his head and groaned loudly. He had dealt with Almina a few times at the furniture store and found her to be a very a harshly opinionated woman with no sense of humility. She was well known for bringing anyone of any age to tears for her sharp tongue.

"Don't tell me that you listened to that woman's opinions," he said, shaking his head.

The starlight from above shimmered off the tear trails along Aubrey's cheeks. He reached out with a fingertip and gently wiped them dry. Aubrey leaned into the touch, her eyes slipping closed.

"I couldn't help it. The whole community knows about what happened last summer and none of them would blame you if you called off our wedding."

"I don't care what others think about us. Let Almina and her harsh mouth think her opinions are important."

"They are important, Jamie. She's a member of our church."

"So are we. Our opinions are just as important."

"Not really. My words never seem to count," Aubrey noted bitterly. She pulled away from him and inhaled unsteadily. "I went for a walk afterward to town and-"

"You went for a walk in the freezing rain?" Jamie cut over her. The unexpected head cold made sense to him now.

"Jah. I know it was stupid," Aubrey said, reading his thoughts. "I ended up getting sick because of it, but I just couldn't stand to be in there after that. Not after hearing Almina say that she wouldn't blame you if you wanted to call off the wedding."

"But that's not what I'm doing. I don't want to call the wedding off."

"Then why haven't you talked to your daed yet?"

A headache began to creep up along the back of his neck and reside in the back of his head. Why hadn't he? There had been plenty of opportunities to talk to Aaron, and his daed had cooled down drastically from what had happened. He stared at Aubrey sitting in the buggy alongside him, her nose slightly red and shiny from her cold. The stars reflected in the surface of her eyes.

Did he want to get to married to her?

With everything that had happened in the past few months, it was beginning to wear him down in many ways. He loved Aubrey, there was no doubt about that, but last summer constantly plagued him. "Because I have to ask you something first."

Aubrey's fingers stopped picking at the stray thread in the blanket, but gesticulated that she was listening.

"You aren't thinking about leaving again, are you?"

A dull click in the distance echoed before the cold spray of water touched them. Sitting perfectly still, Aubrey continued to stare at him unblinkingly, carefully guarding whatever emotions she had within her.

The longer the silence stretched on, the more Jamie

felt his anger levels begin to rise. He tapped his hands anxiously against the wood of his family buggy and arched an eyebrow expectantly at her. "Well?"

"I've had a lot of thoughts since our baptism."

Jamie recoiled at the answer. His gut twisted painfully as he looked away from Aubrey and out at the dark road that was now soaked with irrigated water. He took a deep breath to keep himself under control. "Then why did you take the vow?"

"You aren't letting me finish what I'm saying. You're jumping to conclusions."

At her accusatory tone, Jamie whipped around to glare at her furiously. The past few weeks' emotions, the excitement, the frustration, the longing, swelled inside of him and threatened to burst. "Then tell me what your thoughts are, because it sounds like you are wanting to leave. Again."

"That's not what I'm wanting. I just-" she paused, biting her lip in thought. "I just want to make sure that this is the right thing. It's a huge a decision, Jamie. You can't expect me not to have nerves, because you have them too."

"So, you want to call it off then?"

Aubrey whirled around on him this time. "No!" she snapped, voice echoing in the dark. "That's not what I'm saying. I-I-I'm just... I know how Emma felt now, with everyone constantly saying things to her and putting words in her mouth."

Trepidation grew within him at the mention of Emma's name. He reached out and curled his fingers around Aubrey's jaw. She resisted at first, but allowed him to turn her head slowly around so that their eyes could meet.

"Tell me you aren't talking to her again," he demanded. "Not after everything that has happened."

Tears filled Aubrey's eyes and spilled out from the corners. "Nee," she whispered, shaking her head. "I promise that I haven't been. I couldn't live without you."

He didn't care at that moment whether they were still arguing, that Aubrey hadn't convinced him or that he hadn't convinced himself, and he kissed harder than he ever had before. It wasn't until a buggy trotted by them and laughter reached his ears that Jamie realized how much passion had taken them both over.

Aubrey shoved him hard against the chest and scrambled out from beneath him, cheeks flushed and prayer kapp lost somewhere in the darkness. Blonde tresses of hair reflected in the starlight and were almost a silver color. It would've been a beautiful sight except for the fear in her eyes.

"I'm sorry-" Jamie started, shame quickly filling him. What had he been thinking? Things had nearly gone too far, and in the process had terrified Aubrey, who was already jittery.

"You wonder what is going on with me? Maybe that's what it is going on with me," Aubrey cried, voice trembling in the dark. "It never occurred to you that I'm possibly scared of getting close to you? Or that I'm afraid I won't be able to be a good fraa to you, like the other Amish women are to their mann?"

She vaulted off the side of the buggy with surprising athleticism and ran down the dark road, leaving Jamie sitting alone in the buggy, before he could reply. He looked up to the sky, running his hands through his hair in aggravation. He began to pray, something that he was beginning to do more and more often.

He couldn't help but think that maybe Aubrey was right. Maybe it wasn't the right time.

One thing became clear to him, sitting in the dark with cold water spraying him. If Aubrey was talking to Emma again, he was going to stop it before it could progress any further.

He needed to talk to the church, and fast.

❧ CHAPTER 6 ❧

Monday morning, Jamie rose earlier than normal. He quickly prayed, did whatever chores needed to be done, and left the house as dawn broke across the sky. His breath steamed in front of him as he walked determinedly through the chilly morning air.

Bishop Abraham's house was close to town and he was relieved to see that lamp light flickered in the kitchen despite the early morning hour. A barn dog trotted up to him, barking in greeting before following him down the long road covered in wet leaves. The front porch was cleanly swept and there was a distinctly feminine touch to the area with meticulously-groomed flower beds.

Rapping his knuckles against the front door, Jamie took a step back and listened to the sound of feet scuffling along the floorboards. He took his fur lined hat off as the door opened.

"Jamie," Abraham greeted him, eyebrows arched high in surprise, "is everything alright, son? It's a very early hour."

Jamie nodded. The bishop was still clothed in his sleep wear, but looked awake and fresh from bathing.

"I apologize," he said, running a hand nervously over his own damp hair from bathing earlier, "but I needed to talk to you before work and this is the only time I have free."

"Of course. Come in."

Abraham led him through a narrow hallway and into the small kitchen. He motioned with a trembling hand to the little wood dining table in the corner. "Please, sit down. Would you like some kaffe?"

"Jah, please."

He sat on the edge of his chair as Abraham poured him a cup of kaffe and then set it on the table in front of him.

The older man sat across from him and curled his age spotted fingers around the mug, lifting it up to take a long sip. "What troubles you this morning to come seek advice from me? I pray that it is not your upcoming union with Aubrey in a few weeks. That would be most devastating."

The way Abraham muttered those words it was hard to tell if he was being sarcastic or serious. He took a long sip of the hot kaffe and felt it warm the pit of his stomach. "Nee, sir. The wedding is still being planned," he added, "but I had something to ask of you."

"I'm listening."

"Do you remember what I asked of you last summer, about Aubrey painting and selling her artwork to the Englischers?"

"Jah," Abraham said slowly. His pale blue eyes

narrowed slightly, "but with last summer's circumstances I would say that it was a bad idea."

"Right, I know, but I think there is something going on with Aubrey and I think it might have to do with Emma."

He picked in aggravation at the chip in his mug. Well, he wasn't entirely sure, but he had a suspicion Aubrey's wedding nerves had to deal with more than their growing relationship. He recognized the longing in her eyes, the same longing that had nearly driven her to leave their community.

"You believe she is corresponding with her sister again?" Abraham questioned.

Jamie shook his head and sighed in exhaustion. After last night and watching Aubrey flee from him, sleep had been the last thing in his mind. "I don't think so. I don't know if she is or isn't. I just think she needs something to keep herself occupied."

"I see." Abraham pursed his lips in thought. He swirled a little bit of cream in his mug before replying, "I get that you are asking for me to find a job for Aubrey outside of the bakery. Something that she would enjoy."

"Something like that."

Abraham smiled thinly at his muttered answer. "There is something very important about love and marriage that you need to know. Do you know what it is?" At the negative shake of Jamie's head, Abraham continued. "Trust builds a solid foundation for a marriage. Without trust, there is no love. It's like trying to keep your crops alive without any water or food. It sounds to me that you do not trust her and there has been some discourse on both your parts."

Jamie swallowed the knot in his throat and looked away from the bishop's knowing gaze. It hurt to admit it to himself, but he didn't trust Aubrey. For the past few weeks he had been trying desperately to pin whatever was going on inside him, but finally hearing it out loud made him feel selfish and foolish for trying to ask the bishop to watch over Aubrey.

"Don't worry, son." Abraham reached across the table and patted him on the back of his hand. "All this is very normal before a wedding. It's a lifelong commitment to someone other than Gott and it can be a bit daunting to comprehend all of that. I was nervous too, before my wedding to my fraa."

He looked up curiously at the word fraa. He knew little of Abraham's past beside that his fraa had died a few years prior, when the flu had struck their community hard.

"Jah, I had a fraa once in my life," Abraham said, chuckling in amusement as he read Jamie's expression.

"I'm sorry. I wasn't trying to look surprised."

"Don't be surprised. My daughters come over during the week to take care of the chores around the house and farm."

That explained the groomed flower beds and clean house. Mansleit never had the time or the patience, in Jamie's opinion, to do such things. He was glad that Aubrey was organized and neat.

"Do you understand what I have told you? Without trust, there is no love. Whatever is bothering you, I suggest talking with Aubrey. She came to me the other week, poor girl, drenched in freezing rain."

"What?"

Abraham was the last person Jamie had ever imagined Aubrey would run to with her struggles and her private thoughts.

The bishop nodded. "She has been coming to me since last summer, to talk about her faith and of course, her relationship with you, has come up quite a few times."

Jamie's heart pounded at the news. His fingers clenched his kaffe mug tightly and his chest threatened to burst with curiosity. "What has she talked about?" he asked thickly.

"I cannot say, as it was said confidentially between her and the church, but I can assure you that your suspicions are pointed in the wrong direction. She is quite happy to be marrying you."

He slumped back in his chair, staring numbly in surprise at the table. While one part of him celebrated hearing the news, the other part of him was gnawing on the guilt building within him.

He had done one of the worst things he could've done to his soon-to-be fraa; doubting her faith and accusing her of worldly things. While Aubrey was nervous about their relationship developing, he was worried about her leaving.

"Don't be angry at yourself too much. It's quite understandable where your thoughts had been," Abraham remarked.

"Jah, but what sort of mann am I to question and accuse her of such things?"

"You care deeply about her, that is plain to see. No one wants to see her fall to wicked ways or thoughts."

Bright morning light filled the small kitchen. A gentle knock on the back door interrupted their conversation before it could go any further. A woman a few years older than Aubrey, dressed in a simple grey dress and white kapp, entered the kitchen. Her matching pale blue eyes alerted Jamie that she was one of Abraham's daughters.

"I'm sorry, daed," she started, bowing her head apologetically. "I didn't know you had company."

Abraham waved away the apology. He smiled warmly at his daughter and waved her over to introduce her. "No need for apologizes. Jamie, this is my daughter Bertha. She helps around the house whenever she can spare time from her mann and kinner."

"Pleasure to meet you, Jamie. Would you like to stay for breakfast? There is plenty of food."

"Danka, but I will have to pass," he replied, rising from his chair. "I have to get to work in the next half an hour."

Abraham walked him to the front door. He placed a comforting hand on Jamie's shoulder and squeezed. "Please come by to talk any time, Jamie. That is why I am here. Please take the kaffe to keep you warm on your way to work."

Jamie raised the mug in a wordless thank you before stepping out into the bright morning. He was walking hurriedly in the direction of the furniture store when the loud roar of a car engine coming up from behind startled him. His eyes briefly caught a glimpse of the Englischer driving before the car pulled forward and the back passenger window rolled down to reveal Aubrey's face, pink from the cold and lovely as always. He quickly noted that she didn't seem to have a cold anymore.

"What are you doing?" she asked, shaking her head at him. "It's freezing out and you are walking to work."

His heart lifted to hear her gentle scolding, last night apparently far from her thoughts.

"Hop inside." Aubrey offered. The car stopped and the door opened. "It's warm and you'll get to work on time."

Carefully juggling his mug of kaffe, Jamie slid into the warm car with a grateful sigh. The side of his leg touched Aubrey's, and without thinking, he placed a hand over her knee. To his relief, she didn't tense or pull away. Instead Aubrey scooted a bit closer to him.

"Where is the rest of your family?" he asked curiously.

"Maem is at home with Isaac and Sadie. They unfortunately caught my cold. Well, it was unfortunate for Isaac at least. Sadie brought it on herself by insisting upon helping me with my wedding dress."

Aubrey giggled rather mischievously to herself. He soaked in the sound with a smile, enjoying their light-hearted moment as they drove to town. He was immensely relieved that Aubrey had either forgiven him or let last night go for the time being.

"Where should I drop you off, young man?" the Englischer asked.

"The bakery will be fine, Brandon. The furniture store is only a few blocks down from it," Aubrey replied for him.

When they pulled in front of the bakery, Hannah was standing near the front door.

"Is Hannah working full time for you now?" Jamie asked.

He reluctantly slid out of the warm car, nodding his thanks to the Englischer named Brandon, and helped Aubrey out of the car. They walked hand in hand up to the bakery.

"Jah, with maem taking care of Sadie and Isaac, I've needed the help."

Hannah smiled at them as they approached. "Good morning, Jamie," she said before tugging on the front door. "Open it up. It's freezing out here."

Aubrey unlocked the door and lingered behind as Hannah brushed by her to warm up the ovens. She frowned down at the mug cradled in his free hand.

"Since when do you drink kaffe?" she asked.

He didn't want to admit not sleeping well last night after what had happened, but Aubrey had caught him and knew it.

"I didn't sleep well last night," he admitted, bowing his head. "I couldn't sleep after thinking about what you said."

"Don't worry about it. We have enough to worry about, okay?"

She reached out to cup his cheek tenderly, soft fingers rubbing his shaved cheek. Jamie caught her hand when it retreated, tracing the outline of her fingers before pressing a kiss to the back of them.

"I'll try not to," he said. Then, as an afterthought, he

added, "Danka for forgiving me for what happened last night."

"I didn't exactly tell you to slow down for awhile. We'll just have to be more careful until November," Aubrey said matter-of-factly.

"Jah," he agreed, not liking the idea, but he told himself it was the right thing to do to keep themselves in check.

Standing on her tiptoes, she swept a kiss across his lips before stepping into the bakery. Jamie watched through the screen door as she retreated to the kitchen, shrugging out of her coat before disappearing from sight.

He was thankful at that moment that Aubrey didn't ask where he had been coming from. Telling her what he had asked of Bishop Abraham would've started another fight.

For the first time, he had a secret and had to keep it from Aubrey.

CR&O

"Let me see. Ah! That's better length-wise."

Aubrey stood in front of the floor length mirror with the outline of her wedding dress pinned to her waist. Tears moistened her eyes as she gazed at her reflection. The blue fabric accented her freckles and brought out the blue in her irises.

"What do you think?" Hannah asked. She came to stand behind Aubrey, beaming at her through the mirror's reflection. "You are going to be a lovely bride, Aubrey. I can't wait to see the look on Jamie's face."

They both giggled before setting their measurements, needles and thread on Aubrey's desk.

Hannah sat on the edge of Aubrey's bed, smiling widely at her. "So, how are you feeling? Three more weeks until the big day."

Three more weeks. Exhaustion rolled over her, just thinking about the rest of the wedding preparations. They still had to plan their dishes and finish with the decoration ideas, not to mention how they were going to arrange the house in order to fit everyone that Jamie had invited.

"I feel like I will surely lose my head somewhere, trying to prepare for everything."

Reaching up to grab the sides of her head, she stared at her best friend in mild dismay. Hannah giggled from the bed side.

"You will feel that way all the way up until the end, but it's worth it once it's all over and Jamie is be your mann. Being married..." Hannah trailed off with a dreamy smile before continuing, "I promise it's well worth the wait."

Aubrey watched as Hannah's eyes glazed over in happiness as her thoughts roamed to Jacob. She couldn't wait for that to be her and Jamie in a few weeks, no longer having to restrain themselves from one another.

The other night in Jamie's buggy beside the road flashed through her mind again. Never before had any of their previous kisses or touches ignited the fiery feeling from that night. It left her quivering with an unknown anticipation.

Hannah suddenly gasped. Her hand flew right to her stomach and an odd light filled her eyes.

"What is it?" Aubrey asked, rushing to her side. "Is it the bobli?"

"I-I don't know. It feels like tiny little bubbles tickling the line of my stomach. Feel."

Aubrey hesitated. "I don't know, Hannah. I don't want to hurt you or-"

"Don't be ridiculous. How would you hurt me? Here, feel."

She grabbed Aubrey's hand and placed it firmly against her lower belly. They waited anxiously before a light bubbling sensation trickled against Aubrey's palm. She stared down in wonder at the life growing inside of Hannah, and the fabric of her dress beginning to stretch.

"It is the most amazing feeling," Hannah exclaimed.

"I bet it is. Gott has blessed you."

"You just wait, Aubrey. You will be expecting a bobli shortly afterward too."

"We'll see," she replied, shrugging nervously at the thought. "I don't know if Gott will bless me that way. Not after everything that has happened."

She lifted her hand away from Hannah's stomach and plucked absently at a stray thread in the blanket spread across her bed. Hannah's stare felt like needles poking along her skin.

"What do you mean?"

"I just mean that I wouldn't blame Gott for thinking that I'm not worthy of a bobli right now."

Thinking of what could possibly transpire over the

next few months made Aubrey's heart twinge in an indescribable emotion. A part of her hoped and prayed for the blessing of a bobli with Jamie in the near future, but her recent slips in faith and anxiety over her marriage with Jamie made her doubt that Gott would think her worthy of such things. She certainly didn't think herself worthy of those things.

"How can you say such things about yourself?" Hannah gently chided. "You think so little of yourself because of what happened."

Aubrey drew her legs up and crossed them, sitting Indian style while facing Hannah, who did the same thing. She rubbed at her eyes tiredly before explaining things that had been inside her mind since the church had published her marriage intentions with Jamie.

"After we were published by the church, I couldn't help but think that maybe I didn't deserve Jamie or a family because I had almost thrown them away for an Englischer's life. I still sometimes think about it too. I haven't heard from Emma since I turned the key over to the church and I have no idea where she is. I feel like a bad person, like a bad fraa-to-be, thinking of those things when I shouldn't care or think of it anymore."

For a while Hannah was quiet as she took in Aubrey's words. She rested a soft hand on Aubrey's knee and offered a small smile. "You are not a bad person, Aubrey Forrest. We all go through our troubling, times and yours is no different. I think it's perfectly understandable that you miss your sister and worry over her. The two of you were close."

Tears spilled hotly from Aubrey's eyes. She reached up to dry them with the sleeve of her dress and let out a watery sigh.

"Jah, we were close. I just miss her. I never really cared for everything else that Emma was talking about on the outside. I just missed having someone understand me."

"But you do have people here who understand you," Hannah insisted. "I'm here and I understand how you feel. Jamie understands how you feel. Even your family understands everything. I think your anxiety over marrying Jamie is beginning to cloud your head with doubts."

She stared at the blue fabric dangling over the side of her desk. Maybe Hannah was right. Her anxiety was beginning to put unwanted and illogical thoughts into her mind. "You're right. I guess I'm just more nervous than I thought."

Hannah nodded in understanding. "It's natural like, I've told you before. I would think there was something wrong with you if you were calm and not stressing out over things."

Aubrey giggled before wrapping her arms around Hannah in an appreciative hug. She pulled back, sliding her legs off the side of her bed and standing.

"Danka. Let's do a couple more measurements so I can sew some more later."

As Hannah fretted over perfecting the lengths of her sleeves and neckline while Aubrey stared at herself in the mirror. She briefly wondered what she would look like the day after her wedding--whether she would look the same or like a complete stranger.

Something told her then and there that the reflection would change. After all, she would then be Aubrey Miller, and that gave her a small amount of hope that things would be alright.

CR&O

Jamie bounded up the porch steps of the Forrest's haus and knocked eagerly on the door. The front door opened and revealed Sadie, her nose still red and runny. She blinked a couple of times in confusion.

"Jamie? What are you doing here on a Thursday evening?"

"I was looking for Aubrey," he said, and, smiling tenderly, tugged on the end of Sadie's prayer kapp. "How are you feeling? Aubrey said that you have been pretty sick again."

"Jah. It was all Aubrey's fault too. She drank from my cup and didn't tell me about it."

Sadie opened the door further and ushered him in. She quickly shut the door behind him to keep the cold air out and then turned to yell up the stairs in a surprisingly clear voice.

"Aubrey! Your soon-to-be mann is here to see you."

"Ach, Sadie!" Daniel's irritated voice answered from the living room. "How many times have I told you not to yell in the haus?"

Daniel appeared in the hallway, staring at his youngest daughter in slight irritation before turning to smile in greeting at Jamie.

"How are you feeling, young man?" he asked kindly.

Jamie smiled, bowing his head. "Gut. Very gut. Much better now that the stitches are out and the skin is healing."

"I bet. Are you staying for dinner?"

"Nee. I was hoping that I could show Aubrey something. I promise I won't keep her long."

Aubrey appeared at the top of the stairs and quickly bounded down them. She smiled widely at him. "Jamie, what are you doing here?"

"I wanted to show you something that I've been meaning to show you for a while."

He met Daniel's eyes and they shared a knowing glance. Daniel nodded his approval before handing Aubrey her wool coat from the beg behind him.

"Don't stay out too long. It's getting cold out there."

They walked hand in hand to Jamie's buggy. After helping Aubrey climb up into the seat, he gathered the leather reins in his hand. A pink sky graced their sight as they rode in comfortable silence toward the haus, their haus, down the road. It wasn't much of a haus, but he had done enough of the foundation to show the general gist of the rooms.

When he steered the buggy down a narrow pathway that was still grass and mud, Aubrey turned to look at him curiously. "What are we going?"

Jamie smiled secretively before leaning over and pressing a kiss to her lips. "You'll just have to wait and see."

He laughed when Aubrey rolled her eyes at him, but she waited patiently as they rode further and further down through a series of small hills. He stopped a few feet away from the foundation of their haus and eagerly took Aubrey's cool hand in his.

"You're certainly eager to show me something." Aubrey said, laughing lightly.

They rounded the bend of a hill and a gasp left Aubrey's mouth as she took in the newly built floors and erected walls. Her hand tightened around his as he led her up the front porch steps.

"Is this-," Aubrey swallowed thickly, her wide eyes taking in the living room walls, "-is this our haus?"

"Jah. What do you think?"

Aubrey walked along where the hallway would lead to the kitchen and utility room. She silently took in everything with a small smile.

"I love it. When will you be finished?"

"Hopefully by next spring. I know," he started at the disappointment surfacing in her eyes. "I wanted to have it done sooner than that, but we will have to live with your family until the weather lets up and allows us to build. It's just too cold right now and I've been so worried about the crops that I haven't had the time to build."

His eyes widened in shock when Aubrey suddenly charged toward him, throwing herself into his arms with a peal of delighted laughter.

He stumbled backward at the unexpected weight, but easily regained his footing and twirled them around as their laughter rang out in the cold afternoon.

"So, you will talk to your daed?" Aubrey asked. She looped her arms intimately around his neck and pressed a warm kiss to his forehead, gently pushing back a few errant strands of his hair falling across his brow.

"Jah. I will talk to him tomorrow."

Jamie kissed her before she could say or ask anything else. He wanted to keep this moment as light-hearted as possible. He didn't want to think about talking to Aaron when there was still a good chance he would say no, and that was something he didn't want to think about with Aubrey's taste on the tip of his tongue.

ଔ CHAPTER 7 ଵ

"Pa, I need to talk to you about something."

Aaron glanced up from the pile of hay in the middle of the barn. He arched an eyebrow inquisitively as Jamie climbed down the ladder from the loft.

"Ach? Pray, what is it that you need to talk about?"

Sending a quick prayer to Gott for strength and for his daed's understanding, Jamie came to stand next to Aaron's side. The two of them grabbed armfuls of hay and went to the stalls at the back of the barn, where their horses were currently housed. After the wolf incident, and several other members having their horses or cattle attacked, they had brought all their livestock inside during the evening.

"About Aubrey," Jamie stated.

Aaron paused, arms extended to throw the hay over the stall door. He turned to cast him a furtive glance before allowing the hay to fall to its destination.

"You already know how I feel about this, son," he replied coolly, dusting his hands and sleeves free of hay.

"Jah, I know, but-" Jamie emptied his arms of hay

over the stall door and dusted himself off as well, "I wanted to talk to you about still having your blessing."

When no reply came, he turned to find Aaron with his eyes cast upward. His mouth moved quietly in a prayer before looking down at Jamie once more. His eyes, normally a placid blue, were alight with the stubbornness Jamie had expected. "Son, I don't think it's-"

Jamie shook his head and interrupted his father in a steady voice. "I know you don't think it's right because of what has happened, but I love Aubrey and despite what you think, she loves me. I know that Gott designed us for one another and she is fully committed to the church. Bishop Abraham has even said so. I want to marry her. I don't see myself with anyone else."

"How would you even know that, Jamie? You've only courted one other girl and that was back at Lancaster. You have no idea what marriage or love are really about. Neither of you do."

"Ma was the only woman you ever courted, and you married younger than me."

"That was a different time, son," Aaron said, sighing in exasperation. "Things were much different then. Your Ma and I didn't have much of a choice. We were the only suitable couple at the time."

"So, you're saying that you don't love Ma then? You were just forced into it?"

Aaron's eyes narrowed in a wordless warning. A purple vein began to throb at the corner of his temple. "Don't be ridiculous, Jamie. I love your maem more than life itself."

"Then you can't tell me that my feelings aren't real for Aubrey," Jamie countered.

"I never said your feelings weren't real. I question Aubrey's is all. Marriage is a commitment for the rest of your lives. It's not a decision either one of you should make unless both of you are sure of each other's faith."

Throwing his hands up in frustration, Jamie turned his back on Aaron and glared hotly at the barn wall. He inhaled deeply, trying to keep control of his temper. Trying to talk to Aaron was similar to talking to a concrete wall. Nothing seemed to change or penetrate it. He jerked in surprise when a hand cupped his shoulder and gave a strong, reassuring squeeze.

"I am not trying to dissuade you from what you feel in your heart is right. I am only trying to protect you from having your heart broken. You are not a parent yet, but one day you will understand, when you have kinner, that all you want is for them to be happy and safe," Aaron said softly.

Taken aback by the sudden honesty and openness of Aaron's emotions, he turned around to gaze at him in a mixture of surprised wariness. "I am happy and safe though. Nor is my heart being broken."

"I know that. I-" Aaron interjected, eyes fluttering closed. "I just do not wish to see you think that marriage will keep Aubrey here if her heart is set on leaving."

Jamie's anger softened when it him what his father was really concerned about. As rough and harsh as his daed could be with his kinner over certain things, he still held their best interests as his top priority. No matter their age, he still cared for them and wanted to be assured that they were safe physically and mentally.

"You're worried that Aubrey will leave after we marry."

"Jah. That is my worst fear for you."

"You don't have to worry about that, Pa. If you don't believe me, listen to Aubrey. She will talk to you if you let her."

Or at least he hoped.

After they were published by the church, he'd had a traditional dinner with Aubrey's family, but he had yet to have Aubrey over to his family's haus at all since their courtship. He had been so busy keeping her at a distance from his family to protect their relationship that it had severed her relationship with his own family.

Jamie reached up to give Aaron's hand resting on his shoulder a reassuring pat. "If it wasn't right, Gott would change my mind or not allow this to happen."

A small smile curled up at the corner of Aaron's lips. He took a step back, hand falling away from Jamie's shoulder, and tugged on the end of his beard.

"When did you become so wise?" he asked, amused.

"It might have something to do with the people I'm surrounded with. Or something else. Who knows?"

He grinned when Aaron guffawed. The two finished the rest of their chores in companionable silence and double-checked food and water supplies for the animals before locking the barn doors.

Before they entered the house, Aaron turned to look at Jamie. The moonlight cast shadows across the contours of his face.

"Tell Aubrey she can come over for dinner Saturday night. We'll have a talk then."

Jamie's heart soared and crashed all at the same time. He was relieved to have his father's acceptance finally, but it was still left to Aubrey to convince him fully.

And who knew how that would possibly go.

CRSO

"Aubrey? How do I run the card again?"

Biting her lower lip to keep the exasperated sigh forming within her quiet, Aubrey turned around to face the newest member of their bakery. A line of customers filled the store and the current Englischer, an older woman, huffed in irritation. Joyce Byler's face visibly paled and then stretched into a panicked expression at the line of customers quickly gathering.

Aubrey hurried to the front of the bakery and rushed around the counter. She took the credit card from Joyce's trembling hand and slid it through the machine.

"Just like this. You won't have to push any buttons unless it prompts you. Here you go, ma'am."

She slid the card and receipt over to the older woman, who snatched them up promptly and left the bakery wordlessly. For the next several minutes, Aubrey rang up orders herself while Joyce handed over pastries, pies, or breads. By the time the bakery was finally empty, it was close to lunch time.

"I'm so sorry!" Joyce cried soon as the last customer

left. Tears filled the younger girl's eyes. "I have never worked in a place like this before or used anything like a credit card machine."

At the beginning of the week, Hannah had informed Aubrey and Katie that she would unable to work in the bakery anymore. Her constant morning sickness and fatigue made it impossible to get anything done, and in a way, Aubrey was internally relieved. She would miss working with her best friend, but having to clean up after Hannah and give her extra breaks throughout the afternoon was beginning to take a toll on Aubrey physically and mentally as well. Especially since her maem was spending more and more time at home with Isaac and Sadie with their bouts of sickness.

Hannah had suggested that Joyce Byler, Jacob's youngest sister, approaching her rumspringa and courting days, take her position helping bake and running the register. So far, Joyce had done nothing but burn pies and mess up every order on the register.

At the wide and vulnerable look in Joyce's watery eyes, Aubrey forced a smile on her face and replied, "Don't worry about it. You'll get everything in time."

"I hope so. I am not good at baking like my maem. How will I cook for my mann in the future if I don't even know how to bake a pie?" Joyce looked over at Aubrey with a horrified expression, and to Aubrey's own discomfort, more tears surfaced in her eyes.

"You'll learn as you get older. I did."

"Jah, maybe, but I'm almost sixteen and you're two years older than me and know how to bake."

Aubrey forced herself to keep a patient smile, but was saved an answer when the front door of the bakery opened. Her heart melted at the sight of Jamie's eyes, sparkling brighter than usual, as he approached the counter.

"Good morning, beautiful," Jamie greeted her, placing his hands on the display case with a wide grin.

The center of Aubrey's cheeks flared hotly in response. She felt Joyce squirm next to her and found the younger girl staring down at the register in embarrassment to hear such a public display of affection.

"Jamie Miller," she scolded, a playful smile curling her lips up. "You know better than to say things like that in front of other people."

"I'm sorry. Did it make you uncomfortable, young lady?"

Joyce's face turned a bright shade of red when Jamie swiveled his eyes over to her and grinned charmingly.

"I-I-no. It-I-mean, no. It didn't." Joyce sputtered.

Aubrey stifled a laugh with the back of her hand. Her soon-to-be mann had a habit of paralyzing people with his charm whenever he wanted. She glanced up at the clock above the kitchen doorway before addressing Jamie. "I'll grab your slice of pie and we can go outside."

She returned from the kitchen with Jamie waiting in the same spot, drumming his hands anxiously against the glass display case.

"Get your hands off my display case unless you want to clean it."

Jamie lifted his hands and held them up. "You're not

even my fraa yet and you're already bossing me around."

"Oh stop it. Here's your slice of pie."

She slid her arms through the sleeves of her coat and turned around to catch the anxious look on Joyce's face.

"I'll just be outside there," Aubrey motioned toward the front door. "There's a few pies in the oven that need to be taken out in the next few minutes. The store will probably stay empty until we close."

"Okay."

They exited the bakery and stepped out into the mild afternoon. True to her word, Aubrey sat down on the front porch step and within earshot of the door in case Joyce needed her. Jamie sat down next to her, with his long legs stretched out in front of them, and happily folded the cellophane away from the plate.

"Is that Jacob Byler's younger sister?" Jamie asked. He took a big bite of pie and his eyes closed briefly in bliss.

Aubrey pinched the bridge of his nose in pent up frustration. "Jah," she said, shaking her head in dismay. "She is supposed to replace Hannah, since Hannah is too sick to help me out with the bakery."

"From the look on your face, she has been a lot of help."

"I don't even want to talk about it."

She wound her arm through the crook of Jamie's arm and relaxed her head on his shoulder. When she breathed in the smell of wood shavings and stain clinging to Jamie's clothes and skin, it soothed the headache beginning to make its way to her temples.

"You're in a good mood," Aubrey observed, resting

her chin against his strong shoulder to look at him.

Jamie turned his head to look at her and smiled widely.
A few crumbs of crust clung to his upper lip. She reached
up to brush them away with her fingertips, but stopped
when Jamie easily caught her hand and pressed a kiss to
the back of her hand. The coolness of his lips against her
warm skin drew a shiver from her.

"I have some news that will put you in a good mood
too," Jamie informed her.

"Ach?" She arched an eyebrow at him. "What news
would that be?"

"I talked to my daed last night about the wedding."

Her stomach tightened in a hopeful knot. Aubrey
stared into the blue eyes that matched the fall sky and a
slow grin began to make its way across her face. "You have
his acceptance?"

At the confirmative nod, she let out a squeal of
excitement and threw her arms around Jamie's shoulders.
The relief coursing through her left Aubrey dizzy with
anticipation. She glanced around the parking lot to make
they were alone before pressing a kiss to Jamie's lips.

Jamie's grin faltered slightly. "There's just one thing
that we have to do..."

Her thoughts, full of wedding preparations still left to
do, paused at that. He looked away from her and out at the
parking lot, biting his lower lip.

"Like what?"

"My daed wants to talk to you."

"He does?"

A trickle of fear started at the base of her skull and

down her spine, settling in the pit of her stomach. The thought of talking to Aaron about the wedding crashed her excitement. Something told her that he still wasn't keen on her and would be using this dinner to interrogate her.

"Jah." Jamie reached up to grab her hands in his and held up to his cheek, nuzzling them softly. "Don't worry. Everything will be fine. They've invited you over for dinner next Saturday night."

Staring down at their joined hands, she began to quietly pray. The last thing she wanted was to be questioned, for what felt like the hundredth time, about her commitment to the church and Gott.

"You are coming right?"

She looked up at Jamie's question, soft and vulnerable, and a flicker of uncertainty sparked in his eyes.

"Of course," Aubrey answered, squeezing their joined hands. "I will be there."

The smell of smoke and Joyce's frantic yelling from the bakery door broke the moment. Thick grey smoke curled through the bakery and the smell of burnt pie crusts was strong in the air.

Aubrey reached up to grab the sides of her prayer kapp in an attempt to keep her desperately-fraying patience in check. She stared down through the haze of smoke at the charred pies as Jamie used a damp towel to pat out the little orange flames flickering on the blackened crusts.

"I'm sorry!" Joyce cried. "I forgot to take them out and-"

"Obviously." Aubrey snapped, massaging her temples in aggravation. "You obviously forgot to take out the pies."

Joyce's bottom lip quivered and she bowed her head, tears trailing from the corners of her eyes.

"Aubrey," Jamie started, shooting her a warning glance. "It's fine, Joyce. You know my sister Lily? She used to burn bread all the time."

Setting the damp towel on the counter, Jamie patted Joyce soothingly on the shoulder. The younger girl smiled tremulously up at him, sniffing delicately. A pang of jealousy and anger streaked through Aubrey as she watched the exchange with narrowed eyes.

She looked away sharply when Jamie looked back at her, sensing her gaze, and grabbed the towel from the counter. "We need to get these out before any more customers come in."

Wrapping the towel around the rim of the pies, Aubrey stomped her way out of the bakery and threw the steaming pie into the trash can. Hands grabbed her shoulders and turned her around. Aubrey stared down at the ground, refusing to meet Jamie's concerned stare.

"What's wrong with you, Aubrey Forrest? I have never seen you snap at someone unless there was a reason."

Tears blurred her vision. What was wrong with her? She suddenly felt exhausted and anxious all at once from the morning's events and knowing what was coming Saturday night. She was in desperate need of some time away from the bakery, Joyce, weddings, and even Jamie. "Nothing. It's just been a long day is all."

She kissed Jamie goodbye and helped Joyce clean up

the bakery, forcing herself to remain cheerful while picturing a place in her mind that made her calm. After the bakery closed and before returning home, she would spend a few hours there.

CRSO

Harvesting chores began Saturday morning.

Jamie climbed up into the buggy alongside Henry. The pale morning light filled the road with a pink hue, but there was no warmth within the rising sun. In two weeks there would be nothing left in the fields beside clumps of moist dirt and rotten vegetables that would be churned into the earth for fertilizer. The land would be bare and ready for the winter snow that already threatened them in the distance, grey clouds looming over the snow-capped mountain range.

They raised a hand in greeting to anyone who was already up and working in the fields as they rode toward the Forrest haus.

"What are you harvesting over at the Forrest's haus?" Henry asked.

"The celery for the wedding, as well as the onions and potatoes. Everything else they have done earlier during the week. An Englischer told Aubrey that there will be a cold snap two weeks earlier than normal."

Henry glanced over at him in concern. "Will the celery still be good for the wedding then?"

"I hope so," Jamie said, sighing.

He rubbed his eyes tiredly, thinking of the all dishes

and decorations they would have to redo the night before the wedding. It was traditional for the mann to help out with the dishes and wedding preparations the night before, but if the celery was ruined, then he dreaded helping out.

Especially since Aubrey was already anxious over the wedding preparations. He changed the subject before it could be discussed further. "What are you helping Elizabeth with?" Jamie asked.

"She has potatoes and onions. Like Ma, she already canned the fruits and vegetables as early as possible."

"Jah. This freeze will kill the vegetation. It's a miracle that nothing else has died from how cold these mornings have been."

He wrapped his fingers around the mug of kaffe he had brought with him as the Forrest haus appeared in the distance. Smoke drifted from the chimney and trailed up to the sky.

"Since when do you drink kaffe?"

Jamie raised his eyes to meet Henry's skeptical ones. "I've had kaffe before," he muttered defensively.

"Nee. Not once have I seen you drink kaffe until recently."

Horse hooves crunched down on rocks as Jamie avoided his bruder's keen eyes.

"You aren't sleeping well. Don't think none of us haven't noticed that."

"I'm fine."

Henry pulled on the reins and the buggy wheels ground to a halt in the middle of the road. He set the reins down and turned to look at Jamie in disbelief.

"What?" Jamie asked. He shifted uncomfortably under the weight of Henry's stare and looked around them. "There is a buggy coming-"

"I can't believe that you are lying to me. I'm your brother and you have never lied to me."

"I'm not lying-"

"Jah, you are," Henry said, eyes hardening. "I've known you your whole Jamie Miller. There is something going on. Now what is it?"

A pent up sigh escaped Jamie's lips. He slumped over in his seat in defeat and stared wearily at the landscape around them.

"Is it Aubrey?" Henry prompted gently.

"Nee." Jamie shook his head. He smoothed a hand over his jaw, noting that in two weeks' time that there would be no reason to shave any longer. He would allow a blonde beard to grow there to show his marital status to the Amish community.

"I guess you could say it's wedding anxieties. We have been so busy getting ready for the wedding, and with everything that has happened..." He paused to sigh heavily, a headache beginning to pound in his head. "For a while I thought that Aubrey was going to leave again. I had been so sure that she was planning to leave that I went to Bishop Abraham to talk about it, and turned out that Aubrey has been confiding in the church. I asked him to keep an eye on her."

"What's wrong that?" Henry asked, frowning. "You were concerned over her well being and talked to the church."

"Right, but she wasn't talking to the bishop about leaving. She was talking about her nerves over the wedding and being a fraa."

The frown in Henry's brow furrowed even deeper. "I'm confused. Are you saying you feel guilty for asking the bishop to keep an eye on her?"

"Jah. Among other things. What kind of mann will I be if I don't believe my fraa first?"

"I wouldn't feel guilty for feeling that way, bruder. Going through what you both went through last summer, I would be suspicious myself."

"But it isn't right. A marriage is built on trust and love. Look at Ma and Pa."

They were quiet for a few minutes as a buggy rumbled by them and hellos were briefly exchanged with the other buggy's occupants.

"I think love and trust comes in time. Not right away," Henry said. "Look at Elizabeth and I. Half the time I think she is still in love with the mann who died over a year ago, but I know she also loves me and can grow to trust and love me."

Henry was right.

Love and trust didn't happen over a short period of time. It deepened as the days passed. He had no doubts that once the wedding passed and he settled into his life with Aubrey that all his doubts and anxieties would fade away.

He clapped his brother strongly on the shoulder. "Danka. You are right. As always."

Henry rolled his eyes at the sarcastic statement at the

end and gathered the reins again, flicking them casually. "I'll ignore the last part of that and accept the thank you."

The roar of a car engine broke the quiet morning. Jamie turned around to look at the line of black colored vehicles followed by what he immediately recognized as police officers. He had dealt with them once back at Lancaster, when someone had broken into their haus and after finding nothing valuable, ransacked what few items they had.

"Is that the police?" Henry asked, turning around to look as well. "What are the police doing here?"

Henry pulled the buggy to the side of the road to allow the stream of cars to pass in a cloud of dust and rocks. Jamie watched them drive by, a sickening dread filling him as the line of vehicles went further down the road.

"I don't know. Something isn't right though. They shouldn't be here."

As he said those words, they watched a police car and a black car turn down the road leading to the Forrest's haus. Jamie visibly paled and the contents of his stomach, which consisted of nothing but kaffe, threatened to come back up.

Henry turned to look at him with wide eyes. "Did a police car turn down where I saw it?"

Jamie wordlessly snatched the reins from Henry's hands and flicked them hard. The buggy lurched underneath them as the horses started in surprise. His heart hammered loudly in his ears as the chilly air whipped through his hair.

He wasn't sure why the police where at Aubrey's haus,

but neither scenarios playing through his head were good.

❧ CHAPTER 8 ☙

Something was not right.

Aubrey felt it in the air when she rose before first light to start kaffe for Daniel and Jamie, who would arrive shortly to help harvest the celery and then the rest of their crops. She dressed quickly in a rather ragged grey dress that she wore for harvesting chores and slid her feet into a pair of boots after saying her morning prayers.

"Morning, Papa," She greeted Daniel in the downstairs hallway, shrugging into his wool coat. "Is Mama up yet?"

"She will be down in a minute. Would you mind starting some kaffe?"

"Of course."

The smell of freshly brewed kaffe filled the tiny kitchen. Reaching up to the cupboard, she grabbed a mug for her daed and Jamie when he arrived. She had noticed lately that kaffe always seemed to cling to Jamie's breath. She poured the steaming liquid evenly in the cups and lifted Jamie's cup to her lips, sipping at the hot liquid.

"Are you drinking kaffe?"

Startled, she whirled around to face Katie. A hiss of pain escaped Aubrey's mouth when the hot kaffe spilled over the edge and down along the inside of her wrist. "I-I was just having a sip."

Katie arched an eyebrow at her in disbelief, but didn't push it any further. She dampened a rag with cool water and pressed it to the pink skin curling around Aubrey's wrist.

"I know you are nervous about the wedding," Katie said, voice a soft whisper in the room. "But you need to make sure you are sleeping enough at night. We can't have you fall ill before your own wedding day."

"I will be fine, Mama. I promise. I just didn't sleep very well last night is all."

She gently took the rag from her mother's delicate fingers and wrapped it around her wrist so she could pour another cup of kaffe for Jamie. The two of them wordlessly moved about the kitchen, preparing for breakfast as the pink morning light slowly brightened into another chilly morning.

They had to harvest the celery today and pray that it would survive long enough to use for the wedding. A freeze was coming earlier than usual from what Aubrey had heard from an Englischer, within a week, and would undoubtedly kill whatever crops were left. There would no longer be any warm days left as winter threatened to approach over the mountains. The thought of the celery not lasting for another two weeks made Aubrey's fingers tremble with anxiety.

"I'm sure the celery will be fine until the wedding," Katie spoke up, standing in front of the stove. "We will just have to store them properly until then. If we have to use other decorations and make other dishes, we will. It'll be understandable with this freeze coming earlier than normal."

The headache she woke up with began to pound even harder. Gathering the mugs in her hands, Aubrey smiled tightly at Katie. "I'm going to take these out to daed and Jamie," she said abruptly.

Aubrey hurried out of the kitchen before Katie could reply and stepped out into the morning. She started down the lawn and toward the barn, where Daniel would be readying the horses, mindful not to spill any more kaffe on herself. A quick glance around told her that Jamie had yet to arrive, but the roar of a car engine stopped her midstep.

A line of cars drove down the main road in a cloud of dirt and rocks. Two cars drove down the road leading to her haus and she peered in bewilderment at them as they slowly pulled up. The pit of her stomach churned heavily as she stood there on the lawn, halfway to the barn, feet paralyzed.

Two Englischers, both middle-aged males, dressed in rather fancy-looking suits, slid out of their car. The sunlight reflected of their dark sunglasses as they approached Aubrey with meaningful and confident steps.

"What's going on?" Katie called out.

The back door opened and she peered outside, visibly blanching at the sight of the Englischers. She sprinted down the steps and to Aubrey's side, placing a protective arm around her.

"Daniel! Daniel! There are police officers here."

An Englischer with jet black hair that looked oily in the sunlight came to stand in front of them, hands on his slender hips. Teeth that were tinged a dull yellow flashed at them briefly when he smiled widely. "Good morning, ladies," he said. "It is a lovely morning out here."

Neither of them replied. Hot liquid dribbled down the sides of Aubrey's hands again, but she barely noticed the blistering skin.

"Morning, gentlemen!" Daniel's voice boomed from behind them. He strode from inside the barn, wiping his hands clean with a tattered rag, and stood between the Englischers and them. "What can I help you with?"

"Well, for starters, we would like to talk with your daughters and youngest son."

Katie made a noise inside her throat and tightened her grip on Aubrey possessively. The Englischer's eyes, a pale green color, flicked over to Aubrey and swept her up and down.

Unfazed, Daniel stepped into his line of sight and broke their eye contact. He leveled a suspicious gaze at the Englischer. "What for? There is no trouble going on here," he stated. "You have to have a reason to talk-"

The other Englischer spoke up. He brandished a piece of paper in front of Daniel's face. "This is a search warrant for every house here in this community. We received a anonymous tip that there were possibly underage marriages taking place."

"That is ridiculous!" Katie exclaimed.

"There is no such thing going on here. What do my children have anything do with that accusation?" Daniel asked.

"Your daughter's name," he paused to read something scrawled on the back of the paper. "Aubrey Forrest was named specifically. I am assuming that is her, right there."

He raised a meaty finger and pointed directly at Aubrey, who looked over at her mother and father in confusion.

Daniel's eyes hardened to icy glints and he shook his head. "Whoever supplied that tip to you was wrong. My daughter turns eighteen in-"

"How about we talk to your daughter for ourselves? If you say there is nothing wrong, then a short conversation will have us on our way."

The Englischer smiled in a way that suggested that they had no other choice. He held out a hand for Aubrey. Daniel's shoulders slumped in defeat and he stepped out of the way.

"Come, Aubrey. Let's have a talk, shall we?"

ᏩᏙ

Aubrey was petrified and confused. That much Jamie could read on her pale, stricken face as the buggy came to a quick stop a few feet away. An Englischer with oily black hair beckoned for her to come with him.

"What's going on?" Jamie demanded.

He vaulted out of the buggy, rushing toward Aubrey,

to have a police officer calmly step in front of him and stop mid-stride.

"Who are you, young man?" the other Englischer asked. He was dressed like the other man with him, expensive suit and slicked-back hair. They both reeked of some sort of overbearing cologne.

Jamie instantly felt himself bristle in dislike. He wasn't sure why these Englischers held an air of authority around them, but he wasn't going to let them take Aubrey away.

"I'm Jamie Miller. Who are you?" he shot back, trying to sidestep the police officer restraining him.

"Oh, perfect!" The Englischer smiled widely. "We need to talk to you too. How about we introduce ourselves here and let things calm down a bit, eh? I'm Investigator Graham and this is Investigator Myers. We both work for the police department back-"

"What's going on exactly?" Jamie interrupted shortly. He took a step back from the police officer and crossed his arms, arching an eyebrow at Graham challengingly.

"Jamie," Aubrey breathed, a warning laced in her meek voice. She shook her head at him. "Don't. Everything's fine."

The fear and confusion swirling inside Aubrey's pale blue eyes made his heart constrict in protectiveness. Never before had he ever felt so confrontational or bold with his anger, but the investigators' presence brought out a side of him that he wasn't aware of. A surge of adrenaline pumped through his veins in response.

Graham eyed him carefully, as though sensing the change in Jamie's tense frame. He exchanged a look with

Myers before motioning for the police officer to step aside. "How about we have a private chat? Do you mind if I ask you a few questions?" Graham asked.

Jamie frowned at him. "Questions about what?"

"Nee," Daniel cut in sharply. He pointed to the road. "Jamie, go home to your family. There is nothing going on here, sir, that is illegal. We make sure to obey the laws."

"If that is true, then we will leave. We just need to a ask a couple of questions and we will be on our way," Myers replied smoothly.

He held out a meaty hand and beckoned for Aubrey to follow him again. Jamie watched with narrowed eyes as Aubrey cast him a timid glance before following the Englischer into the fields.

Graham approached him with lithe steps. Sunlight glinted off his sunglasses as they walked in the opposite direction. Jamie led him down the road and turned to catch Henry's puzzled eyes before they disappeared around the haus. They stood awkwardly on the front lawn and out of earshot.

"Beautiful views out here," Graham commented, fumbling around his pocket. When his hand emerged, a cigarette was clutched in his fingers. "I have to give to you compliments for living out here in the peace and quiet. I would give everything I have to silence like this. Cigarette?"

"No danka." At the confused glance, he reiterated with irritation, "I mean, no thank you. I don't smoke."

"Oh, good. Don't ever start. It's a nasty habit."

The smell of tobacco filled Jamie's lungs and burned

them. He took a step back to gulp in the chilly air instead and to keep his fraying concern for Aubrey, his own family, and community at bay.

"What did you want to talk to me about, sir? I have harvesting chores that need to be done."

"Right to business," Graham said, grinning. "I like you. You'd make a good cop."

Jamie scoffed aloud while trying to imagine himself living as an Englischer and a cop. Fumbling through his pockets, Graham pulled out a notepad and pen. He flipped it open and scribbled something on the page. "For starters, what's your age?"

"I'll turn nineteen in two months."

"Okay. How old is Aubrey?"

"Seventeen, but she turns eighteen here shortly. Why do you want to-"

"Best leave the questions for me, Jamie," Graham said without looking up from the notepad. "It'll go much faster if you let me ask the questions and you can return to your harvesting chores. How old are your siblings?"

"Henry is twenty-two, my sister Lily just turned sixteen, and Matilda is five."

"Are your sisters in any arranged marriages?

"No. There are no arranged marriages here. My sister Lily just started courting, but she's too young to be married."

"I see. And have you seen or heard of anything inappropriate around the community?"

"Inappropriate?"

Jamie blinked in confusion, an uneasy feeling causing

his stomach to tighten into knots. He glanced over his shoulder to see where Aubrey was, but couldn't find them out in the field.

"Yes," Graham said, raising his eyes to lock them on Jamie's. "Inappropriate relations. We received a phone call yesterday about an arranged marriage with Aubrey Forrest and an older man. Have such things been happening around here?"

"What?!" Horrified by what Graham was implying, he realized why the investigators were there. "Look, I don't know who told you that I was older or that I was arranged to be married to Aubrey, but they are wrong. Nothing like that ever happens here. We don't believe in arranged marriages."

Graham was silent for a few moments as he took in Jamie's words. He flicked the notebook shut and then slid it into the front pocket of his shirt, followed by the pen he wrote with.

"This tipster claimed to have heard of an arranged wedding," he said slowly. "Does the name 'Emma' sound familiar to you?"

A rush of hot rage filled Jamie as he curled his fingers into a tightly-clenched fist. He cursed under his breath, earning a strange glance from Graham. Jamie turned around to look up at the Forrest haus and up at Aubrey's bedroom window. The white lace curtains were still drawn in attempt to keep some heat in from the chill that always clung to the air now.

"I'm guessing from the pleasant look on your face that you know of her and don't have a good opinion of her,"

Graham noted wryly.

He casually flicked away his cigarette into the frozen grass. Jamie inhaled sharply through his nose to keep his voice steady when he answered. "I don't know Emma personally. All I know is what Aubrey has told me."

"And what has Aubrey told you?"

"The same thing Emma has told you, I'm sure. She left the community when she was about to be married to a church member who was a bit older than her. It wasn't arranged," Jamie stressed the word, "because she agreed to the marriage in the first place and was well over the age of eighteen by then."

Graham looked impressed. "Damn. You obviously know the law regarding what the age is to marry."

Jamie gave a curt nod. He knew of the legal laws that the Englischers had to follow. The Amish followed them too.

"Well, that's all I have to ask of you for now. You can go on your way doing harvesting chores. Whatever that means."

"That's it? That's all you have to ask me."

"You're not under arrest. You're obviously not 'older' as the tip reported."

Graham started around the haus, with Jamie following hotly on his heels.

"What about Emma?"

"What about her?"

"Won't she get into some sort of trouble for making up a false tip?"

Henry stood alongside Katie and Daniel in front of

the barn. Katie's head was permanently swiveled in the direction of the horse pasture directly behind the barn. In the distance he could see the flap of Aubrey's grey dress fluttering in the small breeze and her hands wringing together nervously.

"No." At the scowl on Jamie's face, Graham turned around to face him. "What do you have against her?"

"Nothing."

"Seems to me like you have some sort of grudge. Doesn't seem very Amish to me."

A hand rested on Jamie's arm, where it had drawn back, ready to swing forward. He blinked through the haze that suddenly filled his mind and found Daniel's stern face next to his.

"Go home, Jamie. You need to calm down before you do something irrational."

Jamie didn't answer. He hung his head in shame at the violent feelings coursing through him.

"Come on, Jamie," Henry said, promptly steering him toward the buggy. "Let's go home and make sure our family is alright. Apparently the police are talking to everyone."

He passed by the two cops, who watched him tensely, their hands never far from the hilts of their guns. Turning around to glance over his shoulder one last time in Aubrey's direction, he found that she was already staring at him.

Their eyes met. Even from afar, he could still see the trouble swirling in the blue depths, and the watery surface in them told him that she was crying. He wanted to run out there, sweep her up in his arms, and inhale the sweet scent of sugar that always clung to her skin.

"I love you," he mouthed.

The corner of Aubrey's lips curled up in wavering smile. "I love you too," she mouthed back.

He reluctantly climbed back up into the buggy alongside Henry and threw one last withering stare at Graham, the one Englischer he truly despised. Not for the sarcastic jabs at his faith or culture, but because of what he brought with him.

"What did he talk to you about?" Henry asked.

He glanced anxiously over in the direction of Elizabeth's haus. There were no police cars or black cars parked there.

"We can go," Jamie said, knowing his brother was torn about what to do. "We can at least go tell her what is going on. I don't mind. I need time to think anyways."

Henry smiled gratefully even though it was strained. He pulled the reins to the right and they started down the road toward Elizabeth's haus.

"He wanted to ask me if there were any arranged marriages going on. If I was older than Aubrey."

"What?" Henry gawked at him, shaking his head in disbelief. "That's why they are here? Because they thought there were arranged marriages."

"I don't know. Apparently it was Emma who said something to them."

The name tasted sour on Jamie's lips. He felt them curling back in a sneer before he rubbed it away, praying for Gott to keep him patient and strong. It was hard with the anger for what Emma had done coursing through him like a riptide.

"Aubrey's sister said that?"

"Jah."

They were quiet for a few seconds as they turned down Elizabeth's driveway. Henry let out a long and exhausted sigh.

"I can't imagine how Aubrey and her family are going to react once those investigators tell them who said that. The community is going to be very upset over it too."

Not as much as me, Jamie thought moodily. It wasn't just the accusations that angered him. He had no doubt that the investigator talking to Aubrey was offering her a way out.

If Emma's false statements destroyed their wedding just two weeks away, he would never forgive her.

ଓୠଃ୦

"So, what's with all the celery?" Investigator Myers asked curiously.

He gazed at the green stalks as they passed by them. Aubrey folded her hands nervously in front of her as she led the investigator out to a more secluded spot. Her heart thrummed anxiously inside her chest cavity. This was the first time that she'd ever spoken to an Englischer alone, without her family or another member of the church nearby.

"We use celery for decoration and in dishes for weddings."

Myers arched an eyebrow in bewilderment, but didn't reply. They walked out into the middle of the field and well out of ear shot. Keeping her eyes downcast, she studied the shiny leather of his shoes, caked with mud as she waited for him to speak.

"You look a little bit nervous," Myers observed.

The corner of his lips curled up, but no smile graced his face. The dark shades of his sunglasses kept his eyes shielded and she found it disheartening.

"I-I am a little," Aubrey stammered. A red hue filled the center of her cheeks at how nervous she sounded. "I've never talked to an Englischer before without another church member or my parents present."

"Not even on runchspringa, or whatever it is you call it?"

A bubble of surprised laughter escaped Aubrey's lips. Even though she was still on edge from the natural authority that radiated from him, it was impressive to meet an Englischer that knew a little bit about her faith. Even though he got the name wrong.

"Rumspringa," she said, smiling a little. "And no. I didn't participate in rumspringa."

"Why not?"

She shrugged her shoulders casually. "There was no need for it. I knew that I wanted to stay here with my family."

"I see."

Myers' lips pursed in thought. He reached up to slide his sunglasses over his head, pushing back his black hair. His eyes were a surprising shade of green, vibrant and piercing, as they gazed into hers. "So, tell me, about your wedding. It's in two weeks right?"

"Jah. I mean, yes. In two weeks."

"Who is the groom?"

"His name is Jamie. Why are you asking about my wedding?" Aubrey asked.

She stared at him, warning bells beginning to sound in her head. The accusations he had spoken of before echoed inside her mind and she gasped out loud.

"You think my marriage to Jamie is arranged!" At Myers's nod, she shook her head at him in horror. "That is ridiculous. We don't do arranged marriages or anything like that. No one is married to someone without their consent. Gott would not agree with that."

"So, you're telling me that your marriage to Jamie wasn't arranged."

"Jah!"

"And that he isn't quite a few years older than you?"

"Jah! Who told you all those lies?" Aubrey glared at him, hands propped on her hips. Indignation streamed through her veins at the idea of someone not within their community making up so preposterous a lie.

"Well, that liar was your sister," Myers stated emphatically.

A heavy pause followed.

Her heart stilled before pounding even harder and more sluggishly. He was lying. He had to be. She had not heard from Emma since last summer, when they had parted ways. It didn't seem logical for her sister to make up such things when she had grown up within the community and knew their ways. Emma was an Englischer by all definitions, but lying wasn't one of her characteristics.

"You're lying," Aubrey whispered.

Myers shook his head slowly. "I wish I was. She came to me a few days ago, asking us to investigate and check on your well being. She was quite concerned over you and unsure about your upcoming marriage."

"That..."

She was speechless and in shock. Tears burned the surfaces of her eyes and she blinked them away, turning to gaze over the fields. She sucked in several deep breaths to regain control over her rapidly fraying emotions. Near the barn, Jamie's tall and lithe figure appeared around the corner of her haus and exchanged words briefly with the other investigator. She held her breath when a look of pure anger flashed in Jamie's eyes and he raised his arm, to be restrained by her daed. Thankful for her father's intervention, Aubrey caught Jamie's eyes as they swiveled around to search for hers. Shame flickered in his eyes before a controlled coolness filled them. He climbed up into the buggy alongside Henry.

"She wanted me to tell you that if you wanted to leave, she had a place for you to stay," Myers continued. He placed a hand on Aubrey's tense shoulder. "If you want to come with me, I can take you, no questions asked. If there is anything going on that we need to know about, you can tell me. Everything you tell me is confidential and goes nowhere."

Aubrey fiddled with the strings of her prayer kapp

before sliding it off her head, forgetting the rules temporarily. She wiped away the sweat that had beaded there and felt the familiar tugs of last summer start deep within.

"Can you do me a favor, Investigator Myers?" Her voice was barely a whisper in the morning breeze and trembled as she twisted her hands together nervously.

"Of course."

"Tell my sister that I appreciate her thinking of me and that I am praying for her. There is nothing like that going on here. I love Jamie and I am staying here with him. If she wants to come back, she can come back, but I can't do that to our family. Or to Jamie."

She started back toward the barn and haus before he could reply. Her legs, heavy and wooden, seemed to sink down into the mud and her walk slowly stopped. Keep walking, Aubrey told herself, but her feet remained glued to the ground.

Against her own will, she turned back and said, "Actually. There is something else that you can do for me."

❦ CHAPTER 9 ❧

The following morning, anxious chatter filled the barn. Jamie stood by the doors, waiting for any sign of Aubrey or the Forrest family. Church would start in a few minutes and they were either running late or not coming at all.

Jamie shifted from foot to foot as he replayed yesterday's events. The police had came into their community and talked to every household, separating the kinner from their parents to question them. Initially, the air had been filled with distress and anger, but now it was replaced with a more placating and forgiving mood.

It had been a mistake, a miscommunication. He called it a lie, a filthy lie that had lumped the community in a misplaced stereotype. He was no stranger to the news of corruption and ungodly things happening in other communities, but to think it would happen within his community was infuriating.

Especially since Jamie knew who was the center of it.

Hot anger flashed down his spine. Jamie sighed at the

emotions running rampantly through him. He pinched the bridge of his nose and then palmed ,the tight lines of exhaustion surrounding his eyes.

"Gott give me guidance," Jamie whispered.

He opened his eyes to spot Aubrey finally arriving, sitting on the back seat of her family's buggy, face pale and pinched in a tight expression. All of them appeared equally tired and tense. Aubrey's eyes didn't light up as they usually did whenever she found him. Instead, they looked away pointedly to guard her emotions. His heart clenched at the gesture.

"Jamie," Aaron called out from behind him. "Come inside. Church is starting."

He did as he was told, too exhausted to argue otherwise. Jamie took his respected seat with the mansleit next to Henry, who sat on the other side of Aaron.

Instead of talking about what had happened yesterday, Isaac preached about forgiveness. A part of Jamie didn't expect them to talk about it. It wasn't their way to linger on such things, and he wished that he could have the same sense of serenity that the other church members did by the end of the service.

Ignoring his stomach's growl of hunger, Jamie immediately went to Aubrey's side as she stood with Sadie and Hannah. He didn't care at that moment about the rules of public displays of affection and gathered Aubrey's delicate frame in his arms. She tensed at first, but relaxed slightly against him.

"Are you alright?" he asked, voice muffled from Aubrey's prayer kapp.

"I'm fine."

They pulled back at Sadie's awkward throat clearing and let their hands slip out of each others'.

Aubrey raised an eyebrow at him in faint teasing. "Are you alright?"

He smiled a little bit in relief to hear the jesting in Aubrey's voice. "Jah. I'm fine. Can we go for a walk?"

"Sure."

They walked together along the harvested fields, with their hands brushing lightly. The smell of moist dirt clung to the air, and out of pent up frustration from yesterday, Jamie kicked at a clot of dirt with his shoe. A dainty and soft hand rested on Jamie's bicep as Aubrey stared at him in concern.

"Are you sure you're alright?"

He wanted to laugh then. Not because of what had happened yesterday, but because he was normally the one asking Aubrey those type of questions. When had that changed? Jamie frowned as he wracked his brain to answer that question. He had been so consumed in trying to understand Aubrey's motives and emotions that he had forgotten about himself.

"Jah. I'll be fine once we are finally married," Jamie replied.

Aubrey's hand dropped away from his arm. She turned away to gaze out the mountains, now covered with several feet of snow. It would only be a matter of time before the snow would reach the San Luis valley.

"What? What's wrong?"

"Nothing. I-"

"It doesn't have to do with yesterday, does it?" Jamie interrupted, his heart racing with fear.

"Nee. It doesn't have anything do with that. Will you let me talk instead of interrupting me?" Aubrey asked, annoyance threading her voice. "It's been something that I have been trying to talk to you about for awhile."

"Sorry. Go ahead. I'm listening."

"Bishop Abraham told me that you had come to him about finding me another job to keep me occupied once we are married."

The sides of his neck flared in embarrassment and guilt. Jamie tried to read the composed expression on Aubrey's pale face, but couldn't find any trace of anger like he'd expected.

Aubrey took a deep breath before continuing in a soft voice, "I don't blame you for asking him. I really don't. He offered me a position at the school house, since Bertha Beachey is getting older and I-I accepted it."

Before he could congratulate her or voice his relief, she continued in the same voice. "I haven't been thinking of leaving you or the community. Sometimes it is tempting, given what the community knows and thinks, but I'm not my sister. I can't run away or turn my back on you or Gott. Even out there in the Englischers' world and knowing everything there is possibly to know, I still wouldn't be happy. I'm just scared of what is going to happen after the wedding. Once we speak our vows and whether or not I will make you happy as a fraa..."

The last part was murmured and he had to lean forward to hear the timid words trembling with emotions.

All at once Aubrey's behavior made perfect sense to him. Jamie slid his hands along the curves of Aubrey's cheeks, relishing in the softness and her cold ears against his warm fingers.

"I will be very happy, no matter what happens to us. Is that what has been bothering you?"

"Jah. Among other things."

The center of her cheeks filled with pink and he found it charming. He brushed a kiss on her lips and rested his forehead against hers. "Nothing will go faster than what you feel comfortable with. You are my soon to be fraa and I have nothing but love and respect for you. After all, we have forever to spend together. There's need to rush through things just because we are married. Understood?"

Aubrey smiled widely, nodding her head. His hat brushed against Aubrey's white kapp and he reached up to adjust it before it could fall free. "Gut. Now let's eat."

His stomach growled loudly in agreement. Both of them burst out laughing as they made their way back toward the barn, where Fellowship was on its way. They let go of each other's hand once they rounded the barn.

"Ach, by the way," Jamie said, turning to look at Aubrey walking dutifully alongside him. "My daed thought it'd be best to do dinner this Friday night. That way we can have all day Saturday to prepare."

A shimmer of uncertainty flashed in Aubrey pale blue eyes, but she nodded nonetheless and offered a small smile. "Jah. Sounds good."

He knew that she wanted to ask what Aaron thought of what had happened over the weekend, since the whole community knew it was Emma's doing, but that was a topic he didn't wish to discuss with anyone.

Not when Aaron's acceptance of their marriage was dangerously close to unraveling.

CRSO

Aubrey carefully inspected the celery stalks that were still in the ground. The leaves were perky and not wilted from the cold thankfully. Surprisingly, the crops had held up against the cold. She whispered gratefully to Gott before turning to go back inside the haus, where Katie was pulling out a pie stuffed with stew meat, potatoes, and various vegetables.

"Have you finished your wedding dress?" Katie asked casually.

Aubrey nodded. She moved around the dining table, setting down plates and cutlery as she went. "Jah. I finished it last night."

Her stomach twitched as the butterflies started once again, thinking that by this time next week she would be setting a place for Jamie to eat alongside her. They would have dinner at Jamie's family haus Friday night so they could spend Saturday together, preparing the decorations and dishes.

Katie gently set the oozing pie, which smelled heavenly, onto the pot holder Aubrey placed in the center of the table. When she looked up to gaze at her, Katie's eyes were moist with tears. The sight of it made Aubrey squirm in awkwardness and happiness, since she knew that those tears were ones of joy.

"Mama," Aubrey started, shaking her head, "don't cry. You'll make me cry."

Katie laughed lightly. "I'm sorry," she said, dabbing at her eyes with the sleeves of her dress. "I am just so excited and proud of you all at the same time. My daughter is marrying and there is nothing more beautiful than witnessing such an occasion."

Tears sprung to Aubrey's eyes against her will. She wrapped her maem's slender figure into a hug and rubbed her back soothingly.

"I just wish I could see Emma as happy as you are." Katie said softly. She cupped Aubrey's wet cheeks in her palms and pressed a fond kiss to her forehead.

"She is happy, Mama."

"Nee," Katie said. "She thinks she is happy. Look what living with the Englischers has done to her. Is that really happiness?"

Aubrey bit her lower lip to keep her answer hidden. She had never voiced it to Jamie, who was angry at her sister for a good reason, or to her family, that it had been partly her fault for not clarifying things to Emma. Unable to turn back, Emma had done what she had to do to survive with her family and community--find some sort of happiness in the world. Even if it was considered worldly or wicked.

Instead she answered, "No, Mama. It's not true happiness."

Katie nodded in approval. She moved around the kitchen again, grabbing a pot of string beans heated in butter and little cloves of garlic.

"Are you still having dinner over at the Miller's Saturday night?" she asked.

Sliding another pot holder on the table, Aubrey inclined her head to indicate the positive. Friday night loomed in her mind. She still wasn't sure how Jamie's daed felt about the weekend's events after finding out that it had been her oldest sister behind all of it. Jamie had never mentioned anything beside moving the dinner up to Friday night so they could spend Saturday afternoon at her haus preparing for the wedding on Sunday.

"Jah, but it will be Friday night, so we can prepare everything on Saturday."

"That will be lovely." Katie paused before calling everyone inside for dinner. She laid a calm hand on the back of Aubrey's as she placed a fork beside Isaac's plate. "Everything will be alright. It is a gut sign that the two of you will have dinner over there."

The rest of the night faded away with the soft glow of their lamps and prayers before everyone ventured to their rooms. Aubrey stood out in the dark hallway, listening to the soft breathing of her sleeping family, and with surprising stealth, she tiptoed and opened Emma's door.

The room was still untouched after two years, and the stale smell of dust floated around the chilly room. Mindful of the squeaking floorboards, she walked further into the room and to the closet, which she quietly opened. Dresses, similar to Aubrey's own, hung like they were ready to be worn tomorrow morning.

Aubrey reached out and trailed her fingers over the

dusty and moth-eaten fabric. She fished through them until her fingers found the light blue fabric of what had been Emma's old wedding dress. The fabric had yet to be sewn together, with several pins still holding the skirts, bodice, and sleeves together.

She sat on the edge of the bed with Emma's dress in her lap. Her earlier conversation with the investigator replayed in the back of her mind.

"Actually. There is something else that you can do for me."

Investigator Myer's arched an eyebrow inquisitively. "What is that?"

"Tell Emma that I'm getting married next Sunday and if she wants to come, she could come. Obviously not in the actual ceremony, but standing near the window. Anything. Just as long as she's there."

Aubrey sighed as she traced errant patterns along the fabric.

"I miss you, Emma. Please come Sunday."

And that was what she prayed for, for Emma, a still important part of her life. She only hoped that seeing Emma there, faraway and unreachable, wouldn't change her mind like she had so many times in her dreams.

CR&SO

Friday afternoon arrived with a blast of chilly air and overcast skies. Snowflakes fluttered down and wet the top of Aubrey's kapp. She huddled close to Jamie's side as the buggy made its way toward the Miller's farm and enjoyed the warmth that radiated from his body.

Jamie pulled back on the reins suddenly, before they could turn down the road.

"What-" she started, but warm lips cut her off.

It was over just as quick as it had started, but the kiss warmed her from the inside out. She gently reached out to brush away the snowflakes caught in the curls of Jamie's eyelashes. Sapphire eyes blinked lazily in response to the touch. They remained that way for a few minutes, wiping away snowflakes from each other's faces before reluctantly parting.

"I want you to know," Jamie started, picking up the leather reins, "that no matter what happens tonight, we are still getting married on Sunday. I don't care what my daed says."

"Don't talk like that, Jamie Miller. Everything will be fine. I know what to say to your daed."

Jamie cocked an eyebrow at her in wry amusement and flicked the reins. "Oh really? You suddenly know my daed better than I do?"

"Nee, but I have been rehearsing what I could say to him."

"I see. Hopefully it will work."

Aubrey smiled confidently. "It will. You'll see."

They pulled up to the barn. Aubrey waited patiently for Jamie to unhitch the horses before they walked hand in hand to the back door. Their hands parted right as Aubrey stepped into the narrow hallway. The smell of savory beef stew and onions wafted throughout the haus.

Jamie shrugged out of his coat and waited for Aubrey

to slip out of hers so that he could hang them on a peg in the hallway. He nodded wordlessly toward the kitchen before making his way to the living room, where his bruder and daed were sitting in front of the wood stove.

Food cluttered the small table set for seven people. Steam curled from a large pot of beef stew and a loaf of freshly-baked bread cooled on a plate next to a green bean casserole.

"Aubrey!" Lily exclaimed. "I'm so glad you came to have dinner with us. I can't wait for the wedding this weekend."

"Me too," Aubrey said, laughing. "What can I help with?"

"The bread needs to be sliced," Sarah said. She handed Aubrey a bread knife and a kind smile graced her tired face. "I am glad to have you over as well. I told Jamie it was well past due."

They didn't acknowledge why it had been past due. Aubrey sliced the soft and warm bread carefully as Lily danced around her with the cutlery.

"So, have you finished her wedding dress yet?" Lily asked eagerly. "I bet you are going to look beautiful. I personally can't wait to see Jamie in a bow tie."

Aubrey smiled at Lily's excitement. "I can't wait to see that either, but jah. I finished my dress last night."

"And it fits perfectly?"

"Perfect as it is ever going to be. How is your dress fitting?"

"Perfect as well. I can't wait until I get married..." A dreamy smile curled Lily's lips.

"That won't be for another whole year, Lily," Sarah cut in, shaking a finger at her daughter. "Go fetch your daed and bruders. Dinner is done."

The floorboards shook as they entered the kitchen and took their seats around the table. Jamie caught Aubrey's timid glance and smiled encouragingly at her as he took his seat next to hers. They bowed their heads as Aaron spoke a quick prayer and the kitchen filled with light laughter as dishes were piled with food.

"So, have you harvested the celery yet?" Sarah asked.

Aubrey swallowed a mouthful of buttery mashed potatoes before answering. "Jah. We harvested them yesterday afternoon, before the freeze."

"That's gut. I was worried about the celery freezing."

She had been too, but luckily the weather had somehow stayed reasonable toward the celery crop. Daniel had closed the furniture store early, and with Levi's help, harvested the plants the day before, before the first hard freeze and snowfall. Aubrey had been so relieved that she'd nearly cried.

"Will you be needing extra help with preparing?" Sarah asked. "I can always come over early Sunday morning to help your maem with whatever decorations need to be done. Or cook a dish."

"That would be nice. My maem would appreciate the extra help."

She felt Jamie's hand seeking hers from underneath the table and their fingers twined loosely. His thumb rubbed soothing circles on the inside of her wrists absently as the next hour passed by them in a hazy cloud of warm air from the wood stove and happiness from their full stomachs. The whole time, Aubrey felt Aaron's eyes on them, studying them carefully without saying a word, and her heart began to race nervously.

Aaron belched, a signal of Sarah's good cooking, before pushing his chair back from the table. "We'd better feed the animals one last time and make sure that they have plenty of water. There is a hard freeze in the air."

"I will be right back," Jamie said, squeezing her hand before letting it go. "This won't take long, and afterward I will take you back home before it gets too snowy and cold out."

Aubrey nodded as the three men lumbered out into the cold night. She helped gather up the plates and scrubbed them clean before handing them to Lily to dry as Sarah scooped leftover food into containers. With winter upon them, food hardly went to waste.

As they'd cleaned the kitchen, Aubrey took in the Miller's modest kitchen. There weren't any personal effects, but Sarah's loving touch lingered everywhere, from the way certain cookware was organized to the neatly folded dish towels. Her mind wandered to the haus Jamie had started building for them, mentally mapping out the floor plans of the large kitchen and three bedrooms upstairs.

The men returned a few minutes later, clothes soaked from a cow tipping a water barrel over them. Jamie smiled as he passed by the kitchen door and bounded up the stairs with Henry on his heels.

Aubrey smiled as she turned back to finish washing

the rest of the cutlery. A shiver of anticipation went up her spine, imagining her life with Jamie as his fraa. She tried to picture herself falling asleep in the protective circle of his arms and dropped a fork from the jittery feeling that filled her at the thought. She could hardly wait until they had the privacy to live their lives together.

Her thoughts were interrupted when Aaron walked back into the kitchen and motioned for her to follow him.

"Can I talk to you for a moment alone, Aubrey?" he requested.

Aubrey swallowed thickly. All week she had mentally prepared herself for this conversation with Aaron and what answers could appease him. She handed Lily the dish towel and followed him out the into the hallway.

"Make sure to grab your coat. It's cold outside."

He opened the front door and a blast of cold air blew down the hallway. Aubrey grabbed her wool coat and stepped out into the crisp night. The porch boards groaned as Aaron walked to the other side and put a respectful distance between them. He leaned back against the railing, meaty arms folded across the expanse of his chest, and rested them on top of the slight bulge of his stomach. "I imagine you already know what I want to talk to you about."

"Jah, sir."

Aaron nodded curtly. "Gut. I care about my son. He may not see it or think so, but I love all my kinner. I don't want to give my blessing for your marriage unless I know the truth."

"I'll answer whatever questions you have," Aubrey

responded honestly, albeit nervously.

"Are you fully committed to our Lord, to our faith, and to Jamie?" Before she could answer, Aaron added in a hard tone, "If you lie, I will know."

The threat would've normally sent Aubrey into a stammering mess. She tipped her head back to meet Aaron's piercing gaze bravely. "I have nothing but love for our Lord and the blessings He has given me. I also love your son and would not leave him. I think I have proved myself by joining the church and committing myself to Christ. I wouldn't have joined if I didn't feel like I could commit myself."

"And this past weekend?"

"What about it?"

"It's no secret exactly that your sister was behind the police showing up here."

"Jah, but I had no knowledge of it. My sister is shunned from our community and is happy living an English life. I could never live without your son or my family. That was the reason why I stayed behind. I am not my sister like everyone seems to believe. We are similar, jah, but we are not the same."

Aaron kept his eyes trained on hers unwaveringly for a little while longer before finally glancing away and into the snowy night. He sighed heavily, rubbing the back of his neck with a thick hand. "You must think I am very cruel to question your faith or love for my son. It is not in our way to be involved with our kinner's love life until they are published by the church."

"Nee," Aubrey said, shaking her head. "I don't blame

you for asking questions. With everything that has happened, I would've been surprised if you didn't ask or try to stop the wedding."

"I had no intention of stopping the wedding. I said those words out of anger and fear over my son's life. Jamie has a habit of not using his head when he is angry, and it never ends well."

"I haven't noticed."

The corner of Aaron's lips curled up in a wry smile. "You will, in time. He's quite stubborn, like you are."

"Jah. I noticed that part."

They were quiet for a few minutes longer before the groan of floorboards echoed in the hushed night. Aaron patted Aubrey on her shoulder as he passed to open the front door. "You better have Jamie take you home. After all, you have a wedding to prepare for tomorrow."

A genuine smile spread beneath the shadow of Aaron's honey-colored beard before he opened the door and stepped back inside. Aubrey sagged against the porch railing in relief and rested a hand over her frantically beating heart.

In two days she would be Jamie's fraa and he would be her mann. Nothing sounded sweeter than that. She lifted her eyes up to the dark sky, to where the faint shape of the moon could been seen through the thin clouds.

She first thanked Gott for His strength. Then she prayed for more strength to get through the upcoming weekend without losing her sanity. There was only one question left that would answered on Sunday.

Would her sister be there?

⊂꙰ CHAPTER 10 ℰ੭

The sound of glass shattering and a blast of frigid air startled Aubrey out of a dream. She bolted upright in bed, clutching at her covers for protection as she gazed around the dark room in sleepy confusion. Moonlight glinted off the shards of glass on the floor beneath her window and the white curtains whipped around as a chilly wind whistled through a fist-sized hole in the window.

In the next room over, Aubrey could hear her parents' feet shuffling around and mumbling in alarm at the sound. She slowly pushed the covers back, staring at her broken window in a mixture of alarm and bewilderment. Her eyes spotted a dark mound a few inches away from her desk.

Aubrey squinted at the object, barely making out the envelope tied to it. Her blood pumped frantically as adrenaline shot through her at a dizzying pace. Mindful of the broken glass, she crouched down to grab the rock. Daniel's voice echoed down the hallway, "Sadie, you alright? Katie, go check on Aubrey."

Tugging the bright yellow envelope free, Aubrey

shoved it quickly into her desk right as the door opened. Katie stepped into her room, holding out the lamp to cast a soft glow about the room. Her panicked eyes swept over to Aubrey before landing on the shards of glass surrounding her feet.

"Daniel, in here!" Katie yelled. "What happened, Aubrey?"

"I-I"

She really had no idea what had happened. The floorboards in the hallway groaned as Daniel hurried into her room and paled at the glass shards scattered everywhere. "What happened?" he asked, staring at the glass in shock. "Why are you holding a rock?"

Aubrey dropped said object immediately. It landed on the ground with a heavy thud. "I don't know. I woke up to my window breaking and found the rock on the floor."

Glass crunched beneath the boots Daniel had tugged on. He pushed aside the curtain to gaze outside before turning to look back at Aubrey and Katie. "You didn't hear any voices or weird sounds?"

"Nee. I was sleeping and woke up to this."

"Whoa." Sadie's sleepy head peeked into Aubrey's room. "What happened in here?"

"Go back to your room, Sadie. Everything's fine," Katie reassured her.

Daniel stared at Aubrey for a few more minutes before tiredly running a hand over his face. "Might have been some rowdy English teenagers looking for trouble. You better sleep downstairs until the morning, Aubrey."

"What about my window?"

"I'll have to go to town and buy a new one. Jamie will be over here tomorrow right to help prepare for the wedding?"

"Jah. He won't have time to help though. We have to decorate the room and bake all the dishes."

Her anxiety levels rose thinking of all she had left to do.

"Unless you want to sleep in your room with a broken window in the middle of winter, I am going to need Jamie's help installing a new window," Daniel rationalized.

"Jah. Of course. Danka for your help, Papa."

They exchanged a brief smile before Daniel left to go back to bed. Katie helped Aubrey gather her blankets and pillows before shuffling down the stairs to the living room. When she caught a glimpse of Aubrey's tense face, Katie hugged her reassuringly. "Everything will be fine, Aubrey. I promise. We will get everything done in time." She swept a tendril of hair back from Aubrey's forehead and pressed a fond kiss there. "Get some sleep. We have a busy day tomorrow."

Aubrey slipped underneath the blankets, but sleep evaded her. She twirled her fingers through the strands of her hair anxiously, waiting to hear the soft snores and deep breathing from her family. The wood stove crackled happily in the corner of the room and waves of cozy heat caressed her. Unlike the cool draftiness of upstairs, the living room remained warm and sleep began to tug at her insistently.

There was no doubt in her mind who had thrown the rock.

She rolled over onto her back and stared up at the twinkling stars through the living room above the couch. Somewhere out there in the crisp darkness, Emma had tied an envelope to a rock and threw it up at her window. The yellow envelope sat in her desk drawer, waiting to be opened.

Except something was different this time. The temptation wasn't there like it had been before, when she would've normally been eager to read her sister's message. This time Aubrey felt nothing, no urges to sneak back upstairs, nothing beside excitement for her wedding on Sunday.

Aubrey yawned before rolling back over and curling up facing the wood stove. She would read Emma's message tomorrow night.

CR80

Jamie stared up at the fist sized hole in Aubrey's bedroom window. He kept his hands on the ladder to steady it as Daniel climbed up to pry the broken window loose.

"And you have no idea who would've done this?" Jamie asked. He twisted his head around to look at Aubrey in disbelief. "You heard nothing or anybody saying something?"

Aubrey crossed her arms defensively. "Nee. If I do find out who it is, I'd like to thank them for throwing a rock through my window."

He stared at her intently, noting the way Aubrey's eyes

shifted away to look at everything else but him.

"Coming down!" Daniel called, climbing back down with the broken panel. "It was probably just some English teenagers causing trouble. There have been a lot of issues recently with English teenagers coming around here and acting crazy."

Daniel set the broken panel down on the ground and picked the new one up before climbing back up the ladder with Jamie's hands steadying it. They finished installing the window panel and gladly retreated back inside the warm haus, with November's chill clinging to the air and nipping at their faces.

The next few hours were filled with laughter as Jamie attempted to help in the kitchen by cooking dishes for the next day. Aubrey stood beside the dining room table, never far from his side, placing the crisp celery stalks in glass vases with a smile permanently etched on her face. Whenever their eyes caught, his heart fluttered, and it was impossible to keep his imagination from running wild.

This time tomorrow Aubrey would be his fraa. No matter how many times he said that, it still sounded sweet to him. The thought of falling asleep with Aubrey wrapped in his arms and feeling the soft strands her hair all around him, free from her white kapp, drew shivers. He still remembered last summer when the wind had ripped Aubrey's kapp free from her hair and how the fair strands had tangled around her face wildly.

They finished their preparations for the wedding, decorations placed in the cool pantry to keep the celery as crisp as possible.

"How about you two go for a walk?" Katie suggested then.

Jamie caught her pointed glance and nodded. With Aubrey's birthday today and the wedding tomorrow, her maem knew it would be impossible to shoo Aubrey from the kitchen or haus. That was why she had recruited him to take Aubrey out of the haus for an hour so she could bake a birthday cake and put together a birthday dinner as a surprise.

"That's a gut idea," he said.

Aubrey, however, frowned at them both. "Nee. We still have to bake the cream of celery and-"

"We can do that all when we get back," Jamie said.

She opened her mouth to protest, but Katie shooed them both out of the kitchen. "Get out, both of you. Whatever isn't done we can do in a little bit."

Jamie tugged a resistant Aubrey down the narrow hallway and grabbed their coats from the wooden pegs. He shrugged into his before helping Aubrey into hers and stepped out in the late afternoon with Aubrey's delicate hand entwined with his. They walked along the driveway to the main road and for a while they were both silent other than the gravel crunching underneath their shoes.

"So," Aubrey started, swinging their hands between them. "Are you ready for tomorrow?"

"More than ready. You?"

"Jah. Of course. Just think, tomorrow you won't have to go home."

A grin tugged at Jamie's lips. He let go of Aubrey's hand to wrap his arm around her shoulders firmly, and in return she draped her arm around his waist. They walked slowly past the fields and hauses with smoke curling from the chimneys.

It was the first time since they had been published by the church that a sense of calmness filled him. The past few weeks had been so hectic and stressful, from Jamie's near fatal wounds to Aaron's pending acceptance of their marriage, that Jamie had had little time to enjoy the idea of being married. His nerves had tainted that, but now, with his arm draped around her shoulders like she was made perfectly to fit in the curve of his elbow, all those nerves lifted to the heavens above.

They paused at the split in the road and gazed in the direction of their new haus, which would be done early spring.

"I can't wait until the haus is done," Aubrey commented, snuggling up to him. "I love my family, but I want my alone time with you."

Jamie pressed a kiss to the top of her kapp. "Me too. Although I like your family more than I like mine sometimes."

"That's horrid thing to say about your own family."

"Your family drives you crazy just as much as mine does sometimes."

"Good point. I can't argue with that."

They started back down the road toward Aubrey's haus. A companionable silence filled the space between them as they walked and they returned just in time to find Katie and Sadie frosting a chocolate cake.

"Is this why you wanted me to leave?" Aubrey asked,

grinning widely. "And you're all forgiven for kicking me out since you baked my favorite cake."

Katie laughed as she hugged Aubrey tightly to her and pressed a kiss to her cheek. They all sat around the kitchen table to eat braised beef, buttery mashed potatoes, and green beans with garlic butter before slicing Aubrey's birthday cake. Jamie sat next to Aubrey, with his hand resting on her knee between the table, his jaws aching from the constant smile on his lips.

When ten o'clock approached, Jamie reluctantly left the warm confines of the haus to hitch up his buggy. Aubrey returned shortly after that from the kitchen with a mug of steaming tea for him to take on the ride back.

"Danka," he said, taking the warm mug gratefully. "I don't want to leave, but I'd better get going since we are going to have an early day tomorrow."

"Jah. You better get some rest, but I don't want you to go either."

Aubrey wrapped her arms around his waist and hugged him tightly. Balancing the mug in one hand and careful not to spill any liquid on them, Jamie hugged her back just as tightly. He brushed a soft kiss on her lips and took a step back. If he didn't leave now, he would never leave.

"Come tomorrow you'll be my fraa."

"And come tomorrow you'll be my mann."

"And we won't ever have to part."

"Nee. Not one single night."

He climbed into the buggy, cradling the warm mug between his thighs as he gathered the leather reins and flicked them lightly. Halfway up the road, Jamie turned around to glance one last time at Aubrey. She stood near the barn, arms crossed tightly over her chest to keep warm, and waved goodbye one last time before starting toward the haus.

Come tomorrow night he wouldn't have to make the long ride home in the bitter cold. Tomorrow night he would be asleep alongside Aubrey, and the thought warmed him for the rest of the ride home in the dark.

CRSO

The haus was full of movement for such an early hour. Aubrey sat at the table where her family gathered for breakfast and shoveled a couple of bites of scrambled eggs into her mouth. In less than a few hours, the community would gather in their home and there would be church and then the wedding.

Aubrey fidgeted anxiously in her chair as she waited for the rest of her family to finish eating at what felt like a snail's pace. She shot up the second Daniel set his fork down and grabbed the plates to wash them. Ignoring her daed's teasing stare, she shot to her bedroom with Sadie right behind her.

"I can't believe you are getting married," Sadie said, giggling. "It still doesn't feel real to me."

Carefully pulling out her blue dress from the closet, Aubrey laid it down on her bed so they could stare at it together. Giddiness rushed through her at a dizzying pace. Outside, the trot of horse's hooves drew Aubrey's attention to the window. All three of her bridesmaids had arrived early, as they had all promised.

For the next few hours, Aubrey's room was filled with excited chatter as they readied themselves. Downstairs, their community began to gather in the carefully-arranged living room to fit as many people as possible. Their voices reverberated up through the floorboards as Hannah carefully pinned Aubrey's wedding dress and then motioned for her to sit on her desk chair so Elizabeth could pull her hair back into a smooth bun.

"You look so beautiful, Aubrey!" Lily gushed. "That color brings out your eyes. My bruder is so lucky have you."

Aubrey grinned as Elizabeth gently set her prayer kapp on her head and made sure that it was pinned perfectly as well. "Have you seen Jamie in his bowtie yet?"

"Jah. I wish we Amish could take pictures, because I want to see how goofy he looked ten years from now."

They laughed lightly. Aubrey wished they could take a picture as well, since Jamie would only wear his bowtie once, but mentally told herself that she would have her memories of this day.

Hymns started, as they usually did. Except this time Bishop Abraham ushered both her and Jamie into the kitchen to talk to them privately. Standing there in the stuffy kitchen, with Jamie's hand clutched tightly in hers, a surreal cloud surrounded her as she took in Jamie's bowtie with a smile. Abraham questioned them, as he always did couples to be married, to make sure they were ready for marriage and the lifelong commitment.

Aubrey stared into Jamie's eyes. There was no doubt in her heart. She wanted to be his fraa for the rest of her life and this was where she belonged. Her thoughts flew to her desk, where the yellow envelope was located, but a tender squeeze of Jamie's fingers brought her attention back.

They were ushered back in front of the crowd of beaming faces, where the Bishop Abraham announced them fraa and mann with Gott's blessing. Quiet cheers and clapping broke out as Aubrey clutched at Jamie's hands to keep herself rooted to the ground. Otherwise, she felt like she would've floated away to heaven then and there.

The crowd immediately broke apart to rearrange the furniture and make room for the tables. Aubrey watched as her lovely bridesmaids rushed to grab the celery decorations and set plate after plate of food on the table. Sensing Jamie's eyes, she turned around to look up at him smiling down at her. Not caring that there people bustling around them, she reached up to caress his jaw gently. Starting today, he would allow it to grow as a sign of his marital status, and a possessive thrill filled her, knowing that any Amish women he encountered would know he was married.

The celebration carried on for the next few hours, as all Amish weddings did. They were filled with laughter and joy, but in particular there seemed to be more happiness lingering in the air than usual. Since there were a few hours left in the day and it was relatively warm out, they decided to move things into the barn for further singing and celebration.

Aubrey stood at the edge of the crowded room, a headache beginning to pound from the constant chatter and chairs screeching along the floorboards. She needed a moment alone to soak in the morning's events.

"Are you alright?" Jamie asked.

"Jah. I'm fine. I just need to step out for a moment."

Jamie pressed a kiss to the back of her hand and nodded in understanding. She managed to squeeze through the crowds of well wishers and had to stop several times to exchange hugs. By the time she reached the stairway, her face radiated heat from the stuffiness inside the haus and the crowd inside.

Her room was blissfully quiet. Nee, Aubrey thought with a shake of her head, not her room. The room belonged to her and Jamie now, until they were able to finish their own haus in the early spring.

The cool breeze caught Aubrey's attention. She crossed over to the window, rubbing her arms against the chill, and closed it. Noticing her desk drawer ajar, she rested her fingers on the brass handle for a moment before tugging it open.

A loose piece of paper was folded directly over the yellow envelope. Aubrey's heart thumped hard as she picked up the two items and opened the folded paper first.

Aubrey,

You were the most beautiful bride I've ever seen. The ceremony was wonderful from where I peered in through the living room window. Don't worry. No one saw me, as everyone's attention was on you like it should be.

I wish desperately that I could've been standing there with you as a bridesmaid.

I love you.

Emma

P.S. Check out the card too, and sorry for the broken window. It was the only way I could think of to get things to you. I'm pretty sure daed would've shot me if I'd tried to sneak in.

The card was something an Englischer would buy in a store. On the front, a large cartoon drawing of a mouse was holding a sign that said "Happy 18th Birthday" and the inside was blank beside the mini paragraph Emma had written.

Happy Birthday, my beautiful sister. I think about you every day and night and hope you are well. I wish I could be there to celebrate and have maem's birthday cake, but rules are rules. Don't worry about me. I am doing fine on the outside. If you ever want to find me, contact Michelle Brown, an Englischer who lives in Monte Vista.

Aubrey grinned at the rather cheesy card, but it slowly faded as her sister's words sunk in. She had been here for the wedding, just like Aubrey had asked and prayed for. Except here she was only married for an hour and already holding secrets from Jamie. Her fingers tore the note and card up before she could even think about saving them. This was no longer important or right. After fighting for so long to have happiness and finally be with Jamie, the risk wasn't worth it.

Crossing over to the window, Aubrey pushed it open, allowing the shreds of paper to trickle away in the breeze. She watched them flutter to the ground like a small snowfall and turned around right as Jamie walked in through her bedroom door, no longer having to mind the rules. They were fraa and mann now after all.

Jamie tilted his head to the side curiously. "What are you doing?" he asked, frowning at the open window behind her. "You're letting all the cold air in and we have to sleep in here tonight."

Her stomach twisted at the thought and from the way Jamie's eyes deepened to a sapphire color, as they always did right before they kissed. Before he could lean down to do so, Aubrey placed her palm over his beating heart. The steady thump felt calm and assuring beneath her hand.

"I was throwing away something," she whispered.

"Ach?"

"I lied to you earlier about who threw the rock at my window. It was Emma."

The muscles in Jamie's chest tensed at Emma's name. Aubrey stepped out of the way to motion toward the ground below her window.

"I tore up the letters though, and threw them out the window. Look for yourself."

Jamie pushed the curtain out of the way and peered down at the ground, where pieces of paper fluttered along the ground. He looked back up then, a smile beginning to curl his lips up. "Does that mean you picked me over your sister?"

"I've always picked you. I stayed because of you."

They kissed each other in front of her window, in the patch of sunlight, with a chilly November breeze surrounding them. Mindful of the crowds still gathered downstairs to celebrate their new marriage, they pulled back, but kept their hands twined.

"Together forever?" Jamie said, holding their hands up to kiss them.

"Always and forever."

She prayed then to Gott, thanking Him for the special day and her union with Jamie. None of it would have happened without His blessings. She prayed even harder then that her slips in faith since joining the church wouldn't come back to haunt her in a future that now involved Jamie.

Aubrey glanced out the window before following Jamie out of their room. In the distance, the slender shape of a young woman with blonde hair still streaked black leaned casually against a tree at the edge of their farm. There was no mistaking Emma, even from afar, and she looked like an Englischer.

She turned her back on Emma before the temptation could overwhelm her. This was her life now, Emma no longer a part of it since she had taken the vow, even when her sister seemed determined to be a part of it somehow by hanging back in the shadows.

Aubrey prayed harder then that she could resist it for

Jamie's sake.

End of Book 2

3.AMISH LOSS

ርଃ CHAPTER 1 ᔂ

Spring arrived with warm sunlight and several packets of seeds to plant in the freshly tilled dirt. Aubrey tilted her head back, rejoicing in the warmth on her skin, and a smile graced her face. The clink of a hammer hitting a nail echoed in the quiet Sunday afternoon. Normally, they would've visited with family today since Sunday was their day of rest and Fellowship, but Jamie had insisted upon finishing their haus and farm.

Aubrey turned in the direction of the sound of hammer and to where her mann was currently hunched over a chicken coop. Hammer looped through the belt of his black suspenders, Jamie inspected his work carefully by smoothing his palm over the wood. The midmorning sunlight danced over the blonde fuzz of the beard that tickled the back of her neck in the middle of the night, and he reached up to tug on the end, a habit he'd recently started whenever he was in thought.

She started down the porch steps, a packet of seeds clutched lightly in her hand, and stopped on the other side of the chicken coop. Jamie looked up at her approach and blue orbs sparkled happily up at her.

"What do you think?" Jamie asked. He looked down at the chicken coop in pride, patting the top of it and then propping his hands on his slender hips. "We'll have a couple of chickens to start off with at least."

"It looks wunderbar, Jamie."

They shared a smile before turning their attention to the patch of land that now belonged to them. Their little house, two stories with four bedrooms and two bathrooms, stood strong and proudly in its fresh coat of white paint. Aubrey had set various pots for flowers on the front porch and helped Jamie place a stone path to the front porch. Their days never seemed to end, with Jamie remaining busy at the furniture store carving furniture for their haus and with Aubrey helping her maemm reopen the bakery. After living in her parent's haus during the harsh winter months, they had been more than ready to start building their haus at the first signs of spring. The community held a barn raising after their haus was built, and a few neighbors even offered to trade some livestock for Jamie's talents in furniture carving and Aubrey's knack at baking apple pies.

That had been the first thing they planted--an apple tree that benefited Jamie more than the community--and Aubrey kept busy in the kitchen for the last remaining months of the winter season. Now, with a haus, barn, fenced in fields, and tilled plots for a garden and crops, they were ready to support themselves without the generosity of their community and families.

Jamie lifted his straw hat to dab away the sweat gathering underneath, and his stomach gave a loud rumble. He turned to look at a bemused Aubrey, a sheepish grin spreading across his face. "I guess I'm hungrier than I thought I was earlier."

"I told you to eat more this morning at breakfast." Aubrey said, shaking her head at him in bemusement. "I'll fix you a sandwich to eat."

"Danka."

She left him there to wrap chicken wire around the coop and stepped into the coolness of her roomy kitchen. Jamie had certainly gotten carried away when building, giving them a large kitchen and dining area. Many of their rooms were the same way, and they even had two fireplaces, one on each of the upper and lower levels. Aubrey had originally protested about having two fireplaces, as such luxuries were not really needed in the Amish world, but Jamie's response ended her protests. "I won't let you or our future kinner freeze at night, so we have two fireplaces."

She considered herself one lucky fraa to have a mann who was filled with ambition and an abundant flow of creative projects he always seemed to have inside his mind.

The pantry was directly below the haus, and they stored certain foods down there. She went to their ice box, too big to fit in the kitchen, and grabbed a package of sliced beef her maemm had given them last night. She hurried up the narrow steps and closed the door behind her, walking through the utility room and back to the kitchen. She had just dipped a knife into a jar of mayonnaise they had bought at the English grocery store in Monte Vista when the trot of horse hooves caught her attention.

Aubrey set the knife down on the counter, careful to keep the mayonnaise part propped up on the lid, and leaned over the kitchen sink to peer out the window. She recognized her family's buggy and Sadie's fair head beneath her white kapp. Concerned by her sister's unannounced appearance, Aubrey hurried out of the kitchen and down the back porch steps.

She reached the lawn right as Sadie jumped down from the buggy with Jamie's help and turned to face Aubrey. The tight lines around Sadie's eyes and her pinched lips aroused even more concern. A list of things that could have happened flashed through her mind rapidly: their daed falling ill again or their maemm collapsing in the garden from exhaustion.

"Sadie," Aubrey said, taking her sister's hand in her own, "What is it? Are Mama and Papa all right?"

"Jah. They're fine, I promise."

Aubrey let out a relieved breath, but the tightness in her sister's face didn't fade away. The lines deepened even more as Sadie fidgeted on the balls of her feet, wringing her hands together in an agitated motion.

"I think there is something you need to know that we found out today."

"Ach?"

Sadie let out a heavy sigh. "Last night Mama and I were riding back from the store with some tea for Papa, and we ran into Michael."

"Michael?"

Dread coiled her lower belly. There were only two Michaels that Aubrey knew in their community and one of them had left shortly after Emma was excommunicated. "Don't tell me it's Michael Brenneman that you ran into."

The incline of Sadie's head told her it was. Breathless from the anxiety now coursing through her, Aubrey began to twist her own hands in agitation. She looked up to find Jamie's eyes flicking between them in confusion.

"Who's Michael Brenneman?"

Aubrey debated on telling him, but this was her mann. She had promised no more secrets. "Do you remember what I told you about my sister, Emma?"

"Jah?"

"Well, Michael Brenneman was the one she truly wanted to marry."

Jamie's eyes hardened instantly. He knew what that meant, even if Sadie and Aubrey didn't say it out loud. It meant that Michael Brenneman was in their community, and he would ask the church for forgiveness of his sins and to come back. It also meant that Emma could possibly follow him.

CRISO

"I just thought you should know before anybody else told you," Sadie said, fidgeting with the reins.

"Did you talk to him?" Aubrey asked. She avoided Jamie's eyes, keeping her eyes focused unwaveringly up at her younger sister. "Did he say that he was coming back to the church?"

"Jah. He said that he wanted to come back and planned to talk to the church about it."

Jamie flattened a hand over his hair, sighing in aggravation. This was the last thing he wanted to hear when things were finally peaceful and content. They had recently moved into their new haus, began their planting for the harvest season, and were praying for a bobli to start their family. He studied Aubrey's face from the corner of his eye. She chewed on her bottom lip anxiously, face pinched in an indescribable expression as they fell into a tense silence.

"If the church lets him come back," Jamie said eventually. Coming back to the church after abandoning one's vows wasn't easy. There was a confession of sins in front of the whole church, a reinstatement period that lasted for a couple weeks, and then questioning whether accepting the Ordnung would be a problem again. It wasn't very common for anyone to come back after leaving the church. "There's a good chance that he won't handle coming back. If he left-"

"He left because Emma left," Aubrey cut in, scuffing the bottom of her work boot against the gravel road. "He didn't leave because he couldn't accept the Ordnung. He left because Emma wouldn't confess to the church what they'd done and they were both most likely going to be shunned."

"They were both going to be shunned? What happened?" He looked between Aubrey and Sadie, both their faces a red shade similar to a beet root. At Aubrey's pointed stare, he felt himself redden too in realization. He remembered a couple back in Lancaster that had been caught in a moment of intimacy, and they were both spared the shunning, but their terrified faces were still etched clearly in his mind.

He found himself staring at Aubrey's flat stomach, picturing a baby bump there and their bobli growing safely. He couldn't wait until that day and prayed every night for Gott to bless them with a bobli.

"I better get back home before maemm notices that I've been gone for too long," Sadie said.

They exchanged goodbyes before Sadie turned the buggy around and went back up the road in the direction of her home. Jamie draped an arm over Aubrey's shoulders and drew her into him, resting his chin on top of her head. "Please don't overthink this. Nothing may come out of Michael being here."

"Maybe," Aubrey mumbled, arms wrapping around his waist tightly. "I can't help but wonder why he's coming back here after all this time. You know that people normally never come back after they leave the church."

Jamie sighed. "I have no idea, Aubrey. Maybe he realized that the English life isn't what he thought it was. Either way, it has nothing to do with us now."

"How would either one of us know? We never left the community for rumspringa."

He drew away at that and looked down at his fraa, the one he would spend the rest of his life with. The freckles he dearly loved peppered her cheekbones and there were a couple of new freckles on the curve of her nose. He smoothed a hand down her arm and laced their fingers together, bringing their joined hands up to give hers a brief kiss. A perk of being married meant that they no longer had to hold back from one another.

"Where's all this coming from?" he asked softly, staring down at the pale blue irises shimmering up at him. The center of his chest burned in anxiety at the indecisiveness crossing Aubrey's face. "I thought we moved past all these troubles before we were married."

"I know, and we have moved on from them." She gave him a reassuring squeeze and pecked his lips with a light kiss. "I promise not to overthink it any more. It has nothing to do with us now or in our future. I will fix us a snack and then start on dinner."

She slipped out of his arms before anything else could be said. Jamie remained motionless for a few minutes, gazing around from their tilled garden, haus, and the barn that would shelter animals soon. How blessed were they? Jamie bowed his head in silent appreciation of all the things Gott had given him. It was also the reason he had begun to pray for protection.

Michael Brenneman. The name left a sour aftertaste on the tip of his tongue. He had no idea who he was exactly, but he symbolized a door to Emma from what information he had gathered from Aubrey and the community. If she truly loved Michael, she would consider coming back to the community to follow him, or so he gathered from the conversations he'd had with Aubrey.

Movement in the kitchen window caught Jamie's attention. He watched as Aubrey busied herself preparing them a snack, like a dutiful fraa. If he wanted to be a dutiful mann that meant protecting his family from unsafe situations.

He entered the kitchen through the back door to tell Aubrey, "Make sure to have breakfast an hour early tomorrow."

Aubrey blinked at him in surprise. "Ach? Where are you going tomorrow morning so early?"

"To see Bishop Abraham. I have to talk to him about something tomorrow."

CR80

Aubrey walked along the sidewalk to her maemm's bakery. After accepting her job as a teacher for their community part time, she missed working alongside her family and oftentimes stopped by after school, with Isaac in tow.

She reached the Forrest's bakery with Isaac and found the parking lot empty as they crossed it to the front door. The familiar smells of sugar and freshly baked breads filled Aubrey's nose pleasantly, the smells of her childhood. Her sneakers squeaked on the linoleum floor as she followed Isaac behind the display cases and into the kitchen.

Pies lined the counter and cookies were stacked artfully on plates, but the rest of the kitchen was currently a mess from flour and sugar dusting the counters. Aubrey arched an eyebrow at the scene in front of her.

"What is going on in here?"

Sadie looked up from the pie that she was frantically

crimping. Her face tightened in distress, looking around the messy kitchen and then back at Aubrey. "There was a last minute order and then maemm had to leave to run a quick errand. Can you help me please?"

"Can you wash all the dishes, Isaac?" Aubrey said, nudging her bruder in the direction of the sink. He scowled at her, but gathered the dirty dishes scattered around the kitchen and did what he was told. She rolled up the sleeves of her dress and grabbed the nearest bowl, glancing briefly at the apple mixture. "How did you get so far behind? I told you to-"

"I've had to take over your job after you left, Aubrey. It hasn't been easy trying to run this bakery short one hand."

"Why won't maemm hire anyone else to help?"

"Something about it being too much money right now."

She swallowed down the guilt coating her throat. It hadn't been easy on her family, particularly her maemm, when she'd moved out with Jamie to start their own life and family. They still stopped by every other Sunday to visit, but Aubrey's old responsibilities had fallen upon Sadie's shoulders. Her sister had never complained once though, even when it was stressful.

They worked together wordlessly to finish baking the last of the pies and clean up the kitchen. The front door jingled open as Aubrey pulled an apple pie out of the oven.

"Can you get that?" Sadie asked. Her hands, buried in bread dough, continued to knead without pause.

Aubrey slipped off the oven mitts and hurried to the

front of the bakery, wiping her hands clean on her apron. She froze when she recognized the man standing in front of the display case, shifting from foot to foot a bit nervously.

Michael Brenneman wasn't hard to recognize. He was the tallest man Aubrey had ever seen in her life and big boned (or how Emma put it), easily towering over own daed and Jamie. His jet black hair was tousled and still cut short, but it was the shadow of a beard along his jaw that had Aubrey staring at him in perplexity.

"Wow, Aubrey. You look all grown up now," Michael said, his deep voice booming in the bakery. "And you're wearing a blue dress, so that tells me that you must have gotten married recently."

"Jah. Last November."

A million questions swirled around her mind. Did he know where Emma was? Did he know if Emma would be coming back? This was the one man Emma had truly loved. Aubrey briefly wondered whether Emma would consider coming back to the community to be with Michael.

"Well, congratulations," Michael said and smiled hesitantly. "I'm happy to see that you are happy."

"Danka." When another tense silence followed, Aubrey couldn't stand it any longer. She had to ask, even though she had promised Jamie she wouldn't worry about it. "Do you know where my sister is?"

Michael blinked at the question. He stared at Aubrey in surprise, shoving his hands into the front pockets of his jeans. "I had been hoping you would tell me that she was here..."

Disappointment curled within Aubrey. After seeing her briefly outside their family's home at her wedding, there had been no contact. Despite how happy she was with Jamie, she couldn't help but worry and wonder where she had gone. "Nee. She only came back once last summer and that was because of me. I know she witnessed my wedding too."

"That's because I think she is somewhere here in Monte Vista or close by somewhere. I've seen glimpses of her, but I'm pretty sure she's avoiding me. Who could blame her?"

He grinned humorlessly before tapping a finger on the display case. "Could I possibly buy this one? I haven't had an Amish pie in a while."

"Of course."

Aubrey reached into the display case and grabbed an apple butter pie. She scooted it carefully across the glass counter and waved away the ten-dollar bill held out for her to take. "Don't worry about it. We were just going to take it to someone else after work anyway."

"Danka." Michael smiled appreciatively, scooping up the pie. "You've probably heard that I'm hoping to come back."

I had been hoping that Emma would be coming with you, Aubrey thought with a sigh. "Sadie told me that she ran into you at the general store. Why are you coming back? I mean, Emma will never come back, so why are you coming back?"

"I guess the English life isn't what I thought it would

be," Michael stated, picking at the cellophane absently. "I ended up living in California for a while and met someone there. I couldn't help but think that it wasn't so bad, but then..." Tears suddenly surfaced in Michael's hazel eyes and a flicker of intense pain filled them. "There was a driver who had too much to drink, and you can guess the rest of what happened."

Aubrey's heart ached for him. It seemed like so much tragedy happened after leaving the church, like Gott's grace and protection truly left them. She had seen the same haunted look on Emma's face last summer, the same sort of lost emptiness that they weren't even aware of.

It made her feel incredibly lucky to have stayed behind, to have married Jamie and made the right decision.

"If there is anything you need, don't hesitate to ask," Aubrey said. "I know that the church will put you through a reinstatement period, but I promise to put in a good word for you."

"Unlike your mann?"

Aubrey stared at him in bafflement. At the dark look Michael sent her, dread promptly found its way home in her stomach again.

"I have to talk to Bishop Abraham..."

"What did my mann say to Bishop Abraham?"

Michael shrugged his shoulders indifferently. "Nothing new. I can't be trusted if I left the church to live an English life, and I won't ever be able to accept the Ordnung if I left it before. He really doesn't like Emma, does he?"

She reached up to run her fingers over her face in

wordless frustration. Some part of her really wasn't surprised. Jamie had made it clear several times after they were married that he would take care of her spiritually and protect her; not for control or anything like that, but because he loved her.

Emma's skeletal frame haunted Aubrey's dreams sometimes. For someone who had claimed to be so happy, she had looked so lost and even sick. Michael didn't fare much better from the bags under his eyes and the slight pop of his cheekbones.

"He's afraid that Emma will try to tempt me into leaving again."

"She tried to make you leave before?"

Aubrey pinched the bridge of her nose. She was sure that having this conversation with Michael was inappropriate. Then again, he wasn't part of the church anymore. Though their daeds didn't like each other for whatever their reasons, she had no particular problem with Michael.

"Well, it was mostly my fault. I wasn't sure if I wanted to stay or go."

"Hmm," Michael pursed his lips in thought, "you probably did the right thing though by staying behind. Things aren't all that glorious out there. I've wanted to come back for a while now, but how could I with a wife and kid born outside of our faith? Until now, that is."

The door behind them opened, and Sadie appeared with her arms filled with pies. She stopped at the sight of Michael standing in front of the display case, but shot him a friendly smile.

"Hi, Michael. I thought I heard your voice, but I wasn't sure if it was you."

"It's me, enjoying your pies." He lifted said object to prove his point. "Anyway ladies, I better let you both get back to work. It was nice seeing you both."

Aubrey watched him make his way out the door, stooping down slightly so his head wouldn't hit the top of the door frame. She let out a pent up sigh, praying to Gott that she would keep her patience with Jamie tonight when she arrived home.

"I still can't believe he is coming back," Sadie stated, setting the pies on the counter next to Aubrey. "He doesn't look too good though, like he's unwell-"

"I think he lost his wife and kid in a car accident," Aubrey noted.

Sadie's eyes widened at that. "Ach, that's horrible. I will pray for him."

"He needs a lot more than prayers," Aubrey muttered under her breath. She picked up a rag out of habit and began to wipe down the display cases.

"What do you mean? Is something else going on?"

"I mean it's not going to be easy for him to come back here. He has to confess in front of the church and then a family has to be willing to take him in for a short time to see whether he can accept the Ordnung."

"And that's hard to do?" Sadie asked, frowning.

"It probably is if you think about it. We haven't experienced the English life, but Michael has. I don't think it's easy to leave behind all that, or at least that has been my opinion of it."

They were quiet as they closed up the bakery and waited for Katie to return from her errands. Aubrey stood alongside Sadie on the front porch, head tilted back to warm her cool and sweaty skin.

"Danka for being honest with me," Sadie said suddenly, placing a soft hand on Aubrey's shoulder. "I wanted to ask something that has been on my mind since I saw Michael the other day."

Aubrey opened her eyes to look over at her sister, who looked so much like their daed from their matching frowns to hair color. She gestured that she was listening.

"Do you regret not knowing the English life?"

The answer, or at least the right answer, sat on the edge of her tongue. No one had ever asked her that, and she thought about it for a few moments.

Did she regret it?

A part of her knew the answer to that, the honest one, and it terrified her beyond anything.

CHAPTER 2

"You've seen Emma?"

Sadie nodded affirmatively. Her pale blue eyes stared off into the distance as a spring breeze stirred the straps of her prayer kapp. A twinge of jealousy weaved through Aubrey at the unexpected revelation coming from her younger sister. Then a faint flicker of fear followed and grew stronger with each beat of her heart. Not fear for herself, but for Sadie.

She remembered all too vividly the temptations Emma unknowingly stirred and how they almost led her down a dark path away from everything she loved. She feared for Sadie's willpower with her own rumspringa approaching and how tempting it would be for her to follow Emma's footsteps.

"Are you mad?" Sadie asked eventually. She turned to look at Aubrey, uncertainty flickering in her eyes.

When did keeping secrets become second nature to them? Aubrey chewed anxiously on the inside of her bottom lip, the metallic tang of blood overwhelming her tastebuds.

"Nee. I'm not mad, Sadie. I'm just worried about you is all."

Her brow furrowed in confusion. "Worried about me? Why would you be worried about me?"

Aubrey placed her hands on Sadie's shoulders and squeezed the muscles tenderly. She waited until Sadie's eyes locked on hers before speaking softly. "Because I know how tempting Emma makes things sound. Rumspringa is approaching for you and I don't want to see you make a bad decision that could have bigger consequences than what you think."

"Like leaving?"

"Exactly. It's not easy out there, Sadie. I don't know how Emma is fairing-"

"That's why I wanted to tell you that I saw her," Sadie interrupted, curling her fingers around the porch railing. "She's not doing gut, Aubrey. I've never seen her so lost."

"What do you mean?" Aubrey asked. She slipped back to the summer night when Emma had shown up to their parents' haus and mentally ran over the details she could still remember. If she recalled correctly, by now Emma would have married Derek and be halfway through her schooling in New York. What could have possibly gone wrong during that time?

Sadie sucked in a long a breath through her nose and shook her head in wordless dismay. "I couldn't leave after what Emma told me. Derek died a few months ago in Iraq and after that she suffered a miscarriage. She came back here to live with an Englischer who helped her after she was shunned and to be close to us, although she won't talk to maemm or daed."

Her poor sister who used to be so strong. Aubrey's eyes closed as her heart filled with pain, thinking of how Emma must feeling after losing her mann and bobli. She couldn't even imagine losing Jamie or any of their future kinner. The grief of it would surely kill her.

"I can't even imagine..." she started, but succumbed to the frightening emotions churning within her. A soft hand rested on hers in a gesture of comfort and fingers curled around to her palm. For a while they stared across the parking lot, holding each other's hands as they prayed for their oldest sister. After a few moments of gathering her composure, Aubrey turned to look at Sadie questioningly. "Why hasn't she come to me or any of us? I'd think those circumstances would soften Papa's heart. He misses Emma, even though he doesn't say it out loud."

"I don't know why she hasn't come to any of you," Sadie said, shrugging her shoulders. "She said she doesn't want to interfere with your marriage with Jamie or cause problems with you two."

"She wouldn't do that." Even as the words left Aubrey's lips she knew it wasn't entirely the truth. Jamie's dislike for Emma wasn't a secret, and he had good reasons to be wary of her, but tragic circumstances could surely persuade his mind and possibly their parents'. Who were they to turn away someone in need of spiritual guidance and comfort?

"Do me a favor? Tell Emma to meet me tomorrow at my haus."

Sadie's eyebrow arched in alarm. "Are you sure? I know that Jamie would not agree to-"

"I know he wouldn't agree," Aubrey said, rubbing a hand tiredly over her face. "He has every reason to be suspicious, but I think he would understand if I explained everything to him."

I hope, she thought, with an internal grimace. A dull headache scratched at the inside of her temples, and she massaged them in irritation. The steady clop of horse hooves on the asphalt drew Aubrey's attention to where their maemm steered the buggy into the parking lot easily. Her eyes swept up and down Aubrey in concern, taking in her pale face and the tension in her jaw.

"Are you all right, Aubrey? You look as if you are about to be sick."

Aubrey's stomach twisted at the word "sick" and the contents of her lunch threatened to make an appearance. She cleared her throat, pushing the feeling down, and nodded at Katie.

"Jah, I'm fine. Just need a little bit of fresh air, I think."

Sadie briefly caught her eyes as she brushed by her to walk down the porch steps and to the buggy. She inclined her head ever so slightly, a wordless agreement to her earlier request.

The exchange went unnoticed. Katie held the reins in one hand, gazing at her dubiously. "Are you sure that you don't want a ride home? Maybe you need to lie down and have some tea."

"I'll be fine, Mama. I'm just going to walk over to the

furniture store and wait until Jamie's done with work."

"If you need anything, Aubrey, please don't hesitate to ask me. I know you are married, but you are still my dochtah."

Katie stared at her for a moment longer before relenting and guiding the buggy back around.

That's what Emma needed, their mother's kind hands and warm presence. She ran through a list of possible ways to tell their maemm about Emma without telling their daed. He loved all his kinner, but when it came to picking the church or Emma, he would follow the church.

When Aubrey reached Forrest Furniture, her plans to somehow tell Katie about Emma were futile. She was a dutiful Amish wife and that meant keeping nothing from her mann, even when asked to keep a secret.

Jamie looked up from the table that he was currently brushing stain on, wrists fluidly flicking back and forth along the surface. He paused in surprise to see her, but a grin spread shortly thereafter.

"I didn't know you were going to stop by today," he said, carefully setting the brush on the can of stain. Blonde brows furrowed as sapphire depths took in her pale skin and red eyes. "Is everything okay? You look like you've been crying, or you don't feel well."

He came to stand in front of her, a familiar and soothing presence.

Aubrey rested her head against his chest, soaking up the smell of wood and stain with a small smile. "I'm not feeling well," she admitted softly, tilting her head back to look up at him. "I think it's just the warm weather playing on my nerves is all. Can you take a break?"

Jamie glanced over his shoulder to where Henry was busily sanding down a chair. Her daed had entrusted the daily operations to Jamie when a particularly hard bout of flu hit him and so far everything ran smoother than ever. He seemed to thrive with the new responsibility.

"Of course. I'm taking a short break," Jamie hollered to Henry, who nodded his head and continued sanding the chair without pause.

They walked hand in hand out to the field behind the building and, after carefully folding the dry grass to cover the wet ground, Aubrey sat down in relief. The past week she had felt nothing but exhaustion, which even eight hours of sleep or a two-hour nap after chores didn't seem to fix.

"So," Jamie said, wrapping his arms around his folded knees, "why did you need me to take a break? Are you sure everything is all right?"

How could she bring up Michael's visit to the bakery or what Sadie told her without Jamie getting mad? Aubrey bit her bottom lip at the conundrum she faced presently: concern for her sister's wellbeing and worry of her mann's reaction to it all.

"Michael Brenneman stopped by the bakery today," she began, keeping an eye trained on Jamie's face to gauge his reaction. Like she'd suspected, his face tightened at the mention of Michael. "He told me that you spoke with Bishop Abraham about not having Michael come back to the church."

"I only said that because I wasn't sure if Emma would

be coming back with him."

"What do you have against my sister?"

Jamie stared at her like another head sprouted from her. "You're joking, right? I don't have anything against your sister beside the fact that she tried to get you to leave-"

"That's not fair. I wanted to leave."

"-and then told the police a lie about our wedding," Jamie continued as if she hadn't spoken. "Sometimes I think your sister is deliberately trying to ruin things for us. I don't know why, but that is how it feels sometimes."

Tears slipped free from Aubrey's eyes. "That's not what my sister wants. She would never want any of us to be unhappy."

"Then explain it to me, because I'd be happy to change my mind."

Aubrey reached out to trail her fingers over the dry grass and yanked a fistful from the earth, dirt clinging to the roots. She tossed it away in a surge of aggravation, spraying both of them with dirt. Why weren't things simple? As much as she loved Emma, she complicated things. Just mentioning her name brought Katie to tears and stoked Jamie's temper. She didn't even dare mentioning Emma's name to their daed after what had happened.

"I don't know why she does the things she does," she said then, looking back as Jamie watched her patiently. "I just know that she's in trouble and that she's my sister, even if she isn't a part of our faith anymore. I love her just the same. Wouldn't you do everything in the world to protect Lily if you felt like she was in danger?"

Jamie frowned deeply. "Of course I would, but how do you know that Emma is in trouble? You haven't talked to her in almost two years."

"Because she's here in Monte Vista, Jamie. She came back."

Silence.

A vein throbbed on Jamie's forehead as his lips thinned back into a scowl. He stood up abruptly, pieces of dirt and grass flying everywhere at the sudden movement. "I see where this is going and the answer is no. I don't feel comfortable with you talking to your sister since she left our church and abandoned her vows."

She rose unsteadily to her feet. The world teetered dangerously for a moment before straightening out, and she pointed a finger accusingly at him. "You accuse her of abandoning her vows when you are judging her for the reasons she left."

"I'm not judging her. That is what she did, Aubrey. She left and isn't coming back." Jamie took a step toward her, arms crossed over his broad chest. His sapphire eyes glittered with repressed anger. "You need to choose between me and your sister. I suggest you choose wisely."

A sharp pain low in her belly stopped the retort on her tongue. Aubrey doubled over at the unexpected feeling, a wave of dizziness swooping down upon her again. The pain came again in a sharp cramp that left her breathless and brought her to her knees.

Jamie was at her side in an instant, hands cradling her elbows. "Aubrey? What's wrong?"

"I-" She felt something trickle down the side of her leg and glanced down, visibly blanching at the blood stain on the skirts of her dress. "I have no idea what's going on. Something isn't right."

CƦ&SƆ

Jamie's fingers trembled as he paced around the small hospital room. The pain and bleeding had stopped halfway to the local hospital, but it didn't slow the steady rise of nervous fear within him.

"Can you stop pacing? It's giving me a headache."

He pivoted on his heel at the sound of Aubrey's soft voice and took in his fraa laying on the hospital bed, offering him a brave smile. It awed him to no end sometimes how Aubrey could comfort him with just one smile. He gathered her hand in his, mindful of the IV taped on the back of it, and pressed a kiss to her cool knuckles.

"I'm sorry. Do you want me to get the nurse?"

"Nee. I'm fine, Jamie," she said softly, reaching up to cup his jaw with her free hand. "Just stay by my side and hold my hand. Stop pacing around the room."

Jamie eased himself onto the bed, carefully adjusting the little plastic tube that connected Aubrey to the IV drip, and sat alongside her. With their hands linked, it felt nothing bad could possibly happen.

Guilt threatened to swallow him whole when he thought about the past two hours. They had been arguing over Emma's disconcerting appearance and he'd given her a harsh ultimatum--to pick him or Emma. Now, they waited for Dr. Green to come back in and tell them what was going on. He rubbed a thumb along the inside of Aubrey's wrist and tried to remain positive as they both prayed together.

A gentle knock on the door interrupted their prayers. Jamie slid off the side of the bed, hand still twined firmly with Aubrey's, when Dr. Green walked back in with a folder and a thick packet of papers in hand. He eyed the items nervously, but patiently waited for Dr. Green to speak.

"Well, I do have good news and bad news," Dr. Green started, tucking the packet of papers into his side. "The good news is that we got the blood work back, and it is showing the hormone called Human Chorionic Gondotrophin, or to put it simply, hCG. Do you both know what that means?"

Jamie's heart twisted in a painful knot. He had no idea what hCG meant, but it sounded serious. The pressure around his fingers drew his attention back to Aubrey. Her mouth thinned into a timid line, and fear glimmered brightly in her pale eyes.

"No," Jamie said breathlessly. "We don't know what that means. Is it serious?"

The corners of Dr. Green's lips turned up into a grin. Jamie turned to look at Aubrey in wordless confusion, and she shook her head at him, equally baffled by Dr. Green's behavior.

"It's a hormone that is produced once a placenta is formed." At their still confused looks, he continued on in a jovial voice, "In other words, it's known as the pregnancy hormone."

A shocked silence filled the room. Aubrey's eyes widened drastically until her irises were almost replaced by her pupils. She let out a startled gasp, clamping a hand over her mouth, and looked up at Jamie, who sat alongside her, frozen from his own shock. They were going to have a bobli. So many times he had prayed for it to happen and now it had. A rush of joy tickled its way up his spine and left him breathless.

"I'm pregnant?" Aubrey breathed . A bubble of delighted laughter escaped her at Dr. Green's nod. "Did you hear that Jamie? We're going to have a bobli."

Jamie gathered her in a tight embrace, burying his nose in the cotton fabric of the nightgown the nurses had given Aubrey to wear. The smell of starch and bleach filled his nostrils, but underneath that the faint scent of sugar still clung to Aubrey's skin. He closed his eyes in reverence to the moment--to the surge of pride boiling in his veins-- and drew in a trembling breath before answering.

"I heard. Gott answered our prayers."

Dr. Green waited patiently for them to let go of one another. He smiled when they looked at him, matching grins on their faces.

"I imagine this was planned or hoped for," he commented, holding out the packet of papers for Jamie to take. "Now, the bleeding can be from one or two things: 1) we could be at the very early stages of pregnancy, possibly two to three weeks or 2) we are further along and some sort of stress triggered bleeding. Either way I'd like to have a nurse from the family center do an ultrasound and pelvic examination to check things out and make sure that all is okay in there. With your permission."

"Yes, absolutely," Jamie responded immediately.

"Very well. The nurse will be down in a few moments."

When the door clicked shut, Aubrey let out a pent up breath and placed a hand over her stomach in wonder. She looked up back up at Jamie, eyes brimming with tears of nerves and joy. "Do you think everything will be all right?"

Jamie's heart twisted again. His maemm had suffered through a miscarriage once and the grief that followed had been unimaginable to him then. The pit of his stomach fluttered anxiously as he placed a hand on the flat plane of her belly and quietly prayed for Gott's protection.

"I'm sure it will be alright. We're in good care here if something is wrong," he said and pressed a reassuring kiss to Aubrey's brow. She had taken off her prayer kapp while the nurses helped her slip into a cotton nightgown, and the blonde tresses of hair cascaded around her shoulders. She had never looked more beautiful to him than now from the faint glow around her.

"I better call Henry at the store before the nurse comes in here. Do you want me to have Levi bring your maemm here?"

"Jah, please."

Thankfully, the nurse's station was calmer than it had been when they'd first arrived. He politely asked to use the phone and then called the furniture store.

"Forrest Furniture. This is Levi."

"Levi, it's Jamie."

"Jamie? Is everything okay with Aubrey? Henry told me that she collapsed in the field and you took her to the hospital."

"Everything's fine." I hope, Jamie thought to himself, but continued assuringly. "They will do some tests here in a few minutes, but I wanted to ask if you could get your maemm. I think there will be a certain test Katie might want herhere for, as moral support."

"Of course. I'll close the store now."

"Danka."

He gave the phone back to the nurses and went back to Aubrey's room. The nurse, a middle aged Englischer with grey-streaked hair and dressed in blue scrubs, stood at Aubrey's bedside, writing something on a chart. She turned to smile warmly at Jamie.

"Ah, this must be the new father-to-be. Congratulations, young man," she chirped in a kind tone and flourished her chart. "I was just getting some details from your wife that we needed for our files while we wait to wheel Aubrey over to another room for an ultrasound."

Jamie nodded politely, taking a post by Aubrey's side again.

"I called your bruder and he will tell your maemm," he told her, smoothing a strand of hair back from her forehead. "I thought you'd be more comfortable with her in the room for the, um, other examination."

The center of his cheeks colored, but Aubrey smiled up at him in appreciation.

"We are waiting until your mother arrives for the pelvic exam?" the nurse asked, pausing in her notes.

"Yes. I hope that's-"

"Of course it is, dear. You don't have to explain anything to me. I'm Valerie by the way, the head nurse of the family center here." She offered a hand for Jamie to shake, her frail looking fingers squeezing his with surprising strength. "Now, I know that you both are Amish obviously and where your beliefs are, but I still think it would be a good idea to inform you both as much as possible while you are here."

The next hour flew by in a surreal blur of information. Valerie took every bit of time explaining the stages of pregnancy, some of the symptoms Aubrey would possibly have later, and many things that Jamie didn't understand. A headache pounded dully at the back of his head when they wheeled Aubrey down to an even smaller room filled with strange looking equipment. While another nurse rubbed a blue liquid all over Aubrey's stomach, Valerie took position near a monitor, pointing to certain things.

"So here is the uterus," Valerie said, ignoring the embarrassed grimace on both their faces, "and that little jellybean right there is your baby. From looking at everything, I'd say you are about eight weeks pregnant. Would you like to hear the heartbeat?"

Aubrey nodded eagerly, staring up at the screen in fascination. She grabbed hold of Jamie's hand and squeezed tightly. Images flicked around on the screen before focusing on a small little bundle, and a whooshing noise filled the little room. He stood by Aubrey's side, awed at the sound of a little heartbeat and overwhelmed from the day's events.

They returned to the same room and found Katie waiting inside anxiously. She stood from the chair she had been seated in the second they walked into the room and burst into tears before leaning over the bed to hug Aubrey fiercely.

"The nurses told me. I can't believe you're going to have a bobli!" she cried, tears streaming down her cheeks. "This is wunderbar news! What did they say?"

Aubrey patted her maemm back a bit awkwardly for the emotional display. "They said I'm about eight weeks along, and we heard the heartbeat. The doctor wants...well...could you stay for an exam?"

"Jah, of course," Katie said, nodding her head. She turned to look at Jamie uncertainly. "If you're all right with it Jamie..."

"Jah," Jamie said. He wanted nothing more than a few moments of quiet and peace to digest everything. "You'd be better support than me for this exam."

He had been able to comfort Aubrey through them drawing blood and everything else, but the other exam sounded like a little too much for him.

Katie looked away politely when they exchanged a brief kiss.

"I'll be in the lobby," he informed them before slipping out of the room and down the hallway. Instead of using the elevator, which had been an unnerving experience, Jamie jogged down the stairs to the downstairs lobby and passed what looked to be some sort of food service area where Englischers were seated in leather booths and eating. He had rounded the corner and started toward the sliding glass door when a pair of familiar piercing blue eyes stopped him.

A young woman stopped in front of the automatic sliding glass doors, staring at him in a mixture of surprise and wariness. Strands of blonde hair slicked back stirred in the warm breeze that rushed to greet Jamie as the doors slid open, and tattooed arms crossed over her chest defensively.

It wasn't hard to recognize her from Aubrey's description.

"What are you doing here?"

❧ CHAPTER 3 ❧

"What are you doing here?"

Emma arched a perfectly shaped eyebrow and tilted her chin up in a silent challenge. "I heard that my sister was in the hospital. So, why do you think I'm here?"

He clenched his teeth to keep himself from retorting back. Englischers parted around them and a warm breeze that smelled faintly of lilacs brushed over him. Emma tried to side step him into the hospital, but he fluidly followed the movement. Jamie squared himself in front the sliding glass doors leading back into the hospital. Protectiveness burned in the center of his chest.

"Are you going to move or not?" Emma snapped, tapping her foot in aggravation. "Look, my sister is up in a hospital room. There's no rules that say I can't visit an ill family member or in extreme circumstances."

"I don't care. You won't see Aubrey. I'm her mann and-"

"And what does that mean? You control who Aubrey sees?"

"How would you know? You don't have a husband."

Tears flooded Emma's eyes instantly. Turmoil swirled around in the blue depths, and she sucked in a watery breath, looking away from Jamie. "My husband died a few months ago." Emma spoke in a hauntingly soft voice that was barely detectable above the warm breeze and the whir of the sliding glass doors opening. "He died while serving in Iraq, so I do know what it's like to have a caring husband."

"I'm sorry," Jamie said. That was all he could think to say. He felt only a small amount of sympathy toward Emma for losing someone she had clearly loved, but he still had to protect Aubrey, and now their bobli, from any sort of stress.

"Are my parents here?" Emma asked suddenly, looking around nervously. "I saw a buggy and-"

"Your maemm is here. I'll tell Aubrey that you stopped by," Jamie offered. He hoped that would be enough to deter Emma for the time being.

He turned to go back into the hospital, sure that the exam would be over by now, but heard the sliding glass doors open behind him. Emma followed, all traces of turmoil now replaced by a fiery determination. The neutral moment around them fell away.

"Nee, Emma," Jamie said, shaking his head. "Leave Aubrey alone. She needs to rest and seeing you is only going to work her up more."

"Why? I'm her sister. How would seeing me work her up?"

Because we were fighting about you returning to

Monte Vista and Aubrey collapsed from the stress.

Jamie stared at Emma intently, taking in the tattoos curling across her skin and the eyebrow piercing. The woman standing in front of him felt broken and lost. He feared that just the sight of Emma would cause an already emotional Aubrey more stress. Especially when she seemed to believe that Emma was returning when something told him she wasn't.

Emma tried to side step him again, but bumped into Jamie when he anticipated the move. She sighed in frustration and pushed at his chest before glaring up at him. "What do you have against me? Why do you hate me?"

"I don't hate you," Jamie said calmly. "I'm just protecting Aubrey from any more stress. She's been through enough for one day."

Before their conversation could go any further, Katie's soft voice echoed in the hospital lobby behind them. "Emma? Is that you?"

Katie slowly approached from behind them. Her eyes glistened as she took in her oldest and shunned daughter.

She came to Jamie's side, twisting her hands nervously in front of her. "Hi, maemm," Emma whispered, tears glittering in her eyes. "I know that I'm not supposed to be here, but I heard about Aubrey being in the hospital, and I came here right away. Is she okay?"

"Is Aubrey done with the exam?" Jamie asked tersely.

At Katie's affirmative nod, he quickly started up the stairs to put distance between him and Emma. A wave of anger skittered through him as he reflected on the day's events again. He wanted nothing more than for the rest of the world to fall away and leave him and Aubrey alone to enjoy their blessed news.

When he entered the small hospital room, Aubrey looked up, her fingers absently playing with the hospital ID bracelet around her small wrist. She smiled up at him when he closed the door softly behind him.

"The nurse says that everything looks good. She said that stress can sometimes trigger bleeding."

Jamie breathed out in relief, taking Aubrey's hand in his again. The feel of her fingers sliding through his eased the tension from his encounter with Emma in the hotel lobby.

"That's gut news. How long will they want you to stay here?"

"A few days. They want to give me fluids and monitor things. After that, we can go home and see the midwife in our community."

"Gut."

Aubrey pulled back to look at him with furrowed brows. "What is it? You look like you're mad."

"Nee," he said, shaking his head with a strained smile. "I just have a headache from everything is all."

It wasn't right to keep secrets from his fraa, but when it came to protecting Aubrey and his bobli, he would do everything he could. Even if that meant keeping Emma as far away as possible until he measured her intentions.

☙❧

The soft click of the hospital door startled Aubrey out of a dream she couldn't remember. She blinked a couple of times to clear the fuzziness from her eyes before rolling onto her back. One of the nurses had come into the room sometime during the evening hours and turned the lights off after Jamie left to take care of the chores around their haus.

"Jamie?" she yawned, rubbing her eyes. "Are you back already? I thought it would take longer to-"

A slender figure ghosted the front of her bed, hiding in the shadows of the room. The familiar Romans tattoo on a pale forearm and piercing blue eyes stood out in the dim lighting. Aubrey bolted into a sitting position, ignoring the pain in her hand from the IV being jerked. She peered more intently at the figure in front of her. The monitor beeping in tune with her heart increased dramatically as she took in her sister for the first time since last November. "Emma?" she whispered.

"Yeah, it's me." Emma stepped into the dim light above the hospital bed and offered a quavering smile. Her fingers hesitantly touched the plastic at the edge of the hospital bed and took in the monitors next to Aubrey.

"Calm down," she begged, watching the frantic bleeps on the monitor. "You don't want the nurses to come in here and kick me out."

Aubrey reached up to place a hand over her heart and inhaled deeply to slow down her heart rate. She was confident that this was a dream brought on by exhaustion and the shock of her pregnancy news. Her maemm had said that the hormones would make her feel a bit different for a while.

Little steps that barely made any noise on the tiled floor brought Emma to the side of her bed in a cloud of a perfume that smelled dimly of rose petals. Her black hair shimmered as it shifted around her slender shoulders in waves. Soft fingers grasped hers warmly as Emma smiled down at her.

"How are you feeling?" Emma asked.

"Gut." A heart beat of silence. "How are you here exactly?"

"I told the nurses that I was your sister and they let me in."

Emma eased herself up onto the side of the bed, carefully moving the remote attached to the bed. She kept one leg draped over the side of the bed and her other leg bent, with her knee touching the side of Aubrey's thigh.

Tears moistened Aubrey's eyes suddenly as the day's events flashed through her mind. She was thankful to have Jamie by her side, but her sister's presence offered a different type of comfort and protection that she'd craved often.

"Everything's going to be all right," Emma said reassuringly, stroking a strand of hair back from Aubrey's face. "The nurses told me you're pregnant and about eight weeks along. Have you heard the heartbeat?"

"Jah. They said the bobli is fine. Stress can-" She stopped, realizing what she was saying to Emma, who had gone through a recent miscarriage after her husband's death.

"Stress can trigger bleeding," Emma finished for her,

nodding in agreement. Emma's shoulders slumped downward, and sharp cheekbones were visible through rosy powdered cheeks. A dispiritedness seemed to fill her like the IV pumping fluid into Aubrey's veins.

Despite the relief of seeing her sister, a current of tension filled the room. If Jamie returned earlier than he'd said and found Emma inside her room, there would undoubtedly be a fight. There was supposed to be limited contact with shunned members now that she was baptized. Apprehension floated through Aubrey thinking of her parent's reactions. She was torn about what to say or to do.

"Sadie told me that you are living in Monte Vista again," Aubrey said.

"For a little while at least," Emma said, looking down at the their clasped hands. "After Derek's death and then the miscarriage, I just couldn't say in New York any longer. I know that daed doesn't ever want to see me again, but at least this way I can be somewhat close to you all again."

"I'm sure daed would understand if-"

"He won't, Aubrey. You and I both know that he'll side with the church before he sides with me," Emma smiled sadly. "This is what I chose, so it's what I expect. I don't want to add any extra stress on you. Are you excited about the baby?"

"Of course. Gott has blessed us with a bobli. We couldn't be more excited," Aubrey said, and then after a moment's hesitation, went on gingerly, "Are you sure that you are okay, Emma?"

Emma laughed sarcastically, but tears glistened in her eyes. "You're the one in the hospital and you're asking me if I'm okay. You truly are a compassionate person."

"That's how we've been raised--to care," Aubrey explained, frowning. "I'm glad you're here, but I'm worried about you."

"Don't worry about me. I'll be fine. I better get going before your husband arrives and finds me in here."

She slipped off the bed gracefully, careful not to tangle herself in the plastic tube connected to Aubrey's IV. Emma straightened the front of her shirt and then pressed a kiss to the center of Aubrey's cheek. "Take care of yourself, Aubrey. You've got a little bobli relying on you to be healthy."

"Wait," Aubrey grabbed Emma's retreating wrist, a small cross tattoo catching her eye. She tried to imagine Emma back in plain clothes, covering up all her tattoos and removing the various piercings dotting her sharp face. Or letting the black strands of hair fade back to its original shade of blonde. She inwardly prayed for Gott's guidance for the idea that came to her mind. "Why don't you come back to the church? They'll forgive you if you confess your sins."

A vein pulsated along the dip of Emma's temple. She chewed on her lower lip for a moment while thinking Aubrey's words over. "I don't know if I could come back," she answered slowly.

"Of course you could," Aubrey gushed in exhilaration at the prospect of having her sister back in the community. "Think about it. You could be back around all of us and Gott would want you to come back. You can't deny that."

"I know," Emma agreed, sighing wearily. She pinched

the bridge of her nose. "It's just not that easy to give up what I've worked for so hard out there. I mean, I love to draw, and not worry about the Ordnung. I like wearing these clothes and not wearing prayer kapps. I like going to school every day. There's nothing wrong with going to school and learning about other things besides how to bake an apple pie."

It struck Aubrey then how vain and selfish her sister had become living as an Englischer over the past few years. Maybe it would be better if Emma stayed on the outside. She couldn't adapt back into their lifestyle, not easily at least, without help. A idea popped into her head.

"Do you remember Michael Brenneman?"

She studied Emma's face as she said those words. The subtle tension in her jaw and eyes narrowing to almost icy glints gave Aubrey all the power she needed to put her plan in motion.

"Yes..."

"Would you consider coming back if Michael Brenneman was back too?"

CR80

Two days later, the hospital discharged Aubrey with a clean bill of health. Jamie folded the packet of papers that Valerie had insisted they take and placed them in the back pocket of his trousers. He then helped Aubrey sit in the wheelchair and started down the hallway.

Aubrey turned around in the wheel chair and raised an eyebrow at how fast they were traveling down the long white hallway. "Are you ready to go home?" she asked teasingly.

"Jah. More than you know."

Sleeping in the uncomfortable chair that folded out into a makeshift bed and then rising even earlier to make it home before work in the morning grated on Jamie's nerves. He respected the English doctors and their expertise, but he was more than ready to bring Aubrey home and back to their community. Being surrounded by the white walls and following strict rules made the hospital feel suffocating.

He glanced down at Aubrey as they waited for the elevator doors to open. She looked thinner than normal thanks to the morning sickness that had appeared over the past few mornings, and her freckles stood out starkly against her pale pallor. Despite all that, Aubrey looked relieved to be leaving the hospital as well.

"Just remember what the doctor said," Jamie said once they were in the elevator and riding down to the lobby. He grabbed the railing inside the elevator and held on uneasily. "No stressing out or anything physically exerting for the new few weeks."

"What about the garden and watering?"

"I'll do it."

"And the laundry on Mondays?"

"You can tell me how to do it."

"What about my kinner at the school house?"

"I told Betty that you were feeling ill and would be back once the doctor said you could return."

Aubrey's face contorted into a grimace. Normal

circumstances, no one would know about Aubrey being pregnant. Pregnancies were private, meant to be between mann and fraa and close family, but he had no other choice about telling Betty. He didn't want her working until the midwife in their community said she could. Even then, he wouldn't mind having Aubrey home and resting until their bobli was born.

"I don't want to just sit around and do nothing all day long," Aubrey stated.

The elevator doors opened. Jamie steered the wheelchair through the busy hallway and out into the warm morning air. He breathed in the lilac-scented air with a sigh. The constant smell of bleach and cleaning supplies had given Jamie instant headaches whenever he walked in after a long day working at the furniture store and tending their crops.

"You have to until the midwife says you can do things again. It's called bedrest for a reason," Jamie said.

They crossed the busy parking lot to the buggy. He helped Aubrey stand shakily, the first time she had stood since coming to the hospital, and climb into the passenger side. Once he was sure that Aubrey could sit alone, he pushed the wheelchair back to the hospital lobby and left it with a nurse.

Jamie had climbed into the seat alongside Aubrey when the trails of tears on her cheeks caught his attention. He immediately dropped the leather reins in concern and scooted to Aubrey's side.

"What's wrong, Aubrey? Are you hurting or-"

"Nee. I just--I just--I don't know how I feel," Aubrey

buried her face in her hands and choked back a cry. "I just want to go home and lay down for a while. I think I'm just tired and the nurse said I would be a bit cranky."

Jamie pressed a kiss to the side of Aubrey's head and gathered the reins again, clucking softly. He kept one eye trained on Aubrey as she tilted her head backward to allow the morning sunlight to dry her tears and a small content smile spread across her face.

They rode along in the warm morning, enjoying the fresh air and quietness of their community. Once they arrived home, Aubrey promptly disappeared to wash for the first time in a couple of days. Jamie dashed around the bedroom, putting on the freshly folded sheets that Katie had been kind enough to wash for them. He'd pulled the thick quilt back when Aubrey entered their room dressed in a cotton nightgown.

"Can I ask you something, Jamie?" she asked, sliding on top of the crisp sheets.

Jamie tucked the sheets and quilts around Aubrey's legs. "You don't even have to ask permission."

Pale blue eyes peered up at him intently, a finger reaching up to hook loosely through one of his. "Why didn't you tell me that Emma stopped by the first day I was in the hospital?"

He tensed at the question. No hint of emotion laced Aubrey's voice as she stared up at him, waiting for an answer. "How do you know about that?"

"Because she told me."

"She--?" Jamie's mouth fell open in silent outrage. "I told her to-"

"Shh, Jamie. Don't get mad. Listen to what I have to say."

Aubrey's fingers laced through Jamie's, eyes looking up at him beseechingly. He took a deep breath, controlling the anger now burning inside of him for Aubrey's sake. The last thing she or the bobli needed was another argument revolving around Emma.

"Emma wants to come back to the church. So-"

"She wants to come back?" Jamie blurted, bewildered. "I thought she said she would never come back."

"She's had a lot of bad things happen this past year. Her mann died and she lost their bobli. I think she wants to come back, but doesn't know how."

Dread now replaced the anger within his chest. He squeezed Aubrey's hand softly, but stared at her in exasperation. "I don't know what you are planning, but I don't think this is wise. You can't convince your sister to come back unless she really wants to return."

"But she does want to come back," Aubrey insisted. "She's already talked to me and our maemm about coming back. Maybe talking to the church will help, and I told her that Michael is back as well."

Jamie groaned loudly. "Aubrey, please don't try to set up those two . You have your own life and marriage to worry about rather than your sister's courting life."

"I'm not trying to set them up. I just suggested that maybe it would be easier to come back to the community with Michael."

"But they won't be able to be together for a while. They'll have to stay with someone during the reinstatement--" He trailed off at the pointed look Aubrey gave him and the realization of why they were having this conversation now hit him. "Absolutely not. Your sister is not staying here. You don't even know whether the church will let her come back."

"She can confess to the church and go from there," Aubrey continued stubbornly.

"If she is willing to confess to the church," Jamie corrected, shaking his head. "That was the whole reason she left. She wouldn't confess to the church about what happened with Michael after they both took their vows."

"She left because she loved Michael."

Jamie sighed in aggravation, running a hand down the side of his face. There was just no arguing with Aubrey when she had her heart set on something that could possibly hurt her gentle nature. He didn't know how Aubrey's conversation with Emma (which apparently had happened sometime when he wasn't around) had gone and a nervousness filled him. There was no doubt in his mind that Emma loved her sister, but she loved her English life more and that would hurt Aubrey.

"Please, just think about it?" Aubrey asked timidly, her eyes almost begging him now. "And it may never get to that point. Maemm will talk to daed and then they are going to talk to the church. She's hoping that maybe daed will be forgiving if he knows that she is willing to come back."

"I promise to think about it," Jamie offered. He squeezed Aubrey's soft hand again and pressed a kiss to her warm forehead, smoothing back a couple of strands of her hair.

"I have to go back to work. Your maemm will stop by here shortly and make sure that you are okay."

"I'll be fine," Aubrey yawned, curling up on her left side as the nurses had instructed her.

For a moment he stood by the doorframe, watching the soft rise of Aubrey's chest as she drifted off to sleep quickly. His eyes focused on the flat plane of her belly, trying to imagine her tiny frame growing as their bobli grew over a matter of months.

Jamie shut the door behind him quietly and stood in the hallway, soaking up the silence. He flattened a hand over his hair, shaking from their conversation and the past couple of days. When would they ever have a moment of peace? He prayed then for Gott's strength and help.

He opened the door on the right and stepped into the small bare room. In nine months there would be a crib, a little dresser to hold clothes, and a rocking chair. He stood in the middle of the room, trying to imagine his daughter or son listening to the silence of their haus or stumbling his way here in the middle of the night to tend to their bobli's cries.

That was what he wanted to protect. Aubrey had such a gentle and compassionate nature that it oftentimes blinded her, especially when it came to her sister's whereabouts. Protectiveness surged through him. He wasn't sure what Emma had planned or if she was serious about coming back to the church, but he needed to talk to the one person who knew Emma.

Jamie exited the haus and left the back door unlocked

for Katie to come through in a few hours to check on Aubrey. Instead of hitching up the buggy, he took advantage of the warm afternoon and walked down the road to the one place he knew that Michael Brenneman would be.

❧ CHAPTER 4 ❧

The soft patter of rain filled the haus soothingly. Aubrey stood in the middle of the spare room, the room that would be their bobli's within a few months, and gazed out the window at the grey clouds. Cool air seeped through the crack in the window and stirred the cotton curtains.

Two weeks of bedrest had gone by with little contact with anyone beside her maemm and Jamie when he returned home from work. The midwife of their community, Martha Lapp, agreed with the English doctors on bedrest until the pain stopped--that meant no cooking, cleaning, or tending to her garden.

Aubrey rubbed at her sore eyes. She missed her daily activities and teaching at the schoolhouse. It all provided a pleasant distraction from the turmoil brewing within her. Especially the accursed morning sickness that really didn't happen just in the mornings, but at all hours of the day and night.

She crossed the dusty floorboards to the window. A cloud of dust tickled her nose and she sneezed in response.

Her lower belly tightened instinctively and then slowly eased into a small cramp.

It was hard to share Jamie's joy of having a bobli. Not because she wasn't grateful for Gott's gift to them, but because of the constant bouts of headaches and sickness. Martha assured her it was quite normal to feel the way she did considering her symptoms.

A buggy appeared down the road with Hannah sitting up front and her daughter Naomi sitting patiently alongside her. Even from a distance Aubrey could tell that the two were mother and daughter, from their matching blue eyes to their fair skin. Naomi was drawing close to two years old and she already had such a personality. It was those little things she eagerly awaited that lessened the miserable feeling.

Her heart lifted at the sight of them. Hannah had been gracious and understanding enough to come over to keep Aubrey company on a rainy afternoon. Elizabeth had been by a few times, whenever she had the chance, and even Lily made an occasional appearance with her maemm while bringing meals.

Hannah gave a little wave when she looked up to the bedroom window before disappearing around the haus and to the barn. She shut the window and hurried out of the empty room to greet them at the back door.

"I brought us some fabric to sew and give you something to do while you're on bedrest," Hannah said.

She set down the piles of colored fabrics on the living room table, including the white fabric for a prayer kapp, and the little sewing kit she brought. Aubrey ran her fingers over the fabric appreciatively while looking over at Naomi as she played peek-a-boo by hiding behind Hannah's apron.

"Danka," Aubrey said.

"Naomi, why don't you take these blocks and play with them over there," Hannah directed, opening her sewing kit to reveal a handful of painted blocks.

Naomi eagerly grabbed them and wordlessly sat down a foot away from the women, stacking the blocks and babbling happily to herself.

They sat side by side on the living room couch as the rainfall strengthened to a downpour. Her bad mood lifted for the first time in a few weeks at Hannah's presence.

"So," Hannah said, nimbly threading a needle, "how are you feeling?"

"I still feel sick always. The only thing I can eat is soup with ginger laced in it."

"It'll get better in time. You remember how sick I was with Naomi?"

Aubrey nodded. "I lost count of how frequently I had to make you tea or send you home for the day."

"Exactly, but it's all so worth it. You just wait until your bobli arrives. It's a love that you've never known and could never compare, watching your bobli grow from a tiny baby to a little person."

Hannah shot a loving glance in Naomi's direction. She continued to sew a small grey dress for Naomi while watching Aubrey picked up a roll of fabric. The last time she had even sewn something small was for Isaac and that had been a few years ago. Trying to guess measurements for her bobli seemed impossible.

"Do you need some help?" Hannah offered kindly.

"Jah. Please..."

She smiled gratefully at her best friend. They spent the next few minutes cutting the right amount of fabric and Hannah showed her how to sew little body suits. Once their bobli arrived, she would help with the dresses or little trousers.

"How is Jamie handling the pregnancy?" Hannah asked.

"He's excited over the bobli. He already started building a crib and dresser."

"That's gut. Has he turned into a completely overprotective daed?"

"Jah," Aubrey said, sighing in exasperation. "How did you guess?"

An amused smile curled Hannah's lips upward. She shrugged her shoulders indifferently, holding up the small dress to inspect the length.

"A lucky guess. I remember Jacob being protective and a bit overbearing at times when we first found out that I was pregnant with Naomi. He kept insisting that I had to say inside and avoid anything stressful."

"That's exactly how Jamie is acting. He won't even let me do the laundry and you should see all his crinkled shirts. I'm lucky that dresses don't wrinkle easily like their shirts do."

"They do try though. We have to give them that. There are some manns who aren't as kind to their fraas as ours."

"I can't even imagine handling this pregnancy without Jamie's patience."

Guilt lodged itself in her stomach. All this time she had insisted upon being stubborn and picking meaningless fights with Jamie while he remained steadfast and patient with her moods. Not once did he bat an eyelash or argue with her.

"I heard something very curious the other day," Hannah remarked.

Aubrey stiffened at the abrupt change of topic. She had an idea of what Hannah might have heard. "Ach? What was that?"

"That your sister is thinking about coming back. Jacob overheard Bishop Abraham talking about it with your maemm."

"She's thinking about coming back. I've talked to her a few times and so has Sadie on a few occasions. She lost her mann a few months ago and a bobli, but I think Gott has brought her back here because she wants to come back."

Hannah didn't reply at first. She pursed her lips in contemplation for a few minutes while slowly setting the half-finished dress on her lap.

"Do you really think your sister wants to come back?"

"Jah. Of course I do. Why would she come back around now after all that has happened?"

"I don't want to say this brashly, but I think your sister is a bit too reckless to come back to Gott."

Her pointer finger throbbed when the needle accidentally pricked it. Aubrey wiped the dot of blood on her apron and tried to control the swell of her emotions. It was harder now to keep them under control. She clenched her teeth in a failing attempt to keep her composure. "She can though. I know that she can if she really wants to."

"That's exactly the point, Aubrey. If Emma wants to commit herself to Gott."

Tears stung Aubrey's eyes. First Jamie, now Hannah... Their lack of faith in her sister hurt deeper than anything.

Hannah laid a hand on Aubrey's trembling knee and offered a sympathetic smile. "I know that it has been hard to be without your sister and nobody is doubting her. I'm only suggesting you be cautious when it comes to Emma. She's been living an English lifestyle for a while and that may not be easy for her to leave behind."

The conversation with Emma back at the hospital echoed in Aubrey's mind. It's just not that easy to give up what I've worked for so hard out there. I mean, I love to draw, and not have to worry about the Ordnung. I like wearing these clothes and not wearing prayer kapps. I like going to school every day. There's nothing wrong with going to school and learning about other things beside how to bake an apple pie.

She sank back against the couch pillows in dejection. What was she thinking? Giving herself hope that Emma would return when the chances of her coming back to their community were slim.

"I'm such a fool," Aubrey whispered. She raised tearful eyes up to Hannah's empathetic ones. "What am I doing, Hannah? I've chosen this lifestyle. I've chosen to forever follow Gott and be with Jamie. Yet, I'm still trying to include my sister in everything."

"I don't know what it's like to have a shunned member in my family, but I can imagine how hard it is. You have a bobli on the way and a good life here, Aubrey. If its Gott's will to bring Emma back, then she'll come back. If not, there's nothing anybody can do to change that."

"I know that. I feel so selfish and-"

"You're not selfish."

"-blind for thinking that I could have things back to the way they were before Emma left."

"Aubrey," Hannah started gently, reaching to wipe a tear away from the corner of her eye. "I know that becoming a maemm is a bit daunting, and it made you want to cling to things from the past, because it's new and scary. I promise that when your bobli is here, everything with your sister will fade away because your heart will be occupied with an even greater love. Okay?"

She nodded while wiping her cheeks dry with the edge of her hand. "I'm sorry. I'm such a crying mess these days."

"Don't worry about it. That's what friends and family are for."

A few hours later, Hannah gathered a sleepy Naomi in her arms and pressed a quick kiss to Aubrey's cheek. She ventured out into the balmy afternoon, the rain having lifted. Aubrey watched Hannah's buggy disappear down the road before going to her garden. She sat down on the little wooden bench Jamie had built for her and inhaled the fresh smell of the blooming lilac bushes. The patch of moist earth was dampened from the earlier rainfall, and she imagined the seeds slowly sprouting underneath. One of the few things that gave Aubrey a sense of pride was her gardening skills, and this year she planned to harvest more than her own family could consume.

Approaching hooves alerted Aubrey that Jamie was home earlier than expected. Now they only had one paycheck to live on and plenty of projects around the haus that still needed to be completed. Jamie's shifts usually started before dawn and lasted well into the evening hours. He did all of this quietly and without complaint, even although Aubrey knew how exhausted he felt from the times she caught him dozing off in the rocking chair while reading.

The buggy came into sight, with Jamie tiredly rubbing his face while holding the reins in his other hand. He pulled to a stop in front of the barn and jumped out gracefully before catching sight of Aubrey in the garden.

"Aubrey? What are you doing outside?" he called, approaching the garden with an eyebrow arched.

"I needed some fresh air," she explained and then patted the space next to her. "Sit down with me for a moment. I have to tell you something."

Jamie sat next to her on the bench and turned to look at her expectantly. Most of his face remained impassive, but apprehension flickered in his eyes.

"I wanted to tell you that I'm sorry for the whole Emma ordeal. It was wrong of me to expect you to understand or to try to help when we have other important things to think about."

A small smile spread across Jamie's face. "Like this," he remarked, reaching out to place his hand over Aubrey's stomach. "Danka for the apology, but I have to tell you something before you hear it from anyone else."

She rested a hand over Jamie's and gave his cracked knuckles a tender squeeze. "What's that?"

"It's about Emma."

CR8O

"What about Emma?"

Jamie hesitated at the anxious look Aubrey gave him. He didn't want to give her false hope, but if he didn't tell her, someone else would.

"Your maemm has been talking to the church about Emma possibly coming back."

"She has been?"

He held up a hand as Aubrey straightened in eagerness. "Jah, but the church has to think about it, and Emma will have to confess to the church. It's all up in the air, Aubrey. I wanted to tell you before someone else did, since I promised I would think about things."

"And?"

"We're about to have a bobli, Aubrey. Do you really want your sister around right as we start our own family?"

Aubrey chewed on the inside of her cheek contemplatively. The sunlight warmed the center of her pale cheeks and filled it with color. A sadness filled her eyes when she looked at him resolutely. "Nee. You're right.

I want to enjoy our new family together and not worry about my sister."

"Really?" Jamie said, shocked by answer. He had fully expected some sort of argument, but Aubrey seemed understanding of where his thoughts were coming from. "What's changed your mind?"

Her fingers played with the ridges of his knuckles. The spring air caressed them as they sat on the wooden bench, listening to the birds chirp happily in the trees.

"Talking to Hannah today made me realize a couple of things is all."

"Like what?" he prodded curiously.

"Like how my sister's wellbeing shouldn't be my primary concern and that I was clinging to the past because motherhood is new and scary to me. I wanted to hold something old and familiar."

The admission softened Jamie. He grabbed Aubrey's free hand with his own and squeezed it. "It's scary for me too, Aubrey. That's why we have each other."

Aubrey smiled lovingly at him. "I know that now. All that matters in the world is that we have each other and our bobli. I just hope that my sister makes the right decision, for her sake at least."

"It's her decision to make. She can't come back just to be close to you and your family again. She can only come back if she's serious about devoting herself to Gott again and correcting her ways."

"That's what I realized today too. She may never give up the English life. I hate to say this about my own sister, but I don't think she could even survive through a reinstatement period. She doesn't want to give up anything."

"Then there's the answer."

"Jah. There's my answer." Aubrey said, sighing. "My maemm will be here shortly to bring us dinner, I'm sure. I'm going to wash up now that you are home."

Jamie gave a nod. The past few times Aubrey had gone to wash had ended with her sitting on the floor from being dizzy. Their midwife assured them that this was also normal from the increase of blood coursing through Aubrey's veins and their bobli taking most of whatever Aubrey ate. They'd agreed to have Aubrey wait and wash until someone was present.

He watched her walk up the back porch steps and disappear into the haus before going about the usual chores. When he finished, Aubrey's maemm arrived with two plates full of mashed potatoes and pot roast.

"This has been cooking all day," Katie remarked. She handed the plates of food to Jamie.

His stomach growled hungrily at the smell and he smiled appreciatively at her. "Danka. Would you like to come in?"

"Jah. Just for a few minutes."

They entered the kitchen together. The floorboards upstairs groaned as Aubrey padded around their bedroom softly.

"Have you talked to Aubrey about the conversation we had today with Bishop Abraham?" Katie asked.

She walked around the kitchen easily and set the table for them.

"A little. I told her that the church has to think about it."

Katie nodded. "Danka, by the way, for coming with me to talk to our Bishop. I would've asked Daniel, but I'm afraid that he has been too sick and worried about our farm to talk about Emma."

"Of course." Jamie said, smiling. "I'll admit, I did this more for Aubrey than for Emma."

"Did you talk with Michael Brenneman as well?"

He grimaced at the unpleasant memory. Michael hadn't necessarily been confrontational when it came to Emma, but he wasn't exactly happy while talking about Emma either. He suspected there were feelings still there, but Michael refused to talk about them, and a part of Jamie didn't blame him. Not when Emma had been the main reason that Michael had left in the first place.

"Jah, but no such luck. He says Emma has been avoiding him."

"The poor man," Katie said, clucking her tongue. "I know that he has loved Emma for a long time, but with what happened to him I don't blame him for being angry. You're a good mann, Jamie. I'm so very happy that Aubrey has found someone like you to take care of her and give her a reason to stay. For a while, I was sure that I would lose two daughters."

Their conversation was interrupted when Aubrey's footsteps started down the stairway. She looked refreshed, with her damp hair smoothed back underneath her prayer kapp and skin scrubbed clean. Aubrey's eyes lighted up at the sight of her maemm standing in their kitchen.

Jamie excused himself from the kitchen to give them some privacy to talk. He quickly changed out of his work clothes and splashed cool water on his face to revive himself a bit. The past few weeks had been tiring, from taking on the extra hours at the furniture store to keeping up with the chores around their haus. Next weekend they were going to trade a few pies and new dining table for a cow. That meant he would be staying up late again to try to finish the table in the barn and he felt exhausted thinking about it.

When the sun finally set and filled the sky with pink clouds, Jamie started sanding the table. The exhaustion in his body surprisingly melted away as he fell into the normal motions of working. It provided a distraction from his thoughts, and all the stress that had settled on his shoulders faded.

The sound of a buggy and horse hooves clinking on rocks brought Jamie's attention back. He straightened with a frown and tossed his leather gloves carelessly onto one of the shelves lining the barn walls.

He stopped short in surprise to see Michael Brenneman, still clad in Englischer clothes, jumping out of a buggy. Jamie arched an eyebrow at him, crossing his arms over his chest. "Who lent you a buggy and horse?" Jamie asked.

Michael rubbed the black mare's neck affectionately with the palm of his hand. "My parents did. They have taken me in for the reinstatement and repentance period."

"That's gut news."

"Jah. I know you are wondering why I'm here after

our last conversation."

"I wouldn't call that a conversation exactly. You refused to talk."

"Sorry about that," Michael said, his tone suggesting otherwise. "Can I unhitch and then we can talk in the barn? I don't want to wake Aubrey or-"

"She's asleep upstairs," Jamie noted.

"Then let's talk. Jah?"

Jamie opened the gate to allow the horse to graze while they talked in the barn. He led Michael back into the barn and slipped his hands back into his work gloves. "What do you want to talk about?" Jamie asked.

He picked up the sanding block and adjusted the paper before resuming his task. Michael walked around the edge of the table and brushed off the layer of dust.

"I'll start with why you thought that I knew whether Emma was coming back or not."

"Aubrey told me what happened between you two-"

"She knows only half of what happened between Emma and me."

"No argument there. I just wanted to know whether you had contact with Emma and if you knew her motives about returning."

"I wouldn't know anything, as I told you. I haven't seen Emma in years, and she's been avoiding me since I've been back here," Michael stated bitterly.

Jamie paused his sanding. He studied the tall and rather meaty man standing across from him. There was no mistaking the anger in Michael's eyes as he picked up another sanding block and bent over the table.

"What do you have against Emma?" Michael asked. "The church isn't even that hesitant to let Emma come back."

"I have many reasons. Several of them Aubrey wouldn't agree with."

"Aubrey wouldn't agree with whatever reasons you have. Those two share a close bond and you won't be able to destroy it."

"That's not what I want to do. I just want to protect Aubrey from-"

"From what? What Emma offers?"

His exhaustion came back full throttle and then transformed into irritation. Jamie straightened, with the sanding block in his hand, and pointed a finger at Michael with his free one.

"Would you trust Emma to come back here? She's what drove you out of this community."

A red flush crawled up the side of Michael's neck. He straightened as well, towering over Jamie by a good foot. "I understand that you've got a bobli on the way and that Emma tends to be a bit flighty, but she's a gut person. She wouldn't intentionally hurt Aubrey."

"That's exactly my point. I have never said that Emma would do it intentionally. I just don't want her to get close to Aubrey, give her a sense of hope, and then take off because she can't handle living here again. That would destroy Aubrey more than anything in the world, and I'm her mann. I'm not trying to be controlling or overprotective like you think I'm being, but you loved someone at one point. You'd do everything you could to protect them."

Michael didn't reply at first. He stared down at the tabletop, sand block dangling loosely in his fingertips. With a resigned sigh, he tossed it on the table carelessly. "You're right. I don't blame you for being suspicious of Emma and me returning, but know this. I still love Emma and I will do everything that I can to protect her. We both need Gott back in our lives."

Shame filled Jamie as he thought of how irrational and controlling he had acted since hearing about Emma. He had no right to try to control the situation if Gott meant for them to come back. "I'm sorry. I have no right to judge either of you," Jamie said.

He stretched out a contrite hand for Michael to shake. They grasped hands briefly as Michael smiled at him.

"Danka. I understand where you are coming from. You have every right to protect Aubrey and your unborn bobli."

"Just promise me that you'll help Emma as much as you possibly can. It already sounds like the church is open to her coming back."

Michael smiled a bit darkly. "Jah, but the hard part is now just starting."

"Like convincing Emma?"

"Exactly. Who knows how that will go."

☙ CHAPTER 5 ❧

Martha Lapp's hands were cool and uncomfortably dry against the softness of Aubrey's stomach. She tried not to fidget against the nudges on her stomach or instinctively bat away probing fingers. Instead, she forced herself to look at the lines around the corners of Martha's eyes or where Jamie stood a few feet back to give them space. Every time she looked over in his direction, he offered an encouraging smile.

"No more bleeding?" Martha asked.

"Nee."

"And the cramping?"

"Nothing serious. It's only when I move around a lot."

Her dry hands finally lifted away and politely pulled the skirts of her dress back down. Martha gave a brief nod, and moved back to give Aubrey some space to sit up on the couch.

"Everything feels fine. Your bobli even gave my hand a little kick."

"You felt a kick?" Aubrey asked anxiously. "I have been trying to feel kicking or moving."

"You wouldn't feel anything just yet. Maybe in a few more weeks you will feel movement. First time maemms won't feel kicking until about 16 weeks or so."

She bit her lower lip in disappointment. While laying in bed she oftentimes felt little bubbling sensations in her stomach and imagined their bobli kicking at her palm.

Martha read the disappointment on her face and smiled sympathetically. "Your bobli will be here before you know it. Try to enjoy the pregnancy. Trust me, you'll miss being pregnant once it's over."

Aubrey scoffed. "I don't think so. I won't miss being sick every hour of the day."

"That'll eventually go away once you hit the second trimester. Just drink plenty of tea with ginger and eat small meals," Martha recommended.

She gathered her leather bag from the living room table and turned to give Aubrey a stern look. "I still recommend bed rest for at least a few more weeks, until all the cramping goes away."

"What about church this Sunday?" Aubrey asked. At the disapproval starting to cross Martha's face, she rushed on pleadingly, "Surely it wouldn't hurt to go to church? It's only a mile ride, and I won't stay long afterward."

"I don't know-" Jamie started uncertainly.

"I think that will be just fine. Just take it slow and drink plenty of water," Martha said.

Aubrey clapped her hands eagerly. Being confined to the haus had taken its toll and she missed attending church.

The past two Sundays they'd missed church, Jamie had taken it upon himself to read Scripture to her and pray together. Though she enjoyed sharing those private moments with her mann, she missed being a part of the community.

A wave of nausea rolled through her. While Jamie walked Martha out, she brewed herself some tea with slices of ginger. She took a sip of the hot liquid, exhaling a relieved sigh as the ginger soothed the ill feeling.

"Are you sure about going to church on Sunday?" Jamie entered the kitchen. He sat down on the chair across from her, folding his strong arms on the table.

"Everything will be fine, I promise," Aubrey said. She reached out and pulled one of his hands free. "I can't stay in this haus forever. Fresh air will do me good and so will church."

"If you're sure..."

"I'm positive. You heard Martha. Everything is fine. Our bobli is perfectly fine."

"All right. Just promise to take things slow, Aubrey. I know how you are."

Aubrey grinned playfully at him. "Ach? Pray, tell me how I am."

Jamie rolled his eyes up at the ceiling. He gave her fingers a brief squeeze before standing and adjusting his hat. "I don't have to tell you. I have to go to the Byler's farm for our new cow in a few hours. Since you are feeling cheerful, is it trouble for you to bake a couple of apple pies for them? They've been asking."

"Jah. Of course."

Aubrey danced happily around the kitchen with flour coating her apron for the next two hours. The smell of apples and cinnamon filled the air as her pies bubbled deliciously in the oven. She sipped at her tea whenever a wave of nausea threatened to crash over on her again.

When Jamie entered the kitchen, a layer of sweat covered his forehead. His eyes lit up at the sight of an extra apple pie cooling on a rack and a stew bubbling away.

"You didn't have to make dinner too," Jamie chided gently. He crossed the kitchen and pressed a soft kiss to her lips.

Aubrey rested her chin on his broad chest, tilting her head up to look at him with a smile. "I wanted to. After everyone making us meals for the past few weeks, a home-cooked meal sounded wonderful."

"Jah. It does sound wonderful."

"Furthermore," she said, taking a step back, "I find it only fair that you gain some weight with me."

Aubrey patted his stomach like the times he had done the same to hers. She smiled when Jamie tilted his head back and laughed.

"Gut thing you know all the meals that will make me fat then."

"Jah. That I do."

He kissed her one last time before scooping up the warm pies and promising to be back within an hour. Aubrey stood on the front porch and waved goodbye to Jamie as he turned to glance at her one last time.

The warmth of the afternoon drew Aubrey outside with her sketchbook and pencils. She sat beneath one of the oak trees in their front yard and let her hand draw whatever came to mind. The stillness of the air around her and the distant buzzing of bumble bees relaxed the tension inside her.

The sound of a car engine broke the bubble of contentment. Aubrey frowned at the sound of tires crunching along their driveway. She set her sketchpad on the patch of grass and peered around the tree's trunk to see a white car. Sunlight glinted off the front window and she cupped a hand over her eyes to squint in the direction of the driver. Her hand dropped in surprise as the car stopped alongside her on the road and the engine turned off.

A tanned leg appeared before Emma slid all the way out of the car. When had her sister learned to drive? Some teenagers in their community learned to drive during rumspringa, but she couldn't remember Emma ever mentioning that she knew how to drive.

"When did you learn how to drive?" Aubrey blurted out.

Emma closed the door behind her. A tweezed eyebrow arched above the rim of her sunglasses. "When I first left. I obviously had to learn sometime."

She hopped easily over the ditch filled with water that separated them. An exotic and sweet smell filled Aubrey's nose when Emma folded her lean frame next to her on the ground. Her black-streaked blond hair shimmered as Emma pushed it back over her shoulders and looked around the land in interest.

"This is a nice place," Emma remarked. "Very quiet

and pretty. You have two fireplaces?"

Aubrey smiled despite the tension now coiling within her. "Jah. Jamie put them in because he didn't want me or the bobli to get cold during the winter."

"I'll admit that I miss the whole wood stove thing. There's nothing like a good fire to keep you warm during the winter."

"Do you remember when we used to take all the blankets off our bed and warm them in front of the stove before bed?"

"Of course," Emma said, smiling wistfully. "We used to comb each other's hair in front of the stove too and then race up the stairs to see who got into bed faster."

"You used to let me win though. I remember you'd trip on the top stair so I could win and get warm first."

"That's what big sisters do. We let you win."

They sat in silence for a few minutes. A butterfly danced along in the breeze in front of them and then skimmed along the field. Without even thinking about it, Aubrey rested her head on Emma's shoulder. The smell of her perfume and the touch of her soft skin against Aubrey's cheek felt right--even if it wasn't right.

"Maemm says you've been on bed rest for a while. Are you feeling better?"

"You've been talking to maemm?" Aubrey asked, shocked. It was never in their maemm's nature to go behind their daed's back.

"Only briefly, in passing."

"What about Michael?"

Emma's shoulder stiffened at Michael's name. Her

polished fingernails reached for the blades of grass around them and picked at them in aggravation. "No, and I don't plan to talk to Michael," she said curtly.

Aubrey lifted her head from Emma's shoulder. "Why not? I think it'd help if you talk to him and-"

"What would it help, Aubrey?"

She swiveled her head around to stare at her. The dark tint of Emma's sunglasses guarded whatever emotions were playing in her eyes, but Aubrey could feel them threatening to burn holes in her face. "I just thought having someone go through the same repentance process would make it easier for you."

"Repentance?" Emma echoed, clearly confused. "Who said I would go through the repentance process?"

"Jamie said the church is willing to let you come back. All you have to do is confess and ask for forgiveness in front of the congregation."

"You think they'd let me come back? After what Michael and I did?"

"Gott is forgiving, so the church will be. Why wouldn't they forgive you both?"

"Look at me, Aubrey. I'm a damaged person. I did everything that the Ordnung says not to do. The only real big thing that I haven't done against Gott is committing murder. I sinned against the flesh before my wedding vows, not once, but several times. I carried a baby outside marriage. I've marked myself for life. Can you really see me coming back?"

"Then why are you here?" Aubrey asked.

Anger rose within her rapidly. For the first time since

hearing that Emma had returned to Monte Vista, she could now see Jamie's point. It didn't matter if Emma had the church's forgiveness, or Gott's forgiveness. She had to forgive herself, or else she would never be able to live within their community.

"What do you mean? I'm here because I wanted to be close to my family."

"Nee, you're here because of some other reason and I want to know what it is."

Emma's mouth opened and closed several times as she tried to form an answer. Her curled eyelashes fluttered closed from behind her sunglasses and then opened again. "This is what I feared about coming back," she said quietly.

"What?"

"This," Emma replied, flourishing a hand between them. "I was afraid that you were going to be like this after leaving you."

"Like what?" Aubrey asked indignantly. "What am I doing?"

"You're trying to persuade me to come back like maemm and Sadie. I don't want to come back here. I can't live like all of you. I just can't do it."

Aubrey stood on shaky legs. She stared down at the young woman still sitting on the ground. It seemed funny how a person could be a physical manifestation of someone you once loved, but so strange and different simultaneously.

"You should probably leave then. This is my life, living here with Jamie, and if you can't accept it then-"

"Hold on a second, Aubrey," Emma interrupted,

holding up a hand. "Just take a breather, okay? I see your point. You're right. I-I have to make a decision."

The world around them slowed to a snail's pace. Aubrey stood in front of a contemplative Emma, waiting anxiously for the next few words that would come.

"Well? What is it going to be?"

૱ஐ

"Put wisdom in our hearts while here..."

Jamie closed his eyes and listened to the chorus of voices finish singing the Loblied. Nothing felt more comforting at that moment than church and feeling Gott's presence in the hay-scented air. He prayed for wisdom as a serene blanket draped across his shoulders and comforted him. The headache plaguing the front of his skull faded away temporarily.

What do I do, Gott? What do I do now?

His eyes opened and slid to where Aubrey sat with the women on the other side of the barn. Her eyes were closed as well, a fervent expression on her face. One of her freckled hands rested unconsciously on the small baby bump, and she leaned forward to pray silently even harder.

There was no doubt in Jamie's mind about what she was praying for. Not after what she'd told him yesterday.

Jamie anxiously chewed the inside of his cheek. Why did Emma have to decide to come back now? Something tickled the back of his spine, an unpleasant sensation that filled his soul with worry. When his thoughts returned to yesterday evening, the serene blanket lifted from him.

"Emma's coming back to Gott, and to the Amish church!" Aubrey announced excitedly the moment Jamie walked into the kitchen.

He paused in mid step, too shocked to speak. It took him a few seconds even to voice his disbelief. "She's coming back to the Amish church?"

Aubrey nodded eagerly. The white strings of her prayer kapp swayed at the movement. Her pale blue eyes were bright with unchecked happiness.

"Jah. She told me yesterday that she was coming back. Isn't that gut news, Jamie? I am so excited for her."

"Jah," He managed to croak out, mind still whirling with surprise. "That's very gut news. How did she tell you yesterday?"

"She drove over here after you left. We-"

"She drove here in a car?"

"She can still own a car, Jamie. She isn't back until the church decides she can come back, and if she goes through a reinstatement period."

Jamie rubbed the back of his neck. Sweat had gathered there from the sunlight bearing down on him in the fields. He watched Aubrey dance happily around the kitchen, the first time a flicker of herself had come back since finding out they were expecting a bobli. A part of him rationalized that arguing with Aubrey while pregnant never ended well, but his mouth opened anyway.

"That's a big if, Aubrey. The church still has to talk to Emma, and she has to-"

Just as he'd expected, Aubrey whirled around to glare at him. She held up a jar of seasonings to sprinkle on the fresh chicken and pointed it warningly at him.

"Don't argue with me. I'm pregnant and I'm hungry. Can't you just say this is a gut thing and let it be? Do we have to fight every single time this subject comes up?"

He had let it go then. Once church concluded, he would seek out Bishop Abraham again.

An hour later, they finished with one last hymn and exited the stuffy barn to prepare for lunch. Jamie stood up from the wooden bench and started toward Abraham at the front of the barn. The older man smiled at him warmly and wordlessly flourished an arm to a quieter section of the barn.

"What can I help you with, dear boy?" Abraham asked.

They stood in stall with hay covering the floor and tack hanging on the walls. Jamie absently tugged on the leather rein of a horse's bridle and kept an eye on Aubrey as she walked outside with Sadie glued to her side.

"Do you think this is a gut idea? Bringing Emma back to the church?" he blurted out.

Abraham blinked at the questions. He reached up to stroke his beard thoughtfully for a few minutes.

"Gott has clearly directed her back here," he mused softly, and then lowered his gaze to Jamie. "I cannot turn away from anyone who is in need of spiritual healing or guidance. If it is truly in Gott's plan to bring her back, then that is what will happen."

Jamie tried to hide his disappointment, but Abraham read it clearly with a knowing smile.

"I imagine this makes you nervous, especially with a

bobli on the way and the relationship Aubrey has with Emma."

"You knew about the bobli?"

"It was a passing comment from Betty when she came to me to help her search for another to fill Aubrey's position."

He groaned inwardly at the information. Aubrey loved teaching the local kinner and took her job seriously. She would be devastated at hearing that the position was filled.

"What do you think about Emma returning to our way?" Abraham asked suddenly.

"What do I think?" Jamie asked, confusion lacing his voice. "I don't think that my opinion-"

"Of course it does. You're a part of this church, and as a member you could be called upon someday to minister. What are your thoughts?"

He played with the buckle on the leather saddle next to him. "I guess," he started, "I am a bit skeptical given Emma's past here and her current feelings toward the Amish. I'm not sure if she could follow the Ordnung or let go of the English life."

"You have knowledge of her past discrepancies?"

"Only from word of mouth. I know there's a lot that I don't know."

" 'Do not judge, or you too will be judged,'" Abraham quoted from the Bible.

The center of Jamie's cheeks burned at the subtle reprimand for being judgmental. He buried his face in distress, and rubbed the bristles of his beards in agitation.

"I do not mean to be judgmental or skeptical. I just worry about Aubrey. That is only where my heart and head is at."

Abraham nodded in understanding. "You have every right to feel the way you do. As a mann it's your job to protect the well being of your fraa and bobli. That includes protecting your herd of sheep from spiritual distress."

"Jah. That's all I worry about. Aubrey is so excited over the thought of Emma coming back to the church that it just worries me about what would happen if that didn't happen."

"It would be devastating for Aubrey undoubtedly. The two were very close since the day Aubrey was born. I remember Emma took her job as an older sister quite seriously. They used to look so much alike as well..." Abraham trailed off wistfully.

He doubted that Abraham would think that now. Not with the way Emma looked from her facial piercings, tattoos and blonde hair streaked black.

"If it is any comfort to you," Abraham said, seriousness now lacing his gravelly voice, "this decision will not come easily out of sympathy for Emma's past grievances. She must forgive herself before asking for Gott's and then the church's forgiveness. The option is open to her, but a family must be willing to accept her into their home for reinstatement and repentance."

"I know that Aubrey would be upset over this, but it won't be our home," Jamie decreed firmly.

"I believe Katie has discussed possibly talking to Daniel about letting Emma stay with them temporarily."

"That conversation will not go well. Not after what

happened two summers ago."

The scuffling of feet on the hay-strewn floor interrupted their conversation. Jamie turned in time to see Aubrey approaching tentatively, with a plate of food in hand for him. He wiped his face clean of any apprehension that continued to linger there.

"I brought you some food. I didn't mean to interrupt your conversation," Aubrey said sheepishly.

She extended an arm over the wooden stall door and held it out for him. Jamie took it with a grateful smile at her thoughtfulness.

"We can finish our conversation later. Is that a piece of whoopie pie I see there?" Abraham opened the stall door and brushed by them with a friendly smile.

"What were you two talking about?" Aubrey asked curiously.

He debated on not telling her. Before exchanging their wedding vows, both had promised to no longer keep any secrets. So far, Aubrey had been forthright and honest about everything when asked.

"We were talking about Emma," Jamie said.

"Ach?" Aubrey draped her hands over the stall door, and her blonde eyebrows furrowed in an uneasy frown. "Did he say anything about letting Emma come back?"

"Just the same thing that everyone has already told you. It all relies on Emma and whether she's truly ready to come back to the Amish church."

"I think she is," Aubrey said. After a few seconds passed, doubt clouded her eyes. "At least I think she does. Why am I so concerned about this, Jamie? This isn't my life anymore. You are my life. Our bobli is our life."

Jamie set the plate of food carefully on a wooden post. He grabbed both of Aubrey's hands, marveling in their small size and the soft skin brushing against the calluses on his hands. He laid their palms flatly against each others' and smiled assuredly.

"Jah, it is our life, but Emma is a part of your life as well. I do not mean to be harsh or judgmental when I say what I say. I only wish to protect you from any distress that this might cause if things don't go right."

"I know, but I shouldn't care as much as I do. I'm torn between the two of you sometimes."

"Then know that I'm never going to leave you. Even when you want me to, I won't."

Aubrey's fingers curled around the sides of his palms. "I don't ever want you to leave. I can live without my sister, but I can't live without you."

They stood together for a few moments in silence, enjoying the touch of their hands and the laughter echoing from outside. A gurgling sound from Aubrey's stomach interrupted the peaceful silence.

"Where's your plate of food?" Jamie asked.

He grinned at the color spreading up the side of Aubrey's neck. That had been another thing that changed drastically over the past few weeks. Aubrey's appetite soared, and he constantly caught her nibbling on something. Mainly pies or cookies.

"I didn't get a plate of food. I was too busy preparing yours."

"You need to eat more than I do," Jamie stated.

He handed her the plate of food and opened the gate. They walked side by side out of the Byler's barn and out into the bright sunlight. Kinner chased each other around the wooden tables and the hills of hay stacked near the barn. In the distance, the Sangre de Cristo Mountains were visible from their still snow covered peaks, but the evergreen trees were vibrant in the light. When Jamie breathed in, he could almost taste the pine.

Before they could reach the table where both their families sat, Aubrey slowed her steps At his questioning look, she gave reason to why she'd slowed down.

"My maemm will talk to my daed next weekend about Emma possibly coming back," she commented softly.

Jamie arched an eyebrow. "Jah. I already know that she is."

"Do you think that we could go over as well and talk to my daed?" At the hesitation spreading across Jamie's face, she continued. "I promised Emma that I would try this for her sake. If it doesn't work out, then I won't be involved in any of it anymore. I promise."

Could he trust that promise? Aubrey stared up at him pleadingly, and her jaw worked anxiously as she chewed her cheek. He relented for only one reason.

"Jah, sure. We can go over."

Aubrey sent him a dazzling smile before picking up the pace again. Jamie trailed after her, thumbs hooked on the front of his suspenders.

Emma's return balanced precariously on two things. Even if she decided to come back, Daniel would have to accept her back in their home and there was no way of telling how that would go.

೧ CHAPTER 6 ೧

The smell of cocoa filled Aubrey's lungs pleasantly. She inhaled steadily and whisked the dry ingredients together while keeping one eye trained on the door propped open. Sadie stood behind the cash register, hands folded behind her back nervously. Her soft voice was barely detectable, as was Eli Lapp's, and they conversed quietly for a few minutes.

Aubrey smiled inwardly. After last night's singing, Eli had taken Sadie home in his buggy, and the two were practically inseparable now. Her heart lifted at the thought of the two marrying eventually. Eli would make an excellent mann for Sadie.

She cracked two eggs carefully on the edge of a mixing bowl and then added the wet ingredients. Since she was still under light bed rest, and her days at the schoolhouse were now over, her maemm needed the extra help for a few hours of the day. The whoopie pies were selling fast, and they had trouble keeping up with orders.

The bell on the front jingled. Sadie stepped back into

the kitchen with a wide and silly grin plastered over her face. She absently wiped her hands on the front of her apron before coming to stand next to Aubrey at the counter. They worked alongside each other in companionable silence for a few minutes.

"So, what do you think?" Sadie asked eventually.

Aubrey continued to drop rounded spoonfuls of the dark dough onto the baking sheet. She arched an eyebrow quizzically at her sister's expectant stare. "What do I think of what?"

Sadie rolled her eyes. "You know what I'm talking about. What do you think of Eli? He's wunderbar, right?"

"He seems to be wunderbar. You would know more than I would."

"Jah, but I'm so nervous. He wants to get married soon."

The spoon with a rounded ball of dough paused above the baking sheet. Aubrey tried to imagine her sister announcing marriage at the beginning of fall, but shook her head in dismay. They were much too young to get married within a short a few months.

"How soon is he wanting to get married?"

"Why?" Sadie asked, pausing in latticing an apple pie. "You sound a bit disapproving there."

"I just don't want you to rush into a marriage. It's not as easy as it looks or what you think. Neither of you have even gone on rumspringa nor taken your vows; a lot can change during that time."

"You and Jamie seem fine though. Even after everything that happened, you both are happy and starting a family."

Hope glimmered in Sadie's eyes. Aubrey set the spoon back in the bowl of dough and turned to look at her sister. It was every girl's dream to get married eventually and start a family, but she wanted to protect her young sister from not fully enjoying the process of getting to know the one Gott designed for her.

"Jamie and I are doing well because we took the time to get to know one another. We courted for a while, and we're each other's best friend. Do yourself a favor and don't rush the process because it is a huge commitment, as is joining the church."

Sadie bowed her head, and her fingers absently played with the front of her apron. When she looked back up, her eyes were filled with sadness. "It makes me sad to think that you didn't have Emma talking to you about these things like you are talking to me. Do you think she would have helped you with Jamie?"

Fatigue settled into her bones suddenly. Aubrey rubbed her forehead and then straightened her prayer kapp when it came loose from its pins. She honestly saw no point in trying to imagine how different things could have been if Emma hadn't left. There was nothing that any of them could do to make their lives go back to the way they were.

Even if Emma decided to return, it wouldn't be the same.

"I have no idea, Sadie. I don't really see the point in trying to think about it. I have you, Isaac, maemm and daed, and Jamie. What else do I really need?"

"I suppose you're right." Sadie said, frowning. "I just wonder how different things would have been for everybody if Emma wouldn't have done what she did. I think things would be a lot different for all of us. Daed would have been a minister by now possibly."

"Maybe," Aubrey said tightly.

She finished scooping out the dough for the whoopie pies and set them in the oven to bake. When Katie arrived back at the bakery after checking up on their daed, Aubrey had just finished wrapping the whoopie pies in cellophane. She placed them neatly on a plate in the display case before walking back to her maemm's tiny and neatly organized office.

Katie sat behind a tidy desk with a computer and phone. She rarely used either for work purposes, but today she was busily typing on the keyboard. Her maemm's fingers paused briefly when Aubrey gently rapped her knuckles on the doorframe to signal her presence.

"Is it all right with you if I go?" Aubrey asked, ghosting the doorway. "I am feeling a bit tired and sick. The whoopie pies are finished, and you should get through the day without having to bake anymore."

"You don't need to ask for permission. If you are feeling tired and sick, then go home and rest. That's the best thing you can do for your bobli," Katie said, smiling gently.

She smiled gratefully at her maemm, and turned to go before Katie's soft voice held her back.

"Wait. There is one thing I need to talk with you about before you leave."

"If this has to do with Emma," Aubrey began, turning to face Katie directly. "I already told you. I'm coming to dinner Saturday night, and talking to daed."

Katie's face tightened into a disapproving one. "Are you sure about this, Aubrey? This could go either way knowing your daed, and I don't want you to feel disappointed."

"I know. Daed can be stubborn sometimes," Aubrey said.

They shared a wry, but affectionate, smile. She bid Katie goodbye and left the bakery in the direction of Forrest Furniture. The spring sunshine cheered her as she made her way down the sidewalks and past local businesses. The air smelled of damp dirt, and freshly potted flowers lined the streets.

Aubrey rounded the large building, but found the storage area swept and organized instead of in its usual disarray. It also lacked the usual presence of Jamie, Henry, Levi, and her daed. She frowned as she passed a stained rocking chair and smoothed a hand over the slick wooden spools. The rocking chair tipped forward easily and rocked back in a soothing manner.

She stepped through the open door, and walked down the white hallway that lead to the front of the store. The smell of kaffe was strong in the air, and the faint mumble of conversation reached Aubrey's ears.

"Aubrey?"

Levi emerged from the office. Dark lines circled his normally bright eyes, and his cheekbones were sunken. He also appeared to have lost a few pounds as well, from the flutter of his shirt and suspender slipping from his shoulder. The stress of running the store with Jamie had finally taken a toll on him. Her bruder smiled at her presence, but flicked his eyes over in mild concern.

"What are you doing here? Everything okay?"

She smiled assuredly. "Jah, everything is fine. I was just wondering where Jamie was, and thought we could have lunch together on his break."

"Ach." Levi blinked, and then waved her into the office. "He's with a customer at the moment, but come sit in here with me. Have a chat, so to speak."

The office was like their maemm's at the bakery: tiny and neatly organized. A computer and phone sat on the middle of a desk, but Levi used them for business reasons only. She seated herself uneasily on the edge of a plastic chair as Levi sat across from her.

"So," Levi started, lacing his fingers together in front of him, "you feeling any better? Jamie said you were on bedrest for a while."

"Better, but I'm still restricted to light chores. Nothing too physically exerting. How are things going for you here?"

"I'd be lying if I said it was going gut." He smiled thinly, and his broad shoulders drooped a bit under an invisible weight. "Things aren't going well here. It's been a tough year since daed has been sick, and your mann has been trying to keep up with the orders. It's just been a bit stressful trying to fill orders and make enough to float."

Concern filled her thinking about how stressful things must be for her oldest bruder to be confessing to it. He was always the picture of calm, and filled with positive energy. In many ways he was like Jamie who had never indicated how stressful things were at work. He had been more consumed with her wellbeing than his own.

"There hasn't been any orders coming in for the furniture?" Aubrey asked.

"There has been several requests for certain types of furniture, but the problem lies within time. I have a solution, but Jamie has refused to admit defeat yet."

"What is the solution?"

Levi leaned further back in his chair, and a loud squeak filled the room at the movement. He stared thoughtfully up at the ceiling for a few moments before speaking. "Hire Michael Brenneman as extra help. His daed asked whether I'd be willing to employ him until his testing period is over."

Her eyes fluttered closed in faint annoyance. There was no doubt in her mind what Jamie's response was.

"Let me guess. Jamie has refused that solution."

"You guessed right."

"I'm sorry, Levi," Aubrey said, sighing in exasperation. "He's not very trusting toward Michael nor Emma presently."

"I don't blame him for feeling that way. He has every right to feel the way he does," Levi sighed.

"I know, but still..." She pinched the bridge of her nose. A headache started to throb in her temples, and nausea climbed its way up her throat. When she opened her eyes, Levi was staring at her with an indescribable glint to his eyes.

"How are you feeling about Emma coming back?" he asked.

It was hard trying to read Levi's expression. He kept whatever thoughts and emotions he felt carefully contained. Aubrey focused on the jar filled with various pens, and tried to think of a good answer.

"I hope that she comes back for her sake. She needs Gott back in her life, and so far she seems like she has been interested in returning." Catching sight of Levi's lips thinning in visible disdain, she asked, "How do you feel about it?"

"I don't think it's a good idea. Emma won't make it here for more than an hour," Levi stated bluntly.

Aubrey shrank back in her chair in shock. Never once had she heard Levi talk negatively about someone, let alone a family member. He had been just as devastated over Emma's decision to leave.

"How could you say that?"

"I say that because of what maemm has told me, and from the brief glimpses I have gotten of her around town. She's only coming back here because she has nowhere else to go."

"Why's that a bad thing?" Aubrey asked. She sought to control her boiling temper and curled her fingers into the cold plastic. "Maybe it's a good thing for her to come back now. She needs our family, with everything that has happened to her."

The chair squeaked beneath Levi again when he shifted forward. He focused on her unblinkingly. "That shouldn't be the reason she's coming back. Come on,

Aubrey. You and I both know she won't ever come back. Even if she's serious now, how is she going to handle everyone's opinion?"

"She doesn't care about other's opinions."

"You're wrong. She cares greatly about what other people think of her. If she didn't, she wouldn't be here trying to get back on our good sides."

Aubrey opened her mouth to argue, but the words died on the tip of her tongue. Her conversation with Emma replayed again in her mind. Look at me...

Even if they could convince their daed and the church to let Emma come back, it wouldn't matter. Emma had to live with other's opinions, and who knew how well that would go.

♋⃝

The floorboards groaning broke Jamie's attention from where he sat in a rocking chair near the open window. He looked up from his copy of the Ausband, and caught sight of pale blue through the kitchen door. Soft footsteps padded along the floor as Aubrey finished preparing her cottage cheese salad for dinner.

Jamie focused back on the Ausband. The tension in the haus was palpable, and he had long since given up hope of trying to carry on a conversation with a quiet Aubrey. Whatever thoughts Aubrey had, she wanted to figure out on her own.

Outside, the sun still lingered in the sky above the mountain range; an assuring sign that spring was here to stay. A warm breeze that smelled faintly of pine and lilac trailed in through the open window across from him. Birds chirped happily in the budding trees as the evening approached. He loathed to leave the haus when it was such a beautiful and calm evening. A brief thought of trying to convince Aubrey to stay home for the evening passed through his mind, but he knew that it would be futile. Once Aubrey had her mind convinced about something, there was little he could do to sway her.

"What are you doing?"

A small hand gently grasped his shoulder and gave a tender squeeze. Jamie smiled faintly, leaning back into the touch and reaching up to search for Aubrey's fingers.

"Just thinking is all," he replied, finding her fingers at last to press a kiss to them. They were still damp from washing and smelled of soap. "Are you ready to go?"

"Jah, I guess."

He turned around at the doubt lacing Aubrey's voice. "You guess? This was your idea to go over and talk to your daed."

Aubrey bowed her head to hide the emotions playing in her eyes. In a rather graceful fashion, her hands twisted themselves in the fabric of her apron. "I know," she responded softly. "I just don't know how well this is going to go. My daed won't be happy talking about Emma. I just keep praying that it will all be fine in the end."

"I'm sure that it will be fine, no matter what. After all," Jamie reached out to brush his hand affectionately over the small swell now forming on Aubrey's stomach. "We have this blessing to look forward to, no matter what the result is tonight."

A small smile twitched on Aubrey's lips. She reached down as well to brush a hand along her stomach. "You're right. I just wish the next few months would go by faster so we can finally meet our bobli."

"Jah, me too," Jamie agreed.

"I suppose I'm ready to go over to my parent's house then," she said, withdrawing to the kitchen.

Jamie watched her go with a deep sigh. He quickly prayed that Gott would keep a calming presence in him, and then left the haus to hitch up their horse. A few moments later they were traveling down the dusty and gravel road to Aubrey's parents' haus. Aubrey kept her head turned the other direction, watching the damp fields as they passed them. He felt the tension in her rise steadily when they reached the road leading to her parents' barn.

The Forrest haus remained the same, with pruned flower beds around the haus and a damp patch of ground that little seedlings were poking up through. The windows were open to allow the spring breeze and the faint smell of slow roasting beef reached Jamie's nose. His stomach rumbled hungrily in response as he steered their horse to the barn behind the haus.

It was Sadie who greeted them first. She rounded the corner of the barn with an arm looped through a pail filled with feed for the chickens. Her eyes caught Jamie's briefly in a tense glance, but Sadie offered a hand to help Aubrey climb down.

"How are you feeling today, shveshtah?" Sadie asked.

"Stop asking me that," Aubrey said, tilting her head

back with a sarcastic laugh. "Everyone asks me that every time they see me. It's getting rather annoying. Where's daed?"

Sadie pointed toward the back field. "He's fixing a line for the fields. Somehow one of the lines broke, and part of the field is flooded."

"I'll go help," Jamie offered. He landed gracefully on the gravel road and started to unbuckle their horse from the buggy. Before leading their horse to the field, Jamie carefully grabbed the bowl of cottage cheese salad that sat on the floor and handed it to Aubrey. Their fingers brushed and lingered for a moment longer than they should've before the two sisters walked side by side toward the haus.

The closer Jamie got to the broken line, the muddier the ground became. He beelined around the deeper parts and spotted Daniel standing in the distance. A pile of mud was pushed off to the side and large pails sat along the rim of a large hole. Daniel caught sight of him and lifted a hand in friendly greeting. When he approached, Isaac's mud streaked face peered up at him from inside the hole.

"What happened?" Jamie asked. He took in the broken pipe that Isaac straddled with his feet and the muddy walls around him. "How did the pipe break?"

Daniel tugged on the end of his graying beard. He stared down at the broken pipe with a frown. "I'm thinking it was during the winter, from the deep freezes. We buried these lines a long time ago to help with the watering during the drought, and what good it has done for me. The pipes rusted and cracked."

"We aren't sure if this is the only break or if there are other ones," Isaac stated.

Parts of the field that were particularly muddy had sunk down. The other lines were broken, and fields were being flooded from beneath the earth. Jamie glanced over at Daniel, staring down at Isaac as he scooped even more mud. The tension in his jaw and rigid posture were indicators of his mood. He was rightly worried about his crops and fields. It was one of the few ways that he made up money from not working at the furniture store as often because of his constant bouts of illness. What made it even worse was thinking of what the conversation would be over dinner.

Jamie rolled up his shirt sleeves in determination. He knew Aubrey would be irritated at him for dirtying his clothes, but the least he could do was help. "I can pull up the line and replace it with the new one," he said.

"Danka. Isaac," Daniel motioned for his youngest child to come, "get on up here. Let Jamie pull up the broken line."

Isaac scowled in disappointment, but climbed out of the hole to give Jamie room.

Jamie landed on the heels of his boots and mud squished out from beneath his feet in a watery hiss. He crouched down carefully and buried his hands into the mud to free the broken line. After several attempts, he managed to tug the pipe free finally and replace it with a new one.

"Nice work," Daniel said.

He reached down to offer a hand and pulled him up

with a puff of exertion.

Jamie glanced down at his clothing and let out a groan.

"Aubrey is going to be mad at you," Isaac chuckled, grinning broadly at the mud covering Jamie's trousers and shirt.

"No doubt in that."

He wiped his hands on the back of his pants as they made their way down the field to the haus for dinner. With each step they took, he felt more torn he felt about warning Daniel. He promised himself, like Aubrey had promised, to let things go if the church said no and if Daniel said she couldn't stay with them during her reinstatement period.

The smell of Katie's slow roasted beef filled Jamie's nostrils. His mouth watered the second he stepped into the kitchen to see the table piled with steaming food. He started to a chair, but Aubrey's sharp voice halted him.

"Is that mud all over you?" Aubrey stood in the center of the kitchen with a stack of bowls in her hands. She arched an eyebrow moodily at the mud stains and her lips pursed into an exasperated scowl that Jamie found rather amusing.

"I had to help your daed with the pipe," he explained, shrugging indifferently.

Her eyes narrowed at the nonchalant attitude. "I suppose you just thought to yourself, "'My fraa, who is carrying my bobli, will clean all these mud stains. No problem at all.'"

Snorted laughter echoed in the kitchen. Aubrey raised her eyebrow even higher in a silent challenge. Any other time, he would've reprimanded her for the feisty attitude.

This time, however, Jamie kept his mouth shut and decided to play along.

"That is what I thought. You can read minds pretty well."

Their playful banter eased the tension within him. Aubrey set the bowls on the table and sighed in defeat. She motioned for him to follow her out into the hallway to the tiny washroom.

"I still can't believe you are covered in mud right before dinner," Aubrey chided. She paused in dipping a rag into a sink of soapy water and turned to send him a coy look. "Actually, I can believe it. You are the messiest mann who has ever lived."

Jamie captured her hands easily when they moved to wipe away the dirt on his cheek. The cold water trailed down between their palms and down the inside of his arms. He leaned forward and pressed a warm kiss to her lips.

"But you love me nonetheless," he whispered.

Their foreheads brushed together, and they took solace in their brief moment of privacy before returning to the dinner table. Jamie sat close to Aubrey, with the side of his leg touching hers, and tried to focus on his full plate of food. Pleasant chatter filled the tiny and warm kitchen as the sun disappeared. Katie briefly left the table to light the lanterns, and they sat with full bellies in the warm light. The comfortable evening faded away the second Katie laid a hand on the crook of Daniel's elbow.

"Daniel," Katie started, her voice soft and soothing. "There is something that the kinner and I would like to discuss with you."

Jamie bit the inside of his cheek anxiously. He hadn't ever expected Katie to be the one to bring up the topic of Emma or to go behind her mann's back. His hand unconsciously searched for Aubrey's under the table. Their fingers laced together and a layer of nervous sweat covered Aubrey's palm.

Daniel wiped his mouth clean with a napkin. His eyebrows furrowed into a puzzled frown as he set the napkin aside and pushed his empty plate away.

"Very well. What is it?" he asked, clearly intrigued.

Neither of them answered at first. Aubrey kept her head ducked down, but her eyes swiveled back and forth between her maemm and Sadie. Their courage was wavering, noticeable from the way Aubrey's hand trembled next to his.

"It's about Emma," Sadie blurted out.

A thick silence followed.

Daniel stared across the cluttered dinner table at Sadie with an even more puzzled frown. His youngest daughter dropped her head under the weight of his stare and folded her hands in her lap.

"What about Emma?" he asked, and tension belied his tone.

It was Aubrey who spoke next in a soft voice. "She wants to come back, daed. She wants to come back home."

Another silence fell. The disapproval and anger in the air felt stifling. Jamie watched as a vein pulsated on Daniel's right temple and a red color filled his cheeks. The tension in his jaw increased dramatically as it worked silently. He found himself shrinking back in his chair, waiting for the explosion.

"Nee."

🙞 CHAPTER 7 🙟

"Nee."

A strained silence followed. They sat rigidly in their chairs and focused on the empty plates in front of them. There were very few times in Aubrey's life that she could remember her daed ever getting angry.

This one was the worst.

Daniel rested his palms on the table in front of him and drew in a long breath. The center of his cheeks burned bright red, and the heat radiating off him could be felt throughout the tiny kitchen.

"Daniel, I-" Katie started timidly.

"Nee, Katie." Daniel cut over her firmly. "I know what you will say, and the answer is still the same."

His tone left no room for an argument. Aubrey blinked against the tide of tears threatening to spill out. She had desperately hoped that this wouldn't be their daed's reaction, but it was clear where he stood.

Jamie's clammy fingers rested on her bouncing knee under the table and gave a gentle squeeze. She sucked in a watery sigh, and prayed for Gott's strength. They needed Him now more than ever.

"Daed," Sadie spoke up then, her voice oddly calm. "You've always preached kindness and forgiveness of sins. Why can't that apply for Emma? She wants to come back here, to be with us, to be with Gott."

"Jah, Sadie. I have always said to forgive, and never to judge. That is all in Gott's hands, but I know your sister better than you and Aubrey. She is strong willed, and has never followed the Ordnung. Think of what happened before she left."

"Everyone makes mistakes though. Gott didn't make us perfect beings. What if-"

"Enough, Sadie!"

Daniel's voice boomed sharply in the kitchen, and they all flinched back. The vein on his temple pumped furiously and swelled with his anger. He slapped a palm on the tabletop, and the cutlery clanged together.

"This isn't up for a debate. Emma has made the choice to abandon her vows and to live outside our faith. This was her choice. Understand?"

When Aubrey raised her head, his gaze was focused intently on her. Several emotions flicked through her daed's stare, too many and too fleeting to catch. Her fingers played anxiously with the hemline of her apron before she found the courage to speak. Despite the stern facade, she knew her daed well. He was more hurt than angered by Emma's actions , and knowing that his oldest daughter was going through an emotional hardship would soften his stubbornness.

"Emma lost her mann and bobli," she said softly.

Silence again.

Aubrey watched the stubbornness waver with the news. The hard glints in her daed's eyes softened considerably, and faint concern could be detected in the way his brows furrowed together. He lowered his gaze to the table, jaw clenching tautly.

"Daniel, she needs us," Katie said, resting a hand on his arm again. She peered at him beseechingly and rubbed his tense forearm. "Bishop Abraham is willing to allow Emma back if she agrees to a confession and asks for the congregation's forgiveness. He wants to see her back on the right road with Gott as well."

Wordlessly, he shrugged away from Katie's presence. Chair legs scratched against the wooden floorboards, and Daniel rose from his seat without glancing at them. He left the kitchen in a silence that was punctuated with the back door slamming shut.

They continued to sit around the table for a few minutes, silent with their own thoughts. Fatigue filled Aubrey bone deep at thinking of how Emma would feel once they told her how their daed reacted. She only imagined how it felt to know their daed was upset and angry to the point of never being able to forgive fully. They had always been so close, but a valley had formed between all of them.

They were torn between their love of their family and love of their faith.

Aubrey chewed the inside of her cheek and unconsciously sought Jamie's hand. She breathed in relief when his fingers slid through hers, warm and calloused as always. *It doesn't matter*, she told herself. She had promised Emma that they would try talking to their daed, and if didn't go well, that was it.

"We'd better clean the kitchen before the flies get into the food," Katie stated, her voice guarded from whatever emotions she felt.

They cleared the dishes within a few minutes and washed them clean. Sadie left the room without saying a word to Aubrey or to anyone once they were done, and a few seconds later a door clicked shut upstairs.

"I'll be in the living room when you're ready to leave," Jamie commented.

He rested a hand on Aubrey's lower back briefly before leaving the kitchen to give her and Katie some privacy to talk. Katie stood in front of the drying pots, staring distantly out the window in the direction of the hay field.

"I should've known this was going to happen," Katie said, shaking her head slowly. "I knew that your daed wouldn't allow this. I've gone against him, and now he's angry."

"I'm sure it'll be all right, maemm," Aubrey said. Her heart doubted those words, but she continued reassuringly. "You were just trying to do what's best for Emma. We were all trying to help."

Katie turned to look at Aubrey over her shoulder. She smiled sadly, tears glistening brightly in her eyes. "Jah, we were, but this may have cost us your daed's trust. Even the community's trust if word gets around. This wasn't right,

Aubrey. Your daed is right; Emma has made her decision, and if she truly wants to come back, she knows where to go."

The fragile alliance they had built with Emma shattered at Katie's words. Aubrey rested a hand on the swell of her stomach and rubbed there absently. This was the right decision, to let Emma figure things out for herself. Risking her family, and the community, wasn't worth the struggle any longer.

"You should go home and give your daed some space," Katie said. She turned back to look out the window and whispered, "Pray for strength, and forgiveness of our mistakes."

Aubrey left her maemm standing in front of the window and found Jamie sitting quietly on a chair next to a window. The remaining evening sunlight danced across his face and made his skin appear like pure honey. She wanted nothing more than to run her fingers along his cheekbones and feel the bristles of his beard against her skin.

He glanced up, sensing a presence in the room.

"Let's go home," she told him, nodding to the front door.

They shut the front door quietly behind themselves and rounded the house to the barn. Aubrey stood by their buggy as Jamie ventured into the barn to fetch their horse. She tilted her head to look up at the sky. While the evening gave way to night, a few stars were beginning to pepper the sky.

She prayed then and asked for Gott's forgiveness.

They had been led astray unaware by trying to help Emma. Though she missed her sister, and wanted to help her come back, doubts clouded those feelings.

Jamie returned with their horse trotting behind him happily. A smile crossed Aubrey's face to see that Jamie didn't even have to hold the reins. He was a natural when it came to caring for their growing animals, and his love for them earned their respect.

"How are you feeling?" Jamie asked once they were trotting down the road.

The sway of grass and hay in the darkening night filled Aubrey with comfort. She closed her eyes, basking in the warm spring night and the smell of damp earth.

"Neither happy nor sad really," she answered honestly. "It wasn't unexpected. I know my daed can be very stubborn at times when it comes to certain things."

"I know how he feels. He's only trying to protect his family from heartache."

She opened her eyes at that, and studied Jamie's profile in the dark. He sat confidently alongside her, reins held lazily in one hand while his free hand rested on his knee. The breath in her throat caught when he turned to look at her with an arched eyebrow.

"What? Why are you staring at me like that?"

"Nothing," Aubrey said quickly, turning away to look at the road. "I was just thinking about what you were saying."

"Ach?"

"I never realized how astray we had gone by trying to find a way for Emma to come back. I don't understand how it happened."

Cool fingers grasped hers, and then warm lips pressed against the back of her hand. The bristles of Jamie's beard tickled the sensitive skin of her wrist.

"It's easy to be lead astray," Jamie said softly. "I've been led astray a few times, but all we can do is pray for Gott to help us get back on the right road."

"What is the right road though? Turning my back on Emma, or helping her during this spiritual crisis? What is Gott's purpose for all of this?"

The questions tumbled out of Aubrey's lips from months, even years, of suppressed emotions. She had turned to look back at Jamie in distress, trying desperately to comprehend how things had gotten so messed up. They were starting a family soon, and she was still clinging to the thin hope that maybe she could have her sister back.

Jamie was silent for a moment. He stared thoughtfully at the darkness surrounding them, tugging on the edge of his beard.

"Perhaps," he said, turning to look at her, "it's Gott's way of showing you what you are blessed with. I don't know what the right road is, but I know what blessings that I have. You, our families, our bobli, are all that matter."

She took in his words as their buggy creaked along the road that lead to their haus. Maybe Jamie was right about the blessings. They had several, and these needed to be treated with respect. Her lips curved into a smile when Jamie offered a hand to help her down from the buggy.

"Now, you're smiling funnily at me," Jamie said, arching his eyebrow again. "I can't keep up with you sometimes."

"I don't blame you," Aubrey said, laughing. She reached up smooth her fingertips along the sharp bone of Jamie's cheek, and cradled his face tenderly. "I was just wondering how I ended up with such a wise mann. I'm very blessed indeed."

Jamie chuckled. "Flattery doesn't work on me, but I appreciate the sentiment behind it. Go inside and get ready for prayers. I'll be a minute." He slipped out from beneath her palm and started the task of unbuckling their horse from the buggy.

Aubrey smoothed an affectionate hand along the strong muscles of their horse's neck before walking in the dark to the haus. She stared down at the ground as she walked, mindful of the rocks that poked out from beneath the swaying grass.

When she reached the back porch step, Aubrey turned to watch Jamie's shadowed figure move gracefully toward the field. Her chest burned with love at thinking of how collected he was throughout dinner, and how he'd offered her comfort simply by being there afterward. Not many manns would be willing to do what Jamie had done over the past few weeks.

Above, the stars twinkled happily in the night sky, but it provided little light for anyone to see. Her hand stretched out to touch the wooden railing, thinking about what tomorrow would bring.

She smoothed a hand over her warm face, and then massaged her throbbing temples. Tomorrow meant having to tell Emma about their daed's reaction and knowing what her reaction would be.

Even more than all of that, she dreaded tomorrow, when she would most likely have to say goodbye to her sister. Again.

CR80

Jamie dusted his clothes free of wood shavings. He smoothed a hand over the rough surface, admiring the grain of wood.

"That looks gut," Henry remarked.

He came to stand beside Jamie and hooked his thumbs through his suspenders. The storage room was full of furniture that needed to be finished as soon as possible. There were spaces on the storeroom floor that needed to be filled with new furniture, but with the past few weeks' events, Jamie's mind had been everywhere except work.

"Danka. I think we're almost caught up, inventory wise," Jamie said.

"That's gut news. Will we move all the furniture out now or after lunch?"

"After lunch," Jamie replied, glancing up at the clock above the door. "I promised Aubrey that I would have lunch with her at the bakery."

Both grabbed their lunch pails and walked out into the warm spring morning. Jamie inhaled deeply, soaking in the cloudless sky and the smell of wood.

"Speaking of Aubrey," Henry started, seating himself on the wooden bench outside. "How is she holding up? I've heard some interesting stories..."

Jamie fiddled with the buckle of his lunch pail. His lips thinned in displeasure, already knowing where the conversation would ultimately lead. The whole community was abuzz over the possible return of Michael and Emma, two disgraced members who wanted forgiveness and redemption. While he wasn't sure what Michael's true intentions were, it was Emma's that caused him the most doubt.

However, it didn't matter anymore. That had been the agreement between him and Aubrey after trying to convince her daed about letting Emma stay with them during the reinstatement period.

"From the look on your face, I'm assuming the stories are true then," Henry commented.

"Unfortunately," Jamie remarked, sighing. He pinched the bridge of his nose. "I don't know what will happen next exactly. Emma insists that she wants to come back, and naturally Aubrey wants to help her, but Daniel isn't too keen on her being back."

"Neither is Levi," Henry supplied with a frown. "I overheard him telling Aubrey that Emma shouldn't come back because she can't follow the Ordnung and never did in the first place."

"It doesn't matter anymore. Aubrey had agreed to talk to her daed about possibly letting Emma stay with him, but that door was slammed shut."

"Who can blame him?" Henry said, opening up his lunch pail. "I don't blame you or anyone for being skeptical of it."

Jamie smiled grimly. "I just wish Aubrey could see it

that way. After this weekend, I'm sure she understands now why we feel the way we do."

"That's a gut thing. I guess you don't want to hear what daed has to say about it."

He already imagined what was being said. He grimaced just at thinking of his daed's opinions on what was happening, and made a mental note to keep distance until everything was resolved. He had enough to deal with presently.

"Not really. I can already hear what he would have to say about it."

Henry shrugged and took a bite of his sandwich. "Smart decision. If you plan to move all that furniture soon, you'd better get to the bakery."

While he walked along the sidewalks toward the bakery, Jamie kept his eyes focused on the ground. The past few months had been so busy with the furniture store and Aubrey's pregnancy news coupled with Emma's unnerving appearance that it had distanced him from his own family. Their relationship was strained.

When Jamie had moved out to be with Aubrey and her family after the wedding, his daed hadn't been too happy about losing an extra pair of arms to work around the haus and farm. He grew even unhappier when Jamie could no longer help with the farm since he had his own to look after. They had been so consumed with everything the past few weeks that they hadn't even told his family about Aubrey expecting a bobli.

Guilt gnawed at the bottom of Jamie's ribcage. He reached the bakery to find the parking lot only half-full of cars and the smell of nutmeg in the air. Not bothering with the front door, he crossed the road to the back door of the bakery. Aubrey only baked in the kitchen now, avoiding the front end and customers.

The door was propped open with a large rock and he slipped in with familiar ease. White sugar sparkled on the island, and a couple of bowls were stacked near the sink, waiting to be washed. His eyes landed on Aubrey's petite frame as she leaned down to open the oven door and peer at the cookies baking inside.

A wave of playfulness lessened the heaviness inside his heart. Jamie crept steadily to her and reached out to poke at her slender waist. He was rewarded with a startled squeak and a slap on his arm.

"Don't scare me like that!" Aubrey said, scowling at his laughter. "You'll put me into early labor if you continue playing those types of games."

"I'm sorry. I couldn't resist."

Aubrey rolled her eyes. A small smile curved her lips upward fractionally. "I'm sure it was very hard to resist. Let me tell my maemm that I'm taking a break."

He waited patiently by the door until Aubrey returned from the front with Sadie in tow. After exchanging brief pleasantries with Sadie, he took Aubrey's hand as they walked to the small park a couple of blocks down. The swings and slides were empty, with it being the middle of the day and not quite summer, but they enjoyed the silence.

"How is work?" Aubrey asked.

They sat together at a picnic table under the shade of a large oak tree and watched the shadows of budding

458

leaves dancing across the top. He waited for Aubrey to take a bite of her sandwich before doing the same.

"It's fine. We managed to catch up with inventory," he noted absently.

"That's gut."

He sensed the tension emanating from Aubrey in strong waves. Setting the half-eaten sandwich on the table, he turned so that he straddled the bench and faced Aubrey fully. The sunlight that managed to peek through the oak tree's leafy top danced across her rosy and freckled cheeks. Aubrey kept her eyes focused on the sandwich in her hands, picking absently at the piece of lettuce popping out.

"What's wrong?" Jamie asked.

"Nothing," Aubrey responded quickly.

Too quickly, in Jamie's opinion. Jamie narrowed his eyes at her in a silent warning.

After a few seconds, Aubrey let out a defeated sigh and set the sandwich down as well. She twisted the upper portion of her body to look at him with pained eyes. "It's about Emma. What am I going to say to her about this weekend? She will be devastated knowing daed won't let her stay with them."

Tears trailed down Aubrey's cheeks. Baffled by the sudden emotion, Jamie treaded carefully. With their previous agreement of letting it go after talking to Daniel still in mind, he was confident that the emotions brimming within Aubrey came directly from the shifting moods that accompanied her pregnancy.

"But she knew that was going to be a risk, Aubrey. Didn't you agree to-"

"Jah, I agreed to talk to him, but that still doesn't erase the feeling that I failed to convince him otherwise."

Her shoulders slumped downward in visible defeat. A breeze stirred the whisper of hair underneath Aubrey's kapp, and dark lashes curled against her skin.

Jamie placed a hand on her fidgeting leg and offered an encouraging smile. "Gott will take care of this. He always does in the end, jah?"

"Jah." Aubrey sniffed delicately, but didn't look convinced. "I just wish there was an easy way to tell Emma that I have to say goodbye now. We have a bobli coming, and I can't worry about these problems anymore."

"Would you like me to tell her?" he offered.

A laugh that was mixed with a scoff blew past Aubrey's lips. She raised her head and peered at him in disbelief with red-rimmed eyes. "I already know how that would go, so nee. It needs to come from me," she said, shaking her head.

"I wouldn't be mean about it," Jamie replied defensively. "Your sister already knows where I stand on everything. It wouldn't surprise her at all."

Aubrey stared at him with an indescribable expression. The hair on his arms stood on edge, and he got the eerie feeling that she was trying to read his mind or something similar.

"What?"

She shook her head again. "Is there ever going to be a chance that you would accept my sister?"

The question threw Jamie off guard, and then the guilt set in at the innocent hurt in Aubrey's eyes. He had spent so much time doubting Emma, and trying to convince Aubrey to turn away from the temptations Emma represented at times, but he hadn't stopped to consider how that came across to Aubrey. Family was the center of their world and a core value. Even if Emma were shunned, it didn't make her any less of a sister to Aubrey or a daughter to Katie.

He gathered Aubrey's warm and smaller hand in his to press a tender kiss to the back of it. "I'm sorry, Aubrey. I forget how hard this must be on you and your family. I can only imagine how it feels to be torn between Emma and our faith."

A faint smile crossed Aubrey's face, but it faded to a frown. She gently withdrew her hand and played with the edge of her apron. "I don't want to be torn about it anymore," She said softly.

They were silent for a few moments, listening to the whisper of a breeze in the trees and then the silence of the warm afternoon.

"I better get back to the bakery."

Without sparing a glance at him, Aubrey rose from the picnic table. He watched her walk away with uneasiness burning in him, head bowed and focused on whatever thoughts consumed her. The abrupt goodbye was unsettling, but not wholly unexpected. Whenever it came to anyone disagreeing about Emma's intentions, Aubrey withdrew from the world to pray and reflect. She was sensitive to others' opinions of her sister, and their community had plenty of thoughts regarding Emma Forrest.

Jamie rubbed his face tiredly, and then tilted it backward to look up at the golden light peeking through the budding leaves. Spring had become his favorite season recently. The chill of winter finally floated away and allowed a blanket of warmth to settle on his shoulders. At times, he believed it to be Gott wrapping him in an embrace that filled him with hope.

Spring was the definition of a new cycle of life that Gott used to bless the world. Their fields were beginning to grow, Aubrey's garden was flourishing, and now their bobli was growing within Aubrey.

Maybe he was being too brash in his behavior toward Emma. Maybe everyone deserved a second chance if they were ready to accept Gott's forgiveness, but something foreboding tugged at the back of his hopes. Something told him that this wouldn't end like Aubrey, or her family, prayed that it would.

It wasn't just his job to protect his fraa from possible temptation and hurt spiritually. He loved Aubrey, and wished nothing but happiness for her.

Jamie scooped up their uneaten sandwiches, and placed them back in his lunch pail. He walked back along the sidewalks toward work, praying the entire time. He prayed even harder that Emma wouldn't be the one thing that separated them from one another.

His heart hardened with resolve. There was only one thing left to do.

He needed to speak with Emma again.

෬ CHAPTER 8 ෨

A front of uncomfortably hot and dry air settled into the San Luis Valley. Sweat gathered beneath the line of Aubrey's kapp as she ventured down the sidewalks toward the Farmer's Market. Cradled in her arms were a couple of whoopie pies for Katie's stand, and she was relieved to reach the shaded area that the town of Monte Vista used for their Farmer's Market.

Tables were spread out beneath white tents on a large field of grass to keep everyone shaded from the sun. The trees offered little protection from the strange heat wave. Englischers streamed around the tables of baked goods, preserved jams, and quilts, but the most popular was Jamie's section of the Market. Earlier that morning he had left to pick up Henry and meet her daed and bruder to haul some of the newly-crafted furniture. Several groups of people gathered around the dining room tables, chairs and bed frames with genuine interest.

"They seem to be doing much better with work now, jah?" Elizabeth mentioned.

She appeared at Aubrey's side, taking the whoopie pies from her arms. They exchanged a friendly smile before heading toward Katie's stand.

"Jah. I know that Jamie has worked day and night to catch up," Aubrey commented.

Elizabeth used the sleeve of her blue dress to wipe at the sweat dripping down her temple. Her pale cheeks were red from spending the day out in the sun, and helping Aubrey run the stand whenever her maemm needed a break.

"I can't believe how warm it is!" Elizabeth exclaimed. She set the whoopie pies on the plastic table and arranged them artfully. "I don't remember last spring being this hot so early."

"Me neither," Aubrey said, eyes burning when a small bead of sweat slipped into it from the corner of her eye. "I hope this doesn't mean a drought this summer. That's the last thing any of us want to deal with."

She sat in the chair Jamie brought for her. The heat brought on fatigue more easily, and she constantly sipped at a canteen of water at the suggestion of their midwife, who had checked up on her the other day.

"Plenty of water now that it is getting warmer. Important to stay hydrated, or else you could faint and fall."

The constant thirst and dizzy spells made Aubrey relieved to know that her due date would be in December. She couldn't fathom being nine months pregnant during the middle of the summer, when she was already so exhausted from the heat.

"Especially Henry and the celery crops."

Aubrey blinked in rapid succession. She looked up at Elizabeth, a small grin slowly spreading across her friend's face. It seemed to take forever for the realization behind her words to sink in.

"Does that mean what I think it means?" Aubrey asked. A smile was beginning to make its way across her own flushed face.

Elizabeth nodded, grinning widely with unchecked joy. She jumped out of her chair to hug Elizabeth tightly in congratulations.

"That is exciting news! Congratulations," Aubrey said, beaming.

"Danka. We haven't told anyone else yet..."

"I won't say anything. I promise."

They spent the next few minutes talking over wedding details in hushed whispers so no one else would hear. After selling the last of the apple butter crisps, Elizabeth sat in the other chair alongside Aubrey. A serious expression now filled her joyful face.

"How is your sister?"

The pit of Aubrey's stomach tightened at the mention of Emma's name. She had yet to talk to her sister, who, for the most part, stayed clear of their community now. Michael had also seemingly distanced himself from the community as well. Aubrey frowned at that, wondering if both of their distant behaviors were tied to one another. She wasn't sure what the distance was about exactly, but Aubrey dreaded the time she would have to tell Emma about their daed's reaction, and in return, her own decision to step back from the situation.

"I'm sorry, again," Elizabeth said, reading the turmoil on Aubrey's face perfectly. "Henry told me what has been going on with Jamie, and I can't even imagine how hard it has been. I've been praying every night for you and your family."

Aubrey smiled tiredly in a wordless gratitude. "We are in need of prayers right now, but my sister needs them more than anyone else. She has been through some very hard trials."

"She's still your sister though," Elizabeth said gently. "That's a fact no one can deny. Even yourself."

"Jah, but I promised Jamie that I would stay out of it as much as I could. My sister has always been very flighty and a bit rebellious when it comes to rules. There's no way of knowing whether she could even come back."

"I hope that she does, but I think you're being wise in staying out of it now that you have a life growing inside of you."

"Exactly."

Aubrey sipped some warm water from the canteen and avoided Elizabeth's gaze. She didn't want to think about her sister any longer. The turmoil threatened to trigger her already queasy stomach.

Across the field, Jamie stood proudly alongside a large dresser he had spent weeks creating. He kept one hand on the smooth top, talking easily to an Englischer couple. Her heart warmed at the sight of his smile and sparkling eyes.

When Katie appeared at the table after taking a lunch break, Aubrey rose from her chair and squeezed through the crowds to where Jamie stood. He looked up from the task of counting and smiled at her.

"Everything okay?"

Aubrey nodded. "Jah, all is fine. I just wanted to stretch my legs a bit is all," she said, shrugging her shoulders.

"Well, don't push it too hard. It's hot out here, and-"

"I've been drinking tons of water, Jamie. I'm fine."

His brow pulled into a frown at the sharpness of her tone.

Aubrey flushed at the outburst, and hung her head to look at the grass. "I'm sorry," she apologized softly. "Maybe the heat is getting to be a bit too much for me."

"I can take you home then," Jamie said immediately. He started in the direction of where Henry and Levi stood with Daniel under the shaded area of the Farmer's Market, but stopped when Aubrey caught his wrist.

"Nee. I don't want to go home. Can we go for a walk somewhere and talk?"

The frown on Jamie's face deepened. After excusing himself to Henry and Levi, they walked away from the crowd and off the field. The normally busy town was quiet, with most of the people congregating in the field.

Aubrey led him to a wooden bench on the sidewalk, in front of a secondhand store that stocked used baby clothes, toys, and everything else that was needed. Her eyes lingered on the small crib displayed in the front window, and her hand unconsciously went to the swell of her stomach. In a matter of months their bobli would be occupying a crib like that, and it filled her with overwhelming joy.

"So," Jamie said, stretching out his long legs in front of him. "What's going on? I know you didn't want to walk all the way over here just to be alone with me, but I wouldn't mind that if that's the case."

She laughed lightly. The tension from her conversation with Elizabeth faded to a dull ache temporarily. Instead, she decided to divulge Elizabeth's news.

"I bet. Did you know that Henry and Elizabeth are planning to get married?"

Jamie's eyes widened in shock. He reached up to pull off his hat and wiped away the sweat beading at his hairline. The sunlight bounced off the honey strands of his hair, and it took all Aubrey's self restraint not to reach out and compulsively touch him. Even though they were in privacy, they were still in public.

"I can't believe my own bruder didn't tell me. It's not surprising that Elizabeth told you. According to Henry, she thinks of you as a younger sister after you helped her through the previous winter."

It took a bit of convincing on Aubrey's part, but in the end Elizabeth had accepted Henry's courtship and remained within their community to be surrounded by friends.

"I'm thankful she sees me in that way," Aubrey said, smiling. "You can't go and harass Henry over it either. He'll be mad that Elizabeth told me."

"Jah, secret's a secret," Jamie replied flippantly, but his eyes sparkled with genuine happiness for Henry. He draped an arm over the back of the bench, and his hand brushed against Aubrey's shoulder blades in the process. "What else do you want to talk about? You looked a bit put out earlier. Or is that a pregnancy mood?"

She smacked him playfully on the arm outstretched behind her. "Don't poke fun at my moods." She waved a warning finger under his nose. "You're the one that has to come home and deal with me at the end of the day."

"That's true," Jamie said and easily swiped her finger away from his face. "But seriously. What was bothering you?"

Aubrey leaned against the bench and Jamie's arm with a long sigh. The hot sun above bore down on them, and the smell of dry dirt lingered about the town. Her eyes caught sight of a large pot filled with flowers across the street, the vibrant petals drooping slightly from the heat.

"Elizabeth was asking about Emma," was all she said.

"Ach."

"I'm just so tired of everyone asking what she will do. I love my sister, but this-" Aubrey paused briefly, biting her bottom lip in contemplation. "It's just too much to try to explain the situation."

"You shouldn't have to. It's not your job to explain things to anyone."

"I know, but still..."

Jamie laid a sweaty hand over her forearm and locked eyes with her firmly. The breeze picked up again and carried the smell of freshly carved wood, which clung to Jamie's clothes constantly. The familiar smell soothed the turmoil within her temporarily.

"Don't worry about it, Aubrey. Your sister is an adult, and she can handle whatever is thrown at her. She's tough, I'll give her that. We," he stressed, motioning between the two of them, "have a lot to think about. Let Gott be in control of it."

He clasped her hand tightly in his, and leaned toward her. Aubrey listened to him pray under his breath, but found no comfort in the words. Her thoughts were fixated on the time she would have to face Emma again.

When they finished praying, Aubrey walked to the store behind them to distract herself from her thoughts. She stared at the bucket of stuffed animals, one hand placed protectively over her stomach. Through the reflection of the window, Jamie's tall figure appeared behind her. Strong arms wrapped around her, mindful of the tender swell of her stomach. Her hands strayed to where Jamie's were resting of their own accord.

"It seems so far, but so short a time away," Aubrey commented, rubbing the dryness on Jamie's knuckles.

"What does?"

"The bobli. It feels as if it will be forever, though I know he or she will be here by the end of the December."

She felt Jamie's lips press against the side of her neck and inhaled deeply. Her eyes fluttered closed at the intimate contact, and she felt his lips curl up into a smile against her skin.

"Jah. She'll be here before we know it."

"She?" Aubrey twisted her head to look at Jamie with a arched eyebrow. "You are so sure that this bobli is a she."

"I feel that I'm right on this one."

Aubrey snorted indelicately at the confidence in Jamie's voice. She turned back around, head resting on Jamie's chest, and stared at their reflections in the glass.

"I hope that you're right. I hope you're right about everything."

CRBO

Jamie stared at the collection of stuffed animals in the plastic container. Would the bobli like a stuffed bear or a bunny? He held said objects in his hands, looking down at them with a furrowed brow. Considering the options, he decided to buy both and let the bobli decide which one would be his or her favorite.

The small store in the middle of Monte Vista was filled to the brim with used kinner's clothes, toys, cribs, and anything else a bobli would need. Jamie had stopped in on his way back from the bakery to pick out a stuffed animal for the crib he was in the middle of crafting. He couldn't wait to see Aubrey's expression when he surprised her. It was one of the few things he could contribute to the bobli's room. Aubrey had sewn most of the bobli clothes with Hannah and Elizabeth's help.

He walked through the small aisles and his arms brushed against the racks of pink dresses. The woman behind the counter smiled warmly at him.

"Is that all for you?" she asked kindly, pushing aside a pile of folded clothes. "We have blankets, a crib mattress, and everything else you can imagine."

"Thank you, but this is what I came for," Jamie said,

holding out the two stuffed animals.

"All right then." Her fingers danced across the register, still smiling. "That will be $7.88 with tax."

Jamie reached in his trousers' pocket to grab the small amount of cash he had brought with him, but before he could offer it, a tattooed hand stretched across the counter in front of him. A credit card was held daintily between purple-polished fingernails. He looked up in surprise to find Emma standing alongside him.

Her eyes flicked over to him, one eyebrow arched in a silent challenge. He was too startled even to argue or decline Emma's offer to pay. The woman took Emma's credit card and ran it through her machine.

"Consider it a present from me to the bobli," Emma said. She slid her credit card back in her wallet and then handed the stuffed animals to Jamie. "One of the few things that I can do at least."

Jamie found the resolve to talk again. He started to shake his head, but Emma slipped away from the counter before he could say anything in front of the woman. The afternoon was hot and bright when Jamie stepped out of the store to follow Emma.

"You know that I can't accept gifts from you," Jamie said, holding the stuffed animals toward her.

Emma crossed bare arms and sighed in aggravation. "Do you honestly think anyone will care about that? It's just stuffed animals for your bobli. Besides, I'll be back in the community soon anyway."

He was floored again.

They stood at the middle of the sidewalk in an

awkward silence, with Englischers streaming past them. Jamie's gaze lingered on the diamond piercing on Emma's upper lip and he shook his head in disbelief. He had a hard time imagining Emma ridding herself of all those tattoos and piercings.

"Don't look too enthused there," Emma quipped.

Jamie ignored the snarky jab and crossed his arms over his chest, with the stuffed animals still in hand. "You're really coming back?"

"Jah, I am," Emma said, and tossed the long strands of her back over her tanned shoulder. "Do you have a problem with that?"

He clenched his teeth to keep his own snarky reply back and prayed for patience. "I have no problems with you coming back, if that is what Gott's plans are for you. I am in no position to judge you."

Emma arched a skeptical eyebrow at him, but the defiance in her dissipated slightly. At that moment, she looked uncertain herself. "Well, okay then. Have a gut day."

She turned to go, but stopped short when Jamie reached out to grab her wrist. Her skin felt soft, like Aubrey's, under his fingers, but Emma's wrists were much weaker than Aubrey's, which spent hours kneading bread.

"If you are coming back, we need to get some things settled."

"Like what?"

"Aubrey is an important part of both our lives. We have to learn how to get along for our sakes, but more important, for Aubrey's sake. She doesn't like to hear us fighting."

Emma tugged her wrist free from Jamie's circle of fingers. She combed a hand through her hair with a defeated sigh. "I suppose you're right. So let's make a deal; we will try to get along for Aubrey's sake. Jah?"

"Deal."

He held out a hand for Emma to shake, a truce offering. If Emma were to return, he prayed that the doubts lingering in the back of his mind would fade away. Whatever Gott's purpose was for Emma, he felt right there and then that Gott was trying to teach him something.

"Why do you hate me anyway?" Emma asked casually.

Jamie scuffed the toe of his boot into the concrete sidewalk. "I don't hate you," he said eventually. "I apologize if that is how it seemed-"

"That is how it seems," Emma cut in, arching an eyebrow again. "I don't think I've ever known an Amish man to be so openly hostile."

Blood rushed to Jamie's face in shame. "I-I'm sorry. I know that I have been a bit overprotective, but can you blame me? With everything that has happened and-"

"Aubrey being pregnant. I know. I get it, and it's cool. I'm sorry for everything as well. I didn't help things by doing what I was doing."

A surreal feeling overwhelmed Jamie. He had never expected an apology from Emma about the past few years' events, but he took it gladly. Inwardly, he thanked Gott for His help to resolve the issues between them finally. It had shadowed his mind for a while and contorted his perception. He was cautiously optimistic that they were striding forward.

"Danka for these," Jamie said, waving the stuffed animals. "Aubrey will be excited to put these in the crib once I have it finished."

Emma smiled hesitantly. "You're welcome. I guess I'll be seeing you around then. I have to, you know, go meet with Bishop Abraham."

She turned around before Jamie could reply and started down the sidewalk in the direction of their community. He watched as Emma slowly blended into the Englischers around her before turning toward the furniture store. The warm walk back cleared his thoughts of the turmoil that still clung to him stubbornly, but all that came crashing back when he spotted Michael Brenneman standing in the warehouse with Levi. He was still dressed in Amish clothes, but Jamie's skin prickled in uneasiness at his presence.

"Jamie," Michael said, nodding in acknowledgment.

"What's going on?"

Levi leveled a warning glance from where he stood across a finished table that needed to be put out on the floor.

"Michael has offered to help us catch up on our inventory. He used to work here, and-"

"We don't need to catch up. Everything is caught up."

A tense silence followed.

The bell above the door at the front of the store dinged. Cheerful voiced echoed in the warehouse, and a warm breeze stirred a pile of wood shavings at Jamie's feet. Jamie ignored the pinched expression on Levi's face before he excused himself to go to the front of the store. His conversation with Emma echoed within his mind while he met Michael's distrustful eye.

"Why do you have a problem with me?" Michael asked bluntly.

Surprised by the question, Jamie balled his hands into fists and then shoved them into the pocket of his trousers. He looked away from Michael's gaze, not willing to engage in a full-fledged confrontation. "I don't have a problem with you."

"Jah, you do. I want to know what it is, because I'm working here now, and I'd rather not have any future fights."

"There won't be," Jamie said curtly.

He brushed by Michael stiffly and walked toward the crib he was still staining. Placing the stuffed animals in a corner of the crib, Jamie turned to find Michael right behind him. He tensed at Michael's proximity.

"Did Emma buy those for you?" Michael asked.

Jamie arched an eyebrow at the question.

Michael looked away when he realized what he had just revealed. The two of them were talking again, and if Jamie's suspicions were right, this meant they were coming back to the community together.

"How did you know that?"

A battled plainly raged on Michael's face, but in the end he caved in with a defeated sigh. "Because she told me she wanted to get something for the bobli," he confessed, and grimaced visibly. "I wasn't supposed to tell anyone that we were talking again."

Jamie shook his head in disdain. When one secret was discovered, there was always another one when it came to Emma. A healthy dose of skepticism rushed through Jamie's veins and added to the doubts already circling through him.

"Why?" Jamie asked. "Why are you two hiding that?"

"You obviously don't know what happened if you're asking that question."

Michael smiled grimly. He smoothed a hand over his face before rubbing his temple, and then looked at Jamie with an intense glint to his eyes. "You love Aubrey, jah?"

"Jah. More than anything in the world."

"And you would do whatever it takes to keep her?"

"Jah..." Jamie answered hesitantly, unsure of what Michael was getting at exactly. "Where are you going with this conversation?"

Michael didn't answer right away. Instead, he took a step forward and placed a hand on the crib railing. He turned his face to hide whatever emotions were playing in them, and then gave a firm tug on the crib bars to check its soundness.

"I'm no different from you. I love Emma. Always have, and always will. I look at her, and I just know that Gott brought her to me for a reason. I still dream about getting married someday, and having a family with her. Despite what happened years ago, I-I couldn't lose her now after what's happened."

His voiced wavered thickly with emotion. Michael turned around suddenly, tears glistening on the surfaces of his eyes. "I can't live without my family and Gott. I tried to, but I couldn't do it. Emma-she-I'm trying to convince her to come back."

Something loudly clicked inside Jamie's mind. It made perfect sense now why Emma had acted the way she did with her vague answers and flighty behavior. His other suspicion was right. "She doesn't want to come back."

Michael swallowed thickly, nodding his head. "Nee. She came back initially to find some sort of comfort from being around family, but doesn't want to take the vow again. She doesn't want to face the community and ask for forgiveness."

"So, you're trying to persuade her otherwise?"

"It hasn't been easy. She's stubborn as a mule, and her pride gets in the way. I don't know what to say or do anymore. How did you convince Aubrey to stay in the community?"

"I didn't convince her," Jamie stated, rubbing the back of his neck uncomfortably. "Aubrey wanted to stay in the community. If she'd wanted to leave, she would've left, despite what I would've said to her."

"But you still tried..."

He was searching for answers, for advice. Jamie watched as Michael returned his attention to the crib and stroked his fingers around a railing. He debated on telling him to let Emma go if she was unwilling to come back, but the other part of him understood where Michael's feelings stemmed from. It had been the same feeling Jamie had had when he'd tried to imagine a life without Aubrey, and the void felt so deep that Gott couldn't even fill it.

"Jah. I still tried, but Aubrey is different from Emma."

Michael tugged on the crib railing one last time before letting his hand fall away. He smiled grimly at Jamie once again. "Are you sure about that?"

❧ CHAPTER 9 ☙

A loud and eager knock at the front door paused Aubrey's wrist in mid-seasoning the chicken for dinner. She turned around, heart suddenly beating hard and furiously inside of her chest. The creak of the rocking chair Jamie sat in, and the heavy thumps of his boots, signaled that he had gotten up to answer the door.

What if it was Emma? Was she ready to tell her sister about what had happened?

"Sadie? Is everything-" Jamie's voice started in surprise, but Sadie's voice cut in over him.

"Is Aubrey here? I have to talk to her. Right now."

Aubrey set the jar of seasoning alongside the plucked chicken right as Sadie entered the kitchen. Her tanned face was flushed a bright pink, and her eyes were bright with excitement. A small part of Aubrey relaxed to see that whatever news Sadie carried was gut and apparently exciting.

"Guess what?" Sadie rushed to her, grabbing Aubrey's hands in her sweaty ones. "I'm going to Denver for rumspringa. Isn't that exciting?"

The grin on Sadie's face was contagious, but worry burned inside of Aubrey, thinking of Sadie in a large city experiencing the English lifestyle. Her sweet and gentle sister would undoubtedly attract attention. Over the top of Sadie's kapp, she caught Jamie's eyes, and they exchanged a concerned look. "Are you going with anyone?" Aubrey asked. "A group of friends or-"

Sadie frowned at the question, visibly displeased with her reaction. "Jah, of course. Eli is going, and a whole bunch of us will be together. What are you making? It smells gut."

"It's just a green bean casserole and roasted chicken. Sadie," She caught her sister's arm, stopping her in mid step to inspect the oven's contents, "remember what I told you about rumspringa. Be careful who you trust and don't do anything brash."

"You sound like maemm and daed when they said I could go."

"We don't want you doing anything you'll regret."

There had been the occasional story Aubrey had overheard of girls going a bit crazy during their rumspringa days. Common things like kissing English boys, drinking alcohol or smoking cigarettes, and wearing dresses that barely reached their knees. She tried to picture Sadie experiencing those things, but kept picturing Emma with her tattoos and odd body piercings.

"I won't do anything that I will regret," Sadie said, gently removing Aubrey's clenched hand from her arm. "Don't worry about me, Aubrey. You have other things to worry about than what I'm doing on my rumspringa."

Her hand fondly brushed the swell of Aubrey's stomach before turning to talk to Jamie about the furniture store, and the table he had recently given their family in replacement of their older one.

A queasy feeling started to build within the pit of her stomach. As discreetly as possible, Aubrey stepped out the back door to breathe in the cool spring air. Sprinklers ticked distantly in the fields, and the air felt damp from all the water. She sucked in lungfuls, willing the nausea away with a hand over her stomach.

The door opened up with a soft groan. She glanced over her shoulder to see Sadie exiting the kitchen with a frown.

"Are you all right?" Sadie asked.

Forcing a strained smile, Aubrey nodded briefly. She rested a hand on the porch railing to steady herself just in case a dizzy spell followed. "Jah, I'm fine. Just a bit queasy is all."

They were silent for a few minutes, standing alongside one another on the back porch while watching the sprinklers in the distance. The peaceful silence, with the sun slowly dipping toward the horizon, filled Aubrey with ease. It was times like these that she was grateful she'd stayed behind, and for Gott's creation.

"Have you talked to Emma since the dinner?" Sadie asked abruptly. "I haven't seen or heard from her in a couple days. Now that I think about it, I haven't seen Michael Brenneman anywhere either."

"I have no idea what is going on with her. One minute

she's around and wants to be here, and then the next minute she's disappeared."

"I pray she's coming back. Especially after daed said that she could live with them during the reinstatement period."

Aubrey's jaw dropped in surprise. She had witnessed the hurt and even anger in their daed's eyes and she had already assumed that route wouldn't work. "What changed his mind?"

"I think it was a bit of everything and everyone," Sadie said, shrugging her shoulders. "After dinner he went for a walk and prayed. I think he prayed even harder for the following couple of days, but he told maemm and I that he would allow it if Gott was willing it to happen."

"Wow. Tha-that's gut news."

Sadie turned to her with a smile. "Isn't it though? It'll be nice to have all our family back and not have this dark cloud hanging above us all the time."

Aubrey looked away to hide her doubts, but clung to the frail hope that maybe Sadie would be right. Their family could be whole again.

"I better go. I told maemm I would be back before dinner would be done, and I know that it was probably done a few minutes ago." She pressed a soft kiss to Aubrey's cheek, and gave an encouraging smile. "Everything will be all right. You'll see. I have faith in Gott that He will help us and Emma through this."

The second Sadie was down the road and out of earshot, Jamie emerged from the kitchen with a frown. He came to stand next to Aubrey, eyes focused on the sprinklers as well.

"Did I hear right? Your daed said he would let Emma live with them during the reinstatement period?"

"I guess." Aubrey arched an eyebrow up at Jamie in mock anger. "Were you eavesdropping on our conversation?"

"Perhaps."

The troubled expression didn't leave Jamie's eyes, nor did he return her playfulness. His jaw clenched together a few times as though he was chewing on words and then swallowing them down with force.

"What's wrong, Jamie?"

"Emma doesn't want to come back."

She stiffened at the unexpected and harshly spoken words. Her heart started to thump loudly within the confines of her chest, and a wave of nausea crashed over her again. "What do you mean? How do you know that?"

A heavy sigh escaped Jamie's lips. He reached up to push his hat off and flattened a hand over his hair in mild aggravation. "I know that because Michael Brenneman told me. Your bruder hired him to help out at the furniture store, and that's when he told me that the two of them are talking, or have been talking this whole time."

"That doesn't make any sense. Why would she not tell me something like that?"

"Because Emma has secrets, and she keeps them," Jamie stated, turning his head to fix her with an intense gaze that was hard to decipher. "Michael is the one who wants to come back, and he's trying to convince Emma to stay here with him. I don't get it, but he's still in love with

Emma."

Tears wet Aubrey's eyelashes. She should have expected this, knowing how her sister tended to rebel against the rules. None of that eased the sting and hurt, thinking of the times that Emma had looked her directly in the eye and didn't speak the whole truth.

Strong arms gathered her in a hug, and the steady thump of Jamie's heartbeat echoed inside of her head. She cried without shame into the fabric of his cotton shirt, and clutched at Jamie's shoulders blades as the bottle of emotions tipped forth finally. How long she cried was lost to her. The deep rumbling of Jamie's voice as he prayed began to calm the storm within her. When a sense of peace finally came upon her, Aubrey raised her head to look up at Jamie, who held her without complaint.

"Promise me there will never be any secrets like that between us. I don't think I can handle such things anymore."

"I promise, if you promise to do the same," Jamie whispered softly, tucking an errant strand of hair behind her ear.

"Jah, I promise."

They kissed for a few minutes before Jamie left her standing on the porch to start his evening chores. Aubrey picked up a watering can and started the process of watering her freshly potted flowers. The tender buds, barely beginning to bloom, filled her with loving care as she carefully watered the flowers that needed it the most before moving on to their garden. The smell of wet earth and fresh dill greeted Aubrey's nose as she bent to pluck a weed.

The steady clop of horse's hooves broke the silent evening. Aubrey set the watering can down and turned to face the road in confusion. Maybe Sadie had forgotten something or wanted to tell her something else. Instead, much to her surprise and irritation, it was Emma steering a buggy down the road. Unlike the previous times they had talked, her sister's hair was pulled back in a modest bun that mimicked the one Aubrey wore beneath her kapp. The startling black strands of hair still peeked out, but gone were the eyebrow, lip and ear piercing. Her tanned face was devoid of makeup, and she wore a modest dress with sleeves that covered a majority of the tattoos on her arms.

Emma grinned widely at Aubrey, unaware of the conversation that had just taken place between her and Jamie. "What do you think? I promised to start dressing more modestly and remove the facial piercings until I move back in with maemm and daed."

Her stomach muscles balled up tightly and a queasy feeling filled her. It would never cease to amaze her how easy it was for Emma to continue her act and continue to lie.

"Where's your car?" Aubrey asked abruptly. "Who let you borrow their buggy?"

Groomed eyebrows furrowed into a frown at the questions. Emma set the reins down carefully and hopped out of the buggy with graceful movements. Her sneakered feet sprayed gravel everywhere.

"I'm selling it, and daed let me borrow the buggy. Did anyone tell you the news or not?"

"Tell me what?"

"Daed said that I could stay with them while I ask for the church's forgiveness and-"

"Is that really what you want, Emma?" she interrupted over Emma's excited babble, crossing her arms.

Emma's mouth opened into an 'o' of surprise before quickly shutting her mouth. A panicked, stricken expression occupied her face before it was quickly replaced by an indifferent one. "Of course it is. I thought we already had this conversation, Aubrey. I told you, and I told the church I want to come back. I'm asking for forgiveness."

"But that's not what you want. I know you, Emma. The whole time you were here all you talked about was leaving to live the English life. You said yourself that you didn't want to give up your life. What changed?"

Anger was dictating her words. A small part of her held out that Emma would tell the truth this time. She wanted to give her sister a chance to be truly honest with herself and what she wanted or believed was right.

"I-I-"

Her bottom lip quivered, and tears glossed the blue eyes that Aubrey had once knew. Emma took a step back and let out a watery breath, but remained silent with whatever thoughts that were crossing her mind.

"Tell the truth for once, Emma," Aubrey said softly. "Be honest with yourself and Gott. Is this really what you want or does someone else want this for you?"

Slender shoulders trembled with suppressed cries, but they eventually stilled. A thick silence fell, broken only by the click of sprinklers. From the corner of Aubrey's eye, she caught sight of Jamie standing by the barn doors with a pair of leather gloves clutched tightly in hand.

His eyes flicked over to hers briefly before settling on Emma, waiting for an answer as well.

When no answer came, she tried again. "Well? What's the truth?"

ॐ

Jamie stood by the barn doors, surprised by the scene unfolding in front of him. He twisted his leather gloves together and flicked his eyes between Aubrey and Emma. There was utter silence between the two of them, and neither was willing to speak first.

He watched the emotions play along Emma's face. She was torn between telling the truth and continuing to lie. She was also surprised by Aubrey's confrontation, and he was too.

"How much longer are you going to lie to me? We're sisters, and we've always told each other the truth. We never had any secrets, and now you've kept tons of secrets from me," Aubrey said.

The hurt in Aubrey's voice was unmistakable. Jamie tossed his leather gloves cautiously back into the barn, and headed to comfort Aubrey. He stopped short, however, when Emma turned to look at him with glistening eyes. The hair on his arms raised as Emma ran an assessing gaze over him. When he tried to read the emotions battling within her pale irises, Emma turned her head to look back at Aubrey.

"Did you stay here because of Jamie?"

Aubrey's face contorted at the question. She dropped her head to look at the ground, and refused to look at either one of them. The center of his chest burned as time stretched on without an answer.

"I stayed because I wanted to stay," Aubrey eventually answered in a strained voice.

Emma crossed her tattooed arms. "You stayed here because of Jamie. If you don't want me to lie to you, then don't lie to me either. You were adamant about leaving the community to go to school to be an artist. Remember? Then Jamie arrived and all of that changed within a matter of weeks."

He wasn't sure whether the last statement was a hidden jab, but he bristled nonetheless at it. Jamie opened his mouth to respond, but Aubrey beat him to it.

"Jah. I stayed here because I love Jamie, but I also stayed for our family. You have no idea what your leaving did to our family."

"Actually, I do. Daed refuses to acknowledge my existence, and maemm can barely look me in the eye."

"Then what are you doing here? If you know how-"

"I want to be here because Michael wants to be here," Emma blurted out, and tears flooded her eyes as the words escaped. "He wanted to come back after his wife and kid's death, but I-I-I just don't know if I can come back. I don't know what to do, or what to tell him."

"So, you're lying to our Bishop, to your family, and to yourself. What is wrong with you, Emma?"

Shame stained Emma's tanned cheeks a dusty color.

She ducked her head to hide the tears now freely slipping from the corners of her eyes. A warm spring breeze stirred the light fabric of Emma's dress and also played with the errant strands of hair framing Aubrey's face.

"I don't know what's wrong with me. I'm just so lost," Emma whispered.

The click of sprinklers filled the silence between them. Jamie stood by the barn, torn between going to Aubrey and letting her voice the bottled emotions that Emma needed to hear. He watched the two sisters, forever bound by blood, but separated by their hearts, slowly peel away from one another. A small tinge of sadness filled him briefly. There was nothing worse than to lose a family member in any way, and he only dreamed of how it felt: the heartache, the longing for things to be the way they used to be. He had seen all of it with Aubrey.

"This place-" Emma started in a thick voice, "will never accept people like me back again. I don' think I ever belonged here in the first place."

Aubrey shook her head. "You did belong here, Emma. I don't know why you think you are being judged by the community."

"Because I am being judged."

"You're not being judged. You used to be Amish. You know that we don't judge anyone for their decisions in life."

"Really? Then why can't daed forgive me? Or why can't anyone else forgive me?"

Just like that, the sadness for Emma eased out of him. He stared at the petite blonde in disbelief, and a fire of frustration flickered to life inside of him. "Because not once has anyone ever heard you apologize and mean it," Jamie accused.

Emma's head whipped in his direction, having forgotten his presence briefly. Her eyes narrowed at him. "What do I have to apologize to you for?"

His mouth dropped open in further disbelief. Aubrey sent him a pleading look, but he ignored it. He took a step forward. "How about for trying to ruin my wedding?"

"That was a genuine mistake. I didn't know what was going on-"

"What about you trying to convince Aubrey to leave the community when she really didn't want to?"

He came to stand in front of Emma, who merely arched a challenging eyebrow at him.

"She didn't tell me that she didn't want to leave. Obviously, she was telling you something than different."

"Or she was telling you something different," Jamie corrected. "If you want to be here, do it for Gott. Do it for yourself. Don't do it for Aubrey or for Michael. You know that you'd be forgiven if you asked for it, but you can 't decide if this is what you want. You're just telling everyone what they want to hear until you figure things out."

"That's what you think," Emma replied tightly. She turned on her heel and swung up into the buggy. "Excuse me. I have somewhere to be."

Emma jerked on the reins harder than necessary, and the horse gave a startled start.

Jamie stepped out of the way as Emma guided the buggy around and trotted up the road without sparing either of them a glance.

"She has nowhere to be," Aubrey said softly behind him, sighing heavily. "She's just going to run away again."

"I just don't understand what the deal is with her," he said, turning to look at Aubrey with frustrated eyes. "She made all this effort to be back here, and yet she isn't willing to do anything."

Aubrey smiled thinly. Her eyes were dry but sad when she spoke. "My sister is stubborn. We used to get into fights all the time, and whenever she was called out on a lie, she tried to run away. She cares so much about what people think of her. That's why she believes the community is judging her for what happened."

"In a way they are, but she doesn't help by being that way."

"Nee, but her pride won't let her see that. I just pray she makes the right decision." Aubrey pressed a fleeting kiss to his cheek before venturing back to the haus.

He stared after her slender frame with the barest hint of a baby bump on her lower belly. Michael Brenneman's words echoed inside of his mind once again. "Are you sure about that?"

He swallowed down the doubt threatening to crawl its way up his throat and lost himself in the next few hours of chores. When he laid down, listening to the gentle breaths of Aubrey sleeping next to him with a leg twined around his own, tears made their way to his eyes. He prayed then in the dark room for Gott to help them, to make things right, and to protect their blossoming family.

The following morning, Jamie left the haus after

morning prayers and breakfast. He also left a quiet Aubrey, who was baking in the warm kitchen. After last night's confrontation with Emma, barely a word had been spoken beside prayers before bed. He wished that he could read the thoughts playing inside Aubrey's mind, but it was futile. She was just as good at hiding her thoughts as he was.

The town of Monte Vista was quiet as usual in the early morning hour. Dew clung to the many flower beds located throughout the quiet streets and many of the businesses were in the middle of opening up for the day. He spotted Levi's buggy behind the furniture store, with his horse grazing in the field. It was no surprise to find him there early since he was in charge of the books now that Daniel had given the business to Levi to run.

After unhitching their horse, Jamie grabbed his lunch pail from the buggy and headed toward the warehouse. The familiar scents of wood and stain filled Jamie's nose pleasantly as he positioned himself at a work table.

A few hours of focusing on something else would do his mind wonders.

He'd just picked up a sanding block when Levi entered the warehouse through the back door. Levi looked up in surprise from the notes in his hands that he was reading.

"Jamie? I didn't expect you to be here so early. We're caught up on inventory."

"I know. I just needed to get my mind off some things."

"Ach?' Levi said, lowering the notes with a frown. "Is everything all right? Aubrey doing gut?"

"Jah. She's gut. It's-" He paused, wondering what Levi's reaction would be to what had happened yesterday. Aubrey had never directly mentioned Levi's feelings about Emma, though Jamie was sure he had some sort of knowledge of what was happening. "It's about Emma. We learned some things the other evening, and I think it has really hit Aubrey harder than she admits."

Levi set the notes on Jamie's work table and tugged on the edge of his beard in agitation. At that moment, he looked eerily similar to Daniel, from his graying hair from stress to pale blue eyes pinched with exhaustion.

"Has Emma been bothering her?" he asked.

Jamie paused at the curtness in Levi's voice. "Nee. Well, no more than usual with her wanting to come back to the community."

"She doesn't want to come back here. She never wanted to be here in the first place. The only reason she's here is Michael."

"Michael told you about it?"

Levi laughed dryly. "Nee. I just know how my sister is when it comes to Michael. We used to be close, all of us."

They stood silently for a few minutes as a breeze gently played with the shaving piles on the concrete floor. The occasional sound of car engines passing by filled the warehouse. Levi then placed a reassuring hand on Jamie's shoulder.

"Don't worry too much about Emma. She'll never be able to come back. Not because of daed or the community, but because she doesn't know how to forgive herself first before asking others to forgive her."

"It just seems so simple to say I'm sorry and to move on," Jamie noted, shaking his head.

"Not when it comes to certain things. I've prayed hard about this since it reached my ears and even talked to our Bishop. My sister is sensitive, not like Aubrey, but so sensitive that she can't face the people she's hurt. No one is shunned to be hurt, but Emma has taken it that way because it's easier for her to deal with it." Reading the baffled look on Jamie's face, Levi continued with a strained smile. "Don't get me wrong. I love my sister and always will. She is a gut person, but you're better to keep Aubrey focused on your expanding family than to worry about our sister. It's hopeless trying to get Emma to see things."

He squeezed Jamie's shoulder briefly before gathering his notes and retreating to the front of the store. Jamie picked up the sanding block and trailed his fingers over the coarseness there. It was hopeless, he knew that much, but nonetheless he prayed for Gott to help Emma. Not because of Emma herself, but because he knew Aubrey was quietly holding on to the hope that she could have a relationship with her sister again.

It was only up to Emma at this point whether she truly wanted to be back in their community.

❦ CHAPTER 10 ❧

A spring storm had gathered on the horizon when church concluded in the King's barn. The wind carried the moist scent of rain, and it blew coolly against Aubrey's flushed face as she helped the women set the tables inside the barn. In the distance, thunder boomed, with a promise of lightning. They sat inside the barn with plates of food balanced on their knees and warm conversation filled the hay-strewn barn.

"Let's find a seat," Sadie suggested, twining a steady arm through Aubrey's. They waded through the sea of familiar faces and found an empty table toward the barn doors. Once they were seated, Sadie leaned across the table. "Have you talked to Emma recently?"

Aubrey tensed at the memory of their last interaction. She had assumed that Emma had gone back to their parents' home, but she was nowhere to be seen apparently. Again. It came as no surprise this time, considering what had been revealed and said the previous evening.

"Nee. Why?"

Sadie frowned at her sister's curt reply. "I was just wondering, because Emma said that she was going to visit you yesterday. After that she went for a walk and said she had some things to do, but never came back."

"I have no idea," Aubrey said. Her stomach churned. Maybe Emma had finally had enough. She stared down at the splintered tabletop, and fought back the tears.

"Are you sure about that?" Sadie asked carefully.

She was spared answering when Jamie came to Aubrey's side with a heaping plate of food and sat on the chair next to her.

"We shouldn't stay long," he informed her, nodding at the darkening sky. "I don't want to be caught in a rainstorm."

Aubrey glanced over her shoulder at the grey clouds twisting together in the sky. The weather fits the mood perfectly, she reflected. Even though she was surrounded by smiling faces, there was a sense of foreboding in the distance. She frowned at the trouble mounting within her heart.

The first patter of rain on the barn roof signaled the end of Fellowship. Aubrey quickly waved goodbye to her family as Jamie ushered her out of the barn and to their buggy, helping her climb to the seat. Cold drops of rain soaked through the fabric of Aubrey's prayer kapp and through the fabric of her dress. She shivered as the warm morning rapidly gave way to a stormy and much colder afternoon.

A crack of thunder startled their horse and it took

several seconds for Jamie to regain control of the panicked animal. Aubrey clung uncertainly to the buggy's seat as it twisted at a sharp angle and nearly backed up into another buggy parked beside theirs. The air around them was charged with energy from the rapidly approaching storm, and any second the clouds would release a true downpour.

"Hang on," Jamie called to her, holding the reins tightly in his hands. "We're going to go faster than normal."

Aubrey held the edge of her seat tightly at the daring glint in her mann's eyes. *His love for adrenaline has no boundaries sometimes,* she thought with a small smile. "Danka for the warning. Just get us home in one piece, Jamie. I'd rather live to see another day."

They traveled down the gravel road at a fast trot. The wind ripped at their faces and rain drops stung their cheeks. Aubrey closed her eyes at the sensation of riding fast, faster than they ever had before, and let her hands extend upward to feel the cool wetness on her fingertips. The unease in her heart pattered away with the rain as it poured down on them.

When they reached their haus, Aubrey's cheeks were reddened from the rain drops. She helped Jamie unhitch their buggy before leading their horse into its stall and offering soothing words to the trembling creature. The downpour prevented their attempt to dash across the yard to their haus.

Instead, they turned over empty grain barrels and perched themselves on top of them in front of the barn doors to watch the lightning sizzle across the sky. The steady sound of rain on the barn roof, coupled with the smells of dampening earth and dry hay, swirled around Aubrey as she gazed out at the mud puddles.

"I heard your sister didn't come back home," Jamie said quietly.

"You heard right." She turned to look at Jamie sitting on the barrel with his long legs stretched out in front of him and ankles crossed. His hands rested loosely on his thighs as he stared at the wet land in front of them. Even in the darkening afternoon, his honey blonde hair still shimmered brightly.

This was her life now. Jamie was her mann, and they had a bobli to welcome within a few months. Gott had blessed her with a gut life, and she was no longer willing to put that at risk. "It doesn't matter anymore though. She's gone, and that's probably the best thing for everyone," she murmured sadly.

"Probably." He stretched out a hand, wordlessly offering comfort. Aubrey gladly took it to feel his tough but loving hands in her own. "I want you to know that I truly prayed for things to work out. I really had hoped for your family that Emma could be redeemed, and could enjoy a second chance at life with her family."

"It's never been about redemption, or asking for forgiveness. We just wanted her to see that she was still loved. I still loved her, despite what happened."

"So did Michael."

"My sister is lost within her grief. I just wish there was something I could do to help her through it."

"All you can do is pray. There is nothing else anyone can do. Let Gott do what He can do to help."

He gave her hand a tender squeeze before placing it on his knee, then threaded his fingers through hers. They continued to stare at the storm as it passed over them before the clouds parted, allowing the warm sunlight to shimmer through once again. A large grin spread across Jamie's face. "I have a surprise for you," he exclaimed suddenly. "Now that the storm is over, I want to show you something."

Using the hand that held hers, Jamie tugged her onto her feet and led her across the muddy earth. They wiped their shoes on a mat outside the back door before slipping inside. The smell of kaffee and soap still clung to the morning air trapped inside the haus.

Aubrey mentally noted to open the windows downstairs and let in the fresh rain scent as she climbed up the stairs after Jamie to their soon-to-be bobli's room.

"Ready?"

She nodded, a smile tugging at her lips at his obvious excitement. Jamie pushed the door open and stepped back to let her enter first. Her breath caught in her throat when her eyes landed on the crib along the far right wall.

"Ach, Jamie. It looks wunderbar."

The wood was smooth beneath her fingertips and still smelled faintly of stain. All they needed was a mattress pad and a few blankets for the winter season. Aubrey turned to beam up at Jamie and pressed a kiss to his lips. "I can't wait until our bobli is here," she sighed, looping her arms around his broad shoulders.

Jamie's arms wrapped around her waist and he leaned down so that their foreheads rested together.

"He or she will be here sooner than we think."

"I hope so. I want to see what he or she looks like."

Jamie wrinkled his nose. "If it's a girl, I hope she gets your button nose. That would look cute."

"If it's a boy, I hope he has your blonde hair. Although...I don't know if I can handle another version of you running around."

His chest rumbled with a chuckle. "That's true. We might be in trouble if we have a boy and he's like me."

"Or if we have a girl who's like you."

"Then we are really in trouble."

They stood together lost in their own thoughts of their bobli. She tried to picture a little boy with Jamie's chiseled features and trademark honey-colored hair, plus the charming personality that could sweep anyone off their feet. She then imagined a girl with perhaps Jamie's eyes and her personality.

"What are you praying for?" Aubrey asked. She tilted her head up to look at Jamie's face more thoroughly. "Are you praying for a girl or boy?"

"Hmm." He raised his eyes contemplatively up to the ceiling. "A girl," he said eventually, and at her surprised look went on resolutely, "I am praying for a girl. I've always loved the idea of being daed to a little girl."

"I'm surprised. I imagined you would love to have a boy first so you can teach him how to farm."

"I pray for a boy too. That way he can protect his

sister."

Aubrey smiled at that. She could already picture two little kinner around the dinner table and their laughter in the summer's afternoon air. It filled her with hope that Gott was in control when she needed Him the most.

"I'd better check on our horse and make sure that nothing has flooded with the rain," Jamie stated.

"I'll go with you," she said, smiling up at him. "I love the smell of rain during the springtime."

The fields were damp with rain. Aubrey scanned the tender vegetation in her garden and tested the dirt to make sure the roots had gotten plenty of water. She held open the gate leading to the field when Jamie returned with their horse trotting happily behind him without having to be led. She trailed a hand over the smooth brown coat as their horse followed him into the field and then took off with a playful whinny.

They walked hand in hand through the wetness, with their boots squishing in the mud, until they reached the edge of the field. The air felt markedly cooler with the tall pine trees shading them from the sun and the distant bubble of a creek reached their ears. To their relief, the creek's water level was normal. When the first stretch of warm weather had entered the valley, much of the snow had melted into the creek. A few hauses down, where the creek was shallower, the water had flooded into the fields and a barn. Jamie and the rest of the community had done a barn raising after that to help construct a new one.

"The water level looks gut," Jamie noted, wiping a relieved hand across his brow.

He stood on a flat river stone looking down through the forest. Aubrey bent to pick a purple flower and twirled the stem absently between her fingers.

"At least there won't be any more flooding," she said, relieved as well. Their lives centered around the unpredictable weather that occupied Colorado, and it was always a small bit of relief when it cooperated. She could recall several instances of harsh winter seasons that started early and ended too late, or late winters with no snow that led to a drought during the summers. Nothing was ever predictable.

The roar of a car engine cut through the now quiet afternoon. Aubrey's heart plummeted at the sound, and the dread she had felt during church returned. She looked at Jamie, who turned on the rock to peer out with a hand above his eyes for shade.

"I can't tell who it is," he said.

She followed him back into the field with heavy steps. There was only one person she knew who owned a car.

Jamie stopped at the top of grassy hill and visibly tensed. He turned to look at Aubrey with a frown. "Your sister is here."

C380

Aubrey didn't move, or even blink, for a few long seconds. The clouds parted above them and sunlight poured onto their wet heads. They watched as Emma closed the driver's side door with a distant thud. She was dressed in English clothes--ripped jeans, flimsy shoes, and a white tank top. The long strands of her black-streaked blonde hair were pulled up in a high bun.

She turned in their direction with a hand shielding her eyes. The sight of the car and clothes told Jamie what her disappearance had truly been about.

"Do you wish to talk to her?" he asked, turning to look at a silent Aubrey. "If not, I can tell her to leave. She can't be here anyway now that she isn't rejoining the community."

"It's time to say goodbye. She's here to say goodbye. She's made her decision."

Jamie nodded. He held out a hand again for comfort, and his fraa gladly took it. They walked back through the wet field, with mud squishing beneath their boots.

The car engine hummed beneath the hood when they closed the gate behind them and slowly approached a tense Emma.

"I can't stay long. The Bishop made it clear that I can't be here any longer."

"You weren't allowed back in the community before," Jamie said.

Emma's eyes flicked over to him in annoyance. "That was before I told the Bishop I wished to come back. Big difference."

He opened his mouth to argue, but it was Aubrey that cut in smoothly. "What are you doing here, Emma? It looks like you already made your decision."

"I just wanted to apologize to you for everything. You were right, and I can't come back. Not when I never wanted to be here, and it wouldn't be right to Gott for me to be here for any reason other than devoting myself to Him."

"Well, danka for the apology. Good luck with whatever you want to do on the outside." Aubrey grabbed Jamie's forearm and tugged him in the direction of the haus. He looked to Emma in surprise at the harshness behind Aubrey's tone. The surface of Emma's eyes glazed over with hurt tears.

"Aubrey, wait." She started after them, wringing her hands in agitation. They stopped on the front porch step. "I really didn't mean to hurt you or anyone else in our family. I really wanted to come back. I really did, but after talking to you, I realized that what you said was true. I should be coming back for Gott, and for myself. Not because I don't want to lose Michael again."

"What about Michael? Does he know that you are leaving?"

Guilt spread across her face at the mention of Michael's name. Emma looked down at the wet gravel and scuffed the heel of her shoe on the tiny rocks. "No," she mumbled under her breath. "He doesn't know. It's better that I leave this way. He belongs here in the community. I don't belong here."

"Anyone can belong here if they wish to. You can belong here if you want," Aubrey commented softly.

"That's just it though; I don't. It's harsh, I know, but I just can't live this way ever again. I'm sorry that I made you think otherwise. You're my sister, and I will always love you. A part of me had been hoping that we could have our relationship back again."

Tears were now streaming down her tanned cheeks. A hand rested on Jamie's shoulder and he reached up without thinking to clasp it in his. He glanced up to where Aubrey stood on the top porch step, chewing her bottom lip, with tears in her eyes as well.

"I had hoped that too," she whispered.

Emma wiped her eyes dry with the backs of her hands, turning to head back to the still-running car. She stopped after a few steps and turned back to look at them with a strained smile. "Do me favor? One last thing, I swear." When they didn't decline, she continued in a shaky voice. "Tell Michael that I'm sorry as well. Tell him that I love him and wish that things could've worked between us. Sometimes second chances just don't work like we pray and hope they will."

Together they watched Emma slip into the driver's side and back out into the main road. He was torn between feeling grief for Aubrey and feeling relief. A weight that had been tugging on his heart for the past couple of months, since learning of Emma's intent on returning to the community, finally lifted. Without meaning to, he let out a long-held breath.

"Tell me this is right, Jamie," Aubrey sighed. Her eyes were pinched closed and a hand rested on the swell of her stomach. "Tell me that this was the right thing, to say goodbye, to let go of my sister."

Putting aside his relief to see Emma make a decision finally, the right one at that, he rested a hand on Aubrey's stomach as well. He felt the first flutter of life beneath his

palm. "It was the right thing to do, Aubrey. You have a
bobli on its way and you have me to help you through
this."

Aubrey smiled, but it didn't quite reach her wet eyes.
Their hands brushed together as they rubbed at the bobli
growing steadily within the protection of Aubrey's womb.
More sunlight escaped through the parting clouds, and a
peaceful silence filled the afternoon.

"I know. It just hurts knowing that I'll never have
my big sister again. I wish things would have been
different. I prayed for it so hard so many times."

"If Gott truly wanted Emma back within our
community, it would have happened without any issues.
Maybe it wasn't the right time."

"It was never the right time." Aubrey retreated
backward from his hands before disappearing into their
haus. He could hear the distinct clang of pots and pans
being rummaged through in preparation for dinner. With
the sunlight now bearing down upon the valley, a balmy
air filled the afternoon from the wetness clinging to the
land. Sweat beaded along his forehead in response to it,
and he sat down on the bottom porch step to pray.

He prayed for their bobli's continued health and
growth. He prayed for Aubrey's heart to be mended from
its hurt. He prayed for the Forrest family as they
struggled to cope once more. He prayed even for Emma,
who needed Gott's wisdom and strength.

It was then that guilt tugged at him. When was the
last time he had seen his family, beside Henry? He waved
to them in passing at church, but he couldn't remember

the last time he'd actually sat down for dinner with his parents. He was sad to think that while his family was whole despite their occasional fights, Aubrey's family was forever missing a member, and lines had been drawn.

While the next couple of days passed in a blur of spring storms that filled their quiet haus, Jamie finished the bobli's crib to surprise Aubrey. He prayed that it would cheer her up to see their bobli's bed. Yesterday he had come home to find her staring blankly out the living room window, with a couple of bobli blankets in her lap, along with a needle and thread.

"That looks gut."

Levi peered over Jamie's shoulder with a smile. "Maybe we should sell bobli cribs here in the furniture store. With your talent, they would go very fast."

"Jah, perhaps. I wanted to surprise Aubrey and hoped that it would cheer her up."

"I'm sure that it'll cheer her up. She's been excited about the bobli."

He clasped Jamie on the shoulder firmly before retreating back to the front of the store. Slipping off his work gloves to cool his hands, Jamie set them on his work table before venturing to where Henry was staining a rocking chair. His bruder looked up as the paintbrush glided over the armrest. "What?"

"Do you think that I'm too harsh on Ma and Da?"

Henry frowned as he slowly set the paintbrush back into the bucket of wood stain. He dusted the knees of his trousers before standing with a sigh. "Sometimes, maybe. I understand why you've distanced yourself from them over the past few months."

"I haven't meant to. I know Da was upset about losing help around the farm, but I never wanted to lose them entirely."

"I don't think any of us see it that way. You have your own haus and a bobli on the way. It's not like you have all the spare time in the world to share with us."

"But still..." Jamie trailed off with a sigh.

"Is this about Emma?" At the surprised look Jamie gave him, he continued with a shrug. "I heard Michael asking Levi if anything had been said to him, or if anyone knew where she had gone."

They had promised to tell Michael, but neither of them could do it. Jamie avoided Michael at all costs throughout the work day, and kept his conversations pointedly short and always about work. Either Michael sensed that he didn't wish to talk, or didn't care to ask him about it. The answer was clear, and he didn't have to say anything. There was no need to uphold their promise when Michael knew what Emma's disappearance from the community meant.

"A little bit. I've done a lot of praying over the past few days."

"Perhaps it was Gott testing your faith or teaching you a lesson," Henry said.

Footsteps on the gravel outside permeated their conversation. Michael appeared around the corner with rumpled clothing and dark bags under his eyes. He didn't look in their direction, but merely went to his own work table to set down a lunch pail with a careless thud. The agitation and torment he felt was clear from his stiff movements.

It was a painful memory that Jamie recalled vividly, not too many summers ago, when he had feared that he lost Aubrey. Except his fear stemmed from uncertainty. There was no fear with Michael. Only hurt.

Jamie exchanged a silent look with Henry, who jerked his head in the direction of Michael's stiff back. He smoothed his sweaty palms down the front of his blue button up shirt while walking. "Michael," he started, gingerly laying a hand on a tense shoulder. "I'm sorry about Emma. I know how it feels."

The muscles beneath his palm coiled tautly. He immediately withdrew as Michael turned to look at him with weary but determined eyes.

"I don't want your sympathy, because I know you don't feel that way," he replied.

The words cut through the warm morning like a jagged saw blade. Jamie bristled at the unkind tone and shrugged his shoulders indifferently. "I really did have sympathy for you until now."

Michael laughed loudly at that. "I know you wished that Emma away. Who can blame you when you turned out to be right the whole time? She never wanted to come back here in the first place."

"I never wished that. I was only trying to protect Aubrey from getting hurt again. I prayed to Gott that He would help-"

"You did a gut job protecting her. You're a good mann."

"Danka," Jamie replied, even though he was confident it wasn't a compliment. He'd turned to head back in the direction of his work table when Michael's solemn voice stopped him mid step.

"Don't think that this is over. I know Emma, and I know Aubrey. This is far from ending."

Jamie turned to stare directly into Michael's eyes. "You're wrong if you think Aubrey is anything like Emma," he said lowly.

A grim smile spread across Michael's haggard face again. It was the same expression he'd worn before, when they had previously conversed about Aubrey nearly leaving.

"I wouldn't be so sure in that. They are sisters, and closer than what you think. Like I said, this isn't over. It's just beginning."

End of Book 3

4.AMISH MYSTERY

⪻ CHAPTER 1 ⪼

The stars were exceptionally bright that night. Aubrey stared up at them, sparkling in the cold late October night. There were no clouds in sight as the darkness beyond the stars stretched on forever it seemed. A hushed silence filled the air, everyone and everything sleeping peacefully.

All except for her and the bobli.

A firm kick to the tender insides of Aubrey's rib cage reminded her of why she was the only person awake at this late hour. The bobli's due date was over a month away, and there was little room left. At random hours of the day and night, little arms and legs would stretch out as much as possible.

Aubrey rested a hand on the swell of her stomach, marveling at the tightness of her belly. The remnants of the dream that had initially woke her faded away to the inner recesses of her mind. She didn't wish to think of it on such a beautiful night, not with Gott's creation above her and reminding her that He was ever present.

"A few weeks and you will be free to stretch," she

whispered softly, rubbing in affectionate circles.

They had finished the bobli's room yesterday, setting up the crib and folding all the blankets. Aubrey had stared at the room for some time, not quite believing that in a few weeks their bobli would be sleeping soundly in the crib. While the morning sickness had lessened over the summer, she could feel herself beginning to stretch to accommodate their growing bobli. She was ready to meet him or her, to see Gott's blessing to them.

The squeak of the back porch door opening behind them alerted her that Jamie had awakened to find her gone. She adjusted the blanket wrapped around her shoulders and turned to walk back to the haus. The field was only clumps of dirt now, their harvesting season over a few weeks ago, and firm with the recent frost.

Jamie stood on the top porch step, one hand rubbing his face tiredly. The starlight reflected brightly. He was dressed in his night clothes, but had shoved his feet into boots and slipped on a heavy coat before venturing outside.

"What are you doing out in the field?" he asked.

"I couldn't sleep. The bobli was kicking me so I went on a walk through the fields."

She gladly slipped into the warmth of Jamie's arms. He still smelled of sleep, and soap from when he had bathed earlier. Aubrey buried her head into his chest and felt the chill of the night slowly replaced by Jamie's body heat as he rubbed his hands soothingly along her lower back.

"You shouldn't be out here by yourself at night," he

mumbled into her hair, tightening his hold on her. "The bears are getting closer to our haus in search of food for the winter months."

A few days before, they had spotted a black bear roaming on the fringe of the forest lining their back field. Jamie had spent the evening hours patrolling the back field with a shotgun clasped in his hands, ready to shoot if needed.

"I know, I'm sorry. I wasn't thinking about it."

"Obviously. What else is on your mind? I know you didn't go on a walk to put the bobli to sleep."

A resigned breath left Aubrey as she sagged wearily against Jamie. Tears flooded her eyes thinking of the other reason that she had decided to leave their bed and walk outside in the cold air.

"I had a nightmare," she confessed softly.

Jamie tensed slightly against her, but reached up to tangle his fingers through the strands of her loose hair. He combed through the tangles gently and rested his bearded chin on top of her head.

"What was it about?"

She shook her head, biting her lower lip to keep from crying. There were only a few times throughout her life that she could remember a nightmare haunting her for days, but this one had particularly made her sick with unease. The excruciating pain had felt so real that it stole the breath right of her lungs as wave after wave of pain continued, each more intense than the one before it. Her belly had stretched tautly and hardened to the point that she could feel the bobli kicking frantically from the constriction. Then she remembered the blood coating her fingers and a tiny face staring lifelessly at her.

Just thinking about it already had her stomach tightening with a deep-rooted fear that had her heart racing frantically. Her skin felt flushed and tight with heat, and she stepped back to wipe her brow with the back of her hand.

"I dreamed that our bobli..." She trailed off, unable to put it into words.

Jamie stared down at her, the pale starlight reflecting brightly in his eyes. His jaw clenched as it always did whenever he was chewing the inside of his cheek in contemplation.

"Do you remember what Martha said to you yesterday?" he asked.

"Nee. I mean, I know what she said, but what are you referring to?"

He rested his large hands on the curves of his shoulders. "You are healthy, and so is the bobli. We have every reason to believe that everything will be fine once the bobli decides that it is time to come."

"I know, but still..." She hung her head, feeling exhausted for the first time since waking up. "It's just something that is always at the back of my mind. I don't know why I worry so much over it when I know that Gott is protecting me."

"Because it has happened to others before," Jamie said gently.

"Jah. I can't even imagine how horrible it is to lose a bobli..."

Her heart constricted painfully at the thought. For the first time, she could imagine how Emma must have felt, losing her bobli before he or she was even born. "I know how Emma felt now. It's the worst feeling in the world."

"Don't think about it," Jamie whispered, fingers tightening on her shoulders. "Gott has blessed us with a wunderbar gift, and we shouldn't worry over things that only He can control."

Aubrey smiled weakly. "You're right. I just worry so much over our bobli and our lives afterwards."

"I know you do, but what gut is it doing to worry? Everything will be fine. Come," he said, wrapping an arm around her shoulders. "I don't think Sadie will be very happy with you if you're late tomorrow morning to her wedding."

"Nee," she replied, laughing. "She would be upset knowing that I was up at this hour."

Tomorrow morning would be the start of her sister's new life as a fraa. Aubrey's heart swelled with pride thinking of the beginning of the previous summer, when Sadie had returned from her rumspringa stronger than ever within her own faith. Her relationship with Eli had apparently strengthened as well, and they were baptized together, along with Jamie's sister Lily, who was also to marry in two weekends. Then it would be Elizabeth and Henry's wedding after that.

A joy and peace had filled their community again.

Jamie lead her back into the warm haus and checked the wood stove in the living room. Aubrey sat on the edge of the couch as he stoked the coals, shrugging out of the blanket wrapped around her shoulders when a blast of hot air touched her. She felt the bobli stir at the sensation as well before settling back down into a peaceful slumber with a foot stuck firmly in her ribs.

"I can't wait until our bobli is here," she said with a wince, trying to shift their bobli out from her ribs. "My poor ribs have taken a beating, and I can't breathe anymore."

"A little over a month and your wish will come true," Jamie said.

He placed a few more logs onto the sizzling coals, and kept the door ajar to create a draft. Wiping his hands free from bark, he sat on the edge of the coffee table as the sound of wood crackling filled the silence of their haus. They sat wordlessly together staring at the flames, now crawling up the side of logs, with their hands twined loosely in front of them.

"How many names are we down to now?" Jamie asked suddenly, turning to look at her with a smile.

The strands of Jamie's hair were a rich golden color, almost the shade of a fiery orange sunset during the summers, as the fire light played along the sharp contours of his face. Aubrey reached up to trail her fingers across his cheekbone, feeling the bristles of his beard poke her sensitive skin.

"Two names for both a girl and boy."

"What are they?"

She smiled inwardly. There was nothing more comforting and romantic than Jamie wishing to debate their bobli's name in the late hours.

"Rosella or Grace if it's a girl. Mark or Jonathan if it is a boy."

Jamie's eyes slipped closed under her fingers sweeping along his forehead as he weighed them within his mind. "I like the sound of Grace. We could call her Gracie as a nickname."

"I like that. What about a boy?"

"We aren't having a boy."

"Jamie," Aubrey started with a sigh, exasperated by his confidence. "You will be disappointed if this bobli turns out to be a boy."

"I'll be happy either way, but I have a feeling it is a girl. We can settle on a boy name when the time arrives if that is the case."

"I hope you're right, because the last thing I will want to do with you is debate over a boy name."

"Just wait. You'll see that am I right."

"If you say so."

His hand slipped from hers and came to rest on the swell of her stomach. The tips of his fingers massaged across Aubrey's stretching skin. Aubrey's eyes fell closed at the comforting contact. Behind them, flames within the stove started to swallow the pieces of logs eagerly.

"You weren't up because of what happened the other day, were you?" Jamie asked quietly.

Her stomach jerked at the memory of Michael Brenneman confessing to church members that he had been in contact with Emma since she had left again. While Aubrey had done her best to move on from the decision Emma had made at the beginning of spring, it still lingered painfully within her family. They were lucky not to face the repercussions of socially engaging with a shunned member only because Emma had asked to come back.

Now Emma's chances to return were gone, and it had left a deeper ache than the previous one. There was no reversing the church's decision after stomping on a second chance.

"Nee," she said softly, looking down at their loosely twined hands between their bodies. "I have already accepted Emma's decision and prayed for Gott's guidance."

Jamie's eyes focused on Aubrey, assessing her words carefully for any indications of a lie. He nodded his head slowly after a few moments. "I just wanted to check. I sometimes worry about you keeping your thoughts and emotions to yourself. Especially when you're pregnant and going through enough changes as it is."

"They are gut changes, though. I've always dreamed about this, having a mann, a haus, and now a bobli. Gott has blessed me with many things."

"Jah, He truly has."

The loud pop of wood drew their attention back to the wood stove. Jamie stood, offering a hand for Aubrey to take. He hoisted her up easily before closing the door to the wood stove, and together they walked up the flight of stairs to their room.

Aubrey laid on her side, a spare pillow cushioning the swell of her stomach. She listened to Jamie's breath even as he slipped into dreams and traced the outline of his fingers from where his arm was draped protectively over her.

Unease filled her again from the quietness. She tried to cling to the warmth of Jamie's conversation a few minutes prior, but it slipped away from her grasp.

It was no use trying to convince herself that she wasn't afraid of what was to come. It was no use trying to convince herself that she didn't miss Emma and wish to have her back.

❦ CHAPTER 2 ❧

The smell of freshly baked apple pies filled Aubrey's nose when she stepped into the bakery on a particularly crisp morning. She shrugged out of a light wool coat while walking along the linoleum floor to the kitchen, mentally noting that today the shelves needed to be dusted.

Inside the kitchen, Sadie pulled a bubbling pie from the oven. She used her foot to close the oven door before placing the pie on a cooling rack. A blush filled the center of Sadie's cheeks as she hummed gently to herself before realizing that Aubrey was standing in the door frame.

"Morning."

The corner of Aubrey's lips tugged into a smile at her sister's cheerful mood. She remembered how wunderbar it had felt once she was finally married to Jamie.

"Morning," she replied, hanging her coat on the peg. "How are you feeling this morning?"

"Wunderbar. And you?"

"I'm fine. You had an early start, I see."

"Jah, Eli brought me to work this morning. He's

starting his new job in construction today," Sadie said brightly.

"That's gut. I am so happy for you. Where is maemm?"

Aubrey grabbed a jar of flour from a cupboard and began to measure out the amount needed to start a fresh set of pie crusts.

"She went to check on daed. His fever returned last night..."

A flour cloud puffed up in front of Aubrey when she dumped a measured into the bowl. Lately, their daed's health had declined even more with the winter season approaching. Jamie spent hours over at her parent's farm trying to help whenever Levi couldn't help with physically demanding chores. Every morning Aubrey prayed for Gott to give her daed the strength to overcome whatever illness plagued him.

"Has daed gone to talk to the doctor yet?"

"Nee. I don't know why, but maemm says it's pride. He's too stubborn to get help."

"Let's pray that his health gets better on its own then, if he won't talk to a doctor."

Sadie's face darkened. She stared down at the cooling pies on the racks in front of her, biting her lower lip in thought. "I don't know what it is about daed not wanting to talk to the doctor that seems familiar to me. I keep feeling like there is some sort of story to it, or like someone mentioned something about it," she said.

A trickle of recognition stopped Aubrey while whisking all the dry ingredients together. She frowned down at the bowl, trying to place where she too had heard someone talk about why their daed refused to talk to Larry Brenneman. The only time she had ever seen them talk was the night Jamie had been attacked by wolves on his way home from her parent's haus, and even then it had been tense.

"It could be many reasons why daed doesn't want to go," she said eventually. "Larry Brenneman is Michael's daed, and I'm sure he isn't happy about what happened recently."

"That could be it, but there's something else to it. Haven't you ever noticed that they never look in each other's direction during worship? Or that they avoid each other at Fellowship?"

"Jah, to avoid confrontation, I'm sure. Think about it, Sadie. Michael did leave because Emma refused to remain within the community. They might have forgiven each other, but I'm sure they will never be happy about it."

It abruptly hit her how relieved she was that Emma had made the decision to leave permanently. While Aubrey missed her sister dearly, and even had wished that Emma wouldn't have thrown away a second chance to come back, just thinking of the emotional strain she had put on not only their family, but on the Brenneman family as well. It was in their faith to forgive others no matter the circumstances, but there was still suspicion and wariness. Emma's sensitive nature would never be able to stand that sort of deep rooted opinion of her.

"I guess you're right," Sadie said, sighing heavily. "That is probably why I keep thinking there is something more going on."

"Most likely. What other pies do we need to bake before it is busy?"

"Whoopie pies. They've been a best seller since you've started baking them."

Aubrey smiled, pleased to know that her baking received positive feedback by the community and Englischers who ventured in. She had thrown herself into baking after not being able to work at the schoolhouse with the bobli on the way. Betty had had no other choice but to replace her when Aubrey fell ill from morning sickness. She missed working the kinner every day, but being with her family during the last stages of pregnancy helped her through the torrent of emotions.

"I promise to teach you how to bake them the way I do. You will have to since I will be home with bobli at the beginning of December," she said.

The back door of the bakery opened with a loud squeak from the old hinges. Expecting it to be Katie back from checking on their daed, Aubrey turned with a smile that slowly faded when she recognized who it was.

"Gut morning, ladies," Bishop Abraham said, stepping into the warmth of the kitchen. He shut the door behind himself and frowned up at the hinges of the door when they squeaked again. "Looks as if we need some oil for the hinges in here. What an awful noise to hear every time you open the door."

Sadie looked to Aubrey in confusion, a wordless question in her eyes. The bishop rarely visited their bakery or any of the businesses they had. Something else would have brought him to the bakery.

"Is your maemm around?" he asked, smiling kindly at both of them. "I have a few things that I would like to speak with her about."

"She is checking on our daed," Aubrey said, and then added tentatively, "Is there something we can get you?"

The older Amish man turned his pale blue eyes on her. "Nee, but danka though. I actually would like to talk to you both if you can spare me some time from your baking," he said, nodding to the pies cooling on the pie rack.

Aubrey set the whisk down on the countertop and wiped her floured hands on the front of her apron. When she glanced over at Sadie, her youngest sister was twisting her hands nervously in front of her and refused to look in Aubrey's direction.

"Of course. I will grab a stool for you to sit down," Aubrey said.

Abraham smiled. "That would be wunderbar. My old knees can't seem to hold me up for very long anymore." He laughed, and either didn't notice how Sadie refused to laugh or chose to ignore it. He turned to look at Sadie, "I hope that you and Eli are happy now that you two have exchanged your wedding vows."

She didn't hear Sadie's reply as Aubrey hurried out of the kitchen to the front of the bakery. Grabbing the stool from behind the counter, she came back into the kitchen to place it front of Abraham.

"Danka," he said, and perched himself gladly upon it. Resting his age spotted hands on his thighs, Abraham flicked his gaze between the two of them. "I'm sure you two remember what took place three weekends ago."

Aubrey and Sadie tensed visibly at the reminder of Michael confessing that he had had contact with an excommunicated member. He named no names, but Aubrey was well aware of Michael's old feelings for Emma. A part of her wasn't surprised that he hadn't let go of Emma or hoped that she could come back to the community. She had wanted the same thing too.

Abraham continued, "There has been reason to believe that your sister has been in contact with other members. I believe that it is someone she knows, other than Michael. I was told that she was in the community yesterday during Sadie's exchange of wedding vows."

The center of Aubrey's cheeks flared in indignant anger. Naturally, he would believe that it was someone within Aubrey's family. It had happened before in the past, and they were lucky that they weren't shamed or punished for it. While other Amish orders were much stricter, theirs was a bit more relaxed.

This time, however, Abraham was making it clear that Emma would remain out of their community as an excommunicated member of their church. She'd made her choice by leaving twice.

"I assure you it isn't us," Aubrey said firmly. "The last time I spoke with my sister was in the spring, as I told you."

"I believe you, Aubrey. You have many blessings to look forward to," Abraham said. His eyes swiveled over to where Sadie stood, her chin tucked firmly to her chest. "What about you, Sadie? Have you recently seen your sister?"

Sadie didn't reply. A red blush crawled its way up the sides of her neck, and she refused to look at the both of them. The pit of Aubrey's stomach clenched painfully in dismay. "Please tell me that you haven't been talking to her, Sadie," she said, shaking her head. "Not after being married to Eli, and having so much to look forward to."

"It was-"

The back door opened with a loud squeak. All three of them turned to look as Katie stepped inside, unbuttoning her coat with deft fingers. She blinked in surprise to see Abraham sitting on a stool, legs stretched out in front of him.

"Bishop Abraham," Katie started, trying to sound kind through the frown on her face. "I pray that all is all right if you are here in my bakery. May I ask what is going on?"

Abraham looked over at Sadie, but she had gone silent once more. Her lips were stretched into a thin line, and the red color that had occupied her face drained, leaving a pale pallor.

"We will talk later, Sadie," Abraham said. He didn't give Sadie a chance to reply, and stood from the stool with a grimace of pain. "Katie, maybe we could talk outside for a few minutes? There is something I wish to discuss with you."

Katie nodded her head. "Jah, of course. I'll be right back in to help finish baking."

She followed Abraham outside, closing the back door behind her to give them privacy. The second the door closed, Aubrey rounded on her youngest sister.

"What is going on, Sadie? Why does Bishop Abraham seem to think you know something about Emma?"

"I-I-I don't know anything. I promise, I don't know," Sadie said. Tears surfaced in her eyes, and threatened to spill forth at any second. Her bottom lip trembled as she shrank back against the intensity of Aubrey's gaze. "I honestly don't know, Aubrey. I don't know what is going on."

"I don't believe you. You know something is going on."

"I don't know!"

Aubrey watched as the tears finally slipped from Sadie's eyes. They left wet trails down the delicate curves of her cheeks. Sadie buried her face into her hands, slender shoulders trembling from suppressed sobs. "Sadie," Aubrey said, sighing in confusion. "If you don't know what is going on, then why are you crying so hard?"

"Because you don't believe me, nor does Bishop Abraham! You both think I know something."

"Know what? I don't even know what is going on. Why is Bishop Abraham here?"

"I don't know!"

"Sadie. Tell the truth. What secret are you hiding?"

Sadie peeked at Aubrey through the cracks in her fingers. She shook her head in distress, another sob escaping her lips. "I can't tell you what it is, Aubrey. I promised that I wouldn't say anything. I promised..."

"Promised what?" Aubrey's heart pounded hard. "Who did you promise?"

A green tinge suddenly filled Sadie's cheeks. She

heaved, one hand clapped firmly around her mouth as she bolted out of the kitchen to the bathroom at the front of the bakery.

In her wake, Aubrey stood frozen and baffled in front of the counter. "What is going on?" Aubrey whispered to herself.

❦

Jamie brushed the table free from wood shavings and dust. He smoothed a hand along the corners of the table, feeling for any stray slivers that needed to be sanded. When none poked the skin of his palm, he wiped his hand on his pant leg and went to the metal cabinet they kept all their wood stains in. He contemplated which wood stain would look the best before grabbing a darker stain. The darker stained furniture seemed to be selling with a lot more frequency than the others, and it kept him busy from sunup to sundown.

He had barely dipped the bristles of a brush into the lukewarm liquid when footsteps entering the warehouse alerted him that it was either Michael Brenneman or his bruder coming to work. Jamie spared a glance over his shoulder and immediately wished that he hadn't.

Dark circles lined Michael Brenneman's normally clear eyes, and his once meaty frame seemed to slump over in exhaustion as he wordlessly went to his work bench. His clothes were rumpled and almost two sizes too big on his frame from how loosely they clung to his body.

There was no doubt in Jamie's mind regarding what

his poor health and appearance were all about.

Michael set his lunch pail down on his work bench with a little more force than necessary. He turned to glare expectantly at Jamie. "Is there something you'd like to say to me today? Voice your thoughts?"

Jamie curled his fingers into tightly clenched fists. Confrontation isn't becoming for an Amish man, he told himself. He forced himself to feign indifference by shrugging his shoulders casually. "I was just going to comment on how you look as if you haven't had any sleep for the past couple of nights."

"The female cows were giving birth to their calves."

He suppressed the urge to roll his eyes at the blatant lie or excuse. "Sure. I've spent several nights in a row with our livestock."

Michael opened his mouth to reply, but hurried footsteps coming around the building disrupted the retort. They watched as a red faced and heavily pregnant Aubrey walked into the warehouse with a distressed frown stretched across her brow. Concern filled Jamie as he set the can of stain on his own work bench and hurried to meet Aubrey halfway.

"Aubrey? Are you okay? What's going on? Is the bobli okay?"

Aubrey batted away his concerned questions. She looked over in Michael's direction as he turned his back on them before grabbing Jamie by the hands. "Can you take a break? I have to tell you something."

"Sure. Let's go outside to the field."

He helped Aubrey climb over the wooden fence into

the field, where their horses grazed happily on dead grass. Clouds had gathered above the mountaintops and loomed over them with the promise of a snowfall. He shifted to keep warm against the chilly air, regretting that he hadn't grabbed his coat on their way out.

"What's going on?"

"Bishop Abraham visited us at the bakery this morning," Aubrey said. She twisted her hands in an agitated motion. "He talked to us about my sister having contact with some other members of the community. He thinks it's someone within my family."

"That's because it is someone within your family," Jamie said. At the appearance of tears in Aubrey's eyes, guilt and anger gnawed on the walls of his stomach. He hadn't told Aubrey about Emma being at Sadie's wedding for exactly this reason. Obviously Emma and Sadie hadn't broken ties from one another, but why they hadn't done so was unknown to Jamie. Why Sadie seemed convinced to keep talking to Emma after joining the church and getting married seemed ridiculous him.

"What do you mean? Do you know something?" Aubrey asked.

Jamie rubbed at the back of his neck in frustration. They had promised before they were married not to keep secrets from one another, but he had broken that promise and it would upset Aubrey. It was ungodly of him to wish for another person to disappear simply because his or her presence was unwanted, but he was growing very weary of fighting Emma's ghost and the mess she left behind unknowingly. He prayed every morning and night that

Gott would give him the strength to remain calm and forgiving.

Taking a deep breath to brace himself from the onslaught of anger and tears, Jamie said carefully, "When I went for a walk along the edge of your parent's farm, I saw Emma in the trees. I think Sadie might have invited her to witness the wedding, and they are still talking to one another."

A heavy silence filled the gap between them. Aubrey chewed her bottom lip, absorbing his words with a surprisingly blank face. After a minute of silence with Jamie shifting nervously, she broke it with a watery sigh. "I just don't understand why Sadie would keep something like that from me. I used to be close to my sisters, and now they are keeping secrets from me. I now know what it's like to be the outcast in my own family."

"I don't think that is what they are intending to do, Aubrey," he said, and wrapped her in a consoling hug. "I don't know what they are doing exactly, but they both know you are with a bobli. Sadie doesn't want to upset you."

Aubrey's voice was muffled against his chest when she spoke. "But that doesn't make sense though. Sadie was visibly upset when Bishop Abraham came in, and she nearly puked after telling me that she had promised something."

"Promised something? And maybe she's sick because she's pregnant. You were sick too at the beginning."

"She's only been married for one night, Jamie. It doesn't happen that fast."

"If it's Gott's will."

"Nee, I mean, she wouldn't be sick so quickly. Anyway, I think there is something else going on. Bishop Abraham seems to believe it wasn't just my sister who is talking to Emma."

"We all know that Michael has been in trouble, and is still probably talking to her for whatever reasons he possesses."

She shifted out from beneath his arms. Aubrey peered up at him, hands still resting on the upper portion of his chest. "You weren't the one who told Bishop Abraham about Emma being in the forest on Sadie's wedding day?"

"Nee. I never said a word because I don't want to start this again. We're about to have a bobli. We don't need the extra stress."

"Then someone else is watching my family, because they know that Emma is talking to Sadie."

"Aubrey," Jamie said, sighing wearily. "Please just let it go. We really don't have the time or energy to figure this out. Let the church figure out what is going on."

"I can't just ignore it, Jamie. There is something going on with my family, and I will find out what it is."

Aubrey wrenched herself out of his grasp and stomped back through the field to climb clumsily over the fence. He bit the tip of his tongue to resist the urge to swear underneath his breath as he slowly made his way back to the warehouse. When he reached the doors, Aubrey was already gone, and Gott only knew where she had gone. He prayed that she was on her way back to the bakery, but the other part of him knew that wasn't likely.

His fraa had a sweet and caring side to her, but also a determined and hard headed one. Whenever an idea crossed Aubrey's head, there was no stopping it.

When he entered the warehouse, Michael was wrapping a patch of sandpaper around a sanding block. A very faint smile ghosted his lips, and for a brief second, Jamie wondered if he had been listening in on them. Then again, he reminded himself, something was obviously going on when Aubrey stomped by the warehouse with him following behind with a scowl.

Unable to stand the smile across Michael's face, and already in a sour mood, Jamie snapped, "What are you smiling at?"

An actual smile spread across Michael's face this time. "I told you that this situation was far from over. You didn't want to believe me."

"I wanted to believe that you were on the church's side after you took your vows again."

"I am on the church's side. I told them everything that I know about Emma and what is going on."

"What is going on then?"

Michael shrugged his shoulders noncommittally. "I don't involve myself in gossip when it comes to Emma. I'm trying to righten myself in front of Gott."

"If that's true, then why were you contact with her?"

"As I told Bishop Abraham, I have no idea why Emma is still around. She left the community without saying a word to me when she had promised to come back. I only have a general idea of what is going on."

"Would you like to share what you think is going on?

Because I'm lost on what the deal is."

"Why should I tell you?"

A vein on the side of Jamie's temple throbbed in anger. His head hurt as though he had smacked into something repeatedly. A deep seed of dread filled him thinking of all the possible scenarios of what could be going on within their tight knit community. "All I need to know is if it involves Aubrey in any way. You once had a fraa and a bobli. So, please tell me. I know that you don't think ill of Aubrey in any way."

Michael's face remained impassive. He dipped the bristles of his brush repeatedly in the wood stain, watching the liquid drip back down into the can. "I sometimes wish that Emma would be more like Aubrey," he said quietly. "I promised that I wouldn't tell anyone about why she is here, but I can assure you that it has nothing to do with Aubrey. They're trying to keep Aubrey out of it because she is so close to her due date."

"Danka," Jamie said in relief, letting out a pent up breath. Still confused, he decided to pry a little more. "You said, 'they're.' Is Sadie involved in this somehow? I pray that she's not, since she recently took vows with the church and exchanged vows with Eli."

"Like I said," Michael said, turning his back on Jamie. "I promised to keep quiet, because I don't wish to see anybody get in trouble."

Thoroughly confused with the conversation, and with Michael's back and forth answers, Jamie returned to his own work bench to figure things out. There was no doubt that Sadie and Emma were in touch with one another, but why? What was going on for those two to communicate? He frowned down at the freshly sanded table. Sadie never struck him as the type not to follow the Ordnung. She had participated in rumspringa like everyone else, but had decided to join the church shortly afterward.

He straightened when a chilling thought popped into mind. Aubrey recently commented that it seemed rather odd how fast Sadie wished to join the church and accept Eli's marriage proposal. Normally, the youths of their community took their vows around the age of eighteen, after much thought and prayer whether serving Gott was the right path. Sadie would turn seventeen in a few months.

Something had happened for Sadie to speed up her marriage to Eli, and somehow, Emma was in the middle of it. His heart twisted anxiously when he prayed that it wasn't what came to his mind.

⚬ CHAPTER 3 ⚬

The bobli was more active than usual lately. Aubrey rolled onto her side, sighing in aggravation at a well-placed kick to her ribs. She adjusted the pillow beneath the growing swell of her belly and closed her eyes with the futile hope that exhaustion would eventually pull her into sleep. On the other side of the bed, Jamie slept fitfully. He mumbled incoherently under his breath and jerked harshly every once and awhile. When a kick to the back of her thigh followed their bobli kicking the front of her tummy, Aubrey sat up in a huff of irritation.

"It is impossible to sleep anymore!" she grumbled under her breath.

Aubrey managed to wiggle her way out of the bed without waking Jamie. She sat on the rocking chair next to their dresser, and proceeded, with some difficulty, to pull on a pair of thick wool socks to protect her bare feet from the cold floors. Grabbing a thick robe from their closet, Aubrey left the confines of their room to make herself a cup of chamomile tea. She slid her arms through the sleeves of her robe as she unsteadily made her way down the stairs. With each passing day, it became harder to see where her feet were stepping, and she felt increasingly wobbly from the excess weight on her belly.

The living room was exceptionally hot from when Jamie had loaded it with several logs of white fir. The different type of wood was hard to chop, but wonderful during the cold nights because it burned all night and kept the haus warm without them having to wake up to stoke the fire. Aubrey sank down on the couch with a grateful sigh. A dull ache had recently started in her lower back, and it never seemed to go away unless there was a hot towel against it.

She felt her bobli shift against the warm heat touching the stretched skin of her stomach. Aubrey rested a hand there, and waited patiently for the bobli to settle back into sleep. At this pace, she thought grumpily to herself, I'll be used to being up at all hours of the night with a crying bobli.

Tilting her head back, Aubrey looked upward at the sky. The moon shimmered brightly from beyond the thick blanket of clouds, and the faintest trickle of snow started falling to the ground. She straightened up to turn around on her knees and rest her arms on the window seal, then pressed her warm forehead against the cold glass. There was something beautiful and soothing in witnessing the first snowfall of the season. With how unpredictable the weather could be in the valley, sometimes it was a blessing to have at least two snowfalls.

Time slipped by as she watched the snow trickle down

steadily from the clouds until it dusted the front lawn. It wasn't until Jamie sleepily trudged down the narrow stairs that she realized it had actually been several hours since she'd made her tea. "What are you doing up? It's almost four in the morning."

Red circles lined Jamie's eyes and his face was pale in the moonlight. He sank down on the couch cushions next to Aubrey, glancing out the window as well.

"It's the first snowfall of the season," Aubrey said.

"I see that. Why are you up to see it so early?"

She ignored the reprimand. Both of their normally peaceful nights were being disrupted for various reasons. She wondered what Jamie's dreams were to cause such distress clearly written on his face. "I couldn't sleep because of the bobli kicking me, and you were tossing in your sleep and kicking me."

Jamie's eyes widened in alarm. "I was kicking you?" he asked, horrified by the thought. "I didn't realize that I was hurting you in my sleep. I'm sorry. No wonder you are down here."

"It wasn't just you keeping me awake. Our bobli was kicking me too."

He rested a hand on the back of her calf. Aubrey suppressed a shiver when his calloused fingers touched her skin and massaged the aching muscles there. She let her head drop wearily to the headrest of the couch.

"You've been having bad dreams lately," she commented lazily.

"Jah, they've been getting worse every night."

Aubrey lifted her head at that. It wasn't just normal

exhaustion contributing to Jamie's haggard experience. Something deep down was bothering her mann, and she had a feeling it was related to the news of Emma. She reached out to cup Jamie's cheek in the palm of her hand and offered him an encouraging smile. "What are your dreams about? Maybe I can offer some sort of help."

"I doubt that you would be able to," Jamie said, letting out a pent up breath. "I don't even know whether Gott can explain these dreams to me. They are so strange, and so frightening at times."

"How are they frightening?"

He shook his head. "I don't even want to talk about them, Aubrey. I sometimes feel that it's an attack and talking about it will only give it more fuel."

Concern filled her at his words. Aubrey straightened up fully, leaning back on her heels so she could look at him. "Are you sure? We could always pray if you feel-"

"Don't worry about it, Aubrey. I have been praying, and Gott will protect me from these dreams. Right now, I just want to go back upstairs and go to sleep."

She shrank from the harshness in his tone, but nodded in understanding when he shot her an apologetic look. Whatever plagued his dreams was not a topic Jamie wished to discuss. They wordlessly clasped hands before venturing up the stairs. Shortly afterward, Aubrey listened to Jamie's breathing even out. His chest skimmed her back every time he inhaled deeply, and the hairs on the back of her neck fluttered when his warm breath puffed out.

At some point, Aubrey fell into a fitful sleep. She wasn't sure what woke her, but a pale morning light had entered the warm confines of their bedroom. Her stomach grumbled loudly, and the bobli stirred in response to the noise. Gently lifting Jamie's hand from her hip, Aubrey quickly slid out to dress into a pale grey dress and shoved her socked feet into thick boots. She turned to watch Jamie sleep, undisturbed by her presence as she moved around the room, fingers pulling the strands of her thick hair back into a bun. The lines around his face had smoothed out after falling back asleep.

Aubrey went about her normal chores, letting Jamie sleep a bit more with it being Saturday. They had plenty of chores to attend to, but she worried greatly over her mann's recent exhaustion. She slipped out into the crisp morning to gather the chopped wood that was stacked neatly alongside the haus, but stopped short when down the road she caught sight of an envelope in their mailbox, which stood at the edge of the farm. She frowned at the sight, since mail only came during the week.

Gravel crunched loudly beneath her boots as Aubrey approached the mailbox. Her breath streamed out in front of her in a steady white cloud. The corner of the envelope was damp, and there was no address or return address scrawled on the front. Aubrey slid a curious finger along the edge to tear it open, and pulled out a note written in Pennsylvanian Dutch.

I know your sister and father's secret.

She stared down at the neatly scrawled words, heart pounding furiously. Aubrey hastily shoved the note back into the envelope and looked around at the serene surroundings. A cold mist still lingered above the fields, and she spotted recent hoof prints in the dirt along the ditch. Whoever had left the strange note had come sometime while they had been asleep, and on horseback apparently as well.

Aubrey anxiously chewed her bottom lip as she waddled as fast as she could back up to the haus to wake Jamie. She paused briefly at the porch to catch her breath before entering through the kitchen, and let out a relieved to breath see Jamie dressed in his day clothes and pouring himself a cup of the kaffe that she had brewed. Jamie glanced at her with a sleepy frown. "Where did you-"

"Look at this," she interrupted him, shoving the envelope into his chest. "Read what it says."

Jamie set the cup of kaffe down on the counter, and slid the note free from the envelope. His eyes flicked over the page before looking up at Aubrey in confusion. "I don't get it. What does this mean?"

"I have no idea," Aubrey said anxiously. "Whoever wrote it is in our community, because it's in Dutch, and they know something about my family."

"This doesn't make any sense. Which sister is this note referring to?"

"Maybe Emma? I don't know if Sadie could keep secrets very well, but what would my father have to hide? He's respected by the entire community."

"I have no idea." Jamie said, and he flipped the envelope over to frown at the lack of addresses. "Whoever it was doesn't want you to know who they are, but it seems as though they are trying to hold something over your head or your family's heads."

"Maybe someone from the outside?" Aubrey suggested. She didn't want to think about a member of their beloved community stooping to blackmailing, but she wasn't even sure that she was being blackmailed. "You see what I mean? There is something going on with my family. This note didn't come out of nowhere."

"I hate to say this, Aubrey, but this could be about Emma. The community is forgiving, but they aren't very happy with how she behaved either. She might have angered someone more than anyone else. You don't remember any instances of that, do you?"

"Nee. I don't remember anything like that."

They fell into a tense, but thoughtful silence. Jamie carefully folded the note back into the envelope and placed it on the counter behind him. He picked up his cup of kaffe, and with a heavy sigh, took a very long sip. "I don't know what this note is about or what the intended message is, but I think it'd be a gut idea to take it to Bishop Abraham. If it is someone in the community leaving this message, then it needs to be addressed right away."

"Jah, I agree, but I want to know what these secrets are. I don't understand what has happened when everything was fine a few weeks ago."

Jamie shrugged his shoulders. "Neither do I, Aubrey, but this isn't any of our business. No Amish family is perfect by any means, but we have our own family to worry about in the meantime."

A current of anger shot through Aubrey's veins quickly. She stared at Jamie as he sipped at his kaffe, either oblivious to her glaring or simply choosing to ignore it.

"This isn't right, Jamie. You know that it isn't right, and if this was your family-"

"I love my family, but you and the bobli are the center of my world now. Everything else comes second."

"I never said that you and the bobli aren't the center of my world. I just worry that whoever wrote this note thinks that this secret will hurt my family."

"If the person who wrote it is Amish, then that isn't their intention. Look," he took the envelope, and tucked it in the back pocket of his trousers, "if it really will bother you this much, we can go to your family's haus after going to Bishop Abraham about it. Would that make you feel better?"

"A little bit," she replied, nodding her head. A distant part of her admonished her about continuing in this cycle of secrets, but it was hard to ebb her curiosity. She had said goodbye to Emma and kept true to her word by distancing herself. Whatever secrets Emma possessed were no surprise. The only secrets that Aubrey wanted to know were her daed's.

And what would a devoted mann and daed have to hide?

CRXSD

"And you found this in your mailbox?"

They stood in the tiny kitchen of Bishop Abraham's haus as the older Amish man looked over the envelope and letter. A frown creased his already wrinkled brow as he slowly placed the letter back in the envelope.

Jamie looked to where Aubrey stood uncomfortably next to him, with one hand absently resting on the swell of her stomach. Still wrapped up in a thick wool coat, the heat from the wood stove undoubtedly bothered her.

"Jah, in the early morning hours. Right at dawn actually, when I was fetching wood for our stove."

Abraham tugged on the edge of his white beard, eyebrows furrowed in deep thought. "It is disconcerting to think that someone within our community would write a letter like this with the these types of implications."

"Exactly," Jamie said, nodding his head. "I pray that nothing will come out of this, but I admit that I want to know what the writer of this letter intended."

"Maybe it would be best to let it be for now," Abraham said eventually. He handed the envelope to Jamie. "There are many disheartening things being said at the moment throughout our community. I'm afraid that the evil of gossip has besieged our hearts."

"You don't think this has anything to do with my sister, do you?" Aubrey asked.

Abraham leaned back in his chair, one hand still curled loosely around a mug of kaffe. "I am not sure if the center of the rumors is coming from within the community or without," he said, and then took a long sip of the steaming liquid. "I will make sure to address this letter, among other things, after the wedding ceremonies are over. Jamie, I believe your sister is planning to be married this upcoming weekend. Such a joyous occasion."

"Jah, sir. Lily is very excited to be married in Gott's eyes. My whole family is very excited about this union."

"Well, you two have other things to take care of rather than talking to me," Abraham said with a laugh. "Rest assured that this letter will be addressed. I am sure that we will find the source of the disquiet within our community, and Gott will lead us back to the right path."

They bid their goodbyes and left the stuffy confines of Abraham's haus. The crisp air greeted them the second they stepped out toward their buggy. A thin layer of snow covered the ground and soaked the bottom of Aubrey's dress skirts.

"Well, at least it will be mentioned in church," Jamie said. He tucked the envelope back into the pocket of his pants and then helped Aubrey climb into the buggy. "I'm sure that whoever wrote this letter will come forward and explain their intentions."

"I hope so." Aubrey smiled down at him tiredly. They trotted along steadily in the direction of town, the clop of hooves on the asphalt echoing in the morning air.

"Have you heard any of these rumors Bishop Abraham was speaking of?" Aubrey asked.

Jamie shook his head. "Nee, I haven't."

"Do you find it odd that we haven't heard anything?"

He looked down at the leather reins in his fingers. Whoever had written that letter certainly wanted them to know the rumors that were going around, but no one had mentioned any sort of rumor to him. All he knew was that Emma was in contact with a few church members, Michael and Sadie as known ones, but they had yet to be admonished. "I don't know, Aubrey. Maybe the community is trying to protect you from them since you are carrying a bobli."

"Maybe. Can we visit my daed this weekend?"

"If you want to. Just remember that whatever is going on obviously doesn't concern us. Please be careful," Jamie said, sending Aubrey an imploring look.

She reached out to pat him on the hand reassuringly. "I promise to be careful," she said, and turned to watch the fields as they passed. "Maybe my daed can inform us about what is going on. I know he's sick, but he always seems to be in tune with the rest of the community."

Aubrey let out a sharp breath of pain suddenly. She grabbed at her lower back and belly, eyes clenched tightly together.

Panic swelled within Jamie so fast that his fingers numbly dropped the reins to the floor. He reached for Aubrey, but it was over as quick as it started.

"What is it? Is it the bobli?"

"Nee." She shook her head, still breathless, "It was a sharp pain in my back that went around to my belly."

"Is it still happening?" Jamie asked, clutching Aubrey's hand tightly in his own. Their horse continued to trot down the road, unaware of what was going on. "Maybe we should go to the midwife-"

"Nee. I-"

Her face scrunched up in pain again. Jamie hastily grabbed the reins from the floorboard and turned their buggy back in the direction of the community. He kept one hand on Aubrey's knee, feeling the muscles in her legs tense up and then relax every few minutes.

They pulled up to the midwife's haus right as she was

walking out to the barn. Martha looked over at Aubrey hunched over in a wordless pain and set an empty pail down on a hay bale next to the barn.

"What is going on?" Martha asked them, offering up a hand for Aubrey to climb down from the buggy. "Contractions? Water breaking?"

"Co-contractions," Aubrey breathed out.

Martha wrapped a steady arm around Aubrey's waist and guided her to the haus as Jamie frantically unhitched their horse before setting him free to graze in the field. He jogged to catch up to them, his heart pounding painfully within his chest as he took Aubrey's clammy hand in his own.

They followed Martha up the stairs to a spare room. Jamie kept an arm around Aubrey's shoulders to hold her steady as Martha quickly placed down bedding and towels. Anticipation filled him to the point that he was afraid he would surely boil over or go crazy in the process.

He started praying. The bobli still had a month left before he or she would be able to join them in the world. While Martha had warned them that survival from premature births was possible, Jamie had taken comfort in knowing that Aubrey's pregnancy was normal. Gott surely would not bless them with such a gift only to have it be taken away.

"Everything will be okay, Aubrey," he said, running a thumb over the knuckles of Aubrey's fingers. "Gott is here with us. He will take care of you and the bobli."

A tight smile filled Aubrey's face before she was hunched over again in pain. With Martha's help, he laid

Aubrey back on the bed and fluffed the pillows to keep her propped up. He looked away promptly when Martha started to lift the skirts of Aubrey's dress.

"We're okay," Martha said after a few tense moments passed. "What you're feeling are Braxton-Hicks contractions. They're painful sometimes, but they aren't necessarily a sign of immediate labor."

"These aren't real contractions?" Aubrey gasped.

Jamie turned when he heard Martha straighten out Aubrey's skirts to protect her modesty. He let out a relieved breath, going weak at the knees temporarily.

Martha smiled faintly. "I'm afraid not. These contractions will fade out here shortly, and they'll come back irregularly. Real labor contractions will come steadily and become more painful. I can't feel any thinning or dilation, which is a gut thing. We want that bobli to hang in there for a few more weeks."

The color in Aubrey's face drained as she looked to Jamie. A mixture of anticipation reflected brightly in her eyes, but there was an undercurrent of disappointment as well. The longer her pregnancy continued, the more uncomfortable she grew, and the more anxious they both became.

"It's a gut thing, Aubrey. We don't want the bobli to arrive too early." When tears flooded Aubrey's eyes, he rushed on. "Don't worry. The bobli will be here before we know it. Just wait and see. Thanksgiving will pass us by and before you know it we will have our blessing here."

"Your mann is speaking the truth," Martha said. She patted Aubrey kindly on the back of the hand, "The last month of pregnancy is very hard on soon-to-be maemms. Try to get some rest, even if it feels like as if you can't. Take a moment to yourself before coming downstairs. Jamie, may I speak with you for a moment alone?"

He nodded and waited for Martha to help Aubrey sit up properly before following the middle-aged Amish woman back down the flight of stairs. They paused at the bottom to help Aubrey when she decided to come downstairs.

"May I ask what was going on before the contractions started?"

"We were coming from Bishop Abraham's haus after speaking with him. Why?"

"I'm afraid that at this point, Jamie," Martha said, sighing heavily. "Your bobli will be here too soon if there continues to be any emotional distress."

His heart plummeted to his heels. "What do you mean? I'm afraid I don't understand. You said that those contractions aren't real."

"They weren't real contractions, but there are signs of labor. I didn't wish to tell Aubrey directly because it wouldn't do her any good worrying over it."

"If labor's close..." He stopped, swallowing thickly. "How do we stop it from happening now then?"

Martha's eyes were hard glints in the morning light when she turned a stern gaze over to Jamie. "I'm no fool. I know that there are rumors spreading like wildfire throughout our community. I've heard them. It's best that you keep those rumors from Aubrey's ears. They're only going to upset her greatly, and look what happened today."

"What rumors are going around? No one has mentioned anything to Aubrey or me."

"Gut." Martha gave a sharp nod. "Keep it that way. Don't put your bobli's health in danger over trying to figure out these rumors. Whatever Aubrey feels, your bobli reacts to."

Frustration smoldered inside of Jamie's chest. He stared at Martha, gritting his teeth to contain the sharp words he wanted to say. Instead, he focused on the other part of Martha's words: Aubrey and their bobli's health depended on peace.

"You're upset." He glanced up to find Martha's gaze fixated on him, a wry smile tugging at her lips. "I might be a midwife, but I am also gut at reading other's reactions to certain things. What is it you're upset about?"

Jamie laughed darkly. "Take your pick. The rumors that everyone is so keen on keeping from us, Aubrey's health, the bobli's health…"

"It's overwhelming, I'm sure. The last month of pregnancy is the one of the hardest phases, and dealing with these sort of rumors doesn't help. I pray for you and Aubrey everyday that Gott will keep you both protected."

Footsteps on the floorboards above interrupted their conversation as Aubrey appeared from the shadows. Her face was red and splotchy, undoubtedly crying from the past two days' events and lack of sleep.

Jamie helped Aubrey down the stairs carefully while his thoughts continued to tangle themselves into knots. Never before had he been so confused or lost regarding what was going on within the community. Now, there were secrets hidden behind closed doors, and whispers being shared between members.

He had only one question lingering in his mind: What was Gott protecting them from?

⚮ CHAPTER 4 ❧

The following weekend, Aubrey busied herself in baking with Hannah and Elizabeth while their kinner played happily in the living room. Aubrey smiled fondly while rubbing the swell of her stomach whenever their delighted laughter reached the kitchen. Soon, her own bobli would be joining the laughter.

"So," Hannah said, pulling an apple pie free from the oven. "How are you feeling with the bobli's due date so close?"

Aubrey scooted the wire rack across the counter so Hannah could place the pie on it to cool. The contractions had dulled out over the days of rest at Jamie's bidding, but she occasionally found her stomach muscles tightening painfully until she lost her breath. "Anxious," she said, inhaling the pleasant smell of cinnamon and apples. "Earlier this week, Jamie and I thought the bobli was coming."

Both women paused at that.

"What do you mean?" Elizabeth asked.

"I started having pain in my lower back and it led to contractions. Martha said it was my body practicing for labor."

Hannah exchanged an uneasy look with Elizabeth before saying, "Are you sure it wasn't the start of labor, Aubrey? That sounds like labor to us."

"I don't think so," Aubrey said, frowning at her friends' concerned faces. "Martha told me it was nothing to worry about."

"You can be in labor for weeks sometimes," Elizabeth said. She folded a dish towel and placed it on the counter. "I was in labor with my youngest for almost a week or so. Not saying anything against Martha, but it sounds as if it might be the same for you. Do you still have painful contractions?"

Apprehension filled her. While resting helped, the sometimes painful contractions had continued randomly throughout the week. They sometimes came in evenly timed contractions, while other times they were irregular. Aubrey had taken comfort in Martha's words that it was her body preparing for labor, but was it happening sooner than expected? The thought terrified her.

"Sometimes they are painful," Aubrey said, looking to her friends in alarm. "They aren't regularly timed for the most part. Do you think I'm in labor and don't know it?"

Elizabeth rested a calming hand on Aubrey's trembling shoulder. "Nee. I think you might be in the early stages of labor, and I pray that you will make it another few weeks for the bobli's health. There's nothing to worry about if you feel like everything is fine."

"I-I-I think everything is okay. How do you know?" Hannah smiled. "Trust us. You will know when the bobli is coming," she said.

"I hope so," Aubrey said tiredly. "I am exhausted wondering if every little pain or movement is a sign."

They finished baking the rest of the pies. A new family from Lancaster had arrived to their community earlier during the week. While the mensleit generously built a new haus and were currently working on the barn, Aubrey had volunteered, with the help of Hannah and Elizabeth, to bake the Byler family a few welcoming pies. She had sought out Sadie to help, but her younger sister had politely declined with the reasoning that she had been feeling ill for the past week.

"I don't want to get anyone sick," she had said, sipping some hot water with slices of ginger in it. "I wouldn't forgive myself if I got others sick."

"I think we've baked everything. We could deliver all these now," Hannah said.

Elizabeth scanned the pies one last time. "Perhaps we should prepare lunch for the mensleit? I know Henry is most likely complaining because he is hungry."

They shared a laugh before assembling a lunch of simple ham and cheese sandwiches. Aubrey placed them in a basket as Hannah and Elizabeth gathered their kinner from the living room. With extra hands to carry everything, they managed to squeeze into two buggies and trot through the crisp afternoon air.

The Byler's new haus was a mile down the road, past a few hay fields. Several buggies were parked outside the newly erected haus and smoke curled from the chimney. The mensleit were gathered in front of a barn that appeared to be almost finished, with just a few pieces of the roof missing.

A middle aged Amish woman exited the haus when she caught sight of them climbing out of the buggy with pies and lunch in hand. She smiled warmly at them as they approached.

"Gut morning. I am Katie Byler."

They introduced themselves before following Katie into a tidy kitchen.

A young girl no older than Sadie, in a pale pink dress, paused in taking another set of dishes out of a box. Her green eyes sparkled warmly at them as well. "Hello. I am Naomi Byler."

"My oldest daughter," Kate added. She took the basket of sandwiches from Aubrey's arms with a gentle smile. "You shouldn't be going through all this trouble, dear. Not when you are close to having a bobli, am I right?"

Aubrey smiled at the sincerity in Katie's voice. "Jah, in a few weeks," she said.

"Well, danka for all these lovely pies and food. I heard the men complaining about empty stomachs a few minutes ago. We are still trying to organize our kitchen utensils."

They placed the sandwiches on plates for the mensleit. Naomi disappeared from the warm kitchen to fetch the mensleit for lunch while they wiped down the table and scooted extra chairs into the tiny room. A blast of chilly air followed by male laughter echoed in the haus a few minutes later as a stampede of boots on the floorboards approached the kitchen.

Aubrey looked up from pouring Jamie a cup of water to see him entering the kitchen with Henry at his side. A flash of heat went through her when she caught sight of Naomi following behind the two bruders. Her eyes were fixed longingly on Jamie's back, but he either remained oblivious to it or chose to ignore it. A possessive jealousy shot through Aubrey so fast and intense that it alarmed her. Forcing her fingers to uncurl from fists, she forced herself to smile as Jamie made his way to her.

"I didn't think you would be here. You're supposed to be home resting," he said.

She was too busy fighting jealousy to respond outrightly to the reprimand in Jamie's voice. "I feel fine. Plus, I promised to bake pies. Hannah and Elizabeth did most of the work for me."

Jamie didn't get a chance to reply. The rest of the mensleit and Atlee Byler, as he introduced himself, grabbed their plates to eat as they worked.

"It looks like there is a snow storm coming. We want to finish the roof so there isn't any snow in the barn," Atlee said.

"Make sure to get home before it snows," Jamie said to Aubrey, picking up his plate as well. "This is supposed to be a big storm."

Atlee nodded in wordless appreciation for the meal before slipping out the door. Jamie smiled fleetingly in Aubrey's direction before following them outside as well. Again, she watched with a surge of intense jealousy as

Naomi's eyes followed Jamie.

"We'd better get home ourselves before this storm hits us," Hannah said. "We don't want to be traveling in a buggy when the snow comes."

"Of course," Katie said, nodding. "Danka for the pies again. They are delicious."

They gathered their things before walking out into the cloudy afternoon. The sound of hammers thudding into nails and wood echoed in the silence as they seated themselves comfortably in their buggies.

Aubrey sat moodily in the front, barely listening to what Hannah was saying. "...Naomi is a pretty girl, don't you think? She'll have no troubles finding a mann."

"Jah," Aubrey said thickly, trying not to let anger seep into her voice. "She'll find no trouble here."

"What's with that tone?"

Her eyes fluttered closed at the question. What was wrong with her? A chilly breeze swept along her hairline hidden beneath her kapp. The cold air, coupled with praying, helped calm the jealous tide that had swept over her.

"I'm sorry. I just saw Naomi looking at Jamie and..." Aubrey trailed off. She looked away in embarrassment when Hannah smiled knowingly at her.

"You don't have to explain. Jamie loves you. I don't think you ever have to worry about something like that."

"I know. It was just something that happened so fast. I feel so ridiculous thinking about it now."

Aubrey laughed shortly at her irrational emotions. They waved goodbye to Elizabeth and her kinner as their buggy passed by them on the road. They reached Aubrey's haus as snowflakes started to sprinkle from the cloudy sky. Hannah started to unhitch her horse from the buggy and help Naomi down from the buggy.

"I'll help you clean up the kitchen and get a head start on dinner," Hannah said.

"Nee, you should go home before the snow starts to come down," Aubrey said and smiled appreciatively at her friend. "Danka though. I appreciate all the help."

"If you're sure…"

"I'm sure."

Hannah hugged her briefly, and rested a hand on the swell of Aubrey's stomach. "I can't wait to meet your bobli. It'll be such a wunderbar blessing."

"I can't wait to meet my bobli too," Aubrey said.

Their lighthearted moment faded away at the dark expression on Hannah's face. Before she could ask what was going on, Hannah blurted out, "I think there is something you need to hear."

Aubrey drew back in surprise at the statement. She stared in perplexity at her normally upbeat friend. "What is it?"

"It's about your sister…"

Dread filled the pit of Aubrey's stomach. The bobli kicked at the walls of her womb as if he or she could sense it as well.

"Which sister?" she asked, inwardly praying it wasn't Sadie. Her youngest sister had been acting strangely since her wedding, and effectively avoiding her inquiries by claiming she was too ill to work at the bakery.

"Well, it's about Sadie," Hannah said reluctantly. "Your parents and the church has asked me to not to say anything to you because they don't want to see you upset. They don't want to mention anything until they figure it out, but I can't keep quiet. It's bad Aubrey, if it's true..."

She grabbed Hannah's cold hand tightly in her gloved one. "Tell me, please. I promise not to be upset over it. I've been wishing that someone would tell me what is going on. This past weekend, someone wrote a strange letter saying they knew my sister and daed's secret. No one is telling us anything."

"Do you know who wrote the letter?" Hannah asked, frowning.

Aubrey shook her head. "Nee, Bishop Abraham promised to address it after the weddings are over. What is going on?"

"You have to promise not to say anything and promise that you didn't hear it from me. Your family will be very upset if I speak about this."

Tears flooded Hannah's eyes. She held Aubrey's hand tightly and stared at her in wordless pleading. Snow continued to trickle down around them in a soft blanket that spread itself upon the land. Behind them, Naomi jumped free of the buggy to run happily through the unusually early snowfall.

"I promise I won't say anything."

"I heard it from Jacob's sister, Betty, that Sadie may have sinned while on rumspringa."

Her heart thundered. "Sinned? Sinned how?"

Hannah looked down at the snow covered ground

uncomfortably. "You don't find it odd that Sadie rushed to join the church and then she was married to Eli a month afterward?"

"Of course I found it odd. I had told her to take their courtship slow. I was happy for her, but..."

The realization of what Hannah was implying hit Aubrey hard in the gut. It left her breathless with dismay and denial. The decision to join the church right after rumspringa, to marry Eli within a month after that, the morning sickness. It all added up.

She was pregnant before joining the church.

CR&SO

They finished the Byler's barn right as the snow started to flutter upon them. Jamie sighed in relief as he climbed down the ladder with a hammer in hand while the rest of the mensleit gathered their tools to head home for the evening. Nothing sounded more pleasant than going home to a warm wood stove and to whatever Aubrey had cooked for dinner.

His thoughts of warmth were interrupted when a soft hand gently touched his shoulder. He turned around to find Naomi Byler, the oldest of the Byler family, standing behind him with a steaming cup of tea.

"I thought you might need this," she said, smiling shyly up at him.

Jamie glanced around to see whether anyone else was offered tea before reluctantly, not wishing to be rude, taking the warm cup in his gloved hand. He noted how

Naomi peered up at him through her eyelashes, and groaned inwardly at the sight. This was the last thing that he needed to deal with.

"Danka."

"You're welcome."

Naomi fidgeted nervously on the balls of her feet. They stood in awkward silence as Jamie gulped down the tea, nearly scorching his throat in the process. He handed back the cup with a strained smile.

"You did a gut job on the barn," Naomi said.

He dodged the compliment by taking a step back. "I couldn't have built it without the other men. Excuse me, I have to get home before the snow starts to come down."

Naomi opened her mouth to reply, but he was already striding across the gravel road to where Henry was waiting in the buggy. The tops of his ears burned in embarrassment when he climbed into the buggy to find his bruder smirking at him in amusement. They started back down the road in the direction of Jamie's haus.

"Don't say a word," Jamie warned him. "If you do, I swear I'll do something to you."

"Gut thing Aubrey wasn't here to witness that. I doubt she would have been so nice," Henry replied.

"Don't tease her, Henry. I'm not responsible for you if she loses her temper, and trust me, it happens a lot more being pregnant."

Henry smiled. "I'm sure that I'll find out soon enough." He paused for a moment, shifting the reins to another hand. "How is Aubrey doing, by the way?"

"Better with rest. I'm praying that the bobli will hold

off for a few more weeks."

"Is she still having contractions?"

Jamie shook his head. "If she is, she isn't telling me about them. I didn't want her out of the haus today, but she obviously didn't listen."

"That was my fault. After you told me what happened with the letter, rumors, and contractions, I asked Elizabeth to keep her company."

"You've heard the rumors? And didn't tell me about them?"

Henry glanced away guiltily when Jamie glared angrily at him. "Only some of them," he admitted. "But none of them have to do with Aubrey, if that makes you feel any better."

"What are they about?"

"Bishop Abraham doesn't want to trouble you and Aubrey-"

"It's not troubling me. I didn't care to know at first, but with that letter ending up in our mailbox..." He wiped at his runny nose in aggravation. "I just want to know about it in case I have tell Aubrey. Don't you think I'd be a better person to tell her than someone else?"

They pulled to a stop on the side of the road. Henry pinched the bridge of his nose and sighed heavily. He turned to look at Jamie with a weary smile.

"You're right. I just hope that after I tell you there won't be anything drastic done on your part."

"I pray that it won't have to get to that point."

"Then you'd be relieved to know that none of what is being said is about Aubrey. It's about Sadie."

Jamie frowned. His conversations with Aubrey about her sister's strange behavior replayed in his mind. He prayed that whatever it was, it didn't involve Emma. He was still wary of her unexpected presence on Sadie's wedding day.

"What's going on with Sadie?"

"There have been rumors that Sadie might have physically consummated a relationship before taking her vows. That she and Eli joined the church right after rumspringa to cover up something else."

His stomach soured at the implication behind Henry's words, but also tightened with dread. It wasn't unheard of for couples to consummate their relationships before joining the church and rush the process to hide the consequences. There was something more to it than that, and it involved Emma somehow.

"Is that all you've heard?" Jamie asked.

"That is all I've heard. Why?"

"I can't get the letter out of my mind. There is something else going on, and I know Emma is in the middle of it."

"Don't you think you're being hard on Emma?" Henry asked, sighing. "You don't know her, and she's Aubrey's sister. Why would she be involved when she isn't in our community anymore?"

"I saw her on Sadie's wedding day. She was hiding in the woods and ran away before I could say anything."

"Maybe she just wanted to be here on Sadie's wedding day."

"If she wanted to be a part of this community, she

would've taken her second chance last spring. She's here for a different reason."

"Dear Gott," Henry said, shaking his head in dismay. "Please help us stay on the righteous path. This isn't gut for any of us, Jamie. Do yourself a favor and Aubrey one as well: let it go."

Jamie stared out at the snow covered fields. In his heart, he knew that Henry was right. This wasn't Godly behavior getting wrapped up into idle talk. None of it involved Aubrey or himself. "You're right. This isn't gut for anybody."

They continued down the road with snow crunching beneath the buggy wheels. Smoke from the chimney drifted upwards to the sky, and when Jamie slipped out of the passenger's seat with a wave in Henry's direction, the smells of beef and potatoes washed over him.

Kicking his boots free of snow, Jamie entered through the kitchen door to find Aubrey standing in front of the stove. Strands of fine hair framed Aubrey's flushed cheeks as she stirred what appeared to be a beef stew. He smiled in appreciation at his fraa, who'd baked all morning, prepared sandwiches, and then returned to start a hearty dinner that would soothe away the coldness in his bones.

"Hi," he said, pressing a kiss to her temple. "Danka for the sandwiches and now this meal. I hope you saved me an apple pie."

Aubrey pointed to an apple pie cooling on the pie rack. She tapped the wooden spoon against the bubbling pot of stew before setting it on the counter and placed a lid on the pot. When his stomach gave a loud rumble at the aromatic smells of onions, potatoes, and beef, she tipped her head back with a laugh. "I figured you would be hungry. That's why I started an early dinner. There is bread baking in the oven as well."

"Sounds gut."

"Did you finish the Byler's barn?"

"Jah, we finished it right as the snow was beginning to fall."

He sat on his usual chair at the head of the table. Within a minute, Aubrey placed a hot cup of kaffe with cream and sugar in front of him. "How are you and the bobli feeling this afternoon?" he asked, cradling the cup closely. "No more contractions right?"

Aubrey kept her back to him as she grabbed a set of bowls from the cupboard. Her tone was guarded when she spoke, "Nee, nothing painful. A few contractions happened, but not like what it had been."

"Remember what Martha said. Rest if they start to get too painful."

"I know. I-" She paused, looking down at the bowls held delicately in her hands, "I was talking to Hannah and Elizabeth about them earlier."

"Ach?"

"They said it sounds like labor to them, or at least the start of labor. What happens if this bobli comes too early? I can't even bear the thought of..."

Tears flooded Aubrey's eyes as she set the bowls down with a harsh clang on the table. He rose from the chair and wrapped her trembling frame into his arms. It was times like these that Jamie could feel how truly delicate

Aubrey was from the way her thin frame and bulging stomach pressed against his body. Any weight that she had gained solely went to the bobli. He didn't wish to think of such things either, and had prayed daily since his conversation with Martha that Gott would keep both of them healthy.

"It will be fine, Aubrey, I promise. You just have try to relax for a few weeks and then it will be safe for the bobli to come."

"It's so hard to relax." Aubrey cried into his chest, head bowed wearily. "I am so tired from being kept awake all night from kicks. At least if the bobli were here I wouldn't be so lonely in the middle of the night."

"The bobli will be here before we know it. Then, we will be up all night with each other."

"You don't have to get up in the middle of the night. You have to go to work in the morning."

"I want to be a part of it too. I don't care if I'm tired. I've been doing it for the past couple of days, haven't I?"

"That's true, I guess. I don't know what's wrong with me."

Jamie smiled as he tightened his arms around Aubrey's shoulders. "There's nothing wrong with you, so stop worrying about it. I would be worried if you told me everything was fine all the time."

He was answered with a snort of laughter. Aubrey sucked in a long breath, and then took a step back to look up at him with a smile. He wiped away the rest of the tears that trailed down the corners of Aubrey's eyes.

"That would concern you?"

"Jah. It would concern me quite a bit, actually."

"I just wish the bobli was here, and that I didn't have to worry over every little pain."

She placed her hands on her stomach and rubbed in a soothing fashion. Just as quickly as her face lit up, a frown darkened it. "I finally heard one of the rumors going around," she said quietly, and looked up at Jamie's sigh. "Have you heard it too? The one about Sadie?"

Some part of him argued that he would regret discussing this with Aubrey, but he relented, knowing that she wouldn't let it go easily. "I've heard, jah. It's just a rumor. I don't even know why some are making a big deal out of it."

"But what if it's true?"

"You really want to believe that about Sadie?"

Shame filled Aubrey's eyes. "Nee. I don't... I just keep wondering where Emma falls into all of this, or what my daed's secret is. I know that Sadie and Emma have been in contact with one another."

"They shouldn't be any more now that Sadie took her vows with the church."

"That obviously doesn't stop Emma from coming around," Aubrey said, smiling thinly at him. "It's something else. There is something else going on."

"Aubrey-" he started, a warning lacing his voice.

"I promise not to get involved for the bobli's sake. I'm just wondering is all." She turned around to tend to the bubbling stew once more.

Jamie scoffed at her back, knowing his fraa would be involved somehow. Tomorrow was Lily's wedding, and more than half the community would be there, including Sadie. He had no doubt that Aubrey would be questioning Sadie the second she had the chance tomorrow.

☙ CHAPTER 5 ❧

"I'm so happy you could make it!"

The swell of Aubrey's stomach brushed against Lily as she was swept up into an enthusiastic embrace. She felt the bobli give a protective kick at the contact, and smiled when Lily drew back with wonder in her eyes.

"I'm happy for you. I hope Gott continues to bless your marriage," she said.

Lily grinned happily at her before moving away to talk to other members of their community and family. Jamie's extended family from Lancaster had arrived the previous night, and they swept Aubrey into excited conversation over the bobli. Tables were pushed together and the celery decorations were placed artfully throughout the house. Loud chatter filled the entire haus as the dishes of food for everyone to eat were placed on the tables.

A wave of fatigue swept over Aubrey while she stood by the staircase to take a breather. Her cheeks were flushed from the constant embraces and the warm air that smelled of baked chicken. In the midst of it all, Jamie stood laughing with Henry and Lily as they happily piled food onto their plates.

"Why are you over here by yourself?"

She blinked in surprise to hear Jamie's daed's voice. Aaron came to a stand alongside her, watching his family with a small smile as well. When was the last time she had talked to Aaron? At their wedding, and briefly in passing. They had been so consumed with their own lives and with the events that had happened last spring. Guilt filled her thinking of how much Jamie had isolated his family to build theirs.

"I was just getting fresh air. It's a bit warm in here," Aubrey said, and then turned to offer a friendly smile. "How are you feeling?"

Aaron shrugged his broad shoulders. He tugged on the edge of his greying beard and looked down his nose at her. There was a faint misty quality to his eyes when he spoke. "Time is passing. My sons are and will be married soon. Now my oldest daughter. I only have one child left before the haus is no longer filled."

Sadness touched his voice. She could only imagine how it would feel one day to see her future kinner start their own lives.

"It seems so far away for you both, but it will happen in the blink of an eye," Aaron said.

"I've heard."

"I actually wished to speak with you privately for some time. You know my son is protective over you."

Unease filled Aubrey at the statement. She knew that Aaron had heard the rumors going about, and even voiced his skepticism over Emma's recent appearances. While she was protective over her own family, she didn't wish to have another repeat of what had happened two years prior.

"We could talk outside if you like. I could actually use some cold air."

Aaron accepted the offer by nodding his head. He helped Aubrey slip into a wool jacket before opening the door to greet the snowy and cold morning. Aaron closed the door on the conversations and laughter inside, silence falling upon them.

To hide her nerves, Aubrey swept some snow off the porch railing with the sleeve of her jacket. A chilly sting clung to the air as their breath puffed out in front of them. She marveled at how pure the land appeared to be while covered in a white soft blanket of snow.

"I'm sure you already know what I want to talk to you about," Aaron said, a wry smile tugging at his lips. "I'm afraid I'm old and predictable these days."

A small smile pulled her lips upward. "You aren't old or predictable. I understand you're probably concerned over some things that you have heard."

"Has Minister Isaac or Bishop Abraham talked with you or Jamie?"

"Nee." She shook her head, puzzled with the question, "Regarding what specifically?"

"You know that Minister Isaac is reaching an age where he believes that he cannot fully take care of the community or attend to the Bishop's needs. There will be a new minister selected after the weddings."

"Ach, I haven't heard this before."

"You understandably have been occupied with your bobli arriving soon. We aren't supposed to talk about this as you know, but there has been mention that Jamie's name could be suggested."

Aubrey eyes widened at the news for her mann. She clapped her hands over her mouth to keep herself from screaming in excitement. What an honor! Her heart swelled with pride thinking that Jamie could possibly minister to their humble community if they selected him.

"That is wunderbar!"

"It is a heavy responsibility," Aaron said, "but this is where I want to talk to you. These rumors, whether they are true or false about your family, have to stop. They could sway opinions on whether Jamie could minister."

Her excitement darkened when imagining how upset Jamie would be knowing he'd lost the community's trust to minister to them because of rumors. "I assure you, I am trying to figure out what is going on with my family, and who is behind all the rumors. I don't want to see Jamie lose this responsibility because of my family's past."

"That is gut to hear. I know that Jamie mentioned he wanted to keep you sheltered from these with the bobli so close to being here, but you know your family better than anyone. Are these rumors true?"

"There's more than one?"

The door opened before Aaron could reply. Jamie stepped out into the cold afternoon and frowned at the two of them standing alone on the front porch. His eyes immediately shot to Aaron in a warning stare.

"What is going on out here?" he asked.

"Nothing is going on," Aubrey said, reaching out to soothe him before an argument could ensue. "Your daed and I are talking about the bobli is all. It's been a hard day for him watching all of you grow."

Jamie looked over at his daed skeptically, but he didn't pursue it any further. Instead, he held out a hand for Aubrey to take. "Come inside, Aubrey. It's cold, and the food is delicious."

"Sounds gut. I am starving."

She took his hand, and spared a glance over her shoulder in Aaron's direction before allowing Jamie to lead her back into the warm haus. Cheerful conversations washed over them while Aubrey slipped out of her wool jacket.

"What did my daed want?"

"We were talking about something exciting, I promise," Aubrey said, grinning at him.

"Ach, what was so exciting that he had to talk to you alone?"

Aubrey frowned at him as she spoke beseechingly. "Don't be so suspicious of your daed. I wish you two would just sit and talk things over instead of carrying on with this argument."

While she was uncertain if their relationship had ever been free from tension, something told Aubrey that Jamie had always maintained a tumultuous relationship with his daed. Both of them were equally stubborn and headstrong when it came to their opinions.

"He isn't interested in hearing what I have to say. He's stubborn as an old mule."

"You'd be surprised to know then how proud of you he is," she said, letting the words sink in for a few seconds before continuing. "He told me that the congregation has mentioned your name for possibly replacing Minister Isaac."

Jamie stilled as he stared at Aubrey slack-jawed. For a few long moments, he was speechless as several emotions played across his eyes. "They mentioned my name?" he repeated, surprised.

"Jah," Aubrey said.

He swept her up into a tight embrace before they shared a smile. The joy of the morning and afternoon kept both of them grinning well into the evening hours. Finally exhausted from the celebrations, Aubrey waited patiently near the front door as Jamie wished his family goodbye. Sore from standing on her feet all day, she arched her back in hopeful effort that the ache in her lower back would lessen.

"Heading home?" her daed's voice asked from behind. Daniel smiled warmly as he helped Katie into her own coat.

"In a few minutes. Where is Sadie?" Aubrey asked.

"She's in the outhouse, I believe. Poor girl has been sick every single day," Katie said, and pressed a kiss to the center of Aubrey's cheek. "I will see you tomorrow morning at the bakery, jah?"

"Jah."

She waited until her parents finally stepped out into the cold evening before seizing the opportunity to speak with Sadie alone. Slipping back into her coat, Aubrey told

Jamie that she would be right back before disappearing into the evening as well. Clouds still lingered in the sky, blanketing the entire land in pitch darkness. She kept her eyes focused on the stone pathway that led to the outhouse.

Aubrey held her breath as she listened to what sounded like quiet sobs coming from within the outhouse. Lantern light flicked through the cracks in the walls, and a figured shifted around within the tight confines. She wracked her knuckles on the wooden door, and took a step back in patience.

"Eli?" Sadie's voice called out timidly. "Is that you?"

"It's me. Are you okay, Sadie? Maemm said you weren't feeling gut."

Silence followed.

She waited patiently for the lock on the outhouse door to click out of its place before opening the door gently to peer inside. Sadie straightened up from the crouch she had been in, and turned to hide her tear-soaked face. She folded her arms tightly over her middle.

"Aren't you going to ask?" she mumbled miserably.

"Ask what?"

"You know, what everyone is talking about."

"What is everyone talking about?"

Sadie looked at her with an arched eyebrow, shaking her head in exasperation. The lantern light reflected brightly on the watery surfaces of her puffy eyes. It occurred to Aubrey that she had been out here crying for a while.

"Don't pretend that you haven't heard anything. I

know you have," she said.

"Then maybe you should talk to someone about it," Aubrey said, offering an encouraging smile. "You could always talk to me about it if it would—"

"Nee, it wouldn't help. I already know what you probably believe."

She bristled at Sadie's derisive tone. A particularly strong gust of cold air had both of them shifting on their feet as they hugged their bodies to keep warm. The back door of the haus opened behind them. It was Eli, who called out, "Sadie? Are you ready to come inside to go to bed?"

"In a minute," Sadie yelled back. She took a deep breath and composed her face as she stepped out into the night. "I know what you want to ask me, and I don't want to talk about it. To be fair, you didn't want to talk about it either when you were going through your problems."

"That's exactly the reason I'm offering for you to talk to me. Don't you think that I would understand?"

Sadie buried the toe of her boot into the snow covered ground. "Maybe, but you have to promise to keep it to yourself. Don't tell Jamie or our parents."

Aubrey nodded her head eagerly. Her concern for Sadie's well being, and to understand what was happening to her family, had her making promises that she knew she wouldn't keep.

"I promise I won't say a word to anyone, including Jamie. What's going on?"

"Okay. I'm—"

"Aubrey? Are you out here?"

Jamie's voice cut through the night, dousing them in another blanket of coldness. His silhouetted frame stood at the edge of the porch as he gazed out at them near the outhouse.

She bit back a sight of annoyance at being interrupted again. "Jah. I'll be there in a minute," she said, and turned to look at a pale Sadie. "Let's talk about this later? Okay?"

Sadie sucked in a breath, and then slowly nodded in agreement. "Okay. I'll talk to you tomorrow at the bakery."

CRSO

The warehouse was empty and cold when Jamie stepped into it Monday morning. He set his lunch pail on his work bench, frowning at Henry and Michael's unoccupied benches. They normally arrived around the time he arrived.

Voices from the front of the store caught his attention. Shrugging out of his coat, Jamie walked down the long hallway that led to the front of the store. To his surprise, it was Daniel Forrest's voice that he recognized first as he walked to the front counter. "...Your expertise will help Levi run the store since I haven't been able to help around here much."

Atlee Byler stood alongside Levi with his beefy thumbs hooked through the straps of his suspenders. All three men turned to look at him with a friendly smile.

"Gut morning," Daniel said. "I believe you have met Atlee Byler?"

Jamie nodded. "Jah, I helped build their barn this past

weekend. Gut morning to all of you. What is going on?"

"Mr. Byler here will be helping Levi run the store, and even help you and Henry out in the warehouse if the inventory falls behind," Daniel explained, smiling at the older Amish man. "He owned a furniture store in Lancaster."

The name struck him suddenly. Byler Furniture! He remembered the name from visiting another district of the church when they had lived in Lancaster.

"Jamie here," Daniel said, clapping him sturdily on the shoulder, "is from Lancaster as well. Moved here almost three years ago."

Atlee's eyes sparkled warmly at him. "Ah, we have much in common then. It is wunderbar here with all this room," he said, nodding in the direction of the valley. While Lancaster was Gott's beautiful creation in its own right, it was congested, and sometimes noisy with a stream of traffic that trickled through the community.

"It is wunderbar here," Jamie agreed, and then turned to look at Daniel curiously. "Where is Michael?"

All three men tensed visibly at the name. Daniel's face darkened as he glanced away to mask the tumult of emotions going through him. He flicked his eyes between the three of them, and gauging from Daniel and Levi's expressions, something bitter had happened.

Before he had the chance to ask, Henry strolled into the front part of the store as well. He greeted them all cheerfully, but it dampened largely at the tension now filling the store.

"Gut morning everyone. Mr. Byler, I'm surprised to

see you here," he said, in an attempt to break the awkward silence.

"Mr. Byler will be working here with you gentlemen," Daniel said.

"Ach, that will be gut."

When another awkward silence descended upon them, Jamie caught Henry's attention, and jerked his head pointedly in the direction of the door.

"We'd better get to work," he said.

Henry raised an eyebrow, but didn't argue. The minute they entered the warehouse, Jamie closed the door behind them, and turned to look at a bewildered Henry. "Have you heard from or seen Michael Brenneman recently?"

"Nee…" Henry said slowly. "Why do you ask?"

"I think he might have left the community again. Why else would Atlee Byler be here?"

"Because Levi needs the extra help running the store?"

"It's more than that. When I asked them what happened to Michael, they didn't look me in the eye."

"Jamie —"

"He went back to Emma. I know that there is something going on with her."

"— you're being ridiculous. Are you sure that this isn't a personal grudge against Emma?"

"I'm sure," Jamie said flatly, smoothing an irritated hand across his hair. "If I'm to minister later possibly, then I have to know what is going on within our community, and find what the source is to all this distrust and idle talk."

"You're going to minister?"

He stopped pacing at his bruder's surprised tone. In all the excitement of Lily's wedding and trying to understand Michael's disappearance, he had forgotten to share the news Aubrey had been told.

"Daed told Aubrey that there was a suggestion."

"Well, that's wunderbar. A heavy responsibility, but it is truly an honor," Henry exclaimed.

Jamie smiled widely. The initial excitement from yesterday came bubbling back within him. "Danka. We aren't supposed to be talking about it."

"I know. I bet after our wedding the new minister will be selected. I have noticed that Minister Isaac hasn't been in active in the community as much."

"His health has been a concern for a while," Jamie said. The previous winter had been exceptionally hard on the usually charismatic minister, whose health had slowly been declining over a span of three years.

"I pray for him, but I am proud to hear that my young bruder will possibly minister in the future," Henry said.

Their conversation was cut short when Levi stepped into the warehouse. His face, though pinched from exhaustion, seemed genuinely relieved to have extra help with the daily operations.

"Here is a list of what needs to be replaced on the floor soon," he said, and handed them both a piece of paper. "I think it will start to slow down here now that the winter weather is starting to act up."

"It'll give us time to get caught up," Henry said, glancing down at the paper. "Now that there won't be so many Englischers traveling through."

He went to his work bench, shrugging out of his coat to hang it on a peg next to it. Jamie latched on to the opportunity to question Levi about Michael's whereabouts. "What happened to Michael?"

Levi sighed, "Jamie, for Aubrey's sake, please—"

"You have to admit that something is going on, something strange," he insisted.

"I know there is, but it doesn't involve you or Aubrey. Do yourselves both a favor, and stay clear of this," Levi warned.

"Listen," Jamie said lowly. "I'm only trying to understand what's going on. If it's bad, I don't want someone to tell Aubrey. I'm just trying to protect her from—"

"Our sisters?"

Jamie looked away at the knowing look in Levi's eyes. "I have nothing against your sisters, but I know how much Aubrey cares for them both. With the bobli wanting to arrive early, I've been trying to keep Aubrey rested for her and the bobli's health. We've heard some upsetting things, and the other weekend someone wrote us a strange letter."

"What sort of letter?" Levi asked, frowning. He tucked the clipboard into his side. "I'm assuming it has something to do with my sisters."

"And your daed too, something about a secret."

A cold blast of wind stirred the wood shavings on the ground. Levi's jaw clenched tightly, and with a dejected sigh, he ran a hand over his face tiredly. He straightened his hat when it went askew on his fair head.

"Michael left the community this weekend," he said, grimacing. "That's why our daed asked Atlee to work here. It was too hard to run this store with only three of us doing everything."

Some part of Jamie wasn't surprised by the revelation. He had been anticipating the news since last spring, and quite frankly been more surprised that Michael hadn't left earlier. Relations with his family had been strained when he'd publicly stalled in taking his vows again after admitting to having communication with Emma. He felt a stab of sympathy for the Brenneman family, who were undoubtedly upset with Michael's decision to leave yet again.

"To be with Emma?"

"I'm assuming so. She has been around for the last few months. I don't know why other than waiting for Michael to leave," Levi said.

"You've seen her?"

The smell of gas filled the air as Henry fueled up a saw to start on a table. He kept his back turned toward him, but Jamie knew he was listening intently. Levi also looked in Henry's direction, chin jutting out slightly as anger sparked in his eyes.

"I've asked her what she is doing back here. Typical," Levi rolled his eyes sardonically. "She said it didn't concern me, and that it concerned only Sadie and Daed."

"You don't think she would start rumors for revenge?"

"Nee. I don't think so, at least, not after having rumors about her. Emma isn't the one responsible behind the talk."

Jamie tried to mask the sinking feeling in the pit of his stomach. He pinched the bridge of his nose, a headache beginning to cloud his mind. The hope of discovering who was behind the idle rumors, and what secrets they knew, faded away quickly. They were back at square one again of who was behind the letter.

"That wasn't the news you wanted to hear obviously," Levi said.

"Don't you want to know who is behind these rumors?" he asked, and then added as an afterthought, "Is there anyone who has felt wronged by your family? Maybe they are the source of these rumors."

"Hm," Levi said, tugging on the edge of his beard in contemplation. "Two family names come to mind: it's no secret that my daed and Larry Brenneman don't get along, but Thomas Fields was quite understandably upset when he found out what Emma had done when they were published by the church. I wouldn't get too excited over Thomas, though. His name has been mentioned to replace Minister Isaac along with your own. I don't think anybody from within our community is behind any of this or—"

Levi stopped talking abruptly, with his eyes focused on something over Jamie's shoulder. He turned around to see Naomi Byler standing timidly in the doorframe of the warehouse with a lunch pail in hand. Resisting the urge to sigh in annoyance, he forced a pleasant smile on his face.

"Gut morning, Naomi."

She smiled warmly at him in return, ducking her head shyly to gaze upward through her eyelashes. Naomi wouldn't have any trouble finding a suitable mann, he thought absently, taking in her soft features and wheat colored hair beneath her kapp.

"Gut morning. Is my daed here? I brought him his lunch," she said, and lifted the lunch pail to prove her reasoning for being there. "He forgot it at the haus this morning. Ma sent me to give to him."

"Inside, down the hallway," Levi said, pointing at the door. "He's inside the office on the last door on the right."

"Danka. I'll be back in a moment."

They waited until Naomi had disappeared down the hallway in search of Atlee before resuming their conversation. Jamie caught Henry's curious gaze, and shook his head in a silent "don't ask."

"As I was saying," Levi said, grabbing his clipboard once more, "don't go looking for the source of this. Let Gott work it out for our community."

He clasped Jamie on the shoulder briefly before heading in the same direction as Naomi. Fidgeting with the sleeve of his shirt, Jamie chewed the inside of his cheek in thought while grabbing a can of stain from the metal cabinet. Within his heart, he knew that he should pray for Gott to guide them through these troubling times and thoughts.

Except he couldn't let it go.

Jamie opened the can and stared down at the stain's murky brown surface. Unable to resist what his heart urged him to do, Jamie set the brush down on the rim of the can. He walked to the door and peered down the hallway to where Levi sat hunched on a wooden stool. From afar, it wasn't hard to see the tension in the arch of Levi's back as he scribbled notes.

Determination filled Jamie as he watched Levi rub his face with an exhausted sigh. It occurred to him that the oldest of the Forrest kinner knew more than what he said, and he planned to find out what Levi knew exactly.

❧ CHAPTER 6 ❧

The smell of cocoa powder greeted Aubrey the next morning. Her sneakers squeaked on the floor as she walked through the bakery to the kitchen, where a flurry of sound and movement was present. With one hand massaging the small of her back, she pushed the door open to find Naomi Byler standing in front of the oven with her maemm.

"Gut morning," Katie called cheerfully. She rested a hand on Naomi's slender shoulder, smiling as she said, "Naomi has generously taken over your sister's position for the time being. Her maemm owned a bakery in Lancaster."

Naomi smiled warmly in Aubrey's direction. She forced herself to smile back despite the flare of protectiveness going through her, and tried to ignore the queasy disappointment in her stomach. Her sister's disappearance from the bakery was unsettling, and her maemm's acceptance was equally unsettling.

"That's gut to hear. Is Sadie ill?" Aubrey asked.

"Jah, she isn't feeling well is all," came the neutral answer.

Aubrey sighed in defeat. Whatever was going on, her maemm was clearly not going to divulge in front of Naomi. She mentally noted to have Jamie stop by her parent's haus to check on Sadie.

While her maemm opened the store for the day, Aubrey worked alongside Naomi. She half listened to the younger girl talk about Lancaster, and how she'd just started attending night singings. Her thoughts were elsewhere; mainly on her sisters' strange behavior.

"So, do you know who Jamie is?"

"Who?"

Aubrey looked up from the bread she was kneading when she realized that Naomi was asking about Jamie. The same dreamy look filled Naomi's gentle eyes. A fierce wave of protective jealousy crashed down upon her as she felt her fingers flex into fists.

Naomi continued latticing an apple pie. "I was wondering if you knew him. My Ma mentioned that you knew him when you arrived with the other girls with sandwiches. I was just, well, you know—interested now that I'm old enough to court."

A pretty blush filled the center of Naomi's cheeks. It complimented the golden strands of hair tucked underneath her kapp and smooth skin perfectly. She wouldn't be without a courter for long, judging from her delicate appearance to her slender figure beneath her pale purple dress.

"He's my mann."

"Ach," Naomi's eyes widened with realization. She cupped a hand over her mouth, and shook her head apologetically. "I'm so sorry! I didn't realize that he was your mann."

They fell into an awkward silence. Naomi looked down at the half-latticed apple pie, chewing her bottom lip. Sensing contriteness in her tone, Aubrey calmed herself. "It's all right. We were married last year. You obviously didn't know with being new to our community."

"But still, I am sorry. How horrible you must think of me to speak of interest in your mann."

Tears filled Naomi's eyes. Aubrey wiped her hands free from dough and flour on the front of her apron before placing a hand on the younger girl's shoulder.

"I don't think you are horrible. I'm sure that you will find a mann here in our community soon enough."

"Danka. That is very kind of you to say," Naomi said, and then added, "My Da heard that your mann might possibly minister eventually."

Pride filled Aubrey at the thought of Jamie taking care of their community's spiritual needs. He was already unwavering in his faith and offered a helping hand without being asked. He would be a gut spiritual leader to their troubled community.

She frowned when her conversation with Jamie's daed echoed in her mind again. She prayed that whoever was behind these rumors about her family wouldn't ruin Jamie's chances of becoming a minister. Determination filled her. Somehow, she would discover who was the root of all the troubling talk. Even if it were her own sisters.

"Aubrey?"

"Sorry. What were you saying?"

Naomi frowned. "I was saying that it seems Jamie would be a gut mann," she said, resuming her perfectly sliced strips of pie crust. "He seems very caring and compassionate about the community. He helped Da build the barn more than the other mensleit did."

"Jah, that is how he always is," Aubrey said, smiling. "I hope that our bobli will be like him."

"It is up to Gott."

"Everything is."

The front door of the bakery jingled open, followed by the sound of Jamie's voice greeting her maemm. Aubrey glanced up at the clock above the door with a frown, wondering what Jamie was doing at the bakery so early in the morning.

Jamie entered the door, pausing briefly in surprise to see Naomi working alongside Aubrey. He remained friendly though when he greeted them both with a strained smile before asking Aubrey to step outside with him for a moment.

"What is it?" Aubrey asked, tossing Jamie a baffled look as he helped her down the small steps to stand outside. He closed the bakery door behind them with a soft click before turning to look at her anxiously. "What is it, Jamie? You're starting to worry me."

"Why is Naomi Byler working here? Where is Sadie?"

Aubrey blinked in confusion and alarm at the demanding questions. "My maemm says she is feeling too ill to work," she answered slowly. "With Thanksgiving in a couple of weeks, we needed the extra hand in helping bake. Why? What is going on?"

"I heard something today while I was in the hardware store in town," Jamie said, blowing out a heavy breath. "They didn't know I was listening, or—"

"Hold on," Aubrey cut in, holding up a hand. "You're rambling a bit. Who are 'they?'"

Jamie waved a hand airily. "Members of our community," he said vaguely. "They were talking about the rumors surrounding your daed from years ago."

"What were they talking about?" she asked. Her heart pounded anxiously in the confines of her chest. "I know that there have been things said before, but neither daed or maemm ever talked to us about them."

"For gut reason. I think I know who is behind all the rumors too."

"Who?"

He hesitated for a moment before saying, "I hate to say it, Aubrey, but I think Emma and Michael have been the ones talking."

Disbelief shot through Aubrey, followed by denial. She shook her head at him, not willing to believe that her own sister was behind the disquiet in their community. Emma had never meant to cause turmoil or hurt intentionally, no matter how it appeared. She knew her oldest sister better than that.

"Nee. That's not possible. Emma would never say such things about our daed. She respects and loves him too much."

"I never said it would be intentional," Jamie said.

"Then what are you saying?"

Jamie smoothed a hand through his hair, disheveling the golden strands. Their breath puffed out in front of them in white clouds as they shifted constantly on their feet to keep warm.

"I'm not sure what I'm saying exactly. They were talking about what a shame it was that Sadie was following your daed's lead when it came to rumspringa."

"Rumspringa?" Dread filled Aubrey suddenly when she realized that Jamie held the same suspicions she did. "You think Sadie may have..."

"Jah," Jamie said, nodding grimly. "I don't want to believe it, but something tells me that is why her marriage was so rushed."

"But I don't understand why anyone would imply Sadie was following in my daed's footsteps. He never has done anything against Gott or the Ordnung."

"I don't know why that was said either. All I know is that I believe Emma is here to help Sadie with something. Or was here. Michael Brenneman has left the church."

Aubrey bit down on her bottom lip to keep her emotions in check. She didn't want to believe her youngest sister had made a poor decision on her rumspringa, or that her own daed had made the same decision before. The thought seemed ludicrous to her.

"Have you spoken with Sadie yet?" Jamie asked.

She gave a shake of her head. "Nee, not yet. I have been meaning to, but she has been effectively avoiding me."

"I pray that all this idle talk will fade away," Jamie said, sighing deeply. "Now, that your sister has left, maybe it will."

Or it won't. Not to her at least. She still wanted to know why Emma had lingered in their community, or why there was talk about Sadie behaving like their daed in the past. Her heart ached thinking of the secrets that were ripping her family apart at the seams. They were all unraveling by the day it seemed, and she wanted to sew it back together. She wanted to fix it all back to when things had been so simple.

The door opened behind them. Naomi popped her fair head out, blushing when they both turned to look at her with frowns. The smell of baked pie crusts filled the cold morning air. "I apologize, but Mrs. Forrest is asking for your help, Aubrey. There is a line building, and we need someone to watch the ovens."

Naomi's eyes flickered between the two of them curiously. Aubrey cleared her face of the emotions and thoughts that were lingering there. She didn't wish to have Naomi pry at her curiously about their conversation.

"I'll be there in a minute," she said.

When Naomi retreated inside the warm bakery, Jamie pressed a kiss to the crown of her head. "We will figure this out in time. Gott will help us through this time."

Aubrey smiled up at him. "You will be a great minister if you are chosen."

"If I am selected," he replied, smiling as well. "If it is Gott's will for me to minister, then I will do it without question, though I feel like I'm not ready."

They exchanged goodbyes before going their separate

ways. Aubrey gladly stepped back into the warmth of the kitchen to supervise the pies and to clean up the dirty dishes from earlier that morning. She didn't get a chance to think of what Jamie had told her until well into the late afternoon, when the bakery was finally quiet from the stream of customers who had come in looking for pies for their Thanksgiving meals.

"Whew," Katie said, wiping a hand along her brow. She stood behind the counter with a cleaning rag in one hand. "That was quite the morning and afternoon. I have never seen the bakery so busy!"

"It is never this busy?" Naomi inquired. She too held a cleaning rag, wiping fingerprints from the display case.

Aubrey looked up from the task of sweeping the dirt and clumps of snow from the linoleum floor. She sighed, knowing that she would have to mop the floors after the bakery closed. "There's always an increase of customers around this time, but never to this extent."

Katie frowned in Aubrey's direction. "It is a bit strange, but I won't complain. Not when we are supplying others with food that everyone seems to enjoy."

"If you don't mind, may I take a break outside?" Naomi asked. "I think I am in need of some fresh air. If Aubrey doesn't need a break first..."

Aubrey jumped at the chance to talk to her maemm alone. She shook her head and said, "I'm fine. Go on ahead."

She waited until Naomi disappeared through the front door before turning to look at her maemm with determination. "I have to ask you something."

Katie paused in wiping the countertop. She arched her eyebrows at the glint in Aubrey's eyes. "Ach? What is it?"

"Did something happen to daed on his rumspringa?"

Silence.

Katie's face hardened into a stoic expression that kept her emotions well protected. She looked back down at the counter, wiping more forcefully at a smudge. "Why do you ask?" she asked tightly.

Aubrey carefully avoided the wet spots, where small bits of snow had melted, as she walked to the front counter. She propped the broom against the counter. "Because it's obvious something is going on. Jamie overheard members talking about Sadie following in—"

"Don't," Katie interjected sharply. "Don't fall into that trap of talk. It's not the first time I have heard such things."

"If it weren't true, then why are others asking?"

"I don't know, Aubrey. All I can tell you is to focus on yourself, Gott, and your bobli. Don't try to pursue this. Let it be."

Tears surfaced in Katie's eyes, but before they could fall, the door opened. An Englischer ventured into the bakery, pausing uncertainly at the tension resonating in the air still. All traces of their exchange were gone when Aubrey immediately looked back at her maemm, who smiled kindly and rushed to greet the Englischer.

Another sharp crack made its presence known on Aubrey's heart. She was growing weary of the secrets in her family, but one thing was clear as day a late November sky.

Her maemm knew something, and refused to speak of it.

CRSO

"Congratulations again, my bruder."

Jamie shook Henry's hand with a grin. His heart was filled with joy this morning to be able to witness a long awaited marriage between Elizabeth and Henry. He couldn't be happier for his oldest bruder.

"Danka, bruder," Henry said.

Before anything else could be said, Henry was swept up in other conversation with other members of their extended family. It was quite the celebration within their own family to have two kinner from the Miller family to be married within the same year.

He easily spotted Aubrey carrying a pot of celery soup to the tables where they had arranged to eat. The haus was crowded again with bodies and warm conversation that left the center of Jamie's chest feeling hot. He watched in fondness as his fraa laughed freely, the strands of her fair hair framing her pale face.

The door behind him opened with a blast of cold air. He glanced over his shoulder to find a pale, stricken Sadie bundled up in a heavy coat. She smiled absently at him, pulling wool gloves free from her fingers. "It is getting quite chilly outside now. Winter is undoubtedly coming."

"Jah, very cold," he replied, and then after a few minutes added, "How are you feeling?"

Sadie shrugged her shoulders indifferently. "I've felt

better before, but I know that Gott will give me strength to feel better," she said.

"Aubrey told me that you are no longer working in the bakery. She misses having you there," Jamie said. He hoped to keep Sadie talking and gather insight of what was going on inside the Forrest family.

"Naomi is there to keep her company," Sadie said plainly.

Jamie bit back a sigh of impatience. He prayed for calmness then, and guidance as well. "Is everything all right, Sadie?" he inquired as gently as possible. "You do look quite pale."

Sadie's face tightened into a defensive scowl. "It's called being sick. Nothing is wrong beside that. I wish everyone would stop asking me that question, including my sister."

She stomped away from his side without sparing a glance. Jamie watched in bewilderment as she weaved through the crowd of friends and family to where her mann stood. They bowed their heads as they exchanged what appeared to be tense words before slipping into the kitchen.

Curiosity seized him. Before he could follow, Naomi Byler broke through the crowd of Amish people gathered in the living room. She smiled easily at him, stepping to join him at the edge of the friendly conversations. Jamie shifted on the balls of his feet uneasily. At the last moment, his maemm had made the decision to invite the Byler family to Henry and Elizabeth's wedding to give them more opportunity to get to know their community. He'd accepted the news with unease, not knowing whether Aubrey knew of Naomi's possible interest in him.

"Beautiful wedding," Naomi said, smiling. "Your bruder seems very happy."

"Jah, he is."

"And there are no more weddings after this?"

"This is the last wedding for the community for the year," he said.

"And all the weddings were your family or friends. That must make your family very happy."

"Very."

Naomi fell into silence. The back door squeaked open, followed by a trail of cold air, drawing Jamie's attention down the hallway. Sadie slipped through the door before closing it softly behind her. Unable to resist his curiosity any longer, Jamie quickly excused himself from Naomi's side to slip through the kitchen door as well.

He scanned the snowy fields, following the trail of footprints until he spotted Sadie's bundled frame heading in the direction of the woods. Shoving his hands deep into his trouser pockets, he huddled against the cold morning air as he trudged through the ankle high snow after Sadie. When he reached the forest line, the tip of his nose was red and running from the cold. He ignored the cold seeping into his bones and focused on what sounded like voices echoing beneath the evergreen trees.

Careful not to step on any twigs, Jamie spotted the hemline of Sadie's blue dress through the tangled grey foliage. He leaned against the trunk of a tree wide enough to hide his frame.

Sadie's watery voice echoed under the shade of the evergreen pines. "—I just don't know if I can keep lying to everyone. The whole community is starting to talk about what happened."

The answering voice nearly had Jamie collapsing in surprise against the trunk of the tree. He sucked in a breath to keep himself calm before cautiously peeking around the trunk to see Emma Forrest place a consoling hand on Sadie's trembling shoulder.

"It's going to be fine, Sadie. You just have to keep it cool. Remember what we talked about?"

"Jah," Sadie mumbled, bowing her head. "I just think that I should tell everyone the truth. It isn't right to keep lying about this."

A frown marred Emma's slender face. Gone were the black streaks in the long strands of her hair, and the locks were back to their normal golden color. A warm glow filled the center of her cheeks while her slender figure seemed fuller, healthier than the last time he had seen her.

"Sadie, if you tell anybody about what happened on rumspringa you know what will happen."

"But I hadn't taken the vow yet. I wouldn't be in trouble like you are."

Emma sighed. "You're right, but think about what this is going to do maemm and daed. Think about what Eli would say if you admitted to it."

Sadie burst into tears. She was quickly gathered into Emma's arms, her oldest sister murmuring comfort. "It's going to be okay, Sadie. I promise. You hadn't taken the vow yet, like you said. You have nothing to worry about."

"But I do!" Sadie said, voice muffled by Emma's shoulder. "Everyone is talking about it! I can't keep avoiding Aubrey either. She has been asking questions."

"She's our sister. She cares about your well being," Emma said.

"I know, and I want to tell her, but I can't. She's so close to having her bobli—"

"And you—" Emma said, placing a finger gently beneath her chin, "are also with a bobli. I think Aubrey would agree if she knew that your wellbeing matters too."

Jamie's eyes drifted closed at Emma's words. Long had he suspected that something like this was the center of Sadie's odd behavior, but he had prayed hard it wasn't, with the Forrest family already struggling to maintain their grace and dignity. While Sadie wouldn't face as strict a punishment for consummating a relationship before her vows, the memory would continue to haunt her.

Talking to Emma, a shunned member, would mean consequences from the church. Something that Jamie had to take responsibility for, and shepherd Sadie back to Gott if she wished.

Before he could act, however, Sadie suddenly asked, "Do you know if the rumors are true?"

"What rumors?"

"I've heard others say that I followed in daed's footsteps while on his rumspringa."

Jamie held his breath in anticipation of Emma's answer. A battle waged itself in Emma's eyes as she chewed her bottom lip, staring distantly out into the snowy forest.

"I don't know if it's true either," she answered slowly.

"But you've heard about it before?"

"Yes," Emma said, sighing heavily. "When Michael and I wished to be published by the church, his daed didn't wish for us to be married because he believed I was like daed. That I had physically gone against the Ordnung. I don't know why Michael's daed doesn't like our daed, but I suspect it has something to do with what happened on their rumspringa."

"Did you, well, you know, not wait?" Sadie asked, blushing.

"Yes, I did, and I regret it every day of my life, but my situation is different. Michael and I are together now."

"And expecting too," Sadie said. She reached out a hand to touch Emma's stomach lightly. "I wish you were here still. Aubrey would be so happy to know that you are blessed with a bobli."

Emma smiled sadly. "Jah, I wish that too, but don't mention anything to Aubrey. She has enough going on right now, and I don't want either one of you to get into trouble for talking to me."

Sadie's reply was cut short when Eli's voice called her from a distance. He watched the two sisters wordlessly embrace before Sadie hurried past the tree that he was hiding behind. When he peeked around the tree, the clearing was empty. Jamie leaned up against the trunk of the tree. His head ached from the turmoil brewing inside of him.

What would he tell Aubrey?

He had to inform the Bishop of what he'd witnessed.

He didn't want to see Sadie stir down the path that Aubrey had gone down while trying to maintain a secret correspondence with Emma.

Anxiety filled Jamie's bones, making his steps feel sluggish and weighted across the snowy field. He waited until he was certain that Sadie had gone inside before seeking out Aubrey first. A blast of warm air and friendly conversation blasted Jamie the second he stepped inside. He was also greeted with Bishop Abraham's smiling face in the kitchen.

"A bit chilly to take a walk without a coat, eh?" he said kindly, cradling a mug of kaffe.

The strong smell pulled at Jamie as he poured himself a mug as well to ease the headache and exhaustion. He picked at the rim of his mug nervously before speaking. "There is something I have to tell you about—"

"Bishop Abraham," Aaron called from the living room. "You must try my fraa's soup before the guests have eaten it all up."

Laughter followed. Abraham's eyes bore into his eyes, sensing the urgency behind them. He squeezed Jamie's tense shoulder with an age spotted hand. "Excuse me for one moment, please. Then we can talk about what is bothering you," he said.

Jamie gulped down mouthfuls of the hot liquid. The bitter taste of kaffe comforted him while also filling him with much needed energy. The door swung open to reveal a flushed Aubrey.

"There you are," she said, smiling at him. "I was wondering where you went off to..." She trailed off at the look in Jamie's eyes. Without hesitating, she came to his side, and rested a hand on his chest. "What is it?"

He had to tell Aubrey. If he told Bishop Abraham first, she would hear about it no matter what. He collected Aubrey's tiny hands in his own. "I saw your sisters together."

Aubrey peered up at him in surprise. "You saw my sisters?" she whispered, tears wetting her long eyelashes. "Where? Where were they?"

"Outside in the forest. Aubrey," he shook his head, still in disbelief himself. "Sadie's pregnant. I heard her say it, and I don't think Eli is the daed."

"What?"

"I know. I—"

"Are you sure? Are you sure that you heard right?"

He nodded affirmatively. He was bracing himself for Aubrey's questions; he knew her well enough to know there would be tons. "Jah, I heard it with my own ears."

"But it happened on rumspringa?"

"According to her, jah."

"Well," Aubrey said, letting out a choppy breath. "She won't be in as much trouble, if any, since it was on her rumspringa. It's not gut what she did, but it makes sense now why her marriage seemed so rushed."

He didn't return her wry smile. "But she will be in trouble for talking to a shunned member, on my daed's land of all places."

Aubrey stiffened visibly at that. She looked at him carefully for a few moments before the realization of what he was implying hit her. "Don't," she started, staring up at him pleadingly. "Please, don't say anything. Sadie wouldn't be able to handle it."

"I have to tell someone, Aubrey," Jamie said, shaking his head. "This can't keep happening."

"Please, Jamie—"

The door again opened to reveal a smiling Abraham with a bowl of steaming celery soup in hand. "I apologize, Jamie," he said, setting the bowl on the counter. He smiled at Aubrey, but she didn't return the smile. "What is that you needed to tell me?"

Aubrey ducked her head as she brushed by Abraham, mumbling under her breath that she needed fresh air. She casted a tearful glance in Jamie's direction before disappearing from the kitchen. He closed his eyes in exasperation, torn by Aubrey's pleading and what was right.

"Jamie?"

He sucked in a long breath before saying, "I'm afraid that if I say anything now, this joyous occasion would be disrupted."

"Ach, I see," Abraham said, furrowing his grey eyebrows. "Shall we talk later then, perhaps?"

"Jah, later."

The words felt thick and coarse on the tip of his tongue, but in his heart, Jamie knew that he would have to say something. It was only a matter of time before the time would be right to say something.

ೞ CHAPTER 7 ೞ

A sudden and sharp pain in her lower back jolted Aubrey awake from a dream. Disoriented, she stared up at the darkened ceiling of their bedroom. The pain left her breathless, but it was so short lived that it felt as if it had been part of the dream.

She rubbed a hand over her stomach with a frown. The bobli didn't move under her gentle touch, but the muscles felt tenser than usual. When the pain didn't appear again over the next few minutes, Aubrey settled back down on her left side with heavy eyes. She was on the brink of sleep when it happened again. Pain, sharper than a knife slicing right through her back, coiled in her back before slowly making its way across her stomach.

Aubrey sat up with a gasp. She sucked in air greedily through her nose to help ease the pain, but it did little. The pain lingered for a few more seconds before fading away to a dull ache that left her feeling nauseous.

Mindful of Jamie's sleeping figure on the other side of the bed, Aubrey slid out from beneath the sheets and blankets. Chilly air touched her legs as she hurriedly shoved her feet into boots and wrapped a cotton robe around herself before leaving the room. She'd reached the middle of the stairs when the crippling pain started again, forcing her to sit on the edge of a stair while sucking in deep breaths.

"Nee," she whispered, shaking her head in denial. "Please Gott. This is too soon."

No matter how hard she prayed, the pain only became stronger. By a miracle, Aubrey managed to walk down the remaining stairs before another wave of pain could come. She collapsed on the edge of the couch to welcome the heat of the wood stove before it became too intense. The floorboards groaned beneath her boots as she paced feverishly, rubbing at her lower back as it ached hotly.

Time slowed to a snail's pace. Aubrey stared up at the floorboards between pants, wishing that she could find the strength to get up to stir Jamie from his sleep. When they had arrived home from spending the evening with Jamie's family after celebrating Elizabeth and Henry's blessed wedding, he had barely uttered a word to her. They'd prepared for bed without sparing each other a glance, both lost in their own thoughts over what Jamie had witnessed. She couldn't bring herself to ask whether Jamie had told Bishop Abraham about Sadie's conversing with Emma, but inwardly she was furious with her youngest sister for behaving so irrationally.

When the stairs groaned in the hushed night, she knew that Gott had answered her prayers.

"Aubrey? What's—" Jamie stopped halfway down the

stairs, still rubbing sleepily at his eyes. Alarm filled his face when he took in her flushed and pained face. "What is it? Is it the bobli?"

She sucked in harsh breaths, nodding feverishly when she couldn't find the words to say anything. Jamie came to her side, and taking hold of her hand, pressed a kiss to the crown of her sweaty head.

"We should go to Martha's," he said.

Aubrey shook her head. "Nee, this will stop in a few minutes. It's too early for our bobli to be here."

Fear and calmness shadowed Jamie's face. He squeezed her hand reassuringly before rising to stand. "I know, but if you are in pain... We need to go to Martha's haus."

He sprinted lithely up the stairs before she could reply. Between heavy breaths and pain that threatened to tear her into her pieces, Aubrey stared numbly out the front window at the dark night. She prayed strongly, asking Gott to calm the contractions. However, the stronger they became, the meeker her prayers became.

It became clear that Gott intended for the bobli to arrive soon.

Tears streamed down the corner of Aubrey's eyes. It seemed so petty and foolish to be upset over knowing that tomorrow she would not be able to do the massive pile of laundry that needed to be done. Her mind ran through its usual checklist to serve as a distraction from the increasing agony centering in her lower back and hard belly.

Jamie emerged from the crisp night a few moments later. His rough hands were cold against her hot ones as he helped her stand to her feet.

"We need to get you dressed in something warm," he said, leading her toward the stairs. They'd only reached the bottom steps before another crippling wave of pain had Aubrey crying out as she collapsed to the ground. "I'll grab your clothes. Remember what Martha said? Keep breathing through your nose."

Aubrey rested her head on the back of the stairs. She watched Jamie sprint back up the stairs and disappear from view. A fine layer of sweat covered her skin as the pain faded back to a dull ache. She peeled back the fabric of her nightgown from where it clung to her legs uncomfortably, wiping away the sweat that had gathered on her forehead. Her body felt aflame, every limb sensitive to what was coming. She quivered in fear and anticipation, but still clung to the frail hope that the contractions would eventually stop.

A few minutes later Jamie appeared with two robes. He draped the thick cotton fabric over her shoulders.

"It's too hot for these," Aubrey started, reluctantly pushing her arms through the sleeves. "Feel my head. I'm too hot to wear these."

He didn't heed her words, tying the belt loosely underneath her belly. "It's hot inside, but it's freezing outside. I don't want you catch a cold while we ride to Martha's."

"I still think it will stop in time," she insisted, gritting her teeth as another painful contraction started. She waited until it faded away before speaking again breathlessly. "It's too soon for the bobli to arrive. There's still another month left."

Jamie ushered her toward the back door. Along the way, he slipped into his own jacket and grabbed a blanket from the couch. The first touch of the night's air on her face nearly stole the breath out of her lungs. Her teeth clattered at the contrast of temperature and she clutched Jamie's arm in a vice-like grip. They paused briefly when another contraction hit her alongside the buggy with their horse already hitched and whinnying grumpily from being awoken in the middle of the night.

"I feel like my bones are breaking," Aubrey gritted out.

With a helpful push upward from Jamie, she sat in the buggy. Jamie hopped up to the passenger side and gathered the reins in his gloved hands. She noticed, with a stab of annoyance, how calm he appeared.

"They could be," Jamie said.

She gawked at him in disbelief. The soft moonlight from above gave her the ability to see the corner of his lips curl up into a small smile that had a trace of humor in it. The buggy lurched forward with a firm flick of the reins. They traveled down the road at a steady trot.

"That's not funny. Why are you so calm anyways?" she demanded.

He glanced sideways at her, still smiling. "Why? Would you prefer me to panic?"

"Nee, but stop being so calm. I'm not calm."

"You're in pain, so naturally you wouldn't be calm."

Aubrey glared at him. "I'm not calm because the bobli is coming sooner than expected. Are you—"

"I am worried," Jamie cut in over her, all traces of humor gone. "I'm trying to help keep your mind off it. Being worried won't help."

She stared at him in speechlessness. The words died instantly on her tongue when she realized how foolish she was behaving. Before she could apologize, another contraction erupted in the center of her lower back. Jamie wordlessly reached out to hold her hand through it.

They didn't say a word the rest of the way to Martha's. The moonlight shimmered down upon them, glinting off the snowy fields and road. Aubrey rested her head against the side of the buggy, breathing in the crisp night air while holding the quilt Jamie had brought tightly. It is a beautiful and peaceful night for the bobli to arrive, she thought absently. Not a cloud was in the indigo sky above and the stars twinkled brightly. Her breath puffed out in front of her when she leaned out the window to look at the stars, praying as the night air whipped through her free locks of hair.

Martha's haus was shrouded in darkness when they pulled up to it. Barn dogs barked at their presence and danced around their buggy. Jamie held her hand through another contraction before jumping out of the buggy to knock on the front door. Lamp light flickered to life in the bottom half of the haus before Martha appeared in a hastily tied robe and messy bun. She exchanged words before leaving Jamie on the front doorstep.

Unable to sit any longer, Aubrey managed to climb out of the buggy. She felt something warm gush down her legs before staring down in surprise at the dark puddle beneath her feet.

"Your water broke," Martha's voice cut through the darkness. The old Amish woman was suddenly at her side, still wearing a robe that was tied more securely. "The bobli will be here very shortly. By dawn, perhaps."

"But it's too soon," Aubrey told her, half carried between Jamie and Martha. "You said that if the bobli could wait until the first week of December—"

Martha's lips pulled into a thin smile. "It would've been ideal, but the bobli is coming no matter what now. It is Gott's will for your blessing to be here tonight."

A surreal haze took over Aubrey's mind again as she entered the haus and was ushered upstairs to a room. She had imagined this day for months, to be able to see the bobli finally, but it was too soon. Anxiety filled her entire being. The pain had steadily increased over the past hour since waking. With each contraction that came, Aubrey's doubts continued to increase.

"I don't think I can do this," she whispered to Jamie.

He sat on the bedside, holding her sweaty hand between his dry and cold ones. After Martha did a quick check of her vitals, and how far along her labor had progressed, she agreed it would be a good idea for Jamie to fetch Aubrey's maemm. "The bobli will be here in the morning or thereabout from how everything feels."

"You can do it," Jamie said, smiling encouragingly at her. "When Martha is finished getting everything ready, I'll go get your maemm. Our bobli will be here before we know it."

Before Aubrey could reply, Martha entered the room

dressed in her day clothes and hair smoothed back beneath her kapp. She looked refreshed despite the late hour as she moved around the room.

"I'll be back shortly with your maemm," Jamie said, and then looked to Martha. "Do you think I have time to wake my family as well? I know that my maemm wanted to be here for support."

Martha gave a curt nod. "If you hurry. This bobli won't be waiting any longer," she said.

Jamie pressed a kiss to the back of Aubrey's hand before letting go. The cold air clutched at her warm hand now and it filled her with terror. She opened her mouth to ask Jamie to stay by her side, to get her maemm afterwards, but a contraction silenced her objections. She watched through a haze of tears as Jamie slipped out the bedroom door.

"All will be fine," Martha said, pressing a cool rag to her head. She adjusted the pillows behind Aubrey as well. "With the next couple of contractions, you can start pushing."

Time seemed to stretch as Aubrey waited for the familiar throb of a contraction to start blooming in her lower back. When none came after a few minutes, she turned to a frowning Martha with her own frown.

"The contractions have stopped. Is that normal?"

Martha smoothed her dry hands along Aubrey's stomach before doing another check. When she pulled down Aubrey's nightgown, her face was pale and stretched into worry. She rested a hand on Aubrey's bent knee. "Nee, it's not normal. We have to take you to the hospital."

CRSO

Jamie pounded his fist on the front door of the dark Forrest haus. A lamp light immediately clicked on upstairs, followed by the sound of anxious voices. He bounced on the balls of his feet in impatience. The door jerked open to reveal a sleep tousled Katie and Daniel in their robes.

"What is it?" Daniel asked. "Is it Aubrey?"

He nodded rapidly, still breathless from adrenaline coursing through his veins. "Jah, the bobli is on the way," he said, nodding to Katie. "Aubrey asked for me to come get you. Martha said the bobli will be here within the next hour."

Katie's eyes widened in shock and concern. She hastily began to pull the long strands of her hair up into a bun.

"Are you sure? Is Martha sure? There is still a month left before the bobli is due."

"I'm sure. The bobli is coming tonight," he said firmly.

Despite the joy in Daniel and Katie's faces, concern belied their smiles. They knew just as Jamie knew that going into labor early could lead to problems for the bobli. While Jamie had forced himself to remain light hearted and calm throughout the past few hours, his own heart was beating thickly with concern. He knew that there was a good chance that something could possibly happen to Aubrey and the bobli.

"I will dress fast," Katie told him.

Daniel clapped a hand on Jamie's tense shoulder. "You all right there, son? You look a bit frightened."

"I am, sir. The bobli wasn't supposed to be here for another month," he replied, biting the pad of this thumb. "I am praying that Gott will protect them through this."

"He will. If it is any consolation, both Aubrey and Emma were born a month prior to their due dates," Daniel said.

Jamie grimaced inwardly at the mention of Emma's name. What he'd overheard earlier still lingered in the back of his mind. He shoved those thoughts away for another time to reflect and pray about them.

Kate reappeared at the top of the stairs, dressed for the ride to Martha's. Shadowing behind her was a pale Sadie. Their eyes met at the top of the stairs. Fair hair tumbled around Sadie's shoulders, and it struck them how eerily alike she was to Aubrey, from her innocent eyes to cheeks dusted with freckles.

"I'll be back with news," Katie said. She slipped into her coat with Daniel's help and turned to look up at Sadie. "Make sure to have breakfast ready in the morning for Isaac, Eli, and your daed."

The door closed shut before Sadie could reply. They hurried across the snowy yard to the buggy as Katie asked questions. "How is she doing?"

Jamie helped her climb up to the passenger side before jogging to the other side. "She's doing gut. Martha has been keeping her calm."

They started down the road. Jamie briefly paused to look over his shoulder in the direction of his parent's haus.

While he wished to go to them, something within him filled him with urgency. He needed to return to Martha's. He would go to his family later, once the bobli arrived safely.

A tall figure shadowed the front porch the second Jamie navigated the buggy down the driveway. It was Martha's mann, Isaac, who appeared in the moonlight as he quickly made his way to Jamie's side.

"You better stay in there," he said, shaking his head. "Martha has taken Aubrey to the English hospital."

His heart stopped beating for a few seconds. Jamie stared down at the older Amish man in disbelief, not quite sure if he'd heard correctly. He shook his head. "Are sure? She was fine just a few minutes ago—"

"I'm not sure what happened, but Martha took her to the hospital a few minutes ago. If you hurry, I'm sure you can catch up with her."

The cold wind whipped at Jamie's face as he steered the buggy back around. Wordlessly, Katie reached out for his hand. They both prayed together as they sped through the dark night at a dizzying pace until they reached the hospital parking lot.

Katie pointed in a northerly direction. "There's Martha's buggy," she called out over the wind whistling in their ears. Jamie pulled up next to Martha's buggy and helped Katie down before they both hurried across the empty parking lot. A blast of warm air greeted them when they rushed through the automatic doors.

After climbing a flight of stairs to the maternity floor, they spotted Martha talking to a group of English nurses.

"What's going on?" Jamie asked, looking between Martha and the grave faced nurses. His heart felt sick from how it leaped up in his chest and then plummeted to his feet. "Is Aubrey okay? The bobli?"

Martha laid a cold hand on his forearm. The English nurses left them to talk, darting to a room down the quiet linoleum hallway. "Everything is going to be fine, Jamie. She is in gut hands here with these doctors."

"Why couldn't you deliver the bobli?" he asked.

"The contractions had stopped suddenly—"

His heart leaped back up to its proper place at that. "That's a gut thing though, right? Maybe the bobli has decided to wait for another few weeks."

Martha shook her head gravely. "Nee, I'm afraid it doesn't work like that. The bobli is coming tonight, if not early morning. I brought Aubrey here because I feared that the bobli is in a position of becoming stuck, or having the cord wrapped around its neck."

Jamie didn't reply. His head felt heavy as he took in the white washed walls, the beep of machines in the distance, and a bobli crying in a room nearby. He couldn't imagine a world without Aubrey or the bobli. It was a world he didn't wish to think about.

"All will be well," Martha said, rubbing his arm. "Gott is with them, and I trust and respect these doctors here. They will do everything they can to make sure both Aubrey and the bobli will be okay."

He took hope in her comforting words and touch. Down the hallway, the English nurses congregated outside what was most likely Aubrey's room. "Is that her room down there?"

"Jah, please go see her. The both of you. I will be nearby if you need me," Martha said.

Their shoes squeaked on the clean floors as they approached Aubrey's room. An eerie silence that was punctuated with the nurses' chatter and a bobli crying in a room filled the hospital. The room was spacious, almost too spacious, with a large floor filled with a couch and table for eating. Next to the window, Aubrey lay stretched out on the bed, covered in various blankets and what appeared to be pads.

Tears suddenly sprang to Jamie's eyes at the sight of his fraa lying distraught, with her pale face scrunched up in pain. As quick as it hit him, he pushed away the overwhelming emotion before Aubrey could see it. He took her hot hand in his, staring down at the strange belt strapped across her stomach.

"The English nurse said it is to keep track of the bobli's heartbeat. There," Aubrey said, pointing to a machine that beeped almost in time with Aubrey's own heart. "Is the bobli's heart. They said this way they can tell if the bobli becomes too distressed."

"That's gut," Jamie said, the only thing he could think to say. He turned to look at Katie, who smiled tenderly at Aubrey. "Daniel mentioned that both Emma and Aubrey were born a month early."

"Jah, they were both exactly a month early. I came to this hospital long ago because the midwife of our community feared that both wouldn't be able to breathe," she said.

"And we were fine?" Aubrey asked.

Katie smiled even more. "Blessings from Gott," she said.

Except the bobli didn't come within the next hour like they had hoped. Pale morning light eventually gave way to sunny morning, filling the room with a golden glow. To give Aubrey, who was fraught with pain and exhaustion, some time to rest, the nurses administered a drug to help ease the labor process. While initially against it, Jamie felt immensely relieved when Aubrey fell asleep within a few seconds.

"Rest is the best thing right now," an English nurse named Sally told him kindly. "If she doesn't have the strength to keep going, then the bobli won't arrive easily. We will wake her within the next hour. Get some rest yourself."

Instead of curling up in the chair next to Aubrey, he left the room with Katie to keep an eye on her. He wandered around the halls for a few minutes, hands shoved down into the pockets of his trousers. An antsy energy filled him. He prayed and continued to walk in circles until deciding fresh air would do his lungs and tired mind some good.

A light dusting of snow had covered the parking lot over the past few hours. Jamie sucked in a lungful of cold air with a grateful sigh. He started toward the metal bench a few feet away, but stopped short when he caught sight of a couple walking across the parking lot.

Disbelief and anger filled him.

"What are you two doing here?"

Emma stared at him in aloofness. She kept an arm twined through Michael's, clearly not fazed by the warning glare he was currently directing in their direction.

"I'm here to see, Aubrey. I heard that she was in labor."

"You mean Sadie told you," he said bluntly.

Something glimmered in Emma's eyes, but it was too fleeting for him to read it. He refused to look in Michael's direction as the taller man took a defensive and protective stance next to Emma.

"You shouldn't be here, or talking to Sadie. You've made your decision," Jamie said.

"We aren't here to cause any sort of trouble," Michael said sternly.

Jamie pinched the bridge of his nose in frustration. Of all the things that he needed to deal with, this was the last thing he wanted to fight about.

"You can't expect me not to care about my sister either," Emma said. "I know that I made the decision to leave, but you know that being excommunicated doesn't make me disappear. I'm still very much Aubrey's older sister. We just made different decisions about how we wish to live our lives. There's nothing wrong with that."

"It has never been the rules being broken that bothered me," Jamie said, looking directly at the both of them. "It's the emotional consequences that I've seen and worried about. I don't think either one of you understand what happened to your families. Particularly this last time."

"We understand what it has done to our families," Michael said, and then placed a hand on the small swell of

Emma's stomach. "This is our family now, and we can only pray and hope that one day everyone will understand why we did what we did."

Jamie nodded in tired resignation. He did not have it in him to fight with either of them.

"I'd better get back inside. You can wait if you want. I'm sure Aubrey would like to see you," he said.

A genuine smile filled Emma's face at that. Before they could step inside, however, a sudden nagging thought popped into Jamie's head. "Would you two happen to know what happened to Daniel on his rumspringa?"

"Why?" Emma asked, frowning. "There has been talk about him and Sadie being the same on their rumspringas."

He leveled a knowing glance at Emma. They stared at one another for a few moments before she exchanged a glance with Michael.

"That is for another time," Emma said. "For now, let's focus on Aubrey and the bobli arriving here safely."

ᢙ CHAPTER 8 ᢝ

Time had slipped by Aubrey in a strange blur. One minute she had been in Martha's haus, delirious with fright when the contractions stopped abruptly. The next minute the English nurses were administering a drug to help her sleep, but she couldn't recall if she ever woke up after that. Blurbs of conversation had caught her attention through the waves of pain, or the feel of Jamie's fingers in her own, but a strange darkness had also occupied her mind. The only thing that had snapped her back into full consciousness was the cry of a bobli, and the quivering of her limbs.

Aubrey stared down at the carefully folded pink blankets with a small smile. A small clean face shifted against the crook of her elbow, skin perfectly smooth and soft to the touch. Eyelids flickered briefly before the small but lean little body shifted into a more comfortable sleeping position.

"You look exactly like your daed," Aubrey said, trailing a finger over her soft cheek. She looked up to glance at Jamie, who stood alongside her bed with one arm loosely draped over her shoulders. They shared a smile before she resettled against the pillows that smelled like bleach and starch. "I can't believe that she is finally here, after all this time."

"And I was right about her being a girl too," Jamie said.

She rolled her eyes at the triumph in his voice. "Jah, you were right. Next time, I won't go against your word. I still think it was a lucky guess."

"I just knew Gott would bless us with a daughter. I had a feeling about it from day one," he said.

The door to the small room they were currently staying in opened. Sadie ghosted the door frame, peering into the dimly lit room. She smiled when Aubrey waved her inside.

"Ach!" Sadie gasped, staring down at the bobli in Aubrey's arms. "She is truly a beautiful blessing from Gott. What name did you two choose?"

"Gracelynn," Aubrey said, smiling down the perfectly shaped face of her daughter. "Grace or Gracie for short."

"I like it. Very fitting," Sadie said. She hesitated before asking, "Could I hold her?"

"Of course."

She settled Grace comfortably in the crook of Sadie's secure arms before laying back against Jamie's arm and the pillows. When a minute of silence passed in the room, Jamie leaned down to press a kiss to the top of Aubrey's head. "I have to go home to water and feed the animals. I'll be back within an hour."

He shared a fleeting smile with Sadie before picking up his jacket from where it was thrown carelessly on a chair, and then disappeared out of the room with a click of the door behind him. Aubrey studied the way Sadie's eyes softened while she gazed down at Grace's sleeping form. The pallor of her skin was still pale with a tinge of grey to it. She looked sick, and very exhausted.

"How are you feeling?" Aubrey asked.

Sadie glanced up at the question, but her gaze didn't remain on Aubrey's long. Her eyes drifted back down to Grace. "Fine," she answered eventually, but then added with a sigh, "I guess you've probably heard about rumspringa."

"I haven't made any assumptions about what I've heard. You're my sister, and I love you. I just want to know what is going on."

"I suppose I owe you the truth..." Sadie started, but was cut short when Grace stirred back into wakefulness with a loud cry. She waited patiently, seated on the edge of the bed, while Aubrey tucked Grace up to her breast to nurse. "I-I-I didn't mean to slip in my faith. I wasn't strong enough to resist anything that came my way. If Eli found out that all of that talk was the truth, or if our parents found out...they'd be ashamed of my brash behavior."

"Are you—I mean, are you with a bobli?" she asked as gently as she could. It was clear from her shame filled eyes and wounded smile that Sadie felt bad enough for what had happened. She stroked Grace's soft, downy dark hair, waiting for an answer she prayed wouldn't come.

"I am."

Those timid words of admittance stunned Aubrey into silence. She had suspected since the start of the rumors that something was amiss, but to hear the heart breaking truth finally left her speechless. Her baby sister was with a bobli. The thought seemed surreal. In short, all Aubrey could manage to say was, "I wasn't sure if it was true or not. It's nothing to be ashamed of. Gott has blessed you and your mann with such a beautiful gift."

Sadie smiled grimly. "I wish I had your positivity, Aubrey. I don't think this news will go over so well when I confess to the church what I have done," she said.

"I wouldn't worry so much about it. While they won't like what happened, you hadn't taken the vow yet. You were on your rumspringa."

"That doesn't excuse my poor decision."

Aubrey grasped her sister's hand in her own. She gave a strong squeeze to draw Sadie's tear rimmed eyes to her own. "Forgiveness for our own mistakes, and toward others, releases us from revenge. I know that whoever has talked about your mistake is already forgiven, but it doesn't give them the power to seek revenge."

A tear escaped the corner of Sadie's eyes. She spoke quietly. "For the longest time afterward, I couldn't forgive myself, or her for telling her parents what happened. Then I look down at your bobli and realized that I must forgive because Gott has forgiven."

"Who has spoken about this?" Aubrey asked, curious. She had never been able to figure out who was behind the source of talk. Jamie had his assumptions about it being Emma, but she'd doubted that their oldest sister was that vengeful. She may be an Englischer now by choice, but her Amish upbringing hadn't been a choice.

"My friend Martha. She didn't necessarily mean it as vengeful or anything else. She had mentioned to her parents that she had witnessed something that went against the Ordnung."

"And they mentioned it to the church elders?"

Sadie shrugged her shoulders. She reached out to stroke Grace's warm head with a small smile. "I don't know," she said, shaking her head. "I don't know whether they did or didn't. All I know is that our community has been talking about it. I pray every day for forgiveness."

"You're already forgiven. You don't even have to ask for it. I don't know why there has been talk."

"I don't know either, but let's not talk about it anymore. I don't want to ruin this blessed morning with those troubles. How are you feeling?"

Aubrey gladly let it go. While she was still troubled about her sister's situation, and the idle talk within their community, she didn't wish to tarnish the morning either. She snuggled closer to a now sleeping Grace. "Better," she said quietly, exhaustion starting to tug at her mind. "Better than what I was feeling a few hours ago."

They shared a wry smile. Sadie picked at the hospital blanket, worry still evident in her almond shaped eyes. "Jamie said that Martha rushed you here to save your life and the bobli's," she said.

"Jah, but I don't have any memory of it. She was worried that the bobli had gone feet down and would become stuck."

"That can happen?" Sadie exclaimed, eyes widening in fright. Her hand immediately went to her lower stomach. "Ach! That sounds horrible and frightening! I am glad that Gott protected you and the bobli."

"Me too. I can't even imagine losing Grace or being without her."

She held Grace even closer. It struck her how deep her love went for this tiny little being whom she had only known for a few hours. They watched Grace sleep soundlessly in the crook of Aubrey's elbow until sleep began to hood Aubrey's eyes. She carefully set Grace in the little bassinet next to her bed.

"I'd better go. I still have chores to do," Sadie said.

She gave Aubrey's hand a quick squeeze before leaving the room. Aubrey curled up against the pillows with a sigh of relief. Before she could slip into peaceful dreams, the door clicked open again.

Expecting it to be Jamie or a nurse, she was surprised when it was Emma who walked in. Her oldest sister looked in far better health with a glow to her cheeks and natural blonde hair. She was dressed modestly as well, but Aubrey's joy to see her sister was short lived. It was still hard to look at her after what had happened the previous spring.

"What are you doing here?" Aubrey asked, shocked.

Emma came to stand beside the bassinet. She looked down at Grace with a warm smile, and gently smoothed a hand along the soft skin of her head. "I heard that Martha had taken you to the hospital," she said, hand retreating to hang at her side. "I wanted to make sure that you both were okay."

"I'm fine now. You shouldn't be here. If Jamie or—"

"I already spoke with Jamie. I promised to leave after I made sure you were all right. I doubt that the church will be upset with me checking on you."

Aubrey opened her mouth to argue, but she was too exhausted. She scooted over so Emma could sit on the edge of the bed. They sat in a tense silence, with Emma staring at Grace with a small smile.

"Michael and I are expecting," Emma said eventually. "And also getting married sometime next summer." She held out a hand to show Aubrey the small diamond ring on her left hand.

"Congratulations," Aubrey said, a hesitant smile going across her lips. "I'm happy that you and Michael are finally happy."

"How many years later, right?" Emma said wryly. Her humorous expression gave way to a serious one when she tore her gaze from Grace. "I don't want to make this morning about what you've been hearing, but I wanted to tell you that Sadie has been struggling. She came to me because she believed that she would be asked to leave, and I was convincing her otherwise. Sadie couldn't live without our family."

"I know. She told me everything before you came in here," Aubrey said.

Emma nodded. "Good. I just wanted to make sure you knew, and everyone else knew that I wasn't trying to convince her to leave. I was just trying to help her deal with the talk."

"I know," Aubrey said. A sudden thought crossed her mind now that she had Emma to talk to. "Do you know who is saying all these things? I've heard strange talk about daed."

"You have to ask daed about that," Emma said. "As for who is saying these things, I don't think it is anyone particularly. Our family has a history, and it's natural for others to question things."

"That's what I am thinking too. I don't know who in our community would stoop to such a level. It goes against our faith," Aubrey said. Sighing wearily, she combed a hand through her tangled hair. "I just pray that Sadie will be able to get through this. She didn't pick an easy road."

"Sadie will be fine. She's a lot stronger than we think. I'd better get going," Emma said. She stood on long legs, and leaned down to press a soft kiss to Grace's head. "Your bobli is beautiful. You are very blessed to have everything you have. Don't forget that. Okay?"

Tears blurred Aubrey's vision then. Whether it was the strenuous and emotional past few hours, or knowing that this would be the last time she would see her oldest sister, was lost to her. Emma bent down to press a kiss to the top of Aubrey's head as well. She smiled comfortingly down at her. "Don't cry. You're going to be fine," she said.

"I know. It's just been a long night with everything," Aubrey said, dabbing her eyes dry. She then gave a hopeful glance up at Emma. "Will I see you again?"

Emma's smile didn't waver, but a glimmer of tears filled her eyes. She looked down at Grace as she started to stir in the bassinet. "Maybe. Someday, I pray."

CRᏰᎶᎠ

The haus was eerily quiet when Jamie stepped inside after finishing his chores. A chilled air lingered in the rooms. He stood by the doorframe of the living room, and after a minute, decided to attend to the wood stove before leaving for the hospital.

He wearily walked up the stairs to the bedroom he shared with Aubrey. The past eight hours played heavily on his mind--the fear, the adrenaline, the tears in his eyes at Grace's cries. He thanked Gott that the two of them were in good health. He feared, like the English doctor who'd delivered Grace, that her early arrival could mean an abundance of health issues, but no issues existed. There had also been a brief moment where Martha had feared there was stress on the bobli and Aubrey, but Gott had protected them. He had given them a beautiful blessing.

The bed was still unmade from when he had thrown back the covers to find Aubrey in the middle of the night. He quickly folded the sheets and blankets while smoothing out the wrinkles from the thick coverlet. He then packed a bag of clothes for them both before doing the same for the bobli.

Setting the bags on the couch, he ventured outside to grab an armful of chopped firewood to keep the haus warm for when they returned home. The sound of hoofbeats drew his attention down to the road to the sight of his parents' buggy coming in his direction. His maemm practically bounced in the seat next to his daed when they pulled up alongside him.

"We heard the news!" Rebecca said, beaming widely at him. "How are Aubrey and Grace doing?"

Jamie smiled. His maemm's joy was contagious, despite how exhausted he currently felt from running on two hours of sleep. "They are doing gut. I was planning to go get the both of you before going back to the hospital," he said.

"We caught you in time then," Aaron said, smiling as well. "We'll follow you to the hospital."

"Give me a minute to stoke a fire. The haus is cold," Jamie said. At his daed's nod, he hurried back inside. A few minutes later a fire blazed happily in the wood stove, and he shut the doors after adjusting the metal knobs to allow enough heat into the haus. He carefully set the bags he'd packed into his buggy before leading the way back to the hospital.

While Rebecca eagerly strode forward into the hospital, a hand gently clamped down on Jamie's shoulder to hold him back. He looked up at his daed's serious face in confusion. "What? What is it?"

"I wanted to speak with you alone for a minute," he said.

They lingered in the glass room between the outdoors and the hospital. Blasts of winter air swept in to be greeted by the warm air within the hospital. Jamie's head swam at the rapid changes of temperature sweeping over him. He squinted up at his daed, wondering what was so urgent that it needed to discussed now.

"The rumors going around—"

"Daed, this is the last thing I want to hear right now," Jamie said, sighing in annoyance. "None of that matters at this moment."

Aaron's eyes slipped closed in exasperation. "You didn't let me finish what I was going to say," he said, shaking his head. "I was going to say that I pray you two will be able to forget these idle rumors to focus on caring for your bobli."

"Jah, of course we are. Nothing is more important now than this," Jamie said. He then added, "I appreciate your concerns though, daed. I think in time everything will be resolved."

"I'm sure that it will."

They shared a smile before walking into the hospital. Halfway up the stairs leading to the maternity ward, he spotted Michael and Emma heading directly for them. He tensed at the sight, knowing that his daed would disapprove if shunned members of the church tried to speak with them. Emma looked up from the conversation that she was currently having with Michael to spot them on the stairs as well. She stopped in mid step, reading the tension on Jamie's face. Her gaze flicked over to Aaron climbing the stairs alongside him before giving a brief nod. She tugged on Michael's hand and led him in another direction.

For the first time in years, he felt an intense wave of gratefulness for Emma's actions. She knew well that anyone beyond her family would not be pleased with interactions with shunned members. She wasn't willing to cause any additional stress for Aubrey on this blessed day.

The next few hours passed quickly. Outside the sun had begun its descent, dipping below the rugged mountain ranges covered in snow. A pink light filled the tiny hospital room while Jamie sat in the rocking chair next to the window, with Grace cradled in his arms.

"I talked to Sadie," Aubrey said. She sat up in the hospital bed, alert but exhausted as she adjusted the blankets around her. Her nimble fingers pulled up the long strands of her hair and pulled them tight into the bun she often wore beneath her kapp. "She finally admitted to me that she is indeed with a bobli."

"Did she say who has been talking about it?" Jamie asked.

"Nee, she believes it was a friend, but it wasn't said out of vengeance or anything of that sort. Her friend informed her parents what had apparently happened while on rumspringa. I'm sure you can fill in the rest."

"Jah, I can see how the rumors have started," he said. He wasn't surprised by the information. He had never believed that the talk in their community was done out of vengeance. No one mentioned anything to him or Aubrey specifically. It still didn't explain why others were whispering about what happened on Aubrey's daed's rumspringa, but he knew from his brief interaction with Emma that she knew. "Your sister and Michael came by to see you earlier?"

Aubrey paused in wiping the exhaustion from her eyes. She looked at him carefully, and after gauging his expression, answered slowly. "Jah, they stopped by for a minute. Well, Emma did. Why?"

He shrugged his shoulders. The movement caused Grace to stir, but she continued to slumber. He briefly marveled at her tiny fingers curling up into tiny fists before they went lax again. Gott had truly given them a perfect bobli.

"They were entering the hospital when you were in labor. I ran into them when I stepped outside to get some air. I imagined Emma would eventually come see you once everyone was gone for the time being," he said.

"She doesn't have to hide," Aubrey said, sighing softly. "I think on a day like this…"

"But she made her decision, and you made yours. There's nothing wrong with either one," Jamie finished.

They fell into silence while listening to the sounds of the hospital around them. Down the hallway, a newborn bobli also cried. Voices drifted down the hallway, oddly soothing to them compared to the early morning hours when it had been eerily silent.

Jamie's eyes drifted down to Grace again. It was still surreal—no matter how warm and real she felt in the bundle of blankets in his arms—that she was physically present in their lives. How many times had they imagined her in the crib upstairs? Or wondered how she would look?

His nerves were settling finally. It left him breathless and very exhausted. He sank back against the cushions of the rocking chair with a grateful sigh. When his eyes drifted closed of their own will, Aubrey's voice startled him back awake.

"Here," she said, pushing the blankets back from her legs. "You're exhausted. I can watch Grace while you sleep."

Pain flashed in Aubrey's eyes when she started to rise. The nurse assured them both that soreness, and not being able to move normally, was a normal process of recovering. Concern still shot through Jamie though.

"Stay in bed. You need to rest too," he said.

"I am tired," Aubrey admitted, rubbing at her puffy eyes. "I feel as though the world is spinning around me."

Any minute Grace would wake. For the past few hours she'd slept for intervals of an hour, cried until she was properly soothed, and then slipped back into sleep. Exhaustion tugged nauseatingly at him. A glance in Aubrey's direction told him that she felt the same way from how she slumped over and swayed ever so slightly in bed. They both needed a few hours of undisturbed sleep, and both their families had returned home to attend to their afternoon chores. An idea struck him.

"I'll be right back," he said, depositing Grace into Aubrey's arms.

"Where are you going?"

"You'll see. Stay here."

Jamie left the warm confines of their room. He walked down the hallway to the nurses' station, where he could hear the nurses talking softly among themselves. All three nurses looked up at the sound of his footsteps.

"Can we do something for you, dear?" an older nurse asked kindly.

"I was wondering if it were possible for someone to watch our bobli. My fraa is exhausted and—"

"No worries," a much younger nurse said, waving a

hand. "We were wondering how much longer you two were going to last with how long you both have been awake."

He smiled gratefully at them before returning to the hospital room. Aubrey looked up from Grace's sleeping form when he stepped back into the room. "The nurses will watch Grace for us while we get a few hours of sleep," he told her, coming to the side of the bed. At the nervous look on Aubrey's face, he rested a reassuring hand on her shoulder. "Don't worry. They can handle Grace if she wakes up."

"If you're sure…"

They both had been worried about Grace's health, but there were no signs of any distress. Her lungs work perfectly too, he thought to himself when Grace gave a sharp cry of discontent as Aubrey set her on the bed to rewrap the blankets around her.

When the nurse arrived, Aubrey tentatively handed Grace over to the older woman. "Don't you worry, dear," she said, expertly cradling Grace in her arms. "I've lost count of how many babies I have looked after over the years. She is in good hands here."

"Just wake me if she needs something, or if anything is wrong," Aubrey said.

The nurse nodded before dimming the lights even more in their room. Jamie pulled the blinds closed, and settled himself in the pullout bed next to Aubrey's bed. He took her hand in his as they prayed together before falling into silence again. Before they could fall asleep, he pressed a gentle kiss to the back of Aubrey's hand.

"I'm proud of you," he whispered.

Aubrey turned her head to look at him. A sleepy smile curled her lips up, and her voice was barely a whisper when she answered. "Danka. Gott has truly blessed us both."

"Jah, He truly has."

❧ CHAPTER 9 ❧

Grace's cry cut through the warm haus. Struggling to hold the flailing little body, Aubrey hurried out of the kitchen, where she had been trying to help her maemm and Sadie prepare a Thanksgiving meal. She paced up and down the hallway, the only thing that had worked to keep Grace calm for the past few nights and days. The movement eventually soothed her cries and lulled her back into a peaceful slumber.

Exhausted as well, Aubrey sat on the couch to take a moment to rest. The smell of freshly mashed potatoes with butter and chives filled the stuffy living room. A fire cracked happily in the wood stove as Aubrey leaned back against the cushions of her parents' couch. Exhaustion buried itself in her bones. Her eyes slipped closed at the feeling. While she wouldn't trade the long nights for anything, the lack of sleep was starting to catch up with her in the worst ways.

They'd stayed in the hospital for a few days after Grace's birth, and she had gotten used to the nurse's expert hands or advice. Now, she faced handling Grace alone while Jamie went back to work at the furniture store. It was beyond difficult trying to manage all the household chores and prepare dinner with a newborn that always demanded to be held. Only yesterday she had broken down into tears when Grace had started wailing again. It was Jamie's idea then to visit their families for a Thanksgiving meal instead preparing one for everyone else.

"It'll do you both some gut to be around others and have helpful hands," he said, rocking a sleeping Grace. "It won't be like this all the time, I promise. She's only a little bobli."

The creak of the floorboards drew Aubrey from her thoughts. She opened her eyes, straightening to find that it was her daed who'd entered the living room. He smiled at her while slipping out of a heavy jacket, then placed it on the back of the rocking chair he kept next to the stove.

"I didn't mean to wake you," Daniel said, sitting down on the chair. A long sigh of relief escaped his lips before he started rocking. "Your maemm will be furious at me for waking you."

Aubrey glanced down at Grace still tucked in her arms and lost in dreams. She blinked hazily when she took in the evening sunlight leaking through the drapes in the windows. Wiping away the sleep in her eyes, Aubrey adjusted Grace in her arms. The movement stirred Grace from her sleep and it was immediately followed by a sharp cry of protest.

Before the exhausted and frustrated tears could even start, Grace was easily plucked up into her daed's strong arms. He retreated to his rocking chair and began to hum a lullaby that Aubrey recognized from her own childhood. Grace's cries diminished drastically before tapering off. Her heart swelled with love for her daed's tenderness.

"How long was I asleep?" she asked, settling back into the couch for a moment. The soft clanging in the kitchen, followed by soft whispers, told her that Sadie and her maemm still believed her to be asleep. She took advantage of it to wake up fully.

"Only for an hour," Daniel answered, rocking steadily with Grace sprawled happily against his chest. "Jamie left for a few minutes to talk with his family. He said he would be back shortly."

"Danka."

They sat in collective silence while listening to the absent chatter coming from the kitchen. The smell of turkey caused Aubrey's stomach to rumble in hunger. She knew that she should eventually help with dinner, but she remained seated on the couch. Instead, she studied her daed curiously.

His light beard had the faintest hints of grey in the coarse strands. The lines and bags under his eyes were a telltale sign of his health recently. Constant bouts of the flu and colds while trying to keep up with the farm had taken their toll on him. It didn't seem possible that her daed could do anything similar to what Sadie had done if the talk was true.

Aubrey played with her hands nervously. It wasn't proper of her to ask her daed about his past, or what happened on his rumspringa, but she wanted to know whether there was any truth behind the talk. She wanted to close the door on the rumors if they weren't true.

"Daed."

"Hm?"

"I have to ask you something," she said slowly, waiting until Daniel looked up from studying Grace's sleeping face. "It has to deal with the things that have been said about you on rumspringa."

She watched intently as her daed's gaze shifted back down to Grace. No flicker of emotion indicated if he knew what she was implying or if he was aware of what was being said. Daniel gently stroked a finger down Grace's cheek. "None of us should be divulging in such things as gossip. Not when there is this little blessing here."

"I know. I have done my best to stay clear of it, but I just... I just wanted to know if it were true or not," Aubrey said. She wasn't sure if her parents were aware of Sadie's condition, nor did she wish to cross that bridge if they didn't. Instead, she said, "I remembered what it was like during my rumspringa and not knowing if I was making the right decision. I find it hard that you might have struggled through that."

"I'm not a perfect being, Aubrey," he replied, smiling slightly. "I wondered too at the time if Gott wanted me to take a different course in life."

"Are you on the right course?"

"Jah, I know within my heart that Gott has me here for a reason. If He didn't wish for me to be here, I wouldn't be here. Where is all this coming from exactly?"

She didn't know how to answer. She was treading on

thin ice and knew it. Clearing her throat, Aubrey smoothed the fabric of her dress around her knees. "Nowhere in particular. Just some things that I have been hearing."

"Ah, but you want to know if what you have heard is true then?" Daniel asked, even though it wasn't a question.

"I'm sorry. I shouldn't be asking you about this—"

Daniel held up a hand, stopping her in mid ramble. He shifted Grace's sleeping form to rest more peacefully on the curve of his shoulder. They both held their breath as a small cry escaped Grace's lips at being disturbed, but she settled back into slumber under her daed's peaceful rocking. They remained quiet until a few minutes had passed without Grace stirring back into wakefulness.

"Faith doesn't happen overnight. If you're asking if I have gone against our way of life, against the Ordnung, then I will admit that I did years ago. Before any of you kinner were born. I made mistakes in my spiritual quest to join the church, and some of them I am not proud of. I asked for forgiveness, and Gott has forgiven me in return."

"Why didn't you have faith back when you were younger? On your rumspringa?" Aubrey asked.

Daniel smiled thinly. "Did you on your rumspringa?" When she colored at that, he continued. "No one is a perfect being. I have certainly made my fair share of mistakes, and like you a few years ago, thought perhaps this wasn't the place for me."

"So, what kept you here?"

"Your maemm," Daniel said. He smiled wistfully as he smoothed a hand gently down the back of Grace's head. "We have never told you kinner about our courtship days, but your maemm never left for rumspringa. She couldn't leave the bakery for more than a weekend. I knew that if I left the community I would also lose your maemm, and I didn't know if I could handle that."

"Because maemm wanted to stay here," Aubrey said, smiling. While she knew her parents loved one another, she had never known the depth of their shared love. "I was just curious because some of the things that I heard. I wasn't sure if it was true, or if it was idle talk or a misunderstanding."

"Well, I suppose you are old enough now to know," Daniel said. He sighed heavily and leaned back against the rocking chair. Shadows danced in his normally bright eyes. "My rumspringa was a long one. I was torn between wanting to be on the outside, but also wanting to be here. I prayed every day for an answer. My parents prayed for me as well. I thought if I had indecision about joining the church then that was a sign from Gott. I lived a life as an Englischer with a distant uncle for a few months. I carried on a relationship like I believed an English boy would. My parents weren't pleased with my decision, nor was the community, but they respected it as part of sowing of wild oats. I eventually realized that Gott didn't wish for me to be living the life I had been carrying on. I returned to the community to seek forgiveness for the things I'd done. I then spent the next year preparing to join the church, and I never looked back after that."

Aubrey blinked back tears. It was oddly humbling to know that her daed had suffered with his faith, and even at one point had thought about leaving the community.

Her own doubts that sometimes surfaced felt normal because of her daed's words.

"I never knew that you went through such a hard time," she said.

"All of us do at some point, Aubrey. Faith isn't built on thin air; it's built out of the mistakes we make, and the hope that better things will come along. Which they always do, if we let them."

"I know," Aubrey said, her eyes settling on Grace. A rush of love went through her. "I wouldn't have stayed here in the community if Jamie hadn't come along. I can't even imagine how life would've been if I'd decided differently."

"It makes you appreciate things much more, huh?"

"Very."

They listened to the clang in the kitchen along with the steady crackle from the fire within the wood stove. Aubrey chewed her bottom lip, processing her daed's words before speaking again. "Did you ever tell Emma about this?"

Daniel's eyes closed at the mention of his oldest daughter. Sadness shimmered in his eyes when he opened them again to look at Aubrey. "I tried various times," he said softly, "Your sister has her own ideas about things. She listened to Michael more than she listened to me."

"Listened to Michael?" she echoed, confused. "What does Michael have to do with any of what we just talked about?"

"Michael's daed and I experienced rumspringa together as friends," Daniel said. A hard edge crept into his tone, but no other emotion touched his eyes. "We unfortunately had a falling out after rumspringa, but it is of no consequence now. The past is in the past, and there is no changing what happened between him and I."

Before Aubrey could ask anything else, their conversation was interrupted when Katie emerged from the kitchen. Her face was flushed from spending hours in front of the stove. Stray hairs curled around her neck. "Ach, I didn't know you were awake. Hopefully, your daed didn't wake you," Katie said, shooting her mann a disapproving look. "I warned him that you were sleeping peacefully with Grace."

"Nee, he didn't wake us," Aubrey said, hurriedly. She pushed herself off the couch, albeit slowly still, and gathered a sleeping Grace from her daed's arms. "We were just enjoying the warmth of the stove together. I apologize, maemm. Let me help you and Sadie with setting the table for dinner."

She didn't give her maemm a chance to answer. Aubrey walked into the kitchen with Grace settled securely in the crook of her arm. She wanted a moment to absorb what her daed had said before being lost in the motions of getting ready for dinner.

Emma knew what happened with their daed on rumspringa, and apparently didn't believe him, or didn't heed to his advice. Her heart hardened with determination. She was going to speak with her sister one last time.

CR80

"I don't know if this is a gut idea," Jamie said.

They stood outside a small Englischer diner on the outskirts of Monte Vista. Curiosity had taken hold of him when Aubrey mentioned meeting her oldest sister one last time to understand her daed's past. He knew Emma was aware of Daniel Forrest's past from their brief conversation outside the hospital. Now that they stood in front of the diner, huddled against the cold, he wasn't sure if following this whim was the best idea.

Aubrey glanced up at him from where she stood by his side. The past few nights of getting up every two hours with Grace sometimes crying incessantly for hours showed from the dark bags lining her lower eyelids. She looked beyond exhausted, a feeling that Jamie wholeheartedly felt within himself as well. He refused to remain in bed and let Aubrey handle Grace all on her own.

"I just want to know what she knows. Daed said he talked to her about his rumspringa, and I have a feeling there is something that happened," she said.

"Maybe there is a reason why he hasn't told you."

"I'm sure there is a reason, but Emma will tell me. I know she will if I ask her about it."

Jamie sighed. He shoved his hands deep within the pockets of his coat to fight off the chilly wind. "Why is this so important to you? Why does it matter now?"

She didn't reply right away. His fraa's eyes focused somewhere in the distance, chewing her bottom lip the way she always did whenever she was thinking intently. "If there was something going on within your family, wouldn't you want to know about it? Only because you love them, and want to defend their honor if what's being said isn't true?"

"Maybe," he replied, frowning. Would he care to understand what was going if it were his own family? They were raised to believe that family was the center of their world, but now that he was starting his own family, something told him otherwise. All that mattered to him were Aubrey and Grace. "Our family matters now. We have a bobli waiting for us at your parents' haus. Nothing else should matter. We shouldn't even be having contact with Emma."

He knew his fraa well. She wanted to know because she was fiercely protective of her family's reputation, but also because she was curious. Sometimes he also wondered if this was Aubrey's way of staying connected with a life that she had given up to be with him. Jamie shook those thoughts away before they could tantalize him.

Aubrey didn't get a chance to reply. A tall and slender figure appeared across the street, wearing a loose sweater that showed off a small baby bump. The December wind stirred the long blonde strands of hair around Emma's face as she crossed the street with confident strides. She reached up to tuck a strand of hair behind her pierced ear absently. Her lips pulled up into a cautious smile when she reached them. "Gut morning. How are you both feeling with the new bobli?" she asked.

"Tired," Aubrey said, smiling slightly. "How are you feeling?"

Emma gave a short laugh. "Tired as well. Shall we?" She motioned to the glass door of the diner. They stepped inside the warm building that smelled of mashed potatoes and beef. A blast of warm air from the heater above greeted them as they waited to be seated in a booth along the wall. "So, what is it that you need to talk to me about? So urgent that you both are talking to a shunned member?"

"It's about daed," Aubrey said.

A hostess seated them at a small booth. They ordered kaffe while Emma ordered an ice water with lemon. "A midwife told me to take a bit of lemon whenever I have nausea," she said, biting the yellow fruit when the waitress brought them their drinks. "The sour taste makes you think of something other than puking. Now, what about daed did you want to talk about?"

She set the lemon peel on a napkin and looked across the booth at an anxious looking Aubrey. The two sisters shared a long look before Aubrey let out a pent up sigh. She played with the cutlery absently.

"I want to know what you know," she said.

"Know about what? I'm confused."

"Daed told me he spoke with you about what happened on his rumspringa. I know you know what happened."

They were met with silence at first. Jamie studied Emma's face intently while she stirred the small chunks of ice in her cup. Her eyes caught his eyes before sliding back down to the table.

"I don't know if this is right to—"

"To what? Tell me what happened with our own daed? We made a promise a long time ago not to keep secrets from one another," Aubrey said tensely.

Emma sighed. "Fine, you're right. You just have to promise me not to say anything to Sadie, or that you heard any of this from me. Deal?"

The pit of Jamie's stomach tightened into a nervous ball. He started to pray for Gott's council, and for the strength to get up and walk away. Whatever information Emma had, he didn't wish to know anymore. He wanted to return home to Grace, but before he could say anything, Aubrey spoke up alongside him.

"Jah, of course. I won't say anything."

He bit the tip of his tongue in frustration. How many more secrets were they going to have and be part of? Neither sister heeded the annoyed sigh that slipped past his lips.

Aubrey folded her hands in the pit of her lap and twisted them in an agitated fashion.

Running a hand through her hair, Emma peered at them both through tired eyes. "When I came back from rumspringa, everything was different. I wanted to leave, but I wanted to stay. I wanted to be with Michael, but our daeds would never approve of our relationship. They wanted us to find different partners. I didn't understand why our families disapproved of one another until Michael found out why. At the time, daed was one of the few names selected to minister the community. Michael's daed was as well, but he didn't believe that our daed was fit for the position with what happened over rumspringa. So, he told Michael that daed had carried on a relationship with a young English woman for a while when he was on his rumspringa. He claimed that daed didn't want to leave the

English lifestyle because the young woman he had been in a relationship was carrying a child. Daed never denied it to me, but he never admitted it either."

Shock couldn't even describe how Jamie felt presently. He could never imagine Daniel, a man solid in his faith, behaving the way Emma told them. It became clear then who was possibly behind the rumors.

"Do you think Michael's daed is the one who started talking?" he asked.

"It's a possibility," Emma answered, shrugging her shoulders. "But I doubt that he would do so out of vengeance now. He's still Amish through and through. Back then, I think he was just angry with our daed over what happened on their rumspringa. His name had been selected to minister as well then."

"Maybe not out of vengeance, but as a side comment," Jamie said.

He realized then that Aubrey had yet to respond. She sat alongside him with a guarded expression, lost within her own thoughts.

"Are you okay?" he asked, placing a hand on Aubrey's shoulder. The simple touch finally stirred her back to life.

She gave a brief nod before looking to her sister with a frown. "Why didn't you tell me any of this before?" she asked.

"I'm sorry, but I honestly didn't think it was something that needed to be discussed at the time. I just thought daed was trying to convince me to stay in the community, and to move on from Michael. I didn't know that any of it was actually true," Emma said. She bit down on the lemon peel before taking a sip of water. "I still don't know whether any of it is true. Daed has never said if it was or wasn't."

"I know. He has been vague about it with me," Aubrey said.

Jamie stared down at the plastic table cover. He didn't want to think that a member of their community was speaking out of spite. Except it all made sense now where the source had been, but also why Emma and Michael had left the community. Their daeds were never going to approve of their relationship, no matter how much had changed.

Determination filled him. If he was selected by the community and Gott to minister, then he would guide them through this darkness of gossip. He wanted a loving and peaceful community for the future kinner to grow up in. More than anything, he prayed for Aubrey. Long had she sought peace from the turmoil that had plagued her a few years prior, and now that their family was just beginning, he would do whatever it took to obtain that. He straightened in the booth as Gott's presence filled him.

"If it is or isn't true, it no longer matters," Jamie said, squeezing Aubrey's shoulder to gain her attention. "We both have families to guide and protect and love. Whatever has happened in the past no longer matters here in the present. Gott has blessed us with the greatest gifts anyone could ever ask for--our kinner."

To his surprise, Emma agreed with him. "I agree with what Jamie is saying. Whatever happened to daed in his past doesn't matter any longer. He obviously has been forgiven, and also forgiven himself for the mistakes he made while making his decision to stay with the church."

"I know, but still..." Aubrey started, but trailed off with a sigh. She rubbed her eyes tiredly. "I don't know why it bothers me so much when it is all said and done."

"Because it's our family," Emma said simply. "We've been raised in a loving family who defends one another."

"But why wouldn't maemm or daed ever say anything about this to me? Why only you?" Aubrey asked.

Emma smiled gravely. "You really have to ask that? Think of the things that I have done over the years. They were trying to tell me where my behavior could lead. I'll do the same thing if it comes to that in the future."

"Did he ever tell Sadie?"

"No, Sadie doesn't know. I never told her because Sadie will figure things out for herself. She won't ever leave the community, and that isn't a bad thing. Aubrey." She reached out to grab hold of Aubrey's hands with an encouraging smile. "I know that for the longest time I tried to convince you that being an Englischer was a better fate. There's nothing wrong with how either one of us lives. We both have men who love us, and a family that is blossoming. Look what Gott has given you and I. That's all that matters. Not what happened in the past or the gossip going around. None of us are perfect, even some those of us who remain Amish. It's all about forgiveness, and living our lives. It's about having faith that things will work out. Do you understand?"

Aubrey gave a nod. A wavering smile spread across her face as she squeezed Emma's pale fingers tightly in hers. "Jah, I understand."

"Good. Now go live your life, and love your family. Don't look back when Gott has everything under control. Okay?"

"Okay."

◈ CHAPTER 10 ◈

November gave way to an even chillier December. A thick layer of snow covered the ground and crunched dully beneath the wagon wheels. Bundled up in blankets, Aubrey made sure that Grace was also covered in a thick blanket. She smiled down at her slumbering face, peaceful and innocent.

"Are you excited to be back at church?" Jamie asked.

He smiled over at her, also bundled up in a thick wool jacket. Aubrey never thought he looked more handsome than he did at that moment, with the morning sunshine bringing out the golden color of his beard and the intensity of his eyes. Their breath puffed out in front of them as the horses trotted down the road at a steady pace.

"I am," Aubrey said, smiling as well. She longed to be back within church, to feel Gott's presence in the room, and to be surrounded the warmth of their community. "It has only been a few weeks, but I feel like it has been ages since we were in church."

"Well, Grace did arrive on a weekend that church

took place. The hospital didn't want either one of you to leave until they were sure Grace could feed all right," he said.

"And she has been feeding all right," she said, looking down at Grace's pudgy cheeks with a fond smile. "I don't think she has stopped feeding actually since we left the hospital two weeks ago."

"That's gut. No matter how much weight she gains, she's still going to be a beautiful bobli."

Jamie reached out to smooth his palm over the top of Grace's head tenderly, messing the fine strands of hair out of place. He shifted excitedly in his seat, holding the reins securely in his fingers. Today was the day that their church would officially select a new minister, with Isaac stepping down for health reasons. Today, they would find out who the community and Gott believed would be the new minister.

And how she prayed for her mann! She saw no one better than Jamie, who had been her steadfast spiritual leader and friend with her own personal struggles with faith. Nothing would be a greater honor than having her own mann ministering to them and delivering Gott's message.

They reached the King's barn a few minutes later. With Jamie's help, Aubrey stepped out into the snowy morning. She had barely taken a few steps forward before Elizabeth and Hannah were at her side in excited giggles.

"Ach! Look at those pudgy cheeks," Elizabeth said.

"She looks like both of you," Hannah said.

Aubrey laughed as her two friends cooed over Grace.

She even allowed Elizabeth to hold Grace so she could give her sore arms a rest. "Danka. She is truly a blessing from Gott."

Jamie stepped up behind them after unhitching their horse. "But let's not forget that her charm and cuteness came from me," he said, grinning when all three women rolled their eyes at him.

"I'm sure, Jamie," Hannah said wryly. She scooped up her daughter Naomi from playing happily in the snow. "How is she sleeping and feeding now that it has been a couple of weeks?"

"Better. She is no longer fussy," Aubrey said. This was something that she was very grateful for. There was nothing more frustrating and overwhelming than a screaming bobli and not knowing what to do. Her eyes immediately went to where Jamie walked quietly behind them with a small smile on his face. Those were the times that Jamie had prayed with her and offered a helping hand. He was once again not fazed by anything. "I'm better because of Jamie being there day and night. He has been most helpful whenever I need him."

"We are blessed with wunderbar mensleit," Elizabeth said. She smiled at Henry, who stood waiting for them on the front porch of the King's haus. Together they slipped inside to find their seats before church started. Pleasant chatter filled the room while the smell of freshly baked breads lingered in the air.

A light touch on her elbow startled Aubrey out of a conversation with Hannah over the next sewing frolic. She turned to find Sadie standing behind her, hands folded in the fabric of her white apron.

"Could I speak with you before church starts?" she asked quietly.

Aubrey took in her youngest sister's pale pallor and the bags beneath her eyelids with an uneasy stomach. She excused herself quietly from her group of friends after making sure that Grace was still content in Elizabeth's arms. Together the two sisters walked back out into the snowy morning and came to a stop a few feet away from the barn.

"What's going on? Is everything okay?"

"Jah, all is fine," Sadie said, twisting her hands in a continuous motion. "I just wanted to tell you that I confessed to the Bishop about what happened over rumspringa."

She blinked in surprise at the news. "You went to the Bishop? When?"

"This morning. I've prayed hard about what to do after we talked. Gott spoke with me, and I knew that I needed to tell Eli the truth," Sadie said.

"And?" Aubrey prompted. She inwardly prayed that Eli had taken the news in stride. "What did he say?"

"He was upset, understandably," Sadie said. "I told him how everything happened and that it was a mistake I made before accepting his courtship. He prayed for a few days as well before forgiving me. He suggested that I talk to the Bishop about it, but we will love this bobli no matter what."

Aubrey smiled in relief at that. She drew Sadie in for a tight embrace, filled with the joy and relief she felt at hearing the news.

"I'm happy that Gott has helped you through this hardship and showed both of you the way to handle this. Truly I am happy for you, Sadie."

"Danka. I can feel excited now about this bobli," Sadie said, rubbing the swell of her stomach. A frown suddenly appeared on Sadie's face. "Do you think maemm and daed will be forgiving?"

"They don't know?" Aubrey asked, surprised. She had been confident that their parents knew about Sadie being with a bobli.

Sadie shook her head. "Maemm knows I am with a bobli, but she doesn't know... They will be so upset with me!" she cried, burying her head in her hands. "What am I going to do?"

For the second time, Aubrey drew Sadie into a comforting embrace. Her heart ached thinking of what her sister would have to deal with in the upcoming days and weeks. While she wouldn't be punished by the church since she had yet to take the vow, she would have to cope with their parent's disappointment, which was worse punishment than anything else.

"I will pray that maemm and daed will be forgiving. You made a mistake. I'm sure they will understand," she said.

Sadie mumbled into her shoulder. "I don't think so. Think of how upset they were over what Emma said and did. They are going to be heartbroken."

"They will be," Aubrey said, rubbing soothing circles into Sadie's shoulder blades. "But you are doing the right thing by confessing. I think they will be more forgiving about it."

"You think so?" Sadie lifted her head off Aubrey's shoulder. Her wet eyes were hopeful and vulnerable when they looked at Aubrey. "You really think that they will be forgiving?"

Aubrey nodded. "I'm confident that they will be."

And she was. She could feel it deep within her heart that Gott would help Sadie along the path to confessing about what had happened over rumspringa. She didn't wish to see her little sister carrying such a burden. Their parents would undoubtedly be upset about their daughter's brash behavior over rumspringa, but they would be willing to forgive since Sadie was confessing, unlike Emma, who had denied her own brash decisions.

"I suppose you're right," Sadie said. She dabbed her eyes and face dry with the fabric of her apron. "I'm sure they will be forgiving since I'm admitting to what I did, and not denying it every time someone asks. Emma still denies it to this day."

Aubrey scuffed the bottom of her foot along the muddy barn floor. The smell of wet hay and manure filled her nose. She had never understood her oldest sister's willingness to lie. There were quite a few times she could remember her parents' exasperation whenever they had caught Emma in a blatant lie. Members of their community were still walking up the snowy pathway to the King's haus. A particularly chilly blast of cold air swept through the barn. Both sisters hastily adjusted their coats to fight off the biting air.

"I don't know why she lies. I wish I knew why she felt the need to lie, but I have a feeling it wouldn't be a gut idea for us to know. Who knows what other secrets she has," Aubrey said.

Sadie shrugged her slender shoulders. Their sister carried a heavy burden of lies and secrets that had little do with her decision to leave their community. Aubrey couldn't count how often Emma had snuck out in the middle of the night to be with Michael, but she had consistently lied about it whenever she was questioned the next morning. It was the simplest things she lied about as well. Did you feed the chickens? Jah. Give the horses hay? Jah. Except there was never any feed or hay for the chickens and horses unless Aubrey took on the extra chores to protect her sister.

Her earlier conversation with Emma came back to the surface. She had kept her relationship with Michael a secret because their families didn't approve, but was it worth it? The question burned in Aubrey's mind. At that moment she had the impulse to see Emma and ask that question. Was it worth it? The heartache? The sacrifice of family?

As quickly as it burned, it was extinguished. She knew what the answer would be. If loving Jamie and having a family with him meant letting go of her family, she would let go. No matter how painful it was or how wrong she knew it was.

"We should go inside now," Sadie said, peering out the barn doors. "It looks like church is about to start here soon."

They walked together up the pathway and stopped at

the front porch step to stomp the snow off their boots. Before they could step inside, Aubrey stopped Sadie with a hand on her elbow. "I just wanted to tell you how proud I am of you. Gott has truly given you a blessing," she said.

"Danka, Aubrey. You have many blessings that Gott has given you too."

The sharp cry of a newborn filled the morning air when they opened the front door. Sadie smiled at the grimace that spread across Aubrey's face at the sound. "Speaking of blessings," she said, laughing.

A bubble of warm laughter tumbled out of Aubrey's mouth. For what seemed like a long time, a peace filled her. She had a mann, the grace of her family, and a vocal bobli to start her own family. She was truly lucky and blessed with such things. There was nothing greater than looking Jamie in the eye as he carefully rocked Grace back and forth in the crowded room to soothe her discomfort.

He raised an eyebrow at the smile on her face. "What's with that smile?" he inquired, teasing.

Aubrey shook her head. She stretched out her arms, rejoicing in the feeling of Grace's tiny body occupying her arms. "Nothing in particular. I am just thankful today is all."

"Thankful for what?"

Grace's wide blue eyes peered up at her innocently. Her small pink lips pulled up into a hint of a smile that filled Aubrey's heart with such joy it felt it would surely burst. "Thankful for you, for our families, and our bobli. You all are blessings."

"We are blessed, aren't we?"

"Very."

CR80

Jamie took his usual seat between Henry and their daed. He exchanged a smile with Aubrey before she settled into her seat next Sadie. To his relief, Grace finally returned to slumber under Aubrey's gentle swaying. He sang along as they opened with their usual hymns, but his heart was hammering hard within his chest.

What if he were selected to minister?

The initial excitement over the chance to help others spiritually faded away to the seriousness and heavy responsibility that being a minister carried. If he were selected, it was to be Gott's plan for him. He would dutifully serve for the rest of his life, but it also meant spending less time with Aubrey and Grace. Much of his time would be spent preparing sermons before church and going to member's hauses. He doubted that Aubrey had given very much thought to it either. She'd grown accustomed to him being home most of the time when they weren't working.

A wave of uncertainty crashed upon his mind. He glanced over at his daed sitting alongside him, and then over at Daniel Forrest, who sat a few rows ahead of them with Isaac. Despite their flaws and recent revelations, he saw them as more suited for ministering. He was just starting a family, and while his faith in Gott was strong, he didn't view himself as spiritually wise.

Especially since he had been talking to Emma, a

shunned member of their church by her choice.

He prayed hard when Bishop Abraham announced that they were now to select a new minister, and after a few weeks of prayer, he hoped they were confident in their decisions. He disappeared into a side room to give members the privacy of telling him who they thought should be the new minister. He caught his daed's glance, but they didn't speak with one another.

Jamie stood when it was his turn to speak with Bishop Abraham. He wiped his sweaty palms on the fabric of his trousers before going to the room where Bishop Abraham stood alone. He tried in vain to read Abraham's expression, but the older Amish man kept his face carefully guarded.

"Gut morning," Abraham greeted. "Have you given thought to who should be the new minister?"

"Jah," Jamie replied, swallowing thickly. "I think my daed, Aaron Miller, would be a gut minister."

"Very well. Danka."

He hesitated, unsure about Abraham's curtness, but left the room in a cold sweat. When he took his seat again next to Henry, he searched for Aubrey on the other side of the room. She smiled warmly at him when their eyes finally met.

Minutes ticked by slowly as members of their church shuffled in and out of the room. It seemed like hours had passed before Abraham emerged from the room with five bibles in his hands. He smiled at the anxious sea of faces that undoubtedly looked upon him. Everyone wanted to know who the next minister would be.

"Please stand when I call your name," Abraham instructed, and then looked down at a piece of paper in his hand. "Thomas Fields, Daniel Forrest, Larry Brenneman, Henry Miller and Jamie Miller."

Jamie blinked several times in rapid succession. He felt Henry stiffen in surprise next to him, but they stood together. His eyes scoured the room not only to where Daniel stood in front of him, but also to where Thomas Fields and Larry Brenneman stood in the back. No emotion passed their eyes or gave any indication whether they were upset over Daniel Forrest possibly being a minister. But they wouldn't be when he turned back around, he reasoned. This wasn't about the past or old resentments. This was about Gott's will.

He turned his head ever so slightly to look over at Aubrey. She held Grace anxiously to her chest as she leaned forward in her seat to meet his gaze. They exchanged a look filled with apprehension.

"Please come forward, and select a Bible. There is a sheet of paper tucked in one of these Bibles. Whoever chooses the Bible with the piece of paper is chosen by Gott to minister," Abraham said.

He motioned for them to come forward. A tense silence filled the haus as they each grabbed a Bible from Abraham before standing in front of the room. Jamie willed his hands to steady themselves when he nearly dropped the Bible to the floor because of his nerves. He waited for Abraham to tell them to open the Bibles, but he mostly waited for the other men alongside him.

Daniel opened his first, thumbing through the pages.

When a piece of paper didn't materialize in his hand, he let out what sounded like a relieved breath. He watched as Larry did the same thing, followed by Thomas. His heart pounded so hard in his chest that he was sure that the whole church could hear it. Henry turned to look at him in apprehension, but at Jamie's encouraging nod, started to thumb through the pages.

Nothing.

Relief spread across Henry's face. The silence only grew thicker in the room. With now trembling fingers that he didn't bother to steady, he opened the pages of the Bible. The spine gave a loud crunch from its old age. A piece of white paper fluttered to the ground between his feet. He stared down at it with wide eyes. Shock registered in him.

This was it. Tears filled Jamie's eyes in realization. Gott had chosen him.

A flurry of surreal movement surrounded Jamie. Dimly in the distance, he could hear people talking to him. There were no offered congratulations, as he knew there wouldn't be. He stood stock still as Abraham talked to him, but he couldn't retain any of what the Bishop was telling him. At that moment he wanted to speak with Aubrey, who sat a few seats away in silence, and to hear her comforting words that this was Gott's plan for him. He wanted to hold Grace as a reminder of his previous determination.

After church concluded, Jamie stood with the intention to go straight to Aubrey. He took a step forward, but was held back by his daed's hand on his shoulder.

"Gott has selected you to minister. Remember what we talked about," Aaron said gravely.

Jamie nodded forcibly. A group of church members gathered around him to talk, but he excused himself as politely as possible. A headache clawed its way across the front of his head. "Excuse me for a moment," he said, slipping away from the group that had gathered around him.

Aubrey remained seated in her chair with a slumbering Grace still in her arms. Elizabeth and Hannah flocked her side, whispering something to her.

When he approached, all three looked up at him. Tears wet Aubrey's eyelashes. The realization of what Gott selected him to do had finally set in.

"Can we go for a walk?" he asked.

"Jah," Aubrey said, clearing her throat. "Do you mind Elizabeth? Hannah?"

"Of course not!" Elizabeth said. She gently took Grace into her arms. "We'll look after the bobli while you two talk. Take your time."

They silently dressed in their winter coats before exiting out into the cold afternoon. Sunlight glinted off the snow packed fields, and the drip of icicles melting filled the quietness around them. It wasn't until they were near the King's barn that their hands found each others' in comfort.

"How are you feeling?" Aubrey asked quietly.

They stopped behind the barn, near the hay bales. It gave them the much needed privacy to process Jamie's new status as a spiritual leader within their community. He didn't want his doubts to be seen by the members of their church.

"I'm a bit confused about why Gott selected me. Everyone else would have been a better decision," he said.

"It is Gott's will. I will support you no matter what."

He drew her into a tight embrace. The smells of vanilla and flour clung to Aubrey's skin from baking earlier that morning. He inhaled the soothing smell with a small smile.

"How are you feeling about it?" he asked, drawing back to watch her expression. "Some fraas cry openly in church."

The corner of Aubrey's lips quirked up into a smile. "It's a gut thing I didn't then, right?" she said, and after they shared a laugh she continued. "I'll admit that I hadn't given much thought to the responsibility of being a minister. I realize now that it will be a difficult path for you, but I can't doubt Gott's will. Neither should you."

"I don't have any doubts about Gott's will. I just think that there are better people than me to minister."

"Like who?"

"My daed. Your daed. Take your pick," he said, shrugging his shoulders. "I don't consider myself a spiritual leader."

Aubrey smiled gently. "You don't see it?"

"Nee, I don't."

"You are so humble to think that you aren't a spiritual leader, but obviously the community and Gott think otherwise."

"But think about it. I've had interactions with a shunned member. I—"

"Shush," Aubrey said, laying a finger across his lips. "You were trying to understand what was going on in our community. You were trying to put it all back together. Plus, you didn't have interactions willingly with Emma. You talked to her because I insisted on talking to her to figure things out. Which we did."

"And you understand that now that I am a minister these interactions won't happen anymore right? The past is in the past."

Sadness glimmered in her pale blue eyes. The freckles peppering Aubrey's cheekbones were vibrant thanks to the paleness of her skin and the white landscape around them. She chewed her bottom lip before answering. "I understand. The past is in the past, and for gut reason. I have already said goodbye to my sister."

They stared out at the snow covered land together. Jamie leaned up against the wooden fence, brushing off snow from the sleeves of his coat. A sudden sense of peace filled him as he looked upon Aubrey standing at his side, with her own eyes taking in the landscape around them.

It will be okay, he told himself. They were on the right path, one that Gott intended for them both. They were both blessed with a healthy bobli, loving families, and a warm community that would now be at peace. While he dreaded the responsibility, Jamie felt determination again. He was selected to lead them back to the path intended by Gott.

He took Aubrey's soft hand in his own. For a moment, he marveled at the feeling of her dainty fingers wrapping around his palm securely. He brought them up for a quick kiss and to blow warm air on them. "It's going to be okay. I can feel it," he told her.

"I know. I can feel it too," she replied. "Speaking of our blessings, we should go back inside to check on Grace. I'm sure she is hungry by now."

They shared a soft kiss before walking back to the King's haus hand in hand. When they reached the front door, Aubrey's hand slipped away from his. They smiled one last time at one another before slipping back into a haus filled with the warmth of laughter, and into the rest of their lives.

Meanwhile, Jamie prayed that nothing would disrupt their lives again.

The End

BONUS STORY – AMISH FREEDOM TO LOVE (THE AMISH ROMANCE SERIES)

❧ CHAPTER 1 ☙

It was a few minutes after five and Emma just could not sleep, so she sat at her window enjoying the cool morning air, humming her favorite song from the singing the night before. She liked it because it sounded like a lullaby.

There was a knock at her door and she knew it would be her father even before she opened it.

"Up so early, dochtah?" Her father's tall form filled her doorway as she hugged him around the waist like a child. He ruffled her hair and took her hand as he stepped into her room.

"Why are you not sleeping?" she asked him, sitting on the ledge of her window and staring out into the morning. A bit of fog in the distance was disappearing as the morning drew nearer and she hoped the day wouldn't be as hot as it had been the day before.

"I heard you humming. You worry your Maemm," her father said both things in the same breath, as if they were one and the same and of equal importance.

"Everything worries Maemm," she said with a smile, trying to avoid the conversation she knew would soon follow.

Her father must have sensed her reluctance to pursue the topic, and instead kissed her atop the head and turned to leave.

"Don't fall out that window," he said and pulled her door closed behind him.

She decided against the humming in case her mother was the next to make a visit to her room. That she could not handle at five in the morning. No doubt she would hear that having a husband would keep her calmly asleep in the wee hours before dawn. She had heard intimations of the same nature from her mother many times before.

Instead she sat in silence, and when the first rays of the sun broke over the tops of the trees, she made a run for it. "Maemm! Daed!" Emma hollered as she passed her parents' door, "I am heading to the orchard now!"

"What? But it's just six in the morning," her mother's sleepy voice responded.

She heard her father mumble something, but didn't tarry to find out exactly what it was. She made her great escape as quickly as her frock would let her. Her mother had taken it upon on herself to impress the importance of marriage upon Emma every chance she got, and the breakfast table at six-thirty every morning was where Emma felt she was held hostage and made to listen to the merits of marrying young. Soon to follow that her mother would lament the fact that all the other girls her age had paired off, so Emma had learned to master the art of what she called constructive avoidance.

"You are out early," said her friend Holly, the slightly overweight redheaded and freckled friend she could always count on from before she could remember. "Avoiding again?" Holly asked in a knowing tone.

"Nee!" Emma responded, feigning incredulity at the thought that she would get up this early to do the kind of chore she abhorred just to avoid her mother.

"Yes! You so are!" Holly laughed and nudged her playfully as they made their way to the apple orchards that were ripe for picking.

It was late spring in the Amish community of Pinecraft, Florida and the first day of the apple harvest. It was the time when fruit trees bore their first fruits of the year and the young and able bodied did the harvesting. Most young adults Emma's age would have preferred to find some other task to do than stretching the muscles of their arms all day picking fruit and hauling it to the community barn, and Emma was one of those young adults. But she had learned that early mornings to the orchard and then mid-afternoons sorting, washing and cutting apples to be shared between the houses was a perfect way to avoid being reminded that she was about the only young woman her age that had not already chosen a mate.

"You know," Holly began, "there are worse things than getting married."

"Yeah?" Emma teasingly asked her friend, who was having a bit of a problem balancing on the step ladder she had chosen. "Like what?"

Holly hesitated and someone chose that moment to accidentally brush her ladder. As Emma watched helplessly as her friend fell the short distance to the ground, narrowly missing her basket of apples, she knew exactly what the response was going to be before it came.

"Like being me," Holly giggled with embarrassment.

Emma giggled, "You are just about as awesome as women get; any man would be lucky to have you." She descended her ladder to help her slightly clumsy friend, and brushed away the dried leaves that clung to her dress.

Holly had always been clumsy, while Emma was agile and quick on her feet. For Emma, this made them perfect friends and she even admired Holly for the way she had come to own and strut the woman she had become.

"You girls alright?" Alan, the preacher's son, came over to ask them. His eyes fixed on Emma's heart-shaped face framed by the black hair that lightly blew in the cool morning breeze.

"Jah," Holly responded. "I just tripped over myself."

Even though Holly had spoken, Alan's eyes did not leave Emma's face, and Emma felt like the look from his grey eyes invaded her personal space, so she turned her head away.

"Be careful," Alan said as he finally looked at Holly seconds later and smiled at her before slowly jogging back to the tree he had been picking from.

A few moments passed in silence between the girls as Emma couldn't help but follow the disappearing ginger hair bobbing on Alan's head. She also noted what must be toned legs jogged him back to his task.

"Oh, you fancy him!" Holly piped up, and Emma's attention was once again drawn to the happy grin on Holly's face, smiling as the chip on her front tooth was on full display.

"No, I don't," Emma responded and again climbed her ladder, busying herself with the picking.

Holly did not bother to follow her lead. "Well, he sure fancies you," Holly commented.

Emma followed Holly's suggestive gaze to where Alan was perched on one of the topmost branches of his tree, biting away at an apple and eyeing Emma with intense curiosity. Again Emma quickly averted her gaze. She had been known to be confident, and was a bit disconcerted that Alan's piercing gaze could throw her off.

"I think you both would make me some pretty babies to spoil," Holly said from below, where she had taken to sitting with her back pressed against the trunk of the tree, eating an apple.

"We would have to get married first," Emma replied. "And he is just not my type."

"You won't ever know what your type is since you won't go out with any of the men who have shown an interest." Holly pointed out, and though Emma hated to acknowledge it, she knew Holly was right. "What are you afraid of anyway?"

Emma thought about that question for a moment and realized that it was the first time she had been asked. It was the first time she had also thought that maybe fear was what was holding her back, but fear of what?

"I don't know," she whispered pensively to Holly, as

her eyes were once again drawn to where Alan had been. This time his back was turned to her and his sleeves rolled up as the early morning Floridian sun was making its presence known. She watched the way his shoulders rippled beneath his quaint clothing and admired the way the sun reflected off his ginger hair. He was a catch by physical definition, but it took much more than that to make a happy home.

"So you are afraid of something," Holly gently called up to her, and Emma recognized the concern in her friend's voice. She knew that Holly, who had the calming powers of empathy, would now urge her to analyze the fear and do something about it. She had learned long ago that when Holly urged you to do something, you should do it, because she was always right in the end.

Emma descended, deciding to have their conversation in hushed tones instead of letting the morning wind carry it to the keen ears around them. She had grown up feeling nothing but loved and supported from her small community and her peers, but she had found that the less people knew what was going on with you, the less pitying looks you would get.

"I think I am afraid of choosing the wrong person and not being happy," Emma said as she sat beside Holly, who handed her an apple. Until then she had forgotten that she had dashed out before her mother's scrumptious breakfast.

"Well, that is why you court first," Holly reminded her with a gentle rub on her back.

Just then their one-on-one was interrupted by the stampeding feet of Bret and his cousins. They came rushing into the orchard like a group of elephants strung out on the sheer joy of being alive.

"Hey Emma!" Bret nearly fell over himself trying to stop in front of her. He had inherited his father's urbane good looks and his mother's bright green eyes and playful nature. Emma remembered when they were children how his mother used to make time during the day to chase them around for a few minutes of play. His mother was a stark contrast to her more reserved mother.

Emma had never considered her mother to be stoic and prim; she understood that she was simply reserved. Even though her mother had never missed the opportunity to share a playful moment with her only child, she was just not the mother to go chasing her across the backyard. After all, she was a school teacher, and the community had come to expect a certain decorum from their educators.

As for Emma, she had not only inherited her mother's reserved ways, but also her father's extroversion, and it had made for a very interesting combination growing up. It was a combination that found Bret's playfulness a bit refreshing.

"What about him?" Holly asked, as if reading her mind.

"I do fancy him, but I worry he might never grow up." Emma finished her statement as she watched Bret haul the basket of apples she and Holly had just relieved the tree of back to the community barn, where they would sort them in another couple of hours.

She turned her attention back to where Holly stood

smiling sweetly at her, her chipped tooth complimenting the mischief in her eyes.

"I say you have more than enough choices. The preacher's son, who clearly has an eye for you? Or daring Bret, who just might never grow up?" Holly changed her voice to a more ominous tone. "Who will you choose?"

They laughed and finished their apples as Emma took Holly's words into consideration. She was at a point in her life where she longed for a connection of a more intimate nature, and she knew she wanted a bobli of her own. She also knew that whatever fear she had of relationships would have to be done away with if she was ever going to achieve her dream.

The day flowed by easily and Emma enjoyed the work that took her mind off what was going on around her, but as she sat at the dinner table that night, her mother started in.

Holly, who had stayed over for dinner, tried to ease Emma's discomfort and embarrassment. "She has two suitors, Mrs. Mason," Holly said, to the older woman's delight. "She just didn't want to say anything until she chose one."

Emma knew that Holly meant well, but while that got her mother smiling with hope, the questions would no longer be whether she had a possible male companion, but whether she had chosen one of the two. It got her mother to stop talking about her love life long enough for them to appear normal again, and Emma made a note to thank Holly a bit later.

As Emma walked Holly to the door, they sat as they

usually did when she was there and sighed in unison. The late spring breeze played at the hem of their dresses as they stared out into the night, looking at nothing in particular. It had been another Saturday, but it had felt different to Emma. She couldn't quite put her finger on it.

Maybe it was the fact that she had decided she actually liked someone and that decision meant she would soon no longer be a single woman.

"So are you going to pick one already?" Holly nudged her playfully and she screwed up her face in disdain. Holly was slowly turning into Emma's mother. "Which one though?"

"Well, I think you know which one," Holly said, and Emma took her hands into hers. They had been best friends since the day Emma had accidentally shoved Holly over on their last day of school.

Emma remembered how eager she had been to get home to help make noodles, and that she had all but ran over Holly in an effort not to miss the house chore she enjoyed the most. Seven-year-old Holly had had the greatest misfortune of standing between her and her great escape. But as Holly, who had always been a bit on the plump side, had started howling, with blood running from her mouth from where she had fallen, Emma had stopped and turned back. It turned out that she had caused Holly to chip her newly grown front tooth, and they had been best friends ever since.

Emma sighed. "But he is so serious," she said, referring to the preacher's son.

Holly knew her parents would never approve of Bret

if they knew the preacher's son was an option, so even though she was hesitant, she knew that was the choice she would make if he ever asked her out.

There was to be a wedding the following day, and she would see what happened then.

❧ CHAPTER 2 ❧

"Emma, come on!" Holly called to her impatiently.

Weddings were always a big celebration in the community and Emma had wanted to get there early, but her mother had volunteered to make her famous apple almond pie for the reception and Emma naturally had to help. She really didn't mind it actually, but today was the worst day to be stuck with her mother. A wedding was not hers, but of another young woman her own age, and all her mother could talk about was how when Emma eventually decided to get married there would be lots of apple pies and they would make her favorite truffle cookies. Then came the questions of who her choices were and when was she going to start dating.

Emma picked up the hem of her frock and lightly jogged down the stairs to meet Holly. "The oven was really slow today."

Holly laughed, understanding Emma's reference, and pulled her friend toward where the community had gathered for the celebration. It was a beautiful Tuesday afternoon and the birds chirped all around in joyous coordination with the merry-makings. They sat with the other young people close to the back, waiting on Mary-Ann, the bride, and Paul, the groom. Everyone had known they would get married; they had been dating for a long time.

Emma's eyes wandered the crowd and fell on the parents of the soon-to-be married couple, brimming with joy, and she hoped she would soon make her mother that happy too.

CRBSO

Alan sat at the back of the lot in his Sunday wear, gazing at Emma. He had always admired her, but hadn't quite known how to say it.

"Are you going to go talk to her?" His friend Jason asked from beside him. Alan wouldn't call him a friend, he didn't have many friends, but Jason lived right next door and worked in the stable with him on most days, so they'd had the opportunity of connecting. Plus Alan liked him because he didn't talk too much.

"Jah," he responded to the question, admiring the way the sun danced on her face. He didn't think she was like other girls; she was calmer and her mother was the school teacher, which meant his parents would approve.

"Do you think your parents will approve?" Jason asked. He might not talk much, but he did ask many questions. Jason was just sixteen to Alan's twenty-three, but Alan found him to be mature for his age. The question he had just asked was a valid one.

"Maemm, yes," Alan answered, knowing his mother had taken a liking to Emma. His mother and her mother had been friends when they were younger, but the preacher's wife hardly had time to keep up with friendships between the household of seven that she ran and the duties of the preacher's wife; his mother had hardly found time for herself. But in the few moments she found each day to bond with her oldest son, the question would often come up as to whether or not he liked Emma.

Alan sighed as the rows filled up with people and his father walked down the middle to take his place at the front, where he would officiate the wedding.

"That will be you someday," Jason again piped up, and Alan did nothing but grunt in response.

Very few people knew he had no intentions of becoming a preacher. It was customary in their community that the eldest son from the preacher's family would be trained to lead the community eventually, but Jason had other plans for his life.

The Amish way was the only way of life he saw for himself, but he wanted to be a regular man with the mundane duties that came along with that position. He had always had to bear the burden of being the oldest child, where he was to be the example of all that was good and right. He was tired of that.

He wanted to get baptized, marry the girl of his dreams and live a long boring life where he was not expected to do anything other than be there for his family. He had broached this topic once with his father and the conversation had not gone as planned.

Music began and people stood as the groom entered, and then not far behind him came Mary-Ann, dressed in her traditional blue dress.

Jason muttered his approval and then said, "She's pretty, but Emma will be prettier."

Alan smiled at his subliminal nudging. Jason was worse than his mother, but he happened to agree on that point. Across the way he looked at Emma and Holly, holding hands in pure joy at the spectacle that took place before them. He decided he would ask her out that evening at the reception.

The decision made him nervous, and he hoped his Daed would approve of his choice. Alan knew that for his father he was supposed to be a flawless work of art, and he had been a good son, but he knew he was getting older and Emma was the girl he had a strong pull to marry.

CX&O

As the wedding continued, Emma was oblivious to the eyes that frequently checked to see how she was doing. She was completely caught up in the proceedings, taking in every detail so she would be ready for her big day, and as the wedding came to an end an hour later she had tears in her eyes at how wonderful happy ever after appeared.

"Here it comes," Holly teased as the tears spilled down her face. Holly tried hard to hide her laughter and Emma playfully shoved her.

"Weddings are so sweet," Emma said in her own

defense, giggling with her friend.

"You know you will cry on your wedding day right?"

Emma thought about it for a moment and realized it was highly possible she would be the bride crying from start to finish. She just hoped that would not scare her husband away.

They followed the crowd out to the large oak trees beneath which the reception was to be held and her mother beckoned her to come help with the food. She and Holly willingly took their parents' places, allowing the adults to go congratulate the newlyweds, and to her surprise Alan came to stand beside her.

"Hello," he said, and she lost the ability to speak for a second.

His ginger hair cut into a boyish crop framed his skinny face and highlighted his eyes, and she could see a hint of doubt flash there. Behind her, Holly nudged her and the words came out.

"Hello Alan, how goes the day?" She immediately repeated the words in her head and gave herself a mental slap. She wasn't sure what kind of introduction it was, but Alan didn't seem to mind too much.

"Nice wedding," he took the plate she handed him and placed some food on it for the woman in front of him.

Emma's parents were next in line, and as the singing began Emma saw the twinkle in her mother's eye.

"I was wondering if you would like to hang out with me sometime?" Alan asked just as her mother was about to be served.

Emma froze again. She had no idea why his question

surprised her, because she had long expected it. She felt like a complete klutz; all the confidence she was known for went out the window. Thank God Holly was there, and as Holly nudged her again she found her words, but she waited.

Her mother stood before her, passing questioning glances between her and Alan, but Emma did not think it the time or place to have that conversation. Her father knowingly smiled behind her and Emma was grateful that he was there.

Emma's mother kissed her on the cheek before walking off. "Be sure to get something to eat, and you kids should come sit with us when you are ready." Her mother directed the last bit of her sentence to Alan, who smiled and agreed.

"So will you?" Alan prodded when her parents were out of earshot.

"Okay," Emma smiled back at him, and to her surprise, a smile spread across his face. She didn't think she had ever seen him smile before, but she thought his smile was a beautiful one.

Then she saw him look past her and his expression changed. Following his line of sight, she saw his parents approaching, and he quickly turned away from her and busied himself serving the other people who walked by. When his father stood before him, Emma watched as Alan's shoulders tensed and he seemed to become a whole other person.

"Hello Emma." His mother smiled pleasantly at her and his father inclined his head to say hello. "Holly!" the woman continued cheerfully, reaching across the table to give Holly a hug. Emma did not feel offended by the difference in greetings; Holly was always the forward bubbly one and everyone knew her in the community for the hugs she always gave. Emma had been raised to be more conservative in her actions toward others, but that did not make her impersonal, and the community understood her like they understood her mother.

"Daed," Alan spoke up, looking his father in the eye. "I will be coming home late today; Emma and I are going to meet after the reception."

His father looked between the two young people and then gave his nod of approval.

"Wunderbaar!" his mother exclaimed in delight and gave him a kiss before she walked away.

As soon as it was clear that his parents were not going to coming back, she saw Alan relax and the smile he had given her earlier returned to his face.

She hoped Holly had seen it do that so when she mentioned it later it would not seem like she had up and gone crazy. It made her wonder what might have been going on with Alan.

I guess I will find out, she thought to herself as they served the last of the folks, made their plates and headed toward her parents. Alan stopped short, as there was no space for them there.

"We can go sit by my tree," he said to the girls and gestured toward the tree that young Jason was sitting beneath, waving frantically for them to join him. Holly was the first to head in that direction and Alan took Emma's plate so she could lift her dress to walk across the grass. When she was seated comfortably with her back against the tree, watching as a few people got up to dance, she ate slowly and took Alan in.

Holly had been right; they would make some pretty boblis. But she had a feeling there was a whole lot more going on with Alan than he was really letting on, so she would wait to see.

❦ CHAPTER 3 ❧

As the wedding festivities died down and people trickled away in groups, Emma and Holly stayed behind to help with the cleanup. Emma could feel Alan's eyes watching her every move, but she didn't feel uncomfortable; strangely enough, it made her feel all warm and cuddly inside. She could feel her tummy doing somersaults every time their eyes met and he smiled at her.

"Hey Emma!" Bret said in front of her. She was startled out of her inner ruminations by his strong voice and he always just seemed to pop up out of nowhere. His jovialness was contagious and she smiled back at him.

"Hello, I haven't seen you all day. How are you?"

He smiled back at her, no doubt pleased that she had noticed his absence, but then a flash of uncertainty ran across his face and Emma looked at his clothes and realized he had indeed been at the wedding. She saw that he must have been wondering how it was that she hadn't seen him and she changed the conversation before it might have taken that turn.

"How is your mom?" she asked, honestly concerned. His mother had been sick for a few weeks and despite their best efforts, the community doctors could do nothing about it.

"Better," he said, and the smile returned to his face. "She got up and walked around today, but she couldn't manage to come to the wedding, and you know how she hates missing weddings," Bret responded and rolled his eyes.

His mother had always been a woman on the go and full of energy, so Emma could only imagine just how much it must have made her sad that she was too sick to move about, but she was honestly happy that she was okay.

As the early evening breeze picked up, Bret looked at her as if he was about to say something important.

"Hey Emma, I was wondering if you wanted to hang out after we are all done cleaning up?" he asked her shyly.

She looked up at him in surprise and then at Alan, who had been near enough to hear the invitation- his face turning serious the moment Bret finished. Holly chuckled behind her, finding the situation funny.

"Ahh-ahhmm," Emma stuttered, feeling a little under pressure and awkward at the moment. For a second she thought about telling Bret that he could hang out with her and Alan, but knew that would be inappropriate and even more awkward, so she answered the only way she could.

"I am sorry Bret, but I already agreed with Alan that I would hang with him when we were done here."

She watched the happiness drain from Bret's face, leaving a smile she knew remained out of respect and courtesy.

"Okay," he said and took the garbage bag they had loaded. "Maybe some other time."

Emma was about to respond, but Bret didn't wait around. He simply walked away, his shoulders sagging under the weight of his disappointment.

"Are you sure you are making the right choice?" Holly asked, coming to stand beside her. Emma looked between Alan, who had gone back to raking the small pieces of garbage no doubt dropped by the children into a pile, and Bret's disappearing shoulders.

"I hope so," Emma responded. In all fairness she liked both boys, but Alan had asked first and so she would see if he was the kind of man she wanted to spend the rest of her life with. If he was, then she would make it work. If he wasn't and Bret was still available, she would go that route.

"I feel like I am back in the orchard deciding which apple to pick," she said to Holly as the finished up and sat at the table, waiting for the boys to come collect them.

Jason squealed to their right and ran away from Alan, who chased after him with the rake he had been using. The girls looked on and smiled, because Jason had likely perplexed Alan into action. Emma had been watching the two boys and found they were no different from normal brothers who gave each other trouble. She knew Jason didn't have any siblings, and she thought it sweet of Alan that he would actually take time to hang out with the teenager. If teenage boys were anything like the teenage girls they had been, she knew that could not be easy.

CR£O

As the sun dipped low in the sky, Alan washed himself at the pipe on the outside of the common area and patted his face dry with his handkerchief. He was a bit nervous about Emma because he could see the look she gave him. It was kind and gentle, but a host of expectations wavered below it.

He couldn't blame her, after all he was the preacher's son. The real question was whether or not she would be disappointed after she had met him more personally. He would take it slow at first.

He offered her his hand and she hopped down from the table she had been perched upon, in deep conversation with her friend Holly.

"See you tomorrow." He watched Emma give Holly a kiss on the cheek and they made their way to the edge of the river close by. There were still quite a few others around with the same idea, but Alan knew he didn't quite fit in with the general populace. Mostly because they would all go silent the minute he walked up. By virtue of his parentage, he had always been the outcast.

He really couldn't blame them; during rumspringa he remembered his mother explaining it to him:

"You are the son of a preacher who will one day be the preacher. Your friends will not want to speak about or do the things they want to do at that age when you are around."

"But I won't say anything," he had said, dejected and

feeling like he was on the outside looking in at all the fun.

His mother had smiled at him and given him a kiss. "I know, but they don't, and it is just one of those things you have to live with."

"So Alan, how come I never see you hanging out with anybody except Jason?" Emma asked him as if reading his mind. He wasn't sure if he should give her the long or the short explanation, so he just answered how he usually did.

"Growing up, all the other kids got silent as soon as I stepped into a room. It's like they felt like everything they would say I would take back to my Daed, so I learned to grow up alone."

Emma chuckled a little at that and he found he liked the sound. It wasn't like the loud laugh his sisters would give. It was a soft and feminine sound, full of composure. He found himself wondering if she ever just let go and had fun sometimes.

"But what about your siblings? Sometimes I wish I wasn't an only child."

As she said that, they reached the edge of the river and she took her shoes off to lower her legs into the water. The grassy banks provided cushiony seats and he followed her lead. Around them in the clearing, conversations carried on, and they could hear the groups of boys talking about all forms of madness that intrigued them.

"Be happy that you are an only child," he said to her, splashing the water with his feet. "You get all your parents' attention and love and none of the fussing and fighting with your siblings for every little thing. And my younger brothers would probably tell you that you didn't have to wear hand-me-down clothes."

Emma laughed and agreed. "But then the big disadvantage of being an only child is that all your parents' hopes and dreams are invested in you and you dare not disappoint."

"That also happens if you are the firstborn, so maybe what you should wish for is to be born second in a family of two. That would be your perfect place."

They mumbled their agreements and the conversation flowed effortlessly from there. Alan listened to every word coming out of Emma's mouth. They talked about food, the summer, rumspringa and her desire to become a full-time teacher.

He listened and listened, all the while becoming more engrossed in the beautiful woman who sat beside him. He could tell she would make a perfect wife.

"So are you looking forward to becoming a preacher?" she asked about an hour into their conversation.

He didn't want to answer that the first time they hung out because he really did not want to scare her off. But avoiding the question would just make her suspicious, so he decided to answer once again with the same diplomatic correctness he had chosen before.

"I haven't decided whether I want to be a preacher or just a regular boring old man," he said with a smile, but the look on her face told him that she had not missed the sadness in his voice.

He also knew Emma was smart enough to read between the lines.

"That sounds like you have already decided," she said to him.

He looked back at her and knew his answer was clearly written on his face, and a little bit of joy slipped from hers.

"I just know there are so many more things I would be good at--many more active and fulfilling things. As a preacher I would be bound to know only one life, and do you see how alienated my father is? People hold him in such high regard that they forget he is also human. I don't want to live like that."

He looked at the shocked look on Emma's face, unsure if his mini-rant had pushed her away from him. But then she smiled and he knew she wasn't about to hang him in the town square by his thumbs.

"Just try talking to them about it. There have been exceptions in the past, maybe one can be made for you."

Alan didn't bother telling her that he had already tried that. He left the conversation there as he walked her home for the night. It wasn't that he didn't trust her with his thoughts and situation, it's just that he had learned not to pile it on too heavy.

"Let's hang out on Sunday?" he asked. She nodded as he waited until she was safely inside and then walked away.

He had finally taken the plunge, and now he was sure that she was exactly the kind of woman he needed in his life. Hopefully his father would see that he could be just as good a contribution to the community without being its preacher.

He would have to wait and see, because he had all intentions of speaking to his family before Sunday, when he would see Emma again.

C**R** CHAPTER 4 **S**O

Emma was in a pensive mood the following day as she headed to the orchard. She came out a bit later not in any particular mood to face her mother, who had slept a little late. He father had seen her thoughtful scowl and had questioned what was wrong, but she was not too sure.

"Emma! Over here!" Holly called to her. Holly was never late for anything, including chores, and Emma admired that about her. But today she was not alone. Her younger sister, who was a bit of a talker, was helping Holly pick apples. It would be the last day of the harvest of the first fruits from the tree, and the orchard was a bit scanty.

"How did it go?" Holly asked her excitedly. Emma was sure that if Holly bubbled any more with excitement, she would bubble herself right off the stepladder and break a limb or two.

"How did what go, Emma?" Holly's sister asked as she approached. The young girl was but fourteen and Emma didn't think the conversation would be appropriate for her age, so she only smiled.

"I had a fun time with a friend," Emma said and glanced knowingly at Holly, who took the hint well and sent her sister to the barn with the basket of apples she had already picked.

Holly climbed down from the ladder and looked at Emma with concern. "So how did it go?"

"I am not sure," Emma replied honestly. Holly hugged her and they sat in the grass, with the cool morning breeze blowing around them.

"Tell me," Holly urged.

"Well, when we were at the wedding I saw how his persona changed every time his father came close, and I was wondering if it's just me or there was something else going on there."

Holly handed her an apple and she took a bite, pondering on the things she was about to tell her while she chewed.

"I heard my sister saying that his father has been really hard on him," Holly said.

Emma smiled inwardly, knowing Holly's big family was tapped into all forms of gossip happening around the community. Holly wasn't much like her other sisters. She kept pretty much to herself, but living in a house like that was sure to keep you up to date on all that was happening in the community, so she knew there was truth to the comment.

"Well, turns out he doesn't want to be preacher, so there might be a bit of conflict there."

"Oh, that's not a bit of conflict," Holly said sadly, "that's a lot of conflict. What is he going to do?"

Emma shrugged her shoulders, hoping he could resolve it with his family. She had not had much interaction with the preacher's family, because like Alan had rightly said, they were treated differently in the community. They were held on a pedestal and if you fell from grace then you fell hard. But she was happy that it was not a case where Alan had wanted to leave the community. She would have been deeply saddened by that.

The rest of the day passed quickly with them thinking up possible situations to get Alan out of his bind.

"You could elope to the community down the road," Holly suggested, and they laughed.

"That would not be considered eloping; that would be disobeying our parents and running away. You would have to shun me for that," Emma reminded Holly.

"Oh yes, well it's settled. Poor Alan must become a preacher."

Emma appreciated Holly's ability to make her feel better, and though they were not making light of the situation, she didn't know what else to think.

She lifted her head from the slicing of apples, the assigned task for the afternoon, to see Bret heading toward her. When he saw her, he immediately froze in his tracks and turned back.

Holly sighed beside her, ever the observant one. "I think you need to fix that one before it get any worse."

Emma knew she was right, because Bret had indeed been one of their closest friends and she would hate to lose his friendship because she had bruised his ego. She decided that she would speak to him the following day.

ର୍ଷ୍ଠ

Alan's week slipped by slowly, and he figured it was probably because he was looking forward to spending time with Emma again. He had caught glimpses of her throughout the week, but his chores for that week had been making house visits with his father and working the stables.

He had managed to deliver a bouquet and an apple pie his mother had made her family, and they had spoken for a short while. He smiled at the memory of it; he really liked her. Her calm, soft spoken personality and relaxed, fluid way of moving put his troubled mind at peace and he could see himself waking up to that every day for the rest of his life.

His mother had openly accepted his choice of a date, though that did not mean they were getting married, but his father had been somewhat hesitant. His choice had been someone else, but as Alan had the right to choose his own partner, his father had reluctantly given his blessing.

It was just another thing to drive a wedge between them, but Alan refused to let it bring him down.

As he made his way back home, smelling like the stables and dying for a shower, he thought of the conversation he would have at the table that night. It was time he stopped arguing with his parents and started talking to his family about his choice.

The house was in relative silence as he made his way in, everyone no doubt in their rooms getting ready for dinner. He could hear his sisters playfully taunting each other as they usually did, and the silence coming from his younger brothers' rooms told him they were either sleeping or reading. In his family, the girls were the ones who inherited all the mischievous genes.

They would play pranks on just about anyone that would let them get away with it, but even their mother was not spared. He knew they stayed away from their father, because his very serious persona spoke of the love he had for them all, but it did not hint at any consideration for their childish games. It wasn't that he wasn't fun to be around, because Alan remembered his life as a child as one where his father always made time for his children. He was just not the father to go gallivanting behind them.

He washed up quickly as he heard the family moving downstairs, and as they sat at the table he allowed time for the mundane happenings of the day to be discussed before he brought up the heavy stuff.

"Daed," he said as the table went silent. His four other siblings usually went silent when he spoke. He was not yet sure if that was out of respect for him or the fact that he usually angered his father of late, so they were silently waiting for it. "I have something to tell all of you, and I know you will not want to hear it, but it must be said."

His father looked at him sternly as his mother put her hand over his. He used to sit beside his father, but recent disagreements had caused him to change his seat because he could not be bothered with the angry stares he would get.

All his life he had known that his community was one

that avoided conflicts. Theirs was a way of life that promoted humility and peaceful resolution, but his father could not meet him halfway.

"This is not the time for this, son," he father said, resting his fork on the side of his plate.

Alan sighed. "Yes, Father, it is, because I want to discuss this as a family."

As he waited for his father's approval to speak, he thought of what he would say, and he really was hesitant. When his father nodded, he simply spoke from the heart like he always had. His father gave a curt nod and all eating stopped as he spoke.

"I will not be a preacher. I have decided tha-," his words were cut short by his father.

"That is not your decision to make. It has already been decided; you simply need to settle on a spouse."

Alan resented the way his father spoke about settling on a spouse. One did not simply go the market and choose one, but he did not say what he was thinking. He instead carried on with what he had been about to say.

"Father, I have decided and I will not change my mind. Wouldn't you rather select someone else for the task; someone who would enjoy it?"

He casted a knowing glance at his brother, Peter. His younger brother had always had a passion for church and would make a better preacher. To confirm his thoughts, Peter smiled at him from across the table.

"I will do it, Daed!" Peter piped up eagerly. Alan had known Peter wanted to for years, but he had waited patiently in the background while his father demanded

Alan do something he did not want to do.

"I have already spoken. Alan you will become pastor."

"No, Daed," Alan said, getting up from the table. "I would rather be an Englischer than a pastor, so if you cannot accept that, then I think I will leave."

A gasp went up around the table, and Alan could see his father's face drain of any color. He knew his words saddened his family, but it was simply what it was. He excused himself from the table and went for a walk in the evening air, soon finding himself outside of Emma's house.

He already knew he wanted her, and now his subconscious had pointed at the same thing. The thought that he might have to leave her behind made him sad.

He hoped that when he told her he might leave, she would not think him bad for walking away from the community.

⟡ CHAPTER 5 ⟡

It was late evening, and Emma felt none of the exhaustion she had felt the earlier that day. She took a shower and lay staring at her ceiling. She wasn't quite sure what she was thinking of, but knew that her mind was busy at work.

When she could finally get it to slow down, it went to the lecture that Holly had given her earlier that day. It had been a lecture about love. She had finally mustered up the courage to speak to Holly about the issues Alan faced with his family and the impossible choice he would have to make sooner or later.

"So you chose the wrong one then?" Holly had asked, trying to make her smile, but it hadn't worked.

Emma had known from the first date she'd had with Alan that she liked him much more than just seeing where this would go. She had felt a strong connection to him and his willingness to show her his vulnerable side, despite the stone-coldness everybody else thought he had, was even more endearing.

For the week they had been dating, she'd looked forward to his visits, and smiled as she caught glimpses of him going about his daily chores. Now as she sat staring at her ceiling she couldn't help but smile at the thought of him.

He was definitely not the wrong one, but would his life allow them the chance to build on what she knew they could have?

That was the question of the century.

She bolted upright at the sound of something tapping against her window. At first she thought it was just another night owl with poor vision. They had been seeing quite a few of those around lately, but then it came again, and she rushed to her window and looked out.

Below stood Alan, staring up at her with a sad smile on his face and a small bouquet of flowers in his hand. As much as she wanted to just rush out to him, she knew she had to first get permission to do so.

"Maemm, Daed?" She rapped gently at their door.

"Are you okay?" Her mother came rushing over to the door with worry on her face, looking Emma up and down to see if there was any sign of something wrong. She couldn't blame her mother. In the years she had been alive and well, the only time she bothered her parents after they had gone to bed was if she was sick, and being the only child, her mother's mind always rushed to the worst case scenario.

"Jah!" Emma answered with a smile as her father came to stand behind her Mom. "Alan is outside, can I go see him?"

"Is he alright?" her mother asked, a look of confusion on her face.

Emma wanted to say she was not sure, which would in fact be the honest thing to say, but she did not want to worry her parents, so she smiled and nodded. "I think so," she answered.

Emma's mother smiled at what that could possibly mean. For Emma, his presence meant maybe something had gone wrong, since he had said he would be speaking to his parents that night, or maybe it had gone well. For her mother, it meant that the two were young and in love, and therefore could not stay away from each other.

For her father, it was a strange look of over-protectiveness that flashed across his face.

"Can I go?" Emma asked again eagerly. Her mother looked toward her father for a response, and when he nodded Emma rushed back to her room and threw on her day clothes. As she passed her parents' door again, she could hear her mother speculating about when she would tie the knot with Alan, and her father erring on the side of caution.

As she slowly stepped down the stairs to the waiting area, she thought about her father. She had never been able to hide anything from him when she was growing up, and the look he had given her over her mother's head said he knew something was not quite alright.

"Hi!" She smiled at Alan, who had made his way to her front steps and sat waiting patiently on her.

He stood as she walked to him and he handed her the makeshift bouquet he had picked along the way. She could see a strange sadness in his eyes, and she knew it was the worst that had happened.

"I tried Emma," he said, "but my Daed would not listen."

They sat in silence, each trying to understand what this would mean for their young relationship, but not wanting to say it out loud. Alan took her hand in his as they sat there and she rested her head against his shoulder.

"I told him that if I couldn't be what I wanted to be, I would leave," Alan whispered to her.

Her heart stopped beating for a second or two and she turn her head to look in his eyes. She had figured that would have been a possibility before, but she had never thought it would have come down to it.

What did this mean for them?

In that moment, she remembered Holly's question about whether she had chosen the wrong one or not. She was confident she had not, but she felt like she was on the verge of losing him before they could even begin. "You can't go," she managed, barely above a whisper.

Her eyes were welling up with tears at the thought of him leaving and she fought hard to hold them back. Alan said nothing to her as his eyes apologized for the fear she now felt and the high possibility that he would break her heart.

"I have to go," he said to Emma, squeezing her hand one last time. He waited until she was safely inside and then walked back home.

Emma knew he must be dreading the tension that would now be in his house, but regardless, this was home and he had nowhere else to go at the moment.

"Is everything okay?" her father asked when he saw her shoulders hanging low as she walked back into the house.

Emma had figured her parents would not go back to sleep until she was tucked away safely in her bed, but she had not thought her father would come down to wait for her. He stood before her, looked at the tears welling up in her eyes and pulled her in for a hug.

"He might leave, Daed," she whispered into his night shirt.

"Then he would be missing out on a lifetime of happiness with you. Don't cry; if he does leave, it will be his loss."

She smiled into her father's chest as he walked her back up the stairs and to bed, tucking her in as he had a million times since she was a child.

ᏣᏖᎦ

The merry birds did nothing to lighten her mood the following day, and she hoped for a sign of Alan, but she heard whispers that he had gone with his father to a neighboring town and would be back for the sermon that evening.

She missed him. Even though he had not left for good, she missed knowing he was close by. If this was how it would be if he left, she was not sure she would survive.

"He will be back," Holly said to her as they helped with the children that day. She had filled Holly in on what could possibly happen if he decided to leave, and she knew her friend was just trying to make her feel better, but it wasn't working.

"I think I like someone," Holly said, and that got Emma's attention. She stared at her freckle-faced friend and waited for her to identify the object of her attention.

"So?" She nudged Holly playfully moments later, when she remained silent.

Holly didn't answer, but Emma's eyes followed her gaze to where Jason lay beneath the tree in the yard, chewing on a grass stem and staring up into the leaves of the tree. He had been going about all day and likely needed a rest.

Emma found Holly's liking of him a bit strange, but said nothing to that effect. It wasn't just that he was five years her junior, because when it came to their community, as long as the two were of consenting ages their relationship would not be frowned upon. However, Holly was a much bubblier, empathetic type and Jason did not seem to have grown out of his childish stage of puberty just yet. He ran around all day being helpful and Emma had yet to hear someone complain about him. However, she was not sure how the two would mesh.

"Does he know?" she asked Holly, who was gazing starry-eyed at the teenager who laid beneath the tree, no doubt about to fall asleep.

"No," came Holly's short response and Emma didn't push it. She was really in no position to lecture anyone or give any opinions on the matter of love these days.

"Hey!" Bret called to them from a few meters away.

Emma smiled at him, but he did not return her smile. It was clear his salutation was more out of respect and courtesy than a desire to say hello. She once again felt sad, but she was not about to let Bret walk away again.

She jogged over to where he was standing, looking out at the orchard lost in thought.

"You don't get to just pretend we are not friends anymore," she said to Bret, who turned to look at her in shock. It was clear that he had not been expecting her to approach him, but she was tired of the way he was acting. He had not said anything but "hi" and "hello" to her since the day she had chosen to go out with Alan.

"He asked me first, Bret, and I really like him," she tried to explain to him. She had missed his playfulness and was hoping they could get past this awkwardness.

"Oh," was all he said, and turned back to the orchard.

There was a light thunder rumbling overhead and she lifted her face to look at the rain clouds hanging over them. The weather was mirroring the storm in her soul.

"I didn't know you were into him," Bret said finally. "He doesn't seem like your type."

"I have a type?" she asked him, a bit confused as she stepped up beside him.

He turned and smiled at her, a mischievous twinkle in his eyes. "Yeah, it was supposed to be me."

She laughed at that and then earnestly looked him in the eyes. "You will always be one of my best friends and it doesn't have to change, even though we aren't dating."

He didn't respond with much more than a simple nudge to her shoulder, and she understood that was his way of telling her he was cool with her choice now.

"So how is it going?" he asked her. "Before you answer, please know I am hoping that he is horrible and you are not enjoying a single moment with him."

She laughed at how happy she was that he was finally getting back to himself, but even then she could not tell him what he wanted to know, because it was truly a wonderful thing, except for the elephant in the room.

"It's lovely," she said, not wanting to give him any reason to question further and wanting a bit of distraction from the doom and gloom that now surrounded her budding relationship.

He looked at her again and smiled, and she realized just how sweet a smile he truly had, but his eyes changed as he looked behind her to where Alan was walking toward her.

"Talk to you later," Bret said, and walked away. He nodded at Alan as they passed each other and Emma's heart skipped a beat at the sight of the smile Alan gave her.

"Hello," he said and pulled a flower from behind him, sticking it beneath her bonnet and behind her ear. He held his palm out and she took his hand, and walked toward Holly. Jason screamed and ran toward Alan from behind, roughly throwing him to the ground, and the girls watched in amusement as they rolled around trying to top each other.

By the time Alan was able to pin Jason, they were both huffing, out of breath, with bits of grass sticking out of their hair and Emma knew that Alan would truly miss his life here if he were forced to leave.

They exchanged a knowing glance before he got up and righted himself once again. And in that moment she knew that what she felt for him was love.

❦ CHAPTER 6 ❧

Alan walked into his house that evening and the feeling of dread was enough to make him pause at the door. When he pushed the door open, he realized it was not an unfounded dread, because his entire family sat in the family room, waiting on him to make his entrance.

"Daed?" he said to his father questioningly, knowing the only time a gathering of this nature was called was if his father had called it as some form of intervention.

"We need to talk, son," were his father's only words, resonating within him to the bone. His father motioned to the seat in front of him and Alan sat without hesitation. He knew he was in no position to argue because whatever he would say would just make the situation worse.

"Alan," his mother started, and he realized they had changed the strategy. It usually would have been his father who started with the stern talking, leaving no room for interjections or objections. It would be his way or the highway. Then, when all hopes and dreams had been crushed, his mother's soft voice would come in to calm the battle and convince them all that what Father said was the right and best way to go.

But they had changed the modus operandi. He assumed that meant that whatever his father was about to say could be absolutely nothing good. He sat and listened to his mother, hearing the pain in her voice with every word, and feeling like a horrible son for being responsible for it.

"We want you to know that we hear you and we understand your plight, but you do have a duty to your family and your community. Tradition is tradition and we expect this of you."

"Mom," he interrupted lovingly.

His father shot daggers at him with his eyes. "Let your Maemm speak," he said frostily, and Alan reluctantly complied.

The words that flowed from his mother's mouth fell on deaf ears, because the anger he felt toward his father blocked out everything else. He could hear his heartbeat in his ears and knew without a doubt that his decision had been made for him.

"Alan?" his mother was saying, but he had no idea what he was expected to respond because the tears flowing down his sister's face were just too much for him to bear. He closed his eyes and willed his heart to stop beating and his eyes to hold the tears that threatened to burst free.

He looked at each of his family members and smiled lovingly, but it did nothing to alter his decision.

"You will do as you are told," his father said firmly, and walked out of the room when his mother had finished talking.

"Daed," he called after his father's disappearing back, and the man stopped in his tracks without turning to face him. "Would you rather me serve the people unwillingly, knowing that I wanted nothing to do with that? Knowing I would be a sad and unhappy man, rather than be left to be what I want to be?"

Alan waited patiently for a response that did not come, and he could do nothing but try to keep his sadness contained.

"You will do as you are told," his father finally said and walked away.

His family dispersed with pitiful looks and his mother was the only one to stay. She waited until the other children had left the room before she let the tears fall silently down her face.

Alan walked over to her and took her hand in his, and as their eyes met he knew there was no need for words. He had been preparing for this day since a couple weeks before and now it was finally here. He let go of his mother's hand and walked up the stairs to the bedrooms.

He spent five minutes talking or joking with each of his siblings, until he came to his youngest sister's room.

"You are leaving," she said without looking up from the book she had been reading by candlelight.

He didn't respond. He sat on the edge of her bed and pulled her into his arms. Of all his siblings, she had been his favorite for the mere fact that she was not easily swayed by the thoughts and opinions of others. They had grown really close over the years, and as he hugged her, he knew that of all the things and people he would miss, she would be one of those he would miss the most.

He made his way to his bedroom and pulled his emergency bag from under his bed. He took a minute to look around the room he had spent all his life in, and as the sadness threatened to topple him, he turned and left.

At the foot of his stairs, his mother waited with a wallet and some money, as well as another backpack with food. He dropped his bag and pulled her in to him for one of those hugs that spoke of nothing but love and appreciation for the woman she had been to him.

"You take care of yourself," she said to him. He had no words; rather, he spoke none of the words he wanted to say, because if he did he would break down right there. With a lingering kiss on his cheek and a promise to pray for his guidance, salvation and return, she let him go.

He walked as slowly as he could through the door, forcing himself never to look back, because if he did, he was sure he would forget his happiness and stay with his family.

As the night swallowed him, he made his way to where the love of his life waited.

CRED

Emma saw the shadow walking up the lane to her house. She had been hoping he would pay her another late night visit and her heart leaped with joy at his arrival.

But just as quickly, the joy went leaping through her window.

Why was he waking with two bags? And even in the darkness, she could see the sadness that clung to him like a curse.

No! She thought to herself.

She again knocked on her parents' door to tell them she had a late night visitor and her mother eagerly gave her consent. Again, she could hide nothing from her father and his face frowned with uncertainty at the mixture of emotions that flooded over hers. He opened his mouth to ask if she was okay and she gave him a curt nod, instructing him not to question her mental or emotional condition at the moment.

He took the hint and she ran down the stairs to the porch, where Alan sat waiting.

"Come with me," he urged her as she stepped out of her house, and she stopped before she reached him.

She did not know how to react to the news, though she had known before she stepped outside. "So you are leaving," she stated in total surrender to her current situation.

She sat beside him and he took her hand.

"Come with me," he said again, and for a moment she thought about it. But for Emma, her place was here in this community, with the people she loved and a culture she enjoyed and respected. She didn't want more and she didn't need less; she just wanted to be here where it was home.

"The English world is not for me," she said, speaking to him in German for the first time since they had dated. "My place is here and I don't ever want to leave. You should stay with me."

Even as she hoped he would change his mind, she knew he wouldn't, because a life devoid of happiness and the need to live according to the wishes of others was enough to drive even the sanest person mad. She didn't want that for him.

"It will be different with me out there," Alan pleaded with her, referring to the visits she had made to the English world during her younger years of rumspringa and the fact that she did not like them. Some Amish children went out and never came back, but for her, the loudness and relative lack of peace were just too much, she had chosen her home and this was where she wanted to stay.

"I cannot go with you-," she began, and Alan interrupted her.

"Then wait for me," he begged.

She felt a moment of hope that she quickly shoved to the back of her mind, because she knew that as attractive as the offer was, time had a way of altering all manmade plans, and once he left she would have to shun him.

"How do you know you will come back?"

He sighed and looked her deeply in the eyes. "This is my home Emma, the people I love live here and I am never giving it up. I will give my father some time to change his mind and then I will come back. Just wait for me."

She listened to the hope, desperation and promise in every word yet again, and as she heard her mother's footsteps approaching, she pulled him down the stairs to the street. The corn patch ahead was the way most of the kids snuck out of the community to the English side of town, and it was the way she had managed to leave many years before. She knew the way well and pulled him through it. As they stood at the edge of the corn field, she looked at him.

"I will try to be patient, but no matter what, you come back to me, Alan. Come back to me."

He lifted her face to his and did the one thing she'd never expected--he bent his lips to hers and gave her a long and lingering kiss. She was surprised, but even that felt right with him and for a moment she melted into his kiss and the embrace that followed, and then she quickly stepped back.

It had been her first kiss and it had been an awesome one.

"Wait for me," Alan repeated as she turned to go back home before her parents raised an alarm.

As the corn field swallowed her up and she headed home, she let the tears slip from her eyes, and the broken heart she'd held together so it would not be harder for Alan broke to pieces with each step that took her further from him.

She heard the footsteps running toward her from behind and turned, hoping it was him, but it was Bret's face, red with worry and exhaustion, that greeted her.

"Oh, you came back!" he said, grinning happily. "I saw you go through the cornfield and thought you had left."

She couldn't erase the tears that ran down her face and he pulled her to him as she shook with sadness.

"Alan?" he asked, and she nodded into his shirt.

"I am sorry," Bret said as he hugged her even tighter. She stayed in his embrace a little longer before turning toward her house as the light came on. Bret walked with her until she got to the stairs, then let her go to her mother, who waited with open arms for her ahead.

"I am sorry, my precious daughter," her father said as he nodded his head in gratitude to Bret and took her inside.

For once, her mother understood not to ask questions and they walked her up the stairs and to bed, bending in prayer for Alan and his journey through the English world.

Her mother told her she would be okay and she believed every word of it, because Alan had promised he would be back, and she intended to wait until he returned.

End of Book 1

BLANK PAGE

Acknowledgements

Thank you to my beloved husband for being so patience towards my writing endeavors. And my gratitude to my co-author, Nicole Wright, my cover illustrator, Anita Jovanovic, and to my editor, Melanie Hall-thank you to all for helping me realize my writing dreams. To my 3 beautiful kids for standing by my side during my many writing late nights.

And the biggest thank you of all—to my readers, both old and new. Your support helps keep the series going. You can find me on facebook at: www.facebook.com/saraahsowellbooks/

If You Enjoyed This Book...

....We would really, really appreciate it if you would help us tell other readers how much you have enjoyed this book by leaving us a review.

To us, reviews are like little gold pieces and they help persuade other readers to give the novels a chance.

More readers will encourage our authors to write more quality novels, and that means we will continue to produce highly-entertaining stories.

Please give your unbiased reviews.

Other Books By Saraah Sowell

TORN SERIES

1. Amish Devotion
2. Amish Bride
3. Amish Loss
4. Amish Mystery

FOLLOWING ORDNUNG SERIES

1. Amish Secrets
2. Amish Rebellion
3. Amish Past
4. Amish Nobility

AMISH FREEDOM SERIES

1. Amish Freedom to Love
2. Amish Freedom to Choose
3. Amish Freedom to Live
4. Amish Survival

MYSTERY IN AMISH COUNTRY SERIES

1. Amish Autumn
2. Amish Courtship
3. Amish Falsehood
4. Amish Christmas Wishl

www.facebook.com/saraahsowellbooks

Other Books By Saraah Sowell

AN AMISH RUMSPRINGA SERIES
1. Amish Rumspringa Journal

AMISH LOVE'S CHANGES SERIES
1. An Amish Romance - Promise of Love
2. Amish Romance – Fight for Love
3. Amish Romance – Made to Love

AN AMISH HOPE SERIES
1. Amish Turmoil
2. Amish Trial
3. Amish Maid
4. Amish Saviour

AMISH STRANDS OF LOVE AND CHASTITY SERIES
1. Amish Prayers
2. Amish Tears
3. Amish Conviction
4. Amish Virtues

www.facebook.com/saraahsowellbooks

Other Books By Saraah Sowell

AMISH GARDEN OF FAITH SERIES
1. Amish Dreams
2. Amish Faith
3. Amish Purpose
4. Amish Loyalty

AMISH COUNTRY OF HOPE SERIES
1. Amish Debacle
2. Amish Love & Hatred

THE EXECUTIVE AMISH SERIES
1 Amish Vengeance
2. Amish Acceptance

www.facebook.com/saraahsowellbooks

DISCLAIMER AND/OR LEGAL NOTICES:

Every effort has been made to accurately represent this book and it's potential. Results vary with every individual, and your results may or may not be different from those depicted. No promises, guarantees or warranties, whether stated or implied, have been made that you will produce any specific result from this book. Your efforts are individual and unique, and may vary from those shown. Your success depends on your efforts, background and motivation.

The material in this publication is provided for educational and informational purposes only and is not intended as medical advice. The information contained in this book should not be used to diagnose or treat any illness, metabolic disorder, disease or health problem. Always consult your physician or health care provider before beginning any nutrition or exercise program. Use of the programs, advice, and information contained in this book is at the sole choice and risk of the reader.

CPSIA information can be obtained
at www.ICGtesting.com
Printed in the USA
BVOW08s1336251016

465970BV00001B/4/P